THE
MAMMOTH BOOK OF
NIGHTMARE
STORIES

TWISTED TALES NOT TO BE READ AT NIGHT!

EDITED BY
STEPHEN JONES
ILLUSTRATED BY RANDY BROECKER

Skyhorse Publishing
A Herman Graf Book

Collection and editorial material copyright © Stephen Jones 2002, 2003, 2019
Interior illustrations copyright © Randy Broecker 2002, 2003

Originally published in hardcover as *Keep Out the Night*
and *By Moonlight Only* by PS Publishing.

All rights reserved. No part of this book may be reproduced in any manner
without the express written consent of the publisher, except in the case of brief
excerpts in critical reviews or articles. All inquiries should be addressed to
Skyhorse Publishing, 307 West 36th Street, 11th Floor, New York, NY 10018.

Skyhorse Publishing books may be purchased in bulk at special discounts for
sales promotion, corporate gifts, fund-raising, or educational purposes. Special
editions can also be created to specifications. For details, contact the Special
Sales Department, Skyhorse Publishing, 307 West 36th Street, 11th Floor,
New York, NY 10018 or info@skyhorsepublishing.com.

Skyhorse® and Skyhorse Publishing® are registered trademarks of
Skyhorse Publishing, Inc.®, a Delaware corporation.

Visit our website at www.skyhorsepublishing.com.

10 9 8 7 6 5 4 3 2 1

Library of Congress Cataloging-in-Publication Data is available on file.

Cover design by Brian Peterson
Cover illustration credit: iStockphoto

Print ISBN: 978-1-5107-3644-3
Ebook ISBN: 978-1-5107-3646-7

Printed in the United States of America

CONTENTS

In memory of
Christine Campbell Thomson (1897–1985),
who led the way . . .

INTRODUCTION
NOT TO BE READ AT NIGHT

FOR FANS OF classic horror fiction and collectors of the American pulp magazine *Weird Tales* in particular, the Not at Night series of anthologies is one of the genre's best-kept secrets.

Beginning with the book from which the series took its collective name, *Not at Night*, published in October 1925, literary agent and author Christine Campbell Thomson (1897–1985) edited twelve volumes that appeared from the British publisher Selwyn & Blount during the 1920s and '30s.

These comprised the initial volume, along with *More Not at Night* (1926), *You'll Need a Night Light* (1927), *Gruesome Cargoes* (1928), *By Daylight Only* (1929), *Switch on the Light* (1931), *At Dead of Night* (1931), *Grim Death* (1932), *Keep on the Light* (1933), *Terror By Night* (1934), and *Nightmare By Daylight* (1936). The final volume in the series was *The "Not at Night" Omnibus* (1937), which collected thirty-five stories from the earlier books, before Thomson decided to bring the series to an end because of a lack of material that was good enough.

Thomson had always been a fan of weird fiction, and the Not at Night series drew extensively on stories that were originally published in *Weird Tales*, providing early hardcover publication for such notable authors as

H. P. Lovecraft, Robert E. Howard, Clark Ashton Smith, Hugh B. Cave, Edmond Hamilton, Mary Elizabeth Counselman, August Derleth, Frank Belknap Long, Seabury Quinn, H. Warner Munn, Hazel Heald, David H. Keller, and numerous others.

In fact, after she began selling stories by her husband Oscar Cook to *Weird Tales*, a mutual copyright arrangement meant that the Not at Night series became the "official" British edition of the legendary periodical (as was sometimes indicated in the books' preliminary pages).

Thomson later recalled conceiving the idea for the anthology on the top of an open-top bus and being responsible for the title of the series. Although she never went into detail about her inspiration, as the first volume's dust-jacket flap confirmed: *The Editor has aimed at a collection which should amply justify the title, and be calculated to make any reader disinclined to go to bed after putting down the book.*

When I decided to pay homage to Thomson's series, I wanted to replicate the intention stated in this jacket copy. However, selling the concept of a "non-themed" anthology can sometimes be a difficult business, as I had discovered previously with my volumes *The Mammoth Book of Terror* and *The Mammoth Book of New Terror*. Therefore, just as Thomson had selected many of her stories from among the best *Weird Tales* had to offer, I decided to approach a number of contemporary horror authors and ask them for their favorite stories and novellas that, for one reason or another, they felt had been unjustly overlooked or ignored.

The reaction to my solicitation was overwhelmingly positive—all the authors I contacted had examples of their work that they would like to see gain greater recognition—and so this present volume was born.

Christine Campbell Thomson left behind a legacy of not only one of the first regular series of weird fiction anthologies, but also a dozen volumes that should be considered a cornerstone of any horror reader's library.

I believe this current volume broadly encompasses her views and tastes for the series through an impressive lineup of tales that were out of print for far too long or that appear here for the first time in new or revised versions.

It is my fervent hope that the varied horrors—both supernatural and psychological—that manifest themselves over the following pages will leave a lasting chill down readers' spines long after they have finished this book . . .

But be warned—do not read them at night!

STEPHEN JONES
LONDON, ENGLAND

THE VIADUCT

BRIAN LUMLEY

Brian Lumley produced his early work very much under the influence of the *Weird Tales* authors, H. P. Lovecraft, Robert E. Howard, and Clark Ashton Smith; and his first stories and books were published by the then "dean of macabre publishers," August W. Derleth through his now legendary Arkham House imprint.

Lumley began writing full time in 1980, and four years later he completed his breakthrough novel *Necroscope®* featuring Harry Keogh, a psychically endowed hero who is able to communicate with the teeming dead. Necroscope has now grown to sixteen big volumes, published in fourteen countries and many millions of copies. In addition, Necroscope comic books, graphic novels, a role-playing game, quality figurines, and a series of audio books in Germany have been created from the popular series.

Along with the Necroscope titles, Lumley is also the author of more than forty other books, and his vampire story "Necros" became one of the first episodes of Showtime's erotic horror anthology TV series *The Hunger.*

He is the winner of a British Fantasy Award, a *Fear* Magazine Award, a Lovecraft Film Festival Association "Howie," the World

Horror Convention's Grand Master Award, the Horror Writers Association's Lifetime Achievement Award, and the World Fantasy Convention's Lifetime Achievement Award.

"'The Viaduct' was written in 1974 while I was in the English garrison town of Aldershot," remembers the author. "This was a weird three or four weeks—a strange time in my life—when quite a bit of surreal stuff was happening. (No, I wasn't on medication, illicit pharmaceuticals, booze or anything of that sort . . . I was in fact a S/Sgt in the Royal Military Police on a Unit Quartermaster's course.)

"Anyway, Ramsey Campbell had asked me for a story for an anthology he was editing, and despite that everything around me felt weird—or perhaps because of it—I wrote him one that wasn't. So 'The Viaduct' was something of a departure for me, containing nothing supernatural, no vampires, no intelligent octopuses from outer space, none of that stuff . . . just something terrifying that might actually happen.

"Out of all my stories, there are only a handful which fit this category—more suspense than purely weird tales. Anyway, I liked the finished product, and whatever feeling of reality it musters probably has its source in its setting—the northeast of England where I grew up.

"Oh, and by the way, the town where I was born really does have such a viaduct . . ."

HORROR CAN COME in many different shapes, sizes, and colors; often, like death, which is sometimes its companion, unexpectedly. Some years ago horror came to two boys in the coal-mining area of England's northeast coast.

Pals since they first started school seven years earlier, their names were John and David. John was a big lad and thought himself very brave; David was six months younger, smaller, and he wished he could be more like John.

It was a Saturday in the late spring, warm but not oppressive, and since there was no school the boys were out adventuring on the beach. They had spent most of the morning playing at being starving castaways, turning over rocks in the life-or-death search for crabs and eels— and jumping back startled, hearts racing, whenever their probing revealed too frantic a wriggling in the swirling water, or perhaps a great crab carefully sidling away, one pincer lifted in silent warning—and now they were heading home again for lunch.

But lunch was still almost two hours away, and it would take them less than an hour to get home. In that simple fact were sown the seeds of horror, in that and in one other fact that between the beach and their respective homes there stood the viaduct . . .

Almost as a reflex action, when the boys left the beach they headed in the direction of the viaduct. To do this they turned inland, through the trees and bushes of the narrow dene that came right down to the sand, and followed the path of the river. The river was still fairly deep, from the spring thaw and the rains of April, and as they walked, ran, and hopped they threw stones into the water, seeing who could make the biggest splash.

In no time at all, it seemed, they came to the place where the massive, ominous shadow of the viaduct fell across the dene and the river flowing through it, and there they stared up in awe at the giant arched structure of brick and concrete that bore upon its back one hundred yards of the twin-tracks that formed the coastal railway. Shuddering mightily whenever a train roared overhead, the man-made bridge was a never-ending source of amazement and wonder to them . . . And a challenge, too.

It was as they were standing on the bank of the slow-moving river, perhaps fifty feet wide at this point, that they spotted on the opposite bank the local village idiot, "Wiley Smiley." Now of course, that was not this unfortunate youth's real name; he was Miles Bellamy, victim of cruel genetic fates since the ill-omened day of his birth some nineteen years earlier. But everyone called him Wiley Smiley.

He was fishing, in a river that had supported nothing bigger than a minnow for many years, with a length of string and a bent pin. He looked up and grinned vacuously as John threw a stone into the water to attract his attention. The stone went quite close to the mark, splashing water over the unkempt youth where he stood a little way out from the far bank, balanced none too securely on slippery rocks. His vacant grin immediately slipped from his face; he became angry, gesturing awkwardly and mouthing incoherently.

"He'll come after us," said David to his brash companion, his voice just a trifle alarmed.

"No he won't, stupid," John casually answered, picking up a second, larger stone. "He can't get across, can he." It was a statement, not a question, and it was a fact. Here the river was deeper, overflowing from a large pool directly beneath the viaduct which, in the months ahead, children and adults alike would swim in during the hot weekends of summer.

John threw his second missile, deliberately aiming it at the water as close to the enraged idiot as he could without actually hitting him, shouting: "Yah! Wiley Smiley! Trying to catch a whale, are you?"

Wiley Smiley began to shriek hysterically as the stone splashed down immediately in front of him and a fountain of water geysered over his trousers. Threatening though they now were, his angry caperings upon the rocks looked very funny to the boys (particularly since his rage was impotent), and John began to laugh loudly and jeeringly. David, not a cruel boy by nature, found his friend's laughter so infectious that in a few seconds he joined in, adding his own voice to the hilarity.

Then John stooped yet again, straightening up this time with two stones, one of which he offered to his slightly younger companion. Carried completely away now, David accepted the stone and together they hurled their missiles, dancing and laughing until tears rolled down their cheeks as Wiley Smiley received a further dousing. By that time the rocks upon which their victim stood were thoroughly wet and slippery, so that suddenly he lost his balance and sat down backward into the shallow water.

Climbing clumsily, soggily to his feet, he was greeted by howls of laughter from across the river, which drove him to further excesses of rage. His was a passion which might only find outlet in direct retaliation, revenge. He took a few paces forward, until the water swirled about his knees, then stooped and plunged his arms into the river. There were stones galore beneath the water, and the face of the tormented youth was twisted with hate and fury now as he straightened up and brandished two which were large and jagged.

Where his understanding was painfully slow, Wiley Smiley's strength was prodigious. Had his first stone hit John on the head it might easily have killed him. As it was, the boy ducked at the last moment and the missile flew harmlessly above him. David, too, had to jump to avoid being hurt by a flying rock, and no sooner had the idiot loosed both his stones than he stooped down again to grope in the water for more. Wiley Smiley's aim was too good for the boys, and his continuing rage was making them begin to feel uncomfortable, so they beat a hasty retreat up the steeply wooded slope of the dene and made for the walkway that was fastened and ran parallel to the near-side wall of the viaduct. Soon they had climbed out of sight of the poor soul below, but they could still hear his meaningless squawking and shrieking.

A few minutes more of puffing and panting, climbing steeply through trees and saplings, brought them up above the wood and to the edge of a grassy slope. Another hundred yards and they could go over a fence and onto the viaduct. Though no word had passed between them on the subject, it was inevitable that they should end up on the viaduct, one of the most fascinating places in their entire world . . .

The massive structure had been built when first the collieries of the northeast opened up, long before plans were drawn up for the major coast road, and now it linked twin colliery villages that lay opposite each other across the narrow river valley it spanned. Originally constructed solely to accommodate the railway, and used to that end to this very day, with the addition of a walkway, it also provided miners who lived in one village but worked in the other with a shortcut to their respective coal-mines.

While the viaduct itself was of sturdy brick, designed to withstand decade after decade of the heavy traffic that rumbled and clattered across its triple-arched back, the walkway was a comparatively fragile affair. That is not to say that it was not safe, but there were certain dangers, and notices had been posted at its approaches to warn users of the presence of at least an element of risk.

Supported upon curving metal arms—iron bars about one and one-half inches in diameter which, springing from the brick and mortar of the viaduct wall, were set perhaps twenty inches apart—the walkway itself was of wooden planks protected by a fence five feet high. There were, however, small gaps where rotten planks had been removed and never replaced, but the miners who used the viaduct were careful and knew the walkway's dangers intimately. All in all the walkway served a purpose and was reasonably safe; one might jump from it, certainly, but only a very careless person or an outright fool would fall. Still, it was no place for anyone suffering from vertigo . . .

Now, as they climbed the fence to stand gazing up at those ribs of iron with their burden of planking and railings, the two boys felt a strange, headlong rushing emotion within them. For this day, of course, was *the* day!

It had been coming for almost a year, since the time when John had stood right where he stood now to boast: "One day I'll swing hand over hand along those rungs, all the way across. Just like Tarzan." Yes, they had sensed this day's approach, almost as they might sense Christmas or the end of long, idyllic summer holidays . . . or a visit to the dentist. Something far away, which would eventually arrive, but not yet.

Except that now it had arrived.

"One hundred and sixty rungs," John breathed, his voice a little fluttery, feeling his palms beginning to itch. "Yesterday, in the playground, we both did twenty more than that on the climbing-frame."

"The climbing-frame," answered David, with a naïve insight and vision far ahead of his age, "is only seven feet high. The viaduct is about a hundred and fifty."

John stared at his friend for a second and his eyes narrowed. Suddenly he sneered. "I might have known it—you're scared, aren't you?"

"No," David shook his head, lying, "but it'll soon be lunchtime, and—"

"You *are* scared!" John repeated. "Like a little kid. We've been practicing for months for this, every day of school on the climbing-frame, and now we're ready. You know we can do it." His tone grew more gentle, urging: "Look, it's not as if we can't stop if we want to, is it? There's them holes in the fence, and those big gaps in the planks."

"The first gap," David answered, noticing how very far away and faint his own voice sounded, "is almost a third of the way across . . ."

"That's right," John agreed, nodding his head eagerly. "We've counted the rungs, haven't we? Just fifty of them to that first wide gap. If we're too tired to go on when we get there, we can just climb up through the gap onto the walkway."

David, whose face had been turned toward the ground, looked up. He looked straight into his friend's eyes, not at the viaduct, in whose shade they stood. He shivered, but not because he was cold.

John stared right back at him, steadily, encouragingly, knowing that his smaller friend looked for his approval, his reassurance. And he was right, for despite the fact that their ages were very close, David held him up as some sort of hero. No daredevil, David, but he desperately wished he could be. And now . . . here was his chance.

He simply nodded—then laughed out loud as John gave a wild whoop and shook his young fists at the viaduct. "Today we'll beat you!" he yelled, then turned and clambered furiously up the last few yards of steep grassy slope to where the first rung might easily be reached with an upward spring. David followed him after a moment's pause, but not before he heard the first arch of the viaduct throw back the challenge in a faintly ringing, sardonic echo of John's cry: "Beat you . . . beat you . . . beat you . . ."

As he caught up with his ebullient friend, David finally allowed his eyes to glance upward at those skeletal ribs of iron above him. They looked solid, were solid, he knew—but the air beneath them was very thin indeed. John turned to him, his face flushed with excitement. "You first," he said.

"Me?" David blanched. "But—"

"You'll be up onto the walkway first if we get tired," John pointed out. "Besides, I go faster than you—and you wouldn't want to be left behind, would you?"

David shook his head. "No," he slowly answered, "I wouldn't want to be left behind." Then his voice took on an anxious note: "But you won't hurry me, will you?"

"'Course not," John answered. "We'll just take it nice and easy, like we do at school."

Without another word, but with his ears ringing strangely and his breath already coming faster, David jumped up and caught hold of the first rung. He swung forward, first one hand to the rung in front, then the other, and so on. He heard John grunt as he too jumped and caught the first rung, and then he gave all his concentration to what he was doing. Hand over hand, rung by rung, they made their way out over the abyss. Below them the ground fell sharply away, each swing of their arms adding almost two feet to their height, seeming to add tangibly to their weight. Now they were silent, except for an occasional grunt, saving both breath and strength as they worked their way along the underside of the walkway. There was only the breeze that whispered in their ears and the infrequent toot of a motor's horn on the distant road.

As the bricks of the wall moved slowly by, so the distance between rungs seemed to increase, and already David's arms felt tired. He knew that John, too, must be feeling it, for while his friend was bigger and a little stronger, he was also heavier. And sure enough, at a distance of only twenty-five, maybe thirty rungs out toward the center, John breathlessly called for a rest.

David pulled himself up and hung his arms and his rib-cage over the rung he was on—just as they had practiced in the playground—getting comfortable before carefully turning his head to look back. He was shocked to see that John's face was paler than he'd ever known it, that his eyes were staring. When John saw David's doubt, however, he managed a weak grin.

"It's okay," he said. "I was—I was just a bit worried about you, that's all. Thought your arms might be getting a bit tired. Have you—have you looked down yet?"

"No," David answered, his voice mouse-like. *No*, he said again, this time to himself, *and I'm not going to!* He carefully turned his head back to look ahead, where the diminishing line of rungs seemed to stretch out almost infinitely to the far side of the viaduct.

John had been worried about him. Yes, of course he had; that was why his face had looked so funny, so—shrunken. John thought he was frightened, was worried about his self-control, his ability to carry on. Well, David told himself, he had every right to worry; but all the same he felt ashamed that his weakness was so obvious. Even in a position like that, perched so perilously, David's mind was far more concerned with the other boy's opinion of him than with thoughts of possible disaster. And it never once dawned on him, not for a moment, that John might really only be worried about himself . . .

Almost as if to confirm beyond a doubt the fact that John had little faith in his strength, his courage—as David hung there, breathing deeply, preparing himself for the next stage of the venture—his friend's voice, displaying an unmistakable quaver, came to him again from behind:

"Just another twenty rungs, that's all, then you'll be able to climb up onto the walkway."

Yes, David thought, *I'll be able to climb up. But then I'll know that I'll never be like you—that you'll always be better than me—because you'll carry on all the way across!* He set his teeth and dismissed the thought. It wasn't going to be like that, he told himself, not this time. After all, it was no different up here from in the playground. You were only higher, that was all. The trick was in not looking down—

As if obeying some unheard command, seemingly with a morbid curiosity of their own, David's eyes slowly began to turn downward, defying him. Their motion was only arrested when David's attention suddenly centered upon a spider . . . like a dot that emerged suddenly from the cover of the trees, scampering frantically up the opposite slope of the valley. He recognized the figure immediately from the faded blue shirt and black trousers that it wore. It was Wiley Smiley.

As David lowered himself carefully into the hanging position beneath his rung and swung forward, he said: "Across the valley, there—that's Wiley Smiley. I wonder why he's in such a hurry?" There had been something terribly *urgent* about the idiot's quick movements, as if some rare incentive powered them.

"I see him," said John, sounding more composed now. "Huh! He's just an old nutter. My dad says he'll do something one of these days and have to be taken away."

"Do something?" David queried, pausing briefly between swings. An uneasiness completely divorced from the perilous game they were playing rose churningly in his stomach and mind. "What kind of thing?"

"Dunno," John grunted. "But anyway, don't—*uh!*—talk."

It was good advice: don't talk, conserve wind, strength, take it easy. And yet David suddenly found himself moving faster, dangerously fast, and his fingers were none too sure as they moved from one rung to the next. More than once he was hanging by one hand while the other groped blindly for support.

It was very, very important now to close the distance between himself and the sanctuary of the gap in the planking. True, he had made up his mind just a few moments ago to carry on beyond that gap—as far as he could go before admitting defeat, submitting—but all such resolutions were gone now as quickly as they came. His one thought was of climbing up to safety.

It had something to do with Wiley Smiley and the eager, *determined* way he had been scampering up the far slope. Toward the viaduct. Something to do with that, yes, and with what John had said about Wiley Smiley being taken away one day . . . for *doing* something. David's mind dared not voice its fears too specifically, not even to itself . . .

Now, except for the occasional grunt—that and the private pounding of blood in their ears—the two boys were silent, and only a minute or so later David saw the gap in the planking. He had been searching for it, sweeping the rough wood of the planks stretching away overhead anxiously until he saw the wide, straight crack that quickly enlarged as he swung closer. Two planks were missing here, he knew, just sufficient to allow a boy to squirm through the gap without too much trouble.

His breath coming in sobbing, glad gasps, David was just a few rungs away from safety when he felt the first tremors vibrating through the great structure of the viaduct. It was like the trembling of a palsied giant. "What's that?" he cried out loud, terrified, clinging desperately to the rung above his head.

"It's a—*uh!*—train!" John gasped, his own voice now very hoarse and plainly frightened. "We'll have to—*uh!*—wait until it's gone over."

Quickly, before the approaching train's vibrations could shake them loose, the boys hauled themselves up into positions of relative safety and comfort, perching on their rungs beneath the planks of the walkway. There they waited and shivered in the shadow of the viaduct, while the shuddering rumble of the train drew ever closer, until, in a protracted clattering of wheels on rails, the monster rushed by unseen overhead. The trembling quickly subsided and the train's distant whistle proclaimed its derision; it was finished with them.

Without a word, holding back a sob that threatened to develop into full-scale hysteria, David lowered himself once more into the full-length hanging position; behind him, breathing harshly and with just the hint of a whimper escaping from his lips, John did the same. Two, three more forward swings and the gap was directly overhead. David looked up, straight up to the clear sky.

"Hurry!" said John, his voice the tiniest whisper. "My hands are starting to feel funny . . ."

David pulled himself up and balanced across his rung, tremulously took away one hand and grasped the edge of the wooden planking. Pushing down on the hand that grasped the rung and hauling himself up with the other, finally he kneeled on the rung and his head emerged through the gap in the planks. He looked along the walkway . . .

. . . There, not three feet away, legs widespread and eyes burning with a fanatical hatred, crouched Wiley Smiley. David saw him, saw the pointed stick he held, felt a thrill of purest horror course through him. Then, in the next instant, the idiot lunged forward and his mouth opened in a demented parody of a laugh. David saw the lightning movement of the sharpened stick and tried to avoid its thrust. He felt the point strike his forehead just above his left eye and fell back, off balance, arms flailing. Briefly his left hand made contact with the planking again, then lost it, and he fell with a shriek . . . across the rung that lay directly beneath him. It was not a long fall, but fear and panic had already winded David; he simply closed his eyes and sobbed, hanging on for dear life, motionless. But only for a handful of seconds.

Warm blood trickled from David's forehead, falling on his hands where he gripped the rung. Something was prodding the back of his neck, jabbing viciously. The pain brought him back from the abyss and he opened his eyes to risk one sharp, fearful glance upward. Wiley Smiley was kneeling at the edge of the gap, his stick already moving downward for another jab. Again David moved his head to avoid the thrust of the stick, and once more the point scraped his forehead.

Behind him David could hear John moaning and screaming alternately: "Oh, Mum! Dad! It's Wiley Smiley! It's him, him, *him!* He'll kill us, kill us . . ."

Galvanized into action, David lowered himself for the third time into the hanging position and swung forward, away from the inflamed idiot's deadly stick. Two rungs, three, then he carefully turned about face and hauled himself up to rest. He looked at John through the blood that dripped slowly into one eye, blurring his vision. David blinked to clear his eye of blood, then said: "John, you'll have to turn round and go back, get help. He's got me here. I can't go forward any further, I don't think, and I can't come back. I'm stuck. But it's only fifty rungs back to the start. You can do it easy, and if you get tired you can always rest. I'll wait here until you fetch help."

"Can't, can't, *can't*," John babbled, trembling wildly where he lay half-across his rung. Tears ran down the older boy's cheeks and fell into space like salty rain. He was deathly white, eyes staring, frozen. Suddenly yellow urine flooded from the leg of his short trousers in a long burst. When he saw this, David, too, wet himself, feeling the burning of his water against his legs but not caring. He felt very tiny, very weak now, and he knew that fear and shock were combining to exhaust him.

Then, as a silhouette glimpsed briefly in a flash of lightning, David saw in his mind's eye a means of salvation. "John," he urgently called out to the other boy. "Do you remember near the middle of the viaduct? There are two gaps close together in the walkway, maybe only a dozen or so rungs apart."

Almost imperceptibly, John nodded, never once moving his frozen eyes from David's face. "Well," the younger boy continued, barely managing to keep the hysteria out of his own voice, "if we can swing to—"

Suddenly David's words were cut off by a burst of insane laughter from above, followed immediately by a loud, staccato thumping on the boards as Wiley Smiley leapt crazily up and down.

"No, no, *no*—" John finally cried out in answer to David's proposal. His paralysis broken, he began to sob unashamedly. Then, shaking his head violently, he said: "I can't move—can't move!" His voice became the merest whisper. "Oh, God—Mum—Dad! I'll fall, I'll fall!"

"You won't fall, you git—*coward!*" David shouted. Then his jaw fell open in a gasp. John, a coward! But the other boy didn't even seem to have heard him. Now he was trembling as wildly as before and his eyes were squeezed tight shut. "Listen," David said. "If you don't come . . . then I'll leave you. You wouldn't want to be left on your own, would you?" It was an echo as of something said a million years ago.

John stopped sobbing and opened his eyes. They opened very wide, unbelieving. "Leave me?"

"Listen," David said again. "The next gap is only about twenty rungs away, and the one after that is only another eight or nine more. Wiley Smiley can't get after both of us at once, can he?"

"You go," said John, his voice taking on fresh hope and his eyes blinking rapidly. "You go and maybe he'll follow you. Then I'll climb up and—and chase him off . . ."

"You won't be able to chase him off," said David scornfully, "not just you on your own: you're not big enough."

"Then I'll . . . I'll run and fetch help."

"What if he doesn't follow after me?" David asked. "If we both go, he's bound to follow us."

"David," John said, after a moment or two. "David, I'm . . . frightened."

"You'll have to be quick across the gap," David said, ignoring John's last statement. "He's got that stick—and of course he'll be listening to us."

"I'm frightened," John whispered again.

David nodded. "Okay, you stay where you are, if that's what you want—but I'm going on."

"Don't leave me, don't leave me!" John cried out, his shriek accompanied by a peal of mad and bubbling laughter from the unseen idiot above. "Don't go!"

"I have to, or we're both finished," David answered. He slid down into the hanging position and turned about-face, noting as he did so that John was making to follow him, albeit in a dangerous, panicky fashion. "Wait to see if Wiley Smiley follows me!" he called back over his shoulder.

"No. I'm coming, I'm coming."

From far down below in the valley David heard a horrified shout, then another. They had been spotted. Wiley Smiley heard the shouting, too, and his distraction was sufficient to allow John to pass by beneath him unhindered. From above, the two boys now heard the idiot's worried mutterings and gruntings, and the hesitant sound of his feet as he slowly kept pace with them along the walkway. He could see them through the narrow cracks between the planks, but the cracks weren't wide enough for him to use his stick.

David's arms and hands were terribly numb and aching by the time he reached the second gap, but seeing the gloating, twisted features of Wiley Smiley leering down at him he ducked his head and swung on to where he was once more protected by the planks above him. John had stopped short of the second gap, hauling himself up into the safer, resting position.

Above them Wiley Smiley was mewling viciously like a wild animal, howling as if in torment. He rushed crazily back and forth from gap to gap, jabbing uselessly at the empty air between the vacant rungs. The boys could see the bloodied point of the stick striking down first through one open space, then the other. David achingly waited until he saw the stick appear at the gap in front of him and then, when it retreated and he heard Wiley Smiley's footsteps hurrying overhead, swung swiftly across to the other side. There he turned about to face John, and with what felt like his last ounce of strength pulled himself up to rest.

Now, for the first time, David dared to look down. Below, running up the riverbank and waving frantically, were the ant-like figures of three men. They must have been out for a Saturday morning stroll when they'd spotted the two boys hanging beneath the viaduct's walkway. One of them stopped running and put his hands up to his mouth. His shout floated up to the boys on the clear air: "Hang on, lads, hang on!"

"Help!" David and John cried out together, as loud as they could. "Help!—Help!"

"We're coming, lads," came the answering shout. The men hurriedly began to climb the wooded slope on their side of the river and disappeared into the trees.

"They'll be here soon," David said, wondering if it would be soon enough. His whole body ached and he felt desperately weak and sick.

"Hear that, Wiley Smiley?" John cried hysterically, staring up at the boards above him. "They'll be here soon—and then you'll be taken away and locked up!" There was no answer. A slight wind had come up off the sea and was carrying a salty tang to them where they lay across their rungs.

"They'll take you away and lock you up," John cried again, the ghost of a sob in his voice; but once more the only answer was the slight moaning of the wind. John looked across at David, maybe twenty-five feet away, and said: "I think . . . I think he's gone." Then he gave a wild shout. "He's gone. *He's gone!*"

"I didn't hear him go," said David, dubiously.

John was very much more his old self now. "Oh, he's gone, all right. He saw those men coming and cleared off. David, I'm going up!"

"You'd better wait," David cried out as his friend slid down to hang at arm's length from his rung. John ignored the advice; he swung forward hand over hand until he was under the far gap in the planking. With a grunt of exertion, he forced the tired muscles of his arms to pull his tired body up. He got his rib cage over the rung, flung a hand up and took hold of the naked plank to one side of the gap, then—

In that same instant David sensed rather than heard the furtive movement overhead. "John!" he yelled. "He's still there—*Wiley Smiley's still there!*"

But John had already seen Wiley Smiley; the idiot had made his presence all too plain, and already his victim was screaming. The boy fell back fully into David's view, the hand he had thrown up to grip the edge of the plank returning automatically to the rung, his arms taking the full weight of his falling body, somehow sustaining him. There was a long gash in his cheek from which blood freely flowed.

"Move forward!" David yelled, terror pulling his lips back in a snarling mask. "Forward, where he can't get at you . . ."

John heard him and must have seen in some dim, frightened recess of his mind the common sense of David's advice. Panting hoarsely—partly in dreadful fear, partly from hideous emotional exhaustion—he swung one hand forward and caught at the next rung. And at that precise moment, in the split-second while John hung suspended between the two rungs with his face turned partly upward, Wiley Smiley struck again.

David was witness to it all. He heard the maniac's rising, gibbering shriek of triumph as the sharp point of the stick lanced unerringly down, and John's answering cry of purest agony as his left eye flopped bloodily out onto his cheek, lying there on a white thread of nerve and gristle. He saw John clap *both hands* to his monstrously altered face, and watched in starkest horror as his friend seemed to stand for a moment, defying gravity, on the thin air. Then John was gone, dwindling away down a drafty funnel of air, while rising came the piping, diminishing scream that would haunt David until his dying day, a scream that was cut short after what seemed an impossibly long time.

John had fallen. At first David couldn't accept it, but then it began to sink in. His friend had fallen. He moaned and shut his eyes tightly, lying half across and clinging to his rung so fiercely that he could no longer really feel his bloodless fingers at all. John had fallen . . .

Then—perhaps it was only a minute or so later, perhaps an hour, David didn't know—there broke in on his perceptions the sound of clumping, hurrying feet on the boards above, and a renewed, even more frenzied attack of gibbering and shrieking from Wiley Smiley. David forced his eyes open as the footsteps came to a halt directly overhead. He heard a gruff voice:

"Jim, you keep that bloody—*Thing*—away, will you? He's already killed one boy today. Frank, give us a hand here."

A face, inverted, appeared through the hole in the planks not three feet away from David's own face. The mouth opened and the same voice, but no longer gruff, said: "It's okay now, son. Everything's okay. Can you move?"

In answer, David could only shake his head negatively. Overtaxed muscles, violated nerves had finally given in. He was frozen on his perch; he would stay where he was now until he was either taken off physically or until he fainted.

Dimly the boy heard the voice again, and others raised in an urgent hubbub, but he was too far gone to make out any words that were said. He was barely aware that the face had been withdrawn. A few seconds later there came a banging and tearing from immediately above him; a small shower of tiny pieces of wood, dust, and homogenous debris fell upon his head and shoulders. Then daylight flooded down to illuminate more brightly the shaded area beneath the walkway. Another board was torn away, and another.

The inverted face again appeared, this time at the freshly-made opening, and an exploratory hand reached down. Using its kindly voice, the face said: "Okay, son, we'll have you out of there in a jiffy. I—*uh!*—can't quite seem to reach you, but it's only a matter of a few inches. Do you think you can—"

The voice was cut off by a further outburst of incoherent shrieking and jabbering from Wiley Smiley. The face and hand withdrew momentarily and David heard the voice yet again. This time it was angry. "Look, see if you can keep that damned idiot back, will you? And keep him quiet, for God's sake!"

The hand came back, large and strong, reaching down. David still clung with all his remaining strength to the rung, and though he knew what was expected of him—what he must do to win himself the prize of continued life—all sense of feeling had quite gone from his limbs and even shifting his position was a very doubtful business.

"Boy," said the voice, as the hand crept inches closer and the inverted face stared into his, "if you could just reach up your hand, I—"

"I'll—I'll try to do it," David whispered.

"Good, good," his would-be rescuer calmly, quietly answered. "That's it, lad, just a few inches. Keep your balance, now."

David's hand crept up from the rung and his head, neck, and shoulder slowly turned to allow it free passage. Up it tremblingly went, reaching to meet the hand stretching down from above. The boy and the man, each peered into the other's straining face, and an instant later their fingertips touched—

There came a mad shriek, a frantic pounding of feet and cries of horror and wild consternation from above. The inverted face went white in a moment and disappeared, apparently dragged backward. The hand disappeared, too. And that was the very moment that David had chosen to free himself of the rung and give himself into the protection of his rescuer . . .

He flailed his arms in a vain attempt to regain his balance. Numb, cramped, cold with that singular icy chill experienced only at death's positive approach, his limbs would not obey. He rolled forward over the bar and his legs were no longer strong enough to hold him. He didn't even feel the toes of his shoes as they struck the rung—the last of him to have contact with the viaduct—before his fall began. And if the boy thought anything at all during that fall, well, those thoughts will never be known. Later he could not remember.

Oh, there was to be a later, but David could hardly have believed it while he was falling. And yet he was not unconscious. There were vague impressions: of the sky, the looming arch of the viaduct flying past, trees below, the sea on the horizon, then the sky again, all slowly turning. There was a composite whistling, of air displaced and air ejected from lungs contracted in a high-pitched scream. And then, it seemed a long time later, there was the impact . . .

But David did not strike the ground . . . he struck the pool. The deep swimming hole. The blessed, merciful river!

He had curled into a ball—the fetal position, almost—and this doubtless saved him. His tightly-curled body entered the water with very little injury, however much of a splash it caused. Deep as the water was, nevertheless David struck the bottom with force, the pain and shock awakening whatever facilities remained functional in the motor areas of his brain. Aided by his resultant struggling, however weak, the ballooning air in his clothes bore him surely to the surface. The river carried him a few yards downstream to where the banks formed a bottleneck for the pool.

Through all the pain David felt his knees scrape pebbles, felt his hands on the mud of the bank, and where willpower presumably was lacking, instinct took over. Somehow he crawled from the pool, and somehow he hung on grimly to consciousness. Away from the water, still he kept on crawling, as from the horror of his experience. Unseeing, he moved toward the towering unconquered colossus of the viaduct. He was quite blind as of yet, there was only a red, impenetrable haze before his bloodied eyes; he heard nothing but a sick roaring in his head. Finally his shoulder struck the bole of a tree that stood in the shelter of the looming brick giant, and there he stopped crawling, propped against the tree.

Slowly, very slowly the roaring went out of his ears, the red haze before his eyes was replaced by lightning flashes and kaleidoscopic shapes and colors. Normal sound suddenly returned with a great pain in his ears. A rush of wind rustled the leaves of the trees, snatching away and then giving back a distant shouting which seemed to have its source overhead. Encased in his shell of pain, David did not immediately relate the shouting to his miraculous escape. Sight returned a few moments later and he began to cry wrackingly with relief; he had thought himself permanently blind. And perhaps even now he had not been completely wrong, for his eyes had plainly been knocked out of order. Something was—*must* be—desperately wrong with them.

David tried to shake his head to clear it, but this action only brought fresh, blinding pain. When the nausea subsided he blinked his eyes, clearing them of blood and peering bewilderedly about at his surroundings. It was as he had suspected: the colors were all wrong. No, he blinked again, some of them seemed perfectly normal.

For instance: the bark of the tree against which he leaned was brown enough, and its dangling leaves were a fresh green. The sky above was blue, reflected in the river, and the bricks of the viaduct were a dull orange. Why then was the grass beneath him a lush red streaked with yellow and gray? Why was this unnatural grass wet and sticky, and—

—*And why were these tatters of dimly familiar clothing flung about in exploded, scarlet disorder?*

When his reeling brain at last delivered the answer, David opened his mouth to scream, fainting before he could do so. He fell face down into the sticky embrace of his late friend.

SPINDLESHANKS
(NEW ORLEANS, 1956)

CAITLÍN R. KIERNAN

Caitlín R. Kiernan is the author of the novels *Silk, Threshold, Low Red Moon, Murder of Angels, Daughter of Hounds, The Red Tree,* and *The Drowning Girl: A Memoir.* She also wrote the movie novelization of *Beowulf* and, more recently, she has published the Siobhan Quinn series of urban fantasies (*Blood Oranges, Red Delicious,* and *Cherry Bomb*) under the pseudonym "Kathleen Tierney."

Her shorter tales of the weird, fantastic, and macabre have been collected in a number of volumes, including *Tales of Pain and Wonder; From Weird and Distant Shores, To Charles Fort with Love, Alabaster, A is for Alien, The Ammonite Violin & Others, Two Worlds and In Between: The Best of Caitlín R. Kiernan (Volume One), Confessions of a Five-Chambered Heart, The Ape's Wife and Other Tales, Beneath an Oil-Dark Sea: The Best of Caitlín R. Kiernan (Volume Two),* and *Dear Sweet Filthy World.*

Kiernan is a multiple recipient of the World Fantasy Award, the Bram Stoker Award, the International Horror Guild Award, and the Shirley Jackson Award, as well as a winner of the Nebula Award, the British Fantasy Award, and the Mythopoeic Award.

As the author explains: "'Spindleshanks' is the only story I've ever written that I thought was so good that it would absolutely, definitely, find a place in an annual 'Year's Best' anthology. Previously, I'd almost felt that confident about 'Rats Live on No Evil Star.' Naturally, neither of these stories were chosen for such compilations. As is so often the case, my own reaction to my work was not in line with the opinions of readers and editors, and so 'Spindleshanks' has languished in a somewhat obscure collection.

"In 'Spindleshanks,' I somehow managed to achieve an economy of language I'd not enjoyed before (or since, for that matter). Stylistically, I think it stands apart from the greater body of what I've written. That wasn't intentional, though, just something that happened. When I started work on the piece, I had in mind a story about a ghoul cult living in a necropolis beneath Lafayette Cemetery, with dashes of lycanthropy thrown in, and 'Spindleshanks' is what came out instead. Rather, not instead, but it is a story where I kept the horrific and supernatural elements so low-key that, most of the time, they work more as subtext than overt theme.

"Looking back at the story, I realize that it's actually about the difficulties I was having finishing my second novel, *Threshold* (née *Trilobite*), with Reese Callicott's *The Ecstatic River* standing in for my own unfinished manuscript. I see in it many of the qualities that I so admire in the work of Shirley Jackson, who, as Stephen King so aptly pointed out years ago, 'never needed to raise her voice.'"

THE END OF July, indolent, dog-day swelter inside the big white house on Prytania Street; Greek Revival columns painted as cool and white as a vanilla ice cream cone, and from the second-floor veranda

Reese can see right over the wall into Lafayette Cemetery, if she wants to—Lafayette No. 1, and the black iron letters above the black iron gate to remind anyone who forgets. She doesn't dislike the house, not the way that she began to dislike her apartment in Boston before she finally left, but it's much too big, even with Emma, and she hasn't bothered to take the sheets off most of the furniture downstairs. This one bedroom almost more than she needs, anyway, her typewriter and the electric fan from Woolworths on the table by the wide French doors to the veranda, so she can sit there all day, sip her gin and tonic and stare out at the whitewashed brick walls and the crypts, whenever the words aren't coming.

And these days the words are hardly ever coming, hardly ever there when she goes looking for them, and her editor wanted the novel finished two months ago. Running from that woman and her shiny black patent pumps, her fashionable hats, as surely as she ran from Boston, the people there she was tired of listening to, and so Reese Callicott leased this big white house for the summer and didn't tell anyone where she was going or why. But she might have looked for a house in Vermont or Connecticut, instead, if she'd stopped to take the heat seriously, but the whole summer paid for in advance, all the way through September, and there's no turning back now. Nothing now but cracked ice and Gibley's and her view of the cemetery; her mornings and afternoons sitting at the typewriter and the mocking white paper, sweat and the candy smell of magnolias all day long, then jasmine at night.

Emma's noisy little parties at night, too, all night sometimes, the motley handful of people she drags in like lost puppies and scatters throughout the big house on Prytania Street; this man a philosophy or religion student at Tulane and that woman a poet from somewhere lamentable in Mississippi, that fellow a friend of a friend of Faulkner or Capote. Their accents and pretenses and the last of them hanging around until almost dawn unless Reese finds the energy to run them off sooner. But energy in shorter supply than the words these days, and mostly she just leaves them alone, lets them play their jazz and Fats Domino records too loud and have the run of the place because it makes Emma happy. No point in denying that she feels guilty for dragging poor Emma all the way to New Orleans, making her suffer the heat and mosquitoes because Chapter Eight of *The Ecstatic River* might as well be a cinder-block wall.

Reese lights a cigarette and blows the smoke toward the veranda, toward the cemetery, and a hot breeze catches it and quickly drags her smoke ghost to pieces.

"There's a party in the Quarter tonight," Emma says. She's lying on the bed, four o'clock Friday afternoon and she's still wearing her butter-yellow house coat with one of her odd books and a glass of bourbon and lemonade.

"Isn't there always a party in the Quarter?" Reese asks and now she's watching two old women in the cemetery, one with a bouquet of white flowers. She thinks they're chrysanthemums, but the women are too far away for her to be sure.

"Well, yes. Of course. But this one's going to be something different. I think a real voodoo woman will be there." A pause and she adds, "You should come."

"You know I have too much work."

Reese doesn't have to turn around in her chair to know the pout on Emma's face, the familiar, exaggerated disappointment, and she suspects that it doesn't actually matter to Emma whether or not she comes to the party. But this ritual is something that has to be observed, the way old women have to bring flowers to the graves of relatives who died a hundred years ago, the way she has to spend her days staring at blank pages.

"It might help, with your writing, I mean, if you got out once in a while. Really, sometimes I think you've forgotten how to talk to people."

"I talk to people, Emma. I talked to that Mr . . ." and she has to stop, searching for his name and there it is, "That Mr. Leonard, just the other night. You know, the fat one with the antique shop."

"He's almost *sixty* years old," Emma says; Reese takes another drag off her cigarette, exhales, and "Well, it's not like you want me out looking for a husband," she says.

"Have it your way," Emma says, the way she always says "Have it your way," and she goes back to her book and Reese goes back to staring at the obstinate typewriter and watching the dutiful old women on the other side of the high cemetery wall.

Reese awakens from a nightmare a couple of hours before dawn, sweating and breathless, chilled by a breeze through the open veranda doors. Emma's fast asleep beside her, lying naked on top of the sheets, though Reese didn't hear her come in. If she cried out or made any other noises in her sleep at least it doesn't seem to have disturbed Emma. Reese stares at the veranda a moment, the night beyond, and then she sits up, both feet on the floor, and she reaches for the lamp cord, but that might wake Emma and it *was* only a nightmare after all, a bad dream, and in a minute or two it will all seem at least as absurd as her last novel.

Instead she lights a cigarette and sits smoking in the dark, listening to the restless sounds the big house makes when everyone is still and quiet and it's left to its own devices, its random creaks and thumps, solitary house thoughts and memories filtered through plaster and lathe and burnished oak. The mumbling house and the exotic, piping song of a night bird somewhere outside, mundane birdsong made exotic because she hasn't spent her whole life hearing it, some bird that doesn't fly as far north as Boston. Reese listens to the bird and the settling house, Emma's soft snores, while she smokes the cigarette almost down to the filter, and then she gets up, walks across the wide room to the veranda doors, only meaning to close them. Only meaning to shut out a little of the night and then maybe she can get back to sleep.

But she pauses halfway, distracted by the book on Emma's night-stand, a very old book, by the look of it, something else borrowed from one or another of her Royal Street acquaintances, no doubt. More bayou superstition, Negro tales of voodoo and swamp magic, zombies and grave-robbing, the bogeyman passed off as folklore, and Reese squints to read the cover, fine leather worn by ages of fingers and the title stamped in flaking crimson—*Cultes des Goules* by Comte d'Erlette. The whole volume in French and the few grim illustrations do nothing for Reese's nerves, so she sets it back down on the table, makes a mental note to ask Emma what she sees in such morbid things, and, by the way, why hasn't she ever mentioned that she can read French?

The veranda doors half-shut and she pauses, looks out at the little city of the dead across the street, the marble and cement roofs dull white by the light of the setting half-moon, and a small shred of the dream comes back to her then. Emma, the day they met, a snowy December afternoon in Harvard Square, Reese walking fast past the Old Burying Ground and First Church, waiting in the cold for her train, and Emma standing off in the distance. Dark silhouette against the drifts and the white flakes swirling around her, and Reese tries to think what could possibly have been so frightening about any of that. Some minute detail already fading when she opened her eyes, something about the sound of the wind in the trees, maybe, or a line of footprints in the snow between her and Emma. Reese Callicott stares at Lafayette for a few more minutes and then she closes the veranda doors, locks them, and goes back to bed.

"Oh, that's horrible," Emma says and frowns as she pours a shot of whiskey into her glass of lemonade. "Jesus Christ, I can't believe they found her right down there on the sidewalk and we slept straight through the whole thing."

"Well, there might not have been that much noise," Carlton says helpfully and sips at his own drink, bourbon on the rocks, and he takes off his hat and sets it on the imported wicker table in the center of the veranda. Carlton the only person in New Orleans that Reese would think to call her friend, dapper, middle-aged man with a graying mustache and his Big Easy accent. Someone that she met at a writer's conference in Providence years ago, before Harper finally bought *The Light Beyond Center* and her short stories started selling to *The New Yorker* and *The Atlantic*. Carlton the reason she's spending the summer in exile in the house on Prytania Street, because it belongs to a painter friend of his who's away in Spain or Portugal, some place like that.

"They say her throat, her larynx, was torn out. So she might not have made much of a racket at all."

Reese sets her own drink down on the white veranda rail in front of her, nothing much left of it but melting ice and faintly gin-flavored water, but she didn't bring the bottle of Gibley's out with her and the morning heat's made her too lazy to go inside and fix another. She stares down at the wet spot at the corner of Prytania and Sixth Street, the wet cement very near the cemetery wall drying quickly in the scalding ten o'clock sun.

"Still," Emma says, "I think we would have heard *something*, don't you Reese?"

"Emmie, I think you sleep like the dead," Reese says, the grisly pun unintended but now it's out and no one's seemed to notice anyway.

"Well, the *Picayune*'s claiming it was a rabid stray—" and then Carlton clears his throat, interrupts Emma, and "I have a good friend on the force," he says. "He doesn't think it was an animal, at all. He thinks it's more likely someone was trying to make it *look* like the killer was an animal."

"Who was she?" Reese asks, and now there are two young boys, nine or ten years old, standing near the cemetery wall, pointing at the wet spot and whispering excitedly to one another.

"A colored woman. Mrs. Duquette's new cook," Carlton says. "I don't remember her name offhand. Does it matter?"

The two boys have stooped down to get a better look, maybe hoping for a splotch of blood that the police missed when they hosed off the sidewalk a few hours earlier.

"What was she doing out at that hour anyway?" Emma asks, finishes stirring her drink with an index finger and tests it with the tip of her tongue.

Carlton sighs and leans back in his wicker chair. "No one seems to know, precisely."

"Well, I think I've had about enough of this gruesome business for one day," Reese says. "Just look at those boys down there," and she stands up and shouts at them, hey, you boys, get away from there this very minute, and they stand up and stare at her like she's a crazy woman.

"I said get *away* from there. Go home!"

"They're only boys, Reese," Carlton says, and just then one of them flips Reese his middle finger and they both laugh before squatting back down on the sidewalk to resume their examination of the murder scene.

"They're horrid little *monsters*," Reese says and she sits slowly back down again.

"They're *all* monsters, dear," and Emma smiles and reaches across the table to massage the place between Reese's shoulder blades that's always knotted, always tense.

Carlton rubs at his mustache and "I assume all is *not* well with the book," he says and Reese scowls, still staring down at the two boys on the sidewalk.

"You know better than to ask a question like that."

"Yes, well, I had hoped the change of climate would be good for you."

"I don't think this climate is good for anything but heat rash and mildew," Reese grumbles and swirls the ice in her glass. "I need another drink. And then I need to get back to work."

"Maybe you're trying *too* hard," Carlton says and stops fumbling with his mustache. "Maybe you need to get away from this house for just a little while."

"That's what I keep telling her," Emma says, "But you know she won't listen to anyone."

The pout's in her voice again and it's more than Reese can take, those horrible boys and the murder, Carlton's good intentions and now Emma's pout, and she gets up and leaves them, goes inside, trading the bright sunshine for the gentler bedroom shadows, and leaves her lover and her friend alone on the veranda.

Saturday and Emma's usual sort of ragtag entourage, but tonight she's spending most of her time with a dark-skinned woman named Danielle Thibodaux, someone she met the night before at the party on Esplanade, the party with the fabled voodoo priestess. Reese is getting quietly, sullenly drunk in one corner of the immense dining room, the dining room instead of the bedroom because Emma insisted. "It's such a shame we're letting this place go to waste," she said and Reese was in the middle of a paragraph and didn't have time to argue. Not worth losing her train of thought over, and so here they all are, smoking and drinking around the long mahogany table, candlelight twinkling like starfire in the crystal chandelier, and Reese alone in a Chippendale in the corner. As apart from the others as she can get without offending Emma, and she's pretending that she isn't jealous of the dark-skinned woman with the faint Jamaican accent.

There's a Ouija board in the center of the table, empty and unopened wine bottles, brandy and bourbon, Waterford crystal and sterling silver candlesticks, and the cheap, dime store Ouija board there in the middle. One of the entourage brought it along, because he heard there was a ghost in the big white house on Prytania Street, a girl who hung herself from the top of the stairs when she got the news her young fiancé had died at Appomattox, or some such worn-out Civil War tragedy, and for an hour they've been drinking and trying to summon the ghost of the suicide or anyone else who might have nothing better to do in the after-life than talk to a bunch of drunks.

"I'm bored," Emma says finally and she pushes the Ouija board away, sends the tin planchette skittering toward a bottle of pear brandy. "No one wants to talk to us." The petulance in her voice does nothing at all to improve Reese's mood and she thinks about taking her gin and going upstairs.

And then someone brings up the murdered woman, not even dead a whole day yet and here's some asshole who wants to try and drag her spirit back to Earth. Reese rolls her eyes, thinks that even the typewriter would be less torture than these inane parlor games, and then she notices the uneasy look on the dark woman's face. The woman whispers some-thing to Emma, just a whisper but intimate enough that it draws a fresh pang of jealousy from Reese. Emma looks at her, a long moment of silence exchanged between them, and then she laughs and shakes her head, as if perhaps the woman's just made the most ridiculous sort of suggestion imaginable.

"I hear it was a wild dog," someone at the table says.

"There's always a lot of rabies this time a year," someone else says and Emma leans forward, eyes narrowed and a look of drunken confidence on her face, her I-know-something-*you*-don't smirk, and they all listen as she tells about Carlton's policeman friend and what he said that morning about the murdered woman's throat being cut, about her larynx being severed so she couldn't scream for help. That the cops are looking for a killer who wants everyone to *think* it was only an animal.

"Then let's ask her," the man who brought the Ouija board says to Emma and the blonde woman sitting next to him sniggers, an ugly, shameless sort of a laugh that makes Reese think of the two boys outside the walls of Lafayette, searching the sidewalk for traces of the dead woman's blood.

There's another disapproving glance from Danielle Thibodaux, then, but Emma only shrugs and reaches for the discarded planchette.

"Hell, why not," she says, her words beginning to slur together just a little. "Maybe *she's* still lurking about," but the dark-skinned woman pushes her chair away from the table and stands a few feet behind Emma, watches nervously as seven or eight of the entourage place their fingers on the edges of the planchette.

"We need to talk to the woman who was murdered outside the cemetery this morning," Emma says, affecting a low, spooky whisper, phoney creepshow awe, and fixing her eyes at the dead center of the planchette. "Mrs. Duplett's dead cook," Emma whispers and someone corrects her, "No, honey. It's *Duquette*. Mrs. Duquette," and several people laugh.

"Yeah, right. Mrs. Duquette."

"Jesus," Reese whispers and the dark-skinned woman stares across the room at her, her brown eyes that seem to say *Can't you see things are bad enough already?* The woman frowns and Reese sighs and pours herself another drink.

"We want to talk to Mrs. Duquette's murdered cook," Emma says again. "Are you there?"

A sudden titter of feigned surprise or fright when the tin planchette finally begins to move, circling the wooden board aimlessly for a moment before it swings suddenly to no and is still again.

"Then who are we talking to?" Emma says impatiently, and the planchette starts to move again. Wanders the board for a moment and members of the entourage begin to call out letters as the heart-shaped thing drifts from character to character.

"S . . . P . . . I . . . N," and then the dark-skinned woman takes a step forward and rests her almond hands on Emma's shoulders. Reese thinks that the woman actually looks scared now and sits up straight in her chair so that she has a better view of the board.

"D . . . L," someone says, and "Stop this now, Emma," the dark woman asks. She *sounds* afraid and maybe there's a hint of anger, too, but Emma only shakes her head and doesn't take her eyes off the restless planchette.

"It's okay, Danielle. We're just having a little fun, that's all."

"F . . . no, *E* . . ." and someone whispers the word, "Spindle, it said its name is Spindle," but the planchette is still moving and "*Please*," the dark woman says to Emma.

"S . . . H," and now the woman has taken her hands off Emma's shoulder, has stepped back into the shadows at the edge of the candle-light again. Emma calls out the letters with the others, voices joined in drunken expectation, and Reese has to restrain an urge to join them herself.

"A . . . N . . . K . . . S," and then the planchette is still and everyone's looking at Emma like she knows what they should do next. "Spindle-shanks," she says, and Reese catches the breathless hitch in her voice, as if she's been running or has climbed the stairs too quickly. Fat beads of sweat stand out on her forehead, glimmer wetly in the flickering, orange-white glow of the candles.

"Spindleshanks," she says again, and then, "That's *not* your name," she whispers.

"Ask it something else," one of the women says eagerly. "Ask Spindle-shanks something else, Emmie," but Emma shakes her head, frowns, and takes her hands from the planchette, breaking the mystic circle of fingers pressed against the tin. When the others follow suit, she pushes the Ouija board away from her again.

"I'm tired of this," she says, and Reese can tell that this time the petulance is there to hide something else, something she isn't used to hearing in Emma's voice. "Somebody turn on the lights."

Reese stands up and presses the switch on the dining room wall next to a gaudy, gold-framed reproduction of John Singer Sargent's *The Daughters of Edward Darley Boit*—the pale, secretive faces of five girls and the solid darkness framed between two urns—and in the flood of electric light, the first thing that Reese notices is that the almond-skinned woman has gone, that she no longer stands there behind Emma's chair. And she doesn't see the second thing until one of the women cries out and points frantically at the wall above the window, the white plaster above the drapes. Emma sees it, too, but neither of them says a word, both sit still and silent for a minute, two minutes, while the tall letters written in blood above the brocade valance begin to dry and turn from crimson to a dingy, reddish brown.

When everyone has left, and Emma has taken a couple of sleeping pills and gone upstairs, Reese sits at one end of the table and stares at the writing on the dining room wall. Spindleshanks in sloppy letters that began to drip and run before they began to dry, and she sips at her gin and wonders if they were already there before the reckless séance even started. Wonders, too, if Danielle Thibodaux has some hand in this, playing a clever, nasty trick on Emma's urbane boozers, if maybe they offended her or someone else at the Friday night party and this was their comeuppance, tit for tat, and next time perhaps they'll stick to their own gaudy thrills and leave the natives alone.

The writing is at least twelve feet off the floor and Reese can't imagine how the woman might have pulled it off, unless perhaps Emma was in on the prank as well. Maybe some collusion between the two of them to keep people talking about Emma Goldfarb's parties long after the lease is up and they've gone back to Boston. "Remember the night Emma called up Spindleshanks?" they'll say, or "Remember that dreadful stuff on the dining room wall? It *was* blood, wasn't it?" And yes, Reese thinks, it's a sensible explanation for Emma's insistence that they use the downstairs for the party that night, and that there be no light burning but the candles.

It almost makes Reese smile, the thought that Emma might be half so resourceful, and then she wonders how they're ever going to get the wall clean again. She's seen a ladder in the gardener's shed behind the house and Carlton will probably know someone who'll take care of it, paint over the mess if it can't be washed away.

In the morning, Emma will probably admit her part in the ghostly deceit and then she'll lie in bed laughing at her gullible friends. She'll probably even laugh at Reese and "I got you, too, didn't I?" she'll smirk. "Oh no, don't you try to lie to me, Miss Callicott. *I* saw the look on your face." And in a minute Reese blows out the candles, turns off the lights, and follows Emma upstairs to bed.

A few hours later, almost a quarter of four by the black hands of the alarm clock ticking loud on her bedside table, and Reese awakens from the nightmare of Harvard Square again. The snow storm become a blizzard and this time she didn't even make it past the church, no farther than the little graveyard huddled in the lee of the steeple, and the storm was like icicle daggers. She walked against the wind and kept her eyes directly in front of her, because there was something on the other side of the wrought-iron fence, something past the sharp pickets that wanted her to turn and see it. Something that mumbled and the sound of its feet in the snow was so soft, like footsteps in powdered sugar.

And then Reese was awake and sweating, shivering because the veranda doors were standing open again. The heat and humidity so bad at night, worse at night than in the day, she suspects, and they can't get to sleep without the cranky electric fan and the doors left open. But now even this stingy breeze is making her shiver and she gets up, moving cat-slow and cat-silent so she doesn't wake Emma, and walks across the room to close the doors and switch off the fan.

Reaching for the brass door handles when Emma stirs behind her, her voice groggy from the Valium and alcohol, groggy and confused, and "Reese? Is something wrong?" she asks. "Has something happened?"

"No, dear," Reese answers her, "I had a bad dream, that's all. Go back to sleep," and she's already pulling the tall French doors shut when something down on the sidewalk catches her attention. Some quick movement there in the darkness gathered beneath the ancient magnolias and oaks along Sixth Street; hardly any moon for shadows tonight, but what shadows there are enough to cast a deeper gloom below those shaggy boughs. And Reese stands very still and keeps her eyes on the street, waiting, though she couldn't say for what.

Emma shifts in bed and the mattress creaks and then there's only the noise from the old fan and Reese's heart, the night birds that she doesn't know the names for calling to one another from the trees. Reese squints into the blacker shades of night along the leafy edge of Sixth, directly across from the place where the police found the body of the murdered cook, searches for any hint of the movement she might or might not have seen only a moment before. But there's only the faint moonlight winking dull off the chrome fender of someone's Chrysler, the whole thing nothing more than a trick of her sleep-clouded eyes, the lingering nightmare, and Reese closes the veranda doors and goes back to bed, and Emma.

HOMECOMING

SYDNEY J. BOUNDS

Sydney J. Bounds (1920–2006) was a prolific British author who worked in many genres. He founded the science fiction fan group, the Cosmos Club, during World War II, and his early fiction appeared in the club's fanzine, *Cosmic Cuts*. His first professional sale never appeared, but by the late 1940s he was contributing "spicy" stories to the monthly magazines published by Utopia Press.

Writing under a number of pseudonyms, he became a regular contributor to such SF magazines as *Tales of Tomorrow*, *Worlds of Fantasy*, *New Worlds Science Fiction*, *Other Worlds Science Stories*, and *Fantastic Universe*, among other titles. When the magazine markets began to dry up, Bounds became a reliable contributor to various anthology series, including *New Writings in SF*, *The Fontana Book of Great Ghost Stories*, *The Fontana Book of Great Horror Stories*, *The Armada Monster Book*, and *The Armada Ghost Book*.

Some of the author's best fiction was collected by editor Philip Harbottle in *The Best of Sydney J. Bounds: Strange Portrait and Other Stories* and *The Best of Sydney J. Bounds: The Wayward Ship and Other Stories*, while his short story "The Circus" was adapted by

George A. Romero for a 1986 episode of the syndicated TV series *Tales of the Darkside.*

"Sometimes," revealed Bounds, "a story works because the author comes up with an original idea: this makes everyone happy. And sometimes an old theme can be updated for today's readers; this, too, can work.

"'Homecoming' is one of the latter—the Frankenstein theme is obvious—but this variation, I believe, is still effective."

HE WOKE AS though from a deep sleep, with a feeling of languor, and his first sensation was unpleasant: a smell of rotting flesh. He opened gummy eyes to a blur of faces. Mouths gaped and speech babbled in a meaningless stream. Then he felt the sting of a hypodermic and the fog began to clear.

The blur resolved into two faces, both male and obviously excited. One was young with a straggle of beard, pimply where the skin was naked. The older had fish-eyes behind thick-lensed spectacles, devil's eyebrows above. Each man wore a white gown and latex gloves.

"Can you hear me?"

Of course he could hear them. He wasn't deaf, but the effort needed to reply was beyond him in his present condition. He lay flat on his back, facing a dead-white ceiling. The powerful glare from massed arc-lamps made him blink and look away, toward a blank wall where tubes drained into a stainless-steel tank. It was cold.

"If you hear me, try to move your fingers."

He started to raise an arm which seemed weighted with a hand of lead. But when his hand came into focus, his arm froze. He stared at moldy flesh and sticks of protruding bone . . . his own hand? The sight brought him dismayingly to the here and now and a knowledge of the source of the smell: himself.

Memory began to tickle through the cells of his brain. His name: Michael Wilde, called "Mickey" by his friends. He half-remembered a series of business failures: used car dealer, an antique shop, second-hand books. And a girl. He couldn't recall her name now, only that he'd been crazy about her. That, and the black depression when she'd walked out on him. It seemed moments ago when he'd filled the bath and lay back in it; he tasted again the bitterness of sleeping tablets . . .

He was still drowsy, but the cold cut into him, made him shiver.

"Yes, I can hear you," he croaked, and it felt as though his throat muscles had rusted.

With creaking effort, he swung leaden legs off the tabletop and struggled to a sitting position. He was in a laboratory of some kind, with black boxes and cylinders and a panel studded with dials and switches.

The two doctors looked pleased. "An unqualified success," one commented.

Unqualified? He could be feeling better than this. "Surely you can do something about the smell?"

The young one squeezed an aerosol can, spraying perfume. It didn't kill the sickly-sweet odor, but masked it to some extent.

"That's a bit better." Wilde looked down at his naked body, saw bluish flesh peeling like the aftermath of some obscure disease. He swallowed. "Anyway, thanks for saving my life—guess you got to me barely in time? Don't worry, I won't suicide again."

The young man smiled. "We didn't," he said pleasantly. "You were truly dead—certified and in the grave for seven days. We dug you up secretly, at night, and Doctor Barnes tried out his revival technique on you. The experiment has succeeded beyond our best hopes."

Really dead then, and now resurrected. Uneasiness rumbled in his stomach like the onset of indigestion, his mind churned gruesome thoughts. "This technique of yours—"

"Something quite new in medical history. The body flushed out and refilled with fresh blood, the cells stimulated by bio-electricity, the heart restarted. You've no idea the time and trouble we've spent on you."

Experiment. Fresh blood. A pulse beat in Wilde's head. "Well, thanks again. I suppose you've some clothes that'll fit me?"

Barnes lifted devil's eyebrows. "For the time being you will stay here. You are alive again—and that's miracle enough—but by no means fully recovered. Brain tissue is quickly damaged when starved of oxygen."

"Besides, there'd be a dreadful row if it got about we'd been robbing graves," the young doctor added. "We'll keep you under observation for a bit—we've a lot more tests to make."

Under observation. Tests . . . the words jolted Michael Wilde. He'd never liked the idea of human guinea pigs, and didn't intend to let them continue using him. He slid from the table, stood upright, swaying.

"I feel fine. Nobody asked you to resurrect me—"

"This is a secret experiment for the advancement of medical knowledge. We can't expect the common people to understand."

Anger flared like a Very light. "It wasn't for my benefit then? You don't care what happens to me!"

"Of course we do," the young man said soothingly. "That's why you should stay here and let us take care of you. Full recovery may be a long process." He picked up another aerosol and carefully sprayed Wilde's ribs as bluish flesh sloughed off. "After all, you're our prize specimen."

It may have been the word "specimen" that triggered him off. Anger surged into berserk fury that pumped strength into his muscles. He lumbered forward, uttering a hoarse cry, glaring through a red haze. He'd never liked doctors anyway . . .

His hand grasped a wrench lying on a bench. He swiped drunkenly, connecting with Barnes's head. The doctor fell, blood spurting.

The young one backed away, turned and fled. He tore open a door, bounded up steps three at a time.

Wilde shuffled after him. At the top of the steps, he found another door leading on to the outside world. He saw open country and the doctor streaking across it in a Land Rover.

The sun warmed him, birdsong thrilled him. He breathed deeply of blossom-scented air before returning inside. Searching, he found clothes that fitted him after a fashion, and a mirror.

His hair, once brown and luxurious, was shedding, and he wore a bristle-like hog's hair on his jaw; pus oozed from one ear. He probed with his tongue and worked out a loose tooth. Suppressing a shudder, he turned from the mirror and climbed the steps.

Outside again, he walked down a lane, not recognizing where he was. He soon found it tiring to walk and, startlingly aware of the brittleness of his bones, lowered himself gently on to a grassy bank.

While he rested, a small black-and-white terrier came weaving across the fields. "Good dog," he called. "Here, boy!" The dog trotted toward him and stopped, wagging its tail. Then it sniffed with its sensitive nose and, tail between its legs, bolted, howling.

Wilde felt his depression return. He forced himself to rise, and walked on. The landscape was bleak moorland, deserted, but the doctors would naturally pick a lonely spot for their experiment. An hour passed before he came on an isolated cottage.

He limped up to the front door and knocked. An old man opened it, stared and gulped an inarticulate sound.

"Good afternoon," Wilde said politely. "I wonder if—"

He was slammed back against the doorframe as the old roan rushed past him, running down the lane. Swearing, he entered the cottage and helped himself to bread and cold sausage from the larder. He sat at the table, eating cautiously at first, then greedily. His stomach appeared to be in working order, and he felt stronger afterward.

But what did he do now? Legally dead, he was damned if he was going to perform like a rat in a maze. That was definite. He needed help. It took only a couple of minutes to be sure there was no telephone in the cottage, so he set off again.

The lane wound between hedgerows and, perhaps fifteen minutes later, he knew he had taken the same direction as the old man. The village was a small one and the street cleared quickly as he approached. Shutters closed; bolts slammed home. White faces peered from upstairs windows. He walked almost out of the village before he saw a telephone box.

He pulled open the door and squeezed inside, searching through pockets for a coin. He located one that had slipped through a hole in the lining, and wondered who he should call. Pete? Yes, Pete would think of something. But he couldn't remember the number . . .

He glanced back at the village. There were men on the street, gathering in a compact group, and they had dogs, shotguns, hayforks. Wilde didn't like the way the situation was developing. He shot out of the phone box, hurrying across a field, keeping close to the hedge for cover.

The mob followed him. They didn't seem anxious to catch up; perhaps they only wanted to drive him away. He was able to keep ahead of them, but they didn't give up; still they came after him.

He crossed another field and reached the outskirts of a wood. He was tiring again, heart pounding. There might be safety among the trees, somewhere to hide until dark.

He limped on and saw a teenage girl coming toward him, and desire stirred in him. For the first time since his resurrection, he felt glad to be alive. But he didn't want to scare her away . . .

He waited behind the trunk of a tree till she came close. Then he stepped out, soft words on bloated lips; she gave a choked-off scream and collapsed at his feet.

Cursing, he lifted her and stumbled into the wood, laid her down on a patch of grass. She was pretty, perhaps seventeen or eighteen, with well-shaped legs—tactfully he straightened her mini-skirt. Small breasts heaved convulsively under a thin sweater. His desire mounted.

After a few minutes she came to and looked up into his face. Her scream of terror pierced the sky, sending black rooks flapping.

"Quiet," he pleaded. "Don't be scared—I need your help."

It was no good. Her face off-white, she stared at the ground, body shaking with silent sobs.

Wilde stood angrily over her, realizing she was going to be no help. Then he heard dogs howling. He stumbled deeper into the wood, pushing through undergrowth till he came to a small stream. He waded in, hoping to throw them off the scent. Even to him the smell was getting so bad he could hardly stand it.

He heard men threshing the bushes behind him. It began to rain, large warm drops. In the distance, thunder rolled. The sky darkened. Rain pelted down, soaking his clothes, turning the ground to mud.

His feet dragged like heavy weights and pieces of decayed flesh dropped from hands and face, leaving a rancid trail he hoped the rain would destroy.

The sound of the chase faded as the rain increased and depression returned, black as the sky. Resurrection hadn't done him much good so far. Perhaps he should return to the laboratory before it was too late? His heartbeat seemed to be slowing and every step became an agony. A memory of Dr. Barnes nagged him . . .

He veered through an arc, circling. The sky was dark, the rain a wet curtain obscuring vision. He slipped in the mud and it was too much effort to rise, so he crawled on hands and knees, wondering why he bothered—so much easier just to lie where he was. Another memory, of a man dying in the Arctic.

He crawled on till he felt a rough stone wall, followed it to a gate. He pushed the gate open and crawled inside, imagining a house, medical aid.

Unexpectedly, he fell into a hole. It was a deep hole and he lacked the energy to climb out. He turned over to lie on his back and look up at the sky, felt rain on his face.

Lightning flashed, revealing the tops of bone-white headstones. The soil had the smell of newly dug earth. In a way, he supposed, it was a kind of homecoming—and he settled down to wait for death to catch up with him.

FEEDERS AND EATERS

NEIL GAIMAN

Neil Gaiman is the author of the best-selling 2013 Book of the Year, *The Ocean at the End of the Lane*, the Carnegie Award–winning *The Graveyard Book*, as well as *Coraline*, *Neverwhere*, the essay collection *The View from the Cheap Seats*, and The Sandman series of graphic novels, among many other works.

His fiction has received many awards, including the Carnegie and Newbery medals, and the Hugo, Nebula, World Fantasy, and Eisner awards.

Originally from England, he now divides his time between the UK, where he recently turned *Good Omens*—originally a novel he wrote with Terry Pratchett—into a television series, and the US, where he is professor in the arts at Bard College.

"This story started as a dream I had in 1984," remembers Gaiman, "when I was living in Edgware, North London. I was, in the dream, both me and the man in the story. Normally dreams don't make stories, but this one continued to haunt me, and in 1990-ish I wrote it as a comic for Mark Buckingham to draw. Not many people read it, and it was printed so dark that much of what was happening became almost impossible to make out.

"When I was asked for a story of mine for this anthology, I remembered that one, and I got intrigued by the idea of taking an old horror story I wrote as a comic and rewriting it as prose. It's an odd piece, like a collaboration between me age thirty and me age forty-one, yet I wondered how hard it would be to turn it from a comic into a short story."

As you will see, for a talented storyteller such as Gaiman, it was not hard at all . . .

THIS IS A true story, pretty much. As far as that goes, and whatever good it does anybody.

It was late one night, and I was cold, in a city where I had no right to be. Not at that time of night, anyway. I won't tell you which city. I'd missed my last train, and I wasn't sleepy, so I prowled the streets around the station until I found an all-night café. Somewhere warm to sit.

You know the kind of place; you've been there: café's name on a Pepsi sign above a dirty plate-glass window, dried egg residue between the tines of all their forks. I wasn't hungry, but I bought a slice of toast and a mug of greasy tea, so they'd leave me alone.

There were a couple of other people in there, sitting alone at their tables, derelicts and insomniacs huddled over their empty plates. Dirty coats and donkey jackets, each buttoned up to the neck.

I was walking back from the counter, with my tray, when somebody said, "Hey." It was a man's voice. "You," the voice said, and I knew he was talking to me, not to the room. "I know you. Come here. Sit over here."

I ignored it. You don't want to get involved, not with anyone you'd run into in a place like that.

Then he said my name, and I turned and looked at him. When someone knows your name, you don't have any option.

"I CAN ALREADY HEAR HER STARTING TO EAT."

"Don't you know me?" he asked. I shook my head. I didn't know any-one who looked like that. You don't forget something like that. "It's me," he said, his voice a pleading whisper. "Eddie Barrow. Come on mate. You know me."

And when he said his name I did know him, more or less. I mean, I knew Eddie Barrow. We had worked on a building site together, ten years back, during my only real flirtation with manual work.

Eddie Barrow was tall, and heavily muscled, with a movie star smile and lazy good looks. He was ex-police. Sometimes he'd tell me stories, true tales of fitting-up and doing over, of punishment and crime. He had left the force after some trouble between him and one of the top brass. He said it was the Chief Superintendent's wife forced him to leave. Eddie was always getting into trouble with women. They really liked him, women.

When we were working together on the building site they'd hunt him down, give him sandwiches, little presents, whatever. He never seemed to *do* anything to make them like him; they just liked him. I used to watch him to see how he did it, but it didn't seem to be anything he did. Eventually, I decided it was just the way he was: big, strong, not very bright, and terribly, terribly good-looking.

But that was ten years ago.

The man sitting at the Formica table wasn't good-looking. His eyes were dull, and rimmed with red, and they stared down at the tabletop, without hope. His skin was gray. He was too thin, obscenely thin. I could see his scalp through his filthy hair. I said, "What happened to you?"

"How d'you mean?"

"You look a bit rough," I said, although he looked worse than rough; he looked dead. Eddie Barrow had been a big guy. Now he'd collapsed in on himself. All bones and flaking skin.

"Yeah," he said. Or maybe "Yeah?" I couldn't tell. Then, resigned, flatly, "Happens to us all in the end."

He gestured with his left hand, pointed at the seat opposite him. His right arm hung stiffly at his side, his right hand safe and hidden in the pocket of his coat.

Eddie's table was by the window, where anyone walking past could see you. Not somewhere I'd sit by choice, not if it was up to me. But it was too late now. I sat down facing him and I sipped my tea. I didn't say anything, which could have been a mistake. Small talk might have kept his demons at a distance. But I cradled my mug and said nothing. So I suppose he must have thought that I wanted to know more, that I cared. I didn't care. I had enough problems of my own. I didn't want to know about his struggle with whatever it was that had brought him to this state—drink, or drugs, or disease—but he started to talk, in a gray voice, and I listened.

"I came here a few years back, when they were building the bypass. Stuck around after, the way you do. Got a room in an old place around the back of Prince Regent's Street. Room in the attic. It was a family house, really. They only rented out the top floor, so there were just the two boarders, me and Miss Corvier. We were both up in the attic, but in separate rooms, next door to each other. I'd hear her moving about. And there was a cat. It was the family cat, but it came upstairs to say hello, every now and again, which was more than the family ever did.

"I always had my meals with the family, but Miss Corvier she didn't ever come down for meals, so it was a week before I met her. She was coming out of the upstairs lavvy. She looked so old. Wrinkled face, like an old, old monkey. But long hair, down to her waist, like a young girl.

"It's funny, with old people, you don't think they feel things like we do. I mean, here's her, old enough to be my granny and . . ." He stopped. Licked his lips with a gray tongue. "Anyway . . . I came up to the room one night and there's a brown paper bag of mushrooms outside my door on the ground. It was a present, I knew that straight off. A present for me. Not normal mushrooms, though. So I knocked on her door.

"I says, 'Are these for me?'

"'Picked them meself, Mister Barrow,' she says.

"'They aren't like toadstools or anything?' I asked. 'Y'know, poisonous? Or funny mushrooms?'

"She just laughs. Cackles even. 'They're for eating,' she says. 'They're fine. Shaggy inkcaps, they are. Eat them soon now. They go off quick. They're best fried up with a little butter and garlic.'

"I say, 'Are you having some too?'

"She says, 'No.' She says, 'I used to be a proper one for mushrooms, but not anymore, not with my stomach. But they're lovely. Nothing better than a young shaggy inkcap mushroom. It's astonishing the things that people don't eat. All the things around them that people could eat, if only they knew it.'

"I said 'Thanks,' and went back into my half of the attic. They'd done the conversion a few years before, nice job really. I put the mushrooms down by the sink. After a few days they dissolved into black stuff, like ink, and I had to put the whole mess into a plastic bag and throw it away.

"I'm on my way downstairs with the plastic bag, and I run into her on the stairs, she says 'Hullo Mister B.'

"I say, 'Hello Miss Corvier.'

"'Call me Effie,' she says. 'How were the mushrooms?'

"'Very nice, thank you,' I said. 'They were lovely.'

"She'd leave me other things after that, little presents, flowers in old milk-bottles, things like that, then nothing. I was a bit relieved when the presents suddenly stopped.

"So I'm down at dinner with the family, the lad at the poly, he was home for the holidays. It was August. Really hot. And someone says they hadn't seen her for about a week, and could I look in on her. I said I didn't mind.

"So I did. The door wasn't locked. She was in bed. She had a thin sheet over her, but you could see she was naked under the sheet. Not that I was trying to see anything, it'd be like looking at your gran in the altogether. This old lady. But she looked so pleased to see me.

"'Do you need a doctor?' I says.

"She shakes her head. 'I'm not ill,' she says. 'I'm hungry. That's all.'

"'Are you sure,' I say, 'because I can call someone. It's not a bother. They'll come out for old people.'

"She says, 'Edward? I don't want to be a burden on anyone, but I'm so hungry.'

"'Right. I'll get you something to eat,' I said. 'Something easy on your tummy,' I says. That's when she surprises me. She looks embarrassed. Then she says, very quietly, '*Meat*. It's got to be fresh meat, and raw. I won't let anyone else cook for me. Meat. Please, Edward.'

"'Not a problem,' I says, and I go downstairs. I thought for a moment about nicking it from the cat's bowl, but of course I didn't. It was like, I knew she wanted it, so I had to do it. I had no choice. I went down to Safeway, and I bought her a ReadiPak of best ground sirloin.

"The cat smelled it. Followed me up the stairs. I said, 'You get down, puss. It's not for you. It's for Miss Corvier and she's not feeling well, and she's going to need it for her supper,' and the thing mewed at me as if it hadn't been fed in a week, which I knew wasn't true because its bowl was still half-full. Stupid, that cat was.

"I knock on her door, she says 'Come in.' She's still in the bed, and I give her the pack of meat, and she says 'Thank you Edward, you've got a good heart.' And she starts to tear off the plastic wrap, there in the bed. There's a puddle of brown blood under the plastic tray, and it drips onto her sheet, but she doesn't notice. Makes me shiver.

"I'm going out the door, and I can already hear her starting to eat with her fingers, cramming the raw mince into her mouth. And she hadn't got out of bed.

"But the next day she's up and about, and from there on she's in and out at all hours, in spite of her age, and I think there you are. They say red meat's bad for you, but it did her the world of good. And raw, well, it's just steak tartare, isn't it? You ever eaten raw meat?"

The question came as a surprise. I said, "Me?"

Eddie looked at me with his dead eyes, and he said, "Nobody else at this table."

"Yes. A little. When I was a small boy—four, five years old—my grandmother would take me to the butcher's with her, and he'd give me slices of raw liver, and I'd just eat them, there in the shop, like that. And everyone would laugh."

I hadn't thought of that in twenty years. But it was true.

I still like my liver rare, and sometimes, if I'm cooking and if nobody else is around, I'll cut a thin slice of raw liver before I season it, and I'll eat it, relishing the texture and the naked, iron taste.

"Not me," he said. "I liked my meat properly cooked. So the next thing that happened was Thompson went missing."

"Thompson?"

"The cat. Somebody said there used to be two of them, and they called them Thompson and Thompson. I don't know why. Stupid, giving them both the same name. The first one was squashed by a lorry." He pushed at a small mound of sugar on the Formica top with a fingertip. His left hand, still. I was beginning to wonder whether he had a right arm. Maybe the sleeve was empty. Not that it was any of my business. Nobody gets through life without losing a few things on the way.

I was trying to think of some way of telling him I didn't have any money, just in case he was going to ask me for something when he got to the end of his story. I didn't have any money: just a train ticket and enough pennies for the bus ticket home.

"I was never much of a one for cats," he said suddenly. "Not really. I liked dogs. Big, faithful things. You knew where you were with a dog. Not cats. Go off for days on end, you don't see them. When I was a lad, we had a cat, it was called Ginger. There was a family down the street, they had a cat they called Marmalade. Turned out it was the same cat, getting fed by all of us. Well, I mean. Sneaky little buggers. You can't trust them.

"That was why I didn't think anything when Thompson went away. The family was worried. Not me. I knew it'd come back. They always do.

"Anyway, a few nights later, I heard it. I was trying to sleep, and I couldn't. It was the middle of the night, and I heard this mewing. Going on, and on, and on. It wasn't loud, but when you can't sleep these things just get on your nerves. I thought maybe it was stuck up in the rafters, or out on the roof outside. Wherever it was, there wasn't any point in trying to sleep through it. I knew that. So I got up, and I got dressed—even put my boots on in case I was going to be climbing out onto the roof—and I went looking for the cat.

"I went out in the corridor. It was coming from Miss Corvier's room on the other side of the attic. I knocked on her door, but no one answered. Tried the door. It wasn't locked. So I went in. I thought maybe that the cat was stuck somewhere. Or hurt. I don't know. I just wanted to help, really.

"Miss Corvier wasn't there. I mean, you know sometimes if there's anyone in a room, and that room was empty. Except there's something on the floor in the corner going *mrie, mrie* . . . And I turned on the light to see what it was."

He stopped then for almost a minute, the fingers of his left hand picking at the black goo that had crusted around the neck of the ketchup bottle. It was shaped like a large tomato. Then he said, "What I didn't understand was how it could still be alive. I mean, it was. And from the chest up, it was alive, and breathing, and fur and everything. But its back legs, its rib cage. Like a chicken carcass. Just bones. And what are they called, sinews? And, it lifted its head, and it looked at me.

"It may have been a cat, but I knew what it wanted. It was in its eyes. I mean." He stopped. "Well, I just knew. I'd never seen eyes like that. You would have known what it wanted, all it wanted, if you'd seen those eyes. I did what it wanted. You'd have to be a monster, not to."

"What did you do?"

"I used my boots." Pause. "There wasn't much blood. Not really. I just stamped, and stamped on its head, until there wasn't really anything much left that looked like anything. If you'd seen it looking at you like that, you would have done what I did."

I didn't say anything.

"And then I heard someone coming up the stairs to the attic, and I thought I ought to do something, I mean, it didn't look good. I don't know what it must have looked like really, but I just stood there, feeling stupid, with a stinking mess on my boots, and when the door opens, it's Miss Corvier.

"And she sees it all. She looks at me. And she says, 'You killed him.' I can hear something funny in her voice, and for a moment I don't know what it is, and then she comes closer, and I realize that she's crying.

"That's something about old people, when they cry like children, you don't know where to look, do you? And she says, 'He was all I had to keep me going, and you killed him. After all I've done,' she says, 'making it so the meat stays fresh, so the life stays on. After all I've done.'

"'I'm an old woman,' she says. 'I need my meat.'

"I didn't know what to say.

"She's wiping her eyes with her hand. 'I don't want to be a burden on anybody,' she says. She's crying now. And she's looking at me. She says, 'I never wanted to be a burden.' She says, 'That was my meat. Now,' she says, 'who's going to feed me now?'"

He stopped, rested his gray face in his left hand, as if he was tired. Tired of talking to me, tired of the story, tired of life. Then he shook his head, and looked at me, and said, "If you'd seen that cat, you would have done what I did. Anyone would have done."

He raised his head then, for the first time in his story, looked me in the eyes. I thought I saw an appeal for help in his eyes, something he was too proud to say aloud.

Here it comes, I thought. This is where he asks me for money.

Somebody outside tapped on the window of the café. It wasn't a loud tapping, but Eddie jumped. He said, "I have to go now. That means I have to go."

I just nodded. He got up from the table. He was still a tall man, which almost surprised me: he'd collapsed in on himself in so many other ways. He pushed the table away as he got up, and as he got up he took his right hand out of his coat-pocket. For balance, I suppose. I don't know.

Maybe he wanted me to see it. But if he wanted me to see it, why did he keep it in his pocket the whole time? No, I don't think he wanted me to see it. I think it was an accident.

He wasn't wearing a shirt or a jumper under his coat, so I could see his arm, and his wrist. Nothing wrong with either of them. He had a normal wrist. It was only when you looked below the wrist that you saw most of the flesh had been picked from the bones, chewed like chicken wings, leaving only dried morsels of meat, scraps and crumbs, and little else. He only had three fingers left, and most of a thumb. I suppose the other finger-bones must have just fallen right off, with no skin or flesh to hold them on.

That was what I saw. Only for a moment, then he put his hand back in his pocket, and pushed out of the door, into the chilly night.

I watched him then, through the dirty plate-glass of the café window.

It was funny. From everything he'd said, I'd imagined Miss Corvier to be an old woman. But the woman waiting for him, outside, on the pavement, couldn't have been much over thirty. She had long, long hair, though. The kind of hair you can sit on, as they say, although that always sounds faintly like a line from a dirty joke. She looked a bit like a hippy, I suppose. Sort of pretty, in a hungry kind of way.

She took his arm, and looked up into his eyes, and they walked away out of the café's light for all the world like a couple of teenagers who were just beginning to realize that they were in love.

I went back up to the counter and bought another cup of tea, and a couple of packets of crisps to see me through until the morning, and I sat and thought about the expression on his face when he'd looked at me that last time.

On the milk-train back to the big city I sat opposite a woman carrying a baby. It was floating in formaldehyde, in a heavy glass container. She needed to sell it, rather urgently, and although I was extremely tired we talked about her reasons for selling it, and about other things, for the rest of the journey.

NOTHING OF HIM THAT DOTH FADE

POPPY Z. BRITE

Before announcing his "retirement," for almost twenty years Billy Martin wrote a string of acclaimed and successful horror novels and short stories under the name Poppy Z. Brite.

As Brite he published the novels *Lost Souls*, *Drawing Blood*, *Exquisite Corpse*, and *The Crow: The Lazarus Heart*, along with the story collections *Swamp Foetus* (aka *Wormwood*), *Are You Loathesome Tonight?* (aka *Self-Made Man*), *Wrong Things* (with Caitlín R. Kiernan), *The Devil You Know*, and *Antediluvian Tales*. He also edited the vampire anthologies *Love in Vein* and *Twice Bitten (Love in Vein II)*.

In 1999 he published *Courtney Love: The Real Story*, a semiofficial biography of the singer, and he subsequently wrote a series of novels set in the restaurant world of New Orleans.

His short story "The Sixth Sentinel" was filmed in 1999 (under the title "The Dream Sentinel") for the Showtime TV series *The Hunger*.

"'Nothing of Him That Doth Fade' was first published in *Aqua Erotica*," explains the author, "a good anthology that unfortunately received more attention for its gimmicky format than for the quality of its stories. Billed as 'the first-ever waterproof book for adults,' it was printed on heavy, moisture-resistant paper designed to be read in the bath or (presumably) to repel other fluids that might sully its pages.

"I'm fond of this story because I think it comes closer than anything else I've written to capturing the essence of a dying relationship—that point at which you know you can't continue with a person, but you still love them too much to let go. Its antecedents include Ray Bradbury's 'Interval in Sunlight' and Harlan Ellison's 'Neither Your Jenny Nor Mine.' Though both these authors are best known for their genre fiction, these two stories contain nary a rocket ship or bug-eyed monster—they are small masterpieces about the terrible things people do to the ones they love or have loved.

"I don't believe I have created a masterpiece, but I do think I've written something that doesn't need waterproof paper to be effective."

THE TWO AMERICANS surfaced slowly, dizzy from the sights of the Great Barrier Reef: the endless billowing vistas of coral; the lone, shy, deadly blue-ringed octopus; the crown-of-thorns starfish that was beautiful even as it gradually nibbled away the reef. The boat was nowhere in sight. They removed their mouthpieces, cleared their face-masks of water, and looked again. The boat was still gone.

"I think they've left us," said Theo.

"Don't be stupid," said Jack.

They had arrived in Australia a week and a half ago, starting out in gay-friendly Sydney to acclimatize themselves and avoid hearing, at least for a few days, the age-old but tiresome question, *Are you two . . . together?* Neither of them wanted to answer that, not about each other, not anymore. Both were in their late thirties. Theo, a pastry chef, was broad across the shoulders, handsome in the manner of an aging schoolboy, conciliatory unless his patience was stretched too far. Jack, a freelance writer for magazines, was long and lean, hatchet-faced and red-headed, always ready with a side-of-the mouth barb to stretch Theo's patience. They had spent twelve years in each other's company. The first eight or so had been good. The trip was an attempt to recapture that goodness. In his heart, neither believed it would work, but the idea of having again what they'd once taken for granted was worth the time, money, and chance.

It was impossible to put one's finger on the moment when things had begun to go sour between them. They'd never been one of those couples who got along perfectly, or seemed to: even during the first couple of years their fights were frequent, loud, and passionate. Sometimes they reconciled with furious lovemaking. More often they would wake up the next morning and find that the whole thing just seemed silly. They were friends as well as lovers then. Friends could fight, air it out, then put it behind them. Friends could laugh at such things; they had spent much time laughing together.

It was when they stopped fighting that things had begun to atrophy. Now, instead of fighting, they sniped constantly. A shortcoming pointed out here, an old grievance dredged up there. It was a habit that clung as closely to them as they had once clung to each other. Friends did not snipe. But Jack and Theo were no longer friends.

The Sydney Harbor threw off azure sparkles. The famous silhouette of the Opera House rose above the water like the tail flukes of a white whale diving deep. Jack and Theo chose an outdoor table at a café that promised Harbor-caught seafood.

"It's too windy out here," Jack said after a few minutes, weighing down his flapping paper napkin with his knife.

"It feels good. Smells like the ocean."

"Fine." Jack pulled his windbreaker tightly around his lanky frame and huddled into himself.

"Let's go inside," Theo said after a few minutes.

"No, it's fine, you wanted to stay out here."

"You're cold. You're making that quite obvious. We won't be able to enjoy our lunch. Come on, let's go in."

"Don't worry about it."

Theo rose from the table, grabbing his napkin and silverware. "I said let's go in the fucking restaurant!" He turned and stalked through the double doors of the café, not turning to see if Jack followed. After a minute, Jack did.

The combination platter of prawns, oysters, and Balmain bugs was fresh and delicious. Ten minutes after it was served, Theo started checking his watch.

"What's wrong?" Jack asked.

"The food took so long to come—if we don't get going soon, we'll miss the 1:15 ferry over to the zoo."

"So we'll catch the next one."

"I wanted to get there by two o'clock."

"What difference does it make?"

"It's a big zoo. We won't have time to see it all if we don't get there early enough."

"So we'll see whatever we have time for."

"What's the point of that? If we're not going to see it all, we may as well not go. In fact, let's just not go."

"Oh, come on. Where else are we going to see a live platypus?" This was Jack's feeble attempt at a joke. His once-irrepressible wit still occasionally tossed one out, but Theo never laughed any more.

"We can see one on the Nature Channel back home."

"That's good enough for you, is it? To see something on TV? Figures."

And so it went, over the cracked and sliced bodies of the small sea creatures. As it turned out, they did take the ferry to the Taronga Park Zoo that day, and even saw a live platypus. But neither of them enjoyed it very much.

Two years ago, Jack had discovered that Theo was sleeping with a line cook at the restaurant where he worked. Theo had always maintained that he was bisexual, at least in theory, but the fact that the line cook was a woman made Jack feel doubly betrayed. It was as if Theo had rejected not just him, but his very maleness.

The affair was not serious, and Theo had already broken it off by the time Jack found out. The line cook no longer worked at Theo's restaurant, and Theo swore he didn't know or care where she had gone. They decided to stay together, not so much because they believed they had anything worth saving as because the idea of being alone after so many years frightened them both too much.

It is said that such betrayals may be forgiven, but can never be forgotten. Jack could do neither. Despite how the memory tore at him—or perhaps because of that tearing—he was never able to let it go. For longer than he cared to remember he pictured Theo with the woman and felt disgusted with his own body, could not bear to look at himself in the mirror or let Theo see him unclothed, let alone touch him. Even now, twenty-four months later, he would hurl it at Theo when Theo was least expecting it, in the most irrelevant situations possible, in the ugliest terms possible. "Oh, I'm not good enough for you because I don't have a pussy. Or tits maybe? Is that it?"

Surrender no weapon, even if it is as likely to blow up in your face as it is to hurt your enemy, even if you realize it is impossible for the battle ever to be won.

The afternoon light on the ocean's surface was a punishing thing, glittering coldly like diamonds, reflecting back up into their eyes. Within a couple of hours their faces were painfully sunburned. Small waves lapped against them, momentarily soothing but eventually turning their skin chapped and salty.

"The boat'll come for us," said Theo. "They'll get back to Cairns and see they forgot us. They'll shit themselves. They'll be back."

"But will we still be here?" said Jack. Theo realized it was a good question; they had no way of knowing how far they'd drifted from the site of the dive.

They had inflated their BCDs and lashed together their empty air tanks, creating an unwieldy flotation device to which they could cling. They linked hands across this device, helping to hold each other up.

"They'll come for us," Theo said again, with less conviction.

More time passed; they could not tell how much. They were very thirsty. They had stopped talking at all. The sun sank lower in the sky, and the water took on a bloody tinge.

Suddenly Jack lifted his head. "Listen," he said, and then they both heard it: the sound of rotors chopping air. A helicopter! They could see it in the distance, a chitinous speck in the gloaming. They both began to shout. Jack let go of the air tanks and struggled in the water, trying to remove his swim trunks. When he had them off, he waved them above his head, a red flag that seemed hopelessly small in the vastness.

The helicopter passed far to their right, circled a time or two more, then headed away. They screamed at it until their throats were raw even though they knew the people inside could not possibly hear them over the rotors and the wind. Theo laid his head against the air tanks and began to cry. Jack looked at him, then looked away toward where the helicopter had disappeared.

"We could try to swim back," he said.

Theo choked on a sob, tried to catch his breath. His nose was running, and he ducked his face into the water to clear it. "The hell we could. Weren't you listening to the captain? He said the reef was fifty kilometers from Cairns."

"We may have drifted closer."

"Not that much closer. Not possible. And we wouldn't even know which direction to swim."

"We'd go the way the chopper went."

"Which way was that?"

Jack looked around, started to speak, shook his head. He raised his arm out of the water to point, hesitated, then put it down.

"I don't know either," said Theo, gripping Jack's hands more tightly. They managed to heave themselves high enough on the air tanks to lay their heads together, and each felt a tiny bit of comfort, a spark in the cold salt void.

They'd taken a rental car in Sydney and begun the long drive north along the coastal highway, heading for Cairns, the jumping-off point for dive tours of the Great Barrier Reef. Their love of scuba diving was one of the first things they'd discovered they had in common, a thing they had traveled all over the world to enjoy together. They shared a sense of awe for the depths, an appreciation of the sea's majesty that neither of them had ever encountered in anyone else.

It seemed an eternity since their last diving trip off the western coast of Jamaica, but they knew the Reef was supposed to be one of the most spectacular dives on Earth: it was a big part of what had brought them to Australia. Driving all the way to Cairns had been Theo's idea. He'd wanted to detour into the outback along the way, but Jack had vetoed the idea on the grounds that it would be full of choking dust, black flies, and poofter-hating rednecks.

They made good time the first day, driving almost ten hours, then found a room in a small hotel in Brisbane. They had thought to push on the following day, but in morning's light Brisbane proved to be a lovely city, dotted with fountains and sculptures and even a windmill, frosted here and there with lacy ironwork balconies that reminded them of New Orleans's French Quarter. They had last been in New Orleans nine years ago, so the memories were good. They booked their hotel room for another two nights.

The next day they climbed Mount Coot-tha, an easy two-hour hike through slender trees with sunlight slanting through their branches. At the summit, Brisbane spread before them like an exquisite miniature painting, and they could see the rocky humps of islands in the bay. They lingered on the summit and found themselves alone. Jack came up behind Theo, embraced him and whispered in his ear.

"I *do* love you. You know that, you must know that. I'm sorry I've been so awful the past few days. I could never have come here with anyone else."

"Me either," said Theo, and squeezed Jack's long fingers tightly in his own. "Let's just forget the past few days and enjoy the rest of the trip."

They were too tired from the hike to have sex that night, or perhaps they were just afraid of risking the fragile peace they'd forged. But they talked for hours over dinner and wine, the kind of amiable, inconsequential talk they hadn't had in recent memory, and they slept curled tightly in each other's arms.

The car wouldn't start the next morning, though, and they had to wait four hours for a man from the rental agency to show up with a replacement, and they began to snarl at each other again. By the time they had transferred their luggage to the new car and were heading back up the coastal highway, a heavy silence hung between them. The greatest pain was this: each remembered the magic of the previous day on the mountain and the words they had spoken, but none of it mattered.

The owner of Sea Pearl Diving Tours had been dressing down his instructor for nearly an hour, but this did not change the fact that the instructor had somehow failed to do a head count after the last dive. Only when the boat got back to Cairns did anyone realize that two of the passengers were missing.

"Do you realize the odds of finding those people at this point?"

"Yes," the instructor said miserably.

"Do you realize that you will be directly responsible for their deaths if they aren't found?"

"Yes."

"Do you have any idea how much their families will be able to sue us for? You know how fuckin' litigious Americans are!"

The instructor did not answer this last question, as he had no idea how such things worked. He was just a diver who was barely good enough to teach other people the rudiments of scuba diving, but he tried to take care of his groups. The worst thing that had ever happened on one of his dives prior to this was a German woman who had been badly stung by a box jellyfish. She'd been in a lot of pain and mad as hell, but ultimately she had been fine. He doubted the two Americans were going to be fine.

"They're being searched for?"

"Yes, you fuckin' wanker, they're *being searched for*. We've got a helicopter and three boats combing a hundred-kilometer area of sea. A bit like finding the proverbial needle in the haystack, wouldn't you say?"

The instructor wouldn't say anything at all. He only just managed to stand up and get himself out of the owner's office before the hot tears of his shame began to flow.

North of Brisbane, Theo and Jack crossed into the Tropic of Capricorn. The land became brown and scorched-looking, and they had to turn on the rental car's air conditioner, which first worked abominably, then not at all. The tightening fist of the heat did nothing to improve their tempers. The scenery grew monotonous: jagged volcanic outcroppings stabbing into a dull reddish sky. Closer to Cairns there would be dripping, steaming rain forest, but here there was nothing for the eye to rest upon.

They made their next overnight stop in Mackay, the heart of the sugar cane belt that began north of Brisbane and ran all the way up the coast past Cairns. Something about the cane intrigued Jack, and he wanted to explore the town. Theo, who had driven all day, had a pounding headache. In the hotel, he pulled the curtains and went to bed while it was still light. Jack ventured out alone.

He walked through the straight streets, along the windy riverfront, past an incongruously large shopping mall and a sign notifying him that he was leaving the Mackay town limits. Then he was in the sugar cane fields. Cane towered over his head, dark purple, thick-jointed, leafy. The sky was beginning to darken. In the distance he saw a column of smoke rising over the fields, then orange flames flickering through the cane. Somebody was burning off a field before the harvest! Jack had read of this practice, which removed the leaves and was said to sweeten the cane, but he had not hoped for the extraordinary good luck of actually seeing it done, had not even known it was the right time of year.

He stood at the edge of the road watching the fire for a long time. Its fierce color and wild motion drained the sluggishness of the long car ride from him. He did not wish Theo was with him. He felt unusually free, unusually *himself*. Out here, away from his lover of a dozen years, he was only Jack. He was no longer the bickering, blaming Jack of Jack-and-Theo, though he knew he would be that Jack again tomorrow. He realized he hardly knew this Jack any more, this man standing alone on a country road on the other side of the world from his home, watching sugar cane burn.

For the thousandth or the millionth time, he thought of leaving, of walking on through the cane fields to the next town, of catching a train or a bus back to Sydney. His wallet and his passport were in his pocket. He could go.

He thought about this for a while. Then he remembered Theo's headache; the pain in Theo's eyes had been genuine and slightly desperate. He could not bear the idea of leaving Theo to fall asleep in pain and wake up alone. Perhaps that was only his latest excuse, but it was true.

Jack turned away from the bright flames and retraced his steps back through the cane fields, back into the town, back to the hotel where Theo slept.

Somehow, clinging to each other across the lashed-together air tanks, Jack and Theo dozed fitfully through the night. They were cold when they woke at dawn, but the terrible thirst had eased a little. They both knew it would return in the full light of day.

As the sun rose in the wrong direction across the sky, they saw a plane circling low above the ocean's surface, far away. A little later they saw a boat on the horizon. They shouted and waved just as they had done the day before, but none of it made any difference.

"I'm tired," said Theo.

There was a crack in his voice, and at another time Jack might have latched onto that and shaken it like a pit bull. Instead he only said, "I know."

"Do you think we have any chance at all?"

Jack began to answer, but then his head jerked up and his eyes widened. He stared at Theo, mute, obviously terrified.

"What?"

"I felt something brush my leg," said Jack.

They looked down through the clear water and saw huge dark torpedo-shapes circling lazily below.

"Sharks."

"The dive instructor said they wouldn't bother people."

"Yeah, I'd put a lot of stock in what the dive instructor said."

They were quiet for a while, staring down at the dark circling shapes. The sharks made no attempt to approach them, not yet. But the psychological effect was that of a man lost in the desert who sees the first vultures overhead.

"We're going to die," said Theo. It was not a question, not even a half-veiled plea for denial or comfort; it was nothing but a statement of fact.

"Come here," said Jack, and let go of the air tanks.

They shucked their inflatable life vests and gave them to the current. Theo kicked off his fins and his swim trunks, and they pressed their bodies together, making a line of warmth in the slight chill of the ocean. The water was a great buoyant hand cradling them as they held each other. They sometimes still had sex, but it had been years since they'd really kissed. They kissed now, softly, remembering the feel and taste of each other's mouths; then harder, with teeth and tongues, with fingers tangling in each other's wet hair.

"You've got a one-track mind," said Theo, and they both laughed. It was something he had said to Jack in the early, sex-drenched days of their relationship, when they could not get enough of each other.

Their hands crept lower, beneath the water line. Their cocks were two rigid columns of flesh. They no longer felt the cold water, had no awareness of the depths yawning beneath them; it was like being in bed together years ago, knowing and feeling nothing outside their world of two-made-one.

They did not trust death to give them that fabled final orgasm. They gave it to each other with their hands and the friction of their bodies, and their seed mingled with the ocean, the salty essence of their lives returning to its primordial home, a triumph over the void as well as an acceptance of it.

Then they held each other very tightly and let the tanks float away. They did not want to be taken, to wonder who would go first, to see each other ripped apart, the pool of blood spreading like an oil slick on the water's surface. Instead, they took one last breath in unison, savoring the seldom-noticed sweetness of air, and dived together forever.

THE UNFORTUNATE

TIM LEBBON

Tim Lebbon is a *New York Times* best-selling writer who has had more than forty novels published to date, including a number of collaborations with Christopher Golden, the movie novelizations of *30 Days of Night*, *The Cabin in the Woods*, and *Kong: Skull Island*, and tie-ins to the *Hellboy*, *Star Wars*, *Alien*, *Predator*, and *Alien vs. Predator* franchises.

Some of his own, more recent titles include *Coldbrook*, *The Hunt*, *The Family Man* (as "T. J. Lebbon"), and *Relics*, while his short fiction has been collected in *Nothing as it Seems* and *Last Exit for the Lost*. Lebbon's eponymous short story was made into the movie *Pay the Ghost* starring Nicolas Cage, and his novel *The Silence* was recently filmed featuring Stanley Tucci and Miranda Otto.

He is a winner of the Bram Stoker Award for Short Fiction and the British Fantasy Awards for Best Novel, Best Novella, and Best Short Fiction.

"For a long time I'd wanted to write a story about the nature of luck," explains the author. "Good luck. Bad luck. No luck. It's something that people are very preoccupied with. I bet I'm not the only one who chose his six numbers for the first National Lottery draw with a 'funny feeling' that I was actually going to win. And virtually everyone I know has a lucky charm, number, day, teddy bear, pair of shorts, necklace, pint glass . . . whatever. Even people who claim to be skeptical about such things have their secret superstitions and beliefs.

"I wondered what would happen if we actually knew of the factors that shaped our fates . . . and if it came to paying a price for good fortune, how far would we go?"

Originally written for Lebbon's first hardcover collection, *As the Sun Goes Down*, the powerful novella that follows was significantly revised for its appearance here . . .

"OH, LOOK," SAID Adam, "a four-leafed clover." He stroked the little plant and sighed, pushing himself to his feet, stretching his arms and legs and back. He had been laying on the grass for a long time.

He walked across the lawn and onto the graveled driveway, past the Mercedes parked mock-casual, through the front door of the eight-bedroom house and into the study.

Two walls were lined with books. Portraits of the people he loved stared down at him and he should have felt at peace, should have felt comforted . . . but he did not. There was a large map on one wall, a thousand intended destinations marked in red, half-a-dozen places he had already visited pinned green. Travel was no longer on his agenda, neither was reading, because his family had gone. He was still about to make a journey, however, somewhere even stranger than the places he had seen so recently. Stranger than anyone had ever seen to tell of, more terrifying, more final. After the past year he was keener than ever to find his own way there.

And he had a map. It was in the bureau drawer. A .44 Magnum, gleaming snake-like silver, slick to the touch, cold, impersonal. He warmed it between his legs before using it. May as well feel comfortable when he put it in his mouth.

Outside, the fourth leaf on the clover glowed brightly and disappeared into a pinprick of light. Then, nothing.

"Well," Adam said to the house full of memories, "it wasn't bad to begin with . . . but it could have been better."

He heard footsteps approaching along the graveled driveway, frantic footsteps crunching quickly toward the house.

"Adam!" someone shouted, panic giving their voice an androgynous lilt.

He looked around the room to make sure he was not being observed. He checked his watch and smiled. Then he calmly placed the barrel of the gun inside his mouth, angled it upward, and pulled the trigger.

He had found them in the water.

At least he liked to think he found them but later, in the few dark and furtive moments left to him when his mind was truly his own, he would realize that this was not the case. *They* found *him*. Gods or fairies or angels or demons—mostly just one or another, but sometimes all four— they appeared weak and delicate.

It was not long, however, before Adam knew that looks count for nothing.

Put on your life jackets, the cabin crew had said. *Only inflate them when you're outside the aircraft. Use the whistle to attract attention, and make for one of the life rafts.* As if disaster had any ruling factor, as if control could be gained over something so powerful, devastating, and final.

"THE SHAPES THAT ROSE OUT OF THE WATER WITH HIM
WERE ALL THAT REALLY REGISTERED."

As soon as the 747 hit the water, any semblance of control vanished. This was no smooth crash landing, it was a catastrophe, the shell splitting and the wings slicing through the fuselage and a fire—brief but terrible—taking out First Class and the cockpit. There was no time even to draw away from the flames before everything fell apart, and Adam was pitched into a cool, dark, watery grave. *Alison*, he thought, and although she was not on the flight—she was back at home with Jamie—he felt that she was dead already. Strange, considering it was he who was dying.

Because in the chaos, he *knew* that he was about to die. The sounds of rending metal and splitting flesh had been dampened by their instant submersion in the North Atlantic, but a new form of blind panic had taken over. Bubbles exploded around him, some of them coming from inside torn bodies, and sharp, broken metal struck out at him from all around. The cold water masked the pain for a while, but he could still feel the numbness where his leg had been, the ghostly echo of a lost limb. He wondered whether his leg was floating above or below him. Then he realized that he could not discern up or down, left or right, and so the idea was moot. He was blinded too, and he did not know why. Pain? Blood? Perhaps his eyes were elsewhere, floating around in this deathly soup of waste and suffering, sinking to the seabed where unknown bottom-crawlers would snap them up and steal everything he had ever seen with one dismissive *clack* of their claws.

He had read accounts of how young children could live for up to an hour submerged in freezing water. They still retained a drowning reflex from being in the womb, their vocal chords contracted and drew their throats shut, and as long as they expelled the first rush of water from their lungs they could survive. Body temperature would drift down to match their surroundings, heart rate would halve, oxygen to the brain would be dramatically lessened, brain activity drawn in under a cowl of unconsciousness. So why, then, was he thinking all this now? Why panic? He should be withdrawing into himself, creating his own mini-existence where the tragedies happening all around him, here and now, could not break through.

Why not just let everything happen as it would?

Adam opened his eyes and finally saw through the shock. A torn body floated past him, heading down, trailing something pale and fleshy behind it. It had on a pair of shorts and Bart Simpson socks. No shoes. Most people kicked off their shoes on a long-haul flight.

The roaring sound around him increased as everything began to sink. Great bursts of bubbles stirred the terrible brew of the sea, and Adam felt a rush of something warm brushing his back. A coffee-pot crushed and spewing its contents, he thought. That was all. Not the stewardess holding it being opened up by the thousands of sharp edges, gushing her own warm insides across his body as they floated apart like lost lovers in the night . . .

And then he *really* opened his eyes, although he was so far down now that everything was pitch-black. He opened them not only to what was happening around him, but to what was happening *to* him. He was still strapped in his seat. One of his legs appeared to be missing . . . but maybe not, maybe in the confusion he had only dreamed that he had lost a leg. Perhaps he had been dreaming it when the aircraft took its final plunge, and the nightmares—real and imagined—had merely blended together. He thought he felt a ghost ache there, but perhaps ghosts can be more real than imagination allows, and he held out his hands and felt both knees intact.

Other hands moved up his body from his feet, squeezing the flesh so that he knew it was still there, pinching, lifting . . . dragging him up through the maelstrom and back toward the surface. He gasped in water and felt himself catch on fire, every nerve end screaming at the agony in his chest. His mind began to shut down—

yes, yes, that is the way, go to sleep, be that child again

—and then he broke surface.

The extraordinary dragged his sight from the merely terrifying. He was aware of the scenes around him—the bodies and parts of bodies floating by, the aircraft wreckage bobbing and sinking and still smoldering in places, the broken-spined books sucking up water, suitcases spilling their insides in memory of their shattered owners—but the shapes that rose out of the water with him were all that he really registered, all that he really comprehended. Although true comprehension . . . that was impossible.

They were fairies.

Or demons.

Or angels.

Or gods.

There were four of them, solid yet transparent, strong yet unbelievably delicate. Their skin was clear, but mottled in places with a darker light, striped like a glass tiger. They barely seemed to touch him, yet he could feel the pinch of their fingers on his legs and arms where they held him upright. The pain seemed at odds with their appearance. He closed his eyes and opened them again. The pain was still there, and so were the things.

They were saving him. He was terrified of them. For one crazy moment he looked around at the carnage and wished himself back in the water, struggling against his seat restraint as it dragged him down, feeling his ears crunch in and his eyeballs implode as awful pressures took their toll, sucking out the last of his air and flooding him and filling him. Perhaps he would see Alison again—

she's dead!

—love her as he had always loved her, feel every moment they had shared. He thought it was a fallacy that a drowning man's life flashes before him. But it was a romantic view of death, and if he had to die then a hint of romance . . .

"You are not going to die," a voice said. None of the things seemed to have spoken and the voice appeared in his head, unaccented, pure, like a playback of every voice ever saying the same thing.

He looked around at them. He could see no expressions because their faces were ambiguous, stains on the air at best. He reached out and touched one, and it was warm. It was *alive*. He laid his palm flat against its chest.

"That is all right," the same voice intoned, "feel what you must. You have to trust us. If you have to believe that we are here in order to trust us, then make sure you do. Because we have a gift for you. We can save you, but . . . you must never forget us or deny us."

Adam held out his other hand. "You're there," he whispered as he felt a second heartbeat beneath his palm. For some reason, it felt disgusting.

"So pledge."

He was balanced on a fine line between life and death. He was in no condition to make such a decision. That is why all that happened later was so unfair.

He nodded. And then he realized the truth.

"I'm dead." It was obvious. He had been drifting down, down, following the other bodies deep down, perhaps watched by some of them as he too had watched. He had known his leg had gone, he had felt the water enter him and freeze him and suck out his soul. He was dead.

"No," the voice said, "you are very much alive." And then one of the things scraped its nails across his face.

Adam screamed. The pain was intense. The scratches burned like acid streaks, and he touched his cheek and felt blood there. He took his hand away and saw a red smear. He looked down at his legs; still whole. He looked back up at the four things that were holding him and his wrecked seat just out of reach of the water. Their attitude had not changed, their unclear faces were still just that.

He saw a body floating past, a person merged somehow with a piece of electrical paneling, metallic and biological guts both exposed.

"We have something to show you," the voice said.

And then he was somewhere else.

He actually felt the seat crumple and vanish beneath him, and he was suddenly standing in a long, wide street. His clothes were dry and whole, not ripped by the crash and soaked with seawater and blood. His limbs felt strong, he was warm, he was invigorated. His face still hurt . . .

The four things—the demons, the angels, whatever they were—stood around him, holding out their hands as if to draw his attention to this, to that. They gave the impression that they lived there, but to Adam they did not seem to feel at home.

"Where is this place?" Adam said. "Heaven?"

"How is your face?"

"It still hurts." Adam touched the scratches on his cheek, but the blood had almost ceased flowing now, and already he could feel the wounds scabbing over. They were itching more than burning. He wondered just how long ago the crash had been.

"You are alive, you see," the voice said, "but we brought you here for a while to show you some things. And to give you a gift. Come with us."

"But who are you. *What* are you?"

The things all turned to look at him. They were still transparent but solid, shapes made of flowing glass. Try as he might, he could not discern any features with which to distinguish one from another, yet they all acted in slightly different ways. The one on his far left tilted its head slightly as it watched him, the one to his right leaned forward with unashamed curiosity whenever he spoke.

"Call us Amaranth," the voice said, "for we are eternal."

Adam thought about running, then. He would turn and sprint along the street, shout for help if the things pursued him, slap off their hands if they chose to grasp at him. He would escape them. He *wanted* to escape them . . . even though, as yet, they had done him only good.

Am I really here, he thought, *or am I floating at the bottom of the sea? Fishes darting into my mouth. Crustaceans plucking at my brain as these final insane thoughts seek their escape.*

"For the last time," Amaranth said, and this time two of them attacked him. One held him down, the other reached into his mouth and grasped his tongue. Its hand was sickly warm, the skin—or whatever surface sheen it possessed—slick to the touch. It brought his tongue forward and then pricked at it with an extended finger.

The pain was bright, explosive, exquisite. Blood gushed into Adam's throat as he struggled to stand. The things moved aside to let him up and he spat out a gob of blood, shaking with shock and a strange, subdued fury.

"You are alive," Amaranth said, "and well, and living here for now. We shall not keep you long because we know you wish to return to your world . . . to your Alison and Jamie . . . but the price of our saving you is for you to see some things. Follow us. And do not be afraid. You are one of the lucky ones."

Adam wanted nothing more than to see his family. His conviction that Alison was dead had gone, had surely been a result of his own impending death. And Jamie—sweet little Jamie, eighteen months old and just discovering himself—how cruel for him to suddenly be without a father. How pointless. Yes, he needed to see them soon.

"Thank you," Adam said. "Thank you for saving me."

Amaranth did not reply. Adam was truly alive, the pain in his tongue told him that. This was unreal and impossible, yet he felt completely, undeniably alive. As to whether he really had been saved . . . time would tell.

One of the things gently took his hand and guided him along the street.

At first Adam thought he could have been in London. The buildings on either side presented tall, grubby facades, with their shop fronts all glazing and posters and flashing neon. A bar spewed music and patrons into the street on one corner, some of them sitting at rickety wooden tables, others standing around, mingling, chatting, laughing. They were all laughing. As he watched, a tall man—hair dyed a bright red, body and legs clad in leather, and sporting a monstrous tattoo of a dragon across his forehead, down the side of his neck and onto his collarbone—bumped into a table and spilled several drinks. Glass smashed. Beer flowed and gurgled between brick paviors. The couple at the table stood, stared at the leather-clad man and smiled. He set his own drinks down on their table, sat, and started chatting to them. Adam heard them introducing themselves, and as he and Amaranth passed the bar, the three were laughing and slapping each other's shoulders as if they had been friends forever.

The tall man looked up and nodded at Adam, then again at each of the things with him. His eyes were wide and bright, his face tanned and strong, and it shone. Not literally, not physically, but his good humor showed through. He was an advert for never judging people by their appearances.

Within a few paces the street changed appearance, so quickly that Adam felt as though it was actually shifting around him. He could see nothing strange, but suddenly the buildings were lower, the masonry lighter, eaves adorned with ancient gargoyles growling grotesquely at the buildings opposite, old wooden windows rotting in their frames, pigeons huddling along sills. He could have moved from London to Italy in the space of a second. And if anything the street felt more real, more meant-to-be than he had ever experienced. It was as if nature itself had built this place specifically for these people to inhabit, carving it out of the landscape as perfectly as possible, and even though the windows were rotting and the buildings had cracks scarring their surfaces like old battle wounds, these things made it even more perfect.

"It's like a painting," Adam said.

"It is art, true." The thing holding his hand let go and another took its place, this one warmer, its flesh more silky. "This way."

The sudden music of smashing glass filled the street, followed by a scream and a sickening thud as something hit the road behind them. Adam spun around, heart racing, scalp stretching as he tried not to imagine what he was about to see.

What he did see was certainly not what he expected.

A woman was lying stretched over the high gutter, half on the pavement, half on the road. As he watched, she stood and brushed diamond-shards of broken glass from her clothes. She picked them from her face, too, but they had not torn the skin. Her limbs had not suffered in her tumble from the second story window, her suit trousers and jacket were undamaged, her skull was whole. In fact, as she ruffled up her hair, stretched her back with a groan and glanced up at where she had fallen from, she looked positively radiant. An extreme-sports fan perhaps? Maybe this was just a stunt she was used to doing day-in, day-out?

She saw Adam watching her and threw him a disarmingly calm smile. "That was lucky," she said.

"What the hell's lucky about falling from a window?"

She shrugged. Looked around. Waved at someone further along the street. "I didn't die," she said, not even looking at Adam anymore. And without saying another word she walked past him and Amaranth to a small Italian café.

Amaranth steered Adam past the café and into a side alley. Again, scenery changed without actually shifting, as if flickering from place to place in the instant that it took him to blink. This new setting was straight out of all the American cops and robbers television shows he had ever seen. There was a gutter running down the center of the alley overflowing with rubbish and excrement, boxes piled high against one wall just begging a speeding car to send them flying, pull-down fire escapes hanging above head-height, promising disaster. Doorways were hidden back under the shadows of walls, and in some of those shadows darker shadows shifted.

Someone rolled from a doorway into their path. Adam stopped, caught his breath, ready for the gleam of metal and the demand for money.

Amaranth paused as well. Were they scared?

And then he realized something else. People had seen him and Amaranth, he had noticed them looking—looking and smiling—and they were not out of place.

"This isn't real," he said, and a shape stood before him.

The man wore a long coat. His hair was an explosion of dirt and fleas and other insects, his shoes had burst and his toes stuck out, as if seeking escape from the wretched body they belonged to.

He looked up.

"My friend!" he said, although Adam had never seen him before. "My friend, how are you? Welcome here, welcome everywhere, I'm sure. Oh, so I see they've found you too?" He nodded at the shapes around Adam and they shifted slightly, as if embarrassed at being noticed. "They're angels, you know," the man said quietly. "Look at me. Down-and-out, you'd guess? Ready to blow you or stab you for the money to buy a bottle of paint-stripper."

"The thought had crossed my mind," Adam said, but only because he knew, already, that he was wrong. There was something far stranger, far more wonderful at work here.

"Maybe years ago," the man nodded, "but not anymore. See, I'm one of the lucky ones. Take a look!" He opened up his coat to display a glimmering, golden suit. It looked ridiculous, but comfortable. The man *himself* looked comfortable. In fact, Adam had rarely seen anyone looking so contented with their lot, so at home with where and what they were.

"It's . . . nice," Adam said.

"It's fucking awful! Garish and grotesque, but if that's what I want to be sometimes, hey, who's to deny me that? Nobody, right? In the perfect world, nobody. In the perfect world, I can do and be what I want to do and be, whenever I want. Yesterday I was making love with a princess, tomorrow I may decide to crash a car. Today . . . today I'm just reliving how I used to be. I hated it, of course; who wouldn't? Today, here . . . in the perfect world, it's not so bad."

"But just where are we?" Adam asked, hoping—realizing—that perhaps this man could tell him what Amaranth would not. "I was in a plane crash, I was sinking, I was dying—"

"Right," the man said, nodding and blinking slowly. "And then you were rescued. And they brought you here for a look around. Well . . . you're one of the lucky ones. We're all lucky ones here."

There was the sound of something moving quickly down the alley, still hidden by shadows but approaching rapidly. For an instant Adam thought it could be gunfire and he prepared to dive for cover, but then he saw the magnificent shape emerge into the sunlight.

"Hold up!" the man said with a distinctly Cockney accent, "'ere comes my ride."

Adam and Amaranth stood aside, and Adam watched aghast as the unicorn galloped along the alley. It did not slow down—did not even seem to notice the man—but he grasped onto its mane as it ran, swung himself easily up onto its back and rode it out into the street. It paused for a moment and reared up, and Adam was certain it was a show just for him. The man in the golden suit waved an imaginary hat back at Adam, then he nudged the unicorn with his knees and they disappeared out of sight along the street.

He heard the staccato beat of hooves for a long time.

For the first time he wondered whether it was *all* a display put on for him, and him alone. The red-haired man . . . the jumper . . . the down-and-out. They had all looked at him. Somehow, it was all too perfect.

He pressed his sore tongue against the roof of his mouth.

"Do you get the idea?" Amaranth asked.

"What idea?"

The things milled around him, touching him, and now their touch was more pleasant than repulsive. His skin jumped wherever they made contact. He found himself aroused and he went with the feeling. It did not feel shameful or inappropriate. It felt just right. While he was here, why not enjoy it?

"The idea that good luck is a gift," Amaranth said.

A talent or a present? Adam wanted to ask, but already they were pulling him farther along the alley toward whatever lay beyond its far end.

He smelled the water before he saw it, rich and cloying, heavy with effluent and rubbish. As they emerged from the mouth of the alley and turned a corner, the lake came into view. It was huge, not just a city lake, more like a sea. Adam was reminded briefly of Venice, but there were no Gondoliers here, and the waters were rougher and more violent than Venice ever experienced. And there were things among the waves, far out from the shore, shiny gray things breaking the surface and screeching before heading back down to whatever depths they came from.

A woman walked past them whistling, nodded a hello, indicated the lake with a nod of her head and looked skyward, as if to say: *oh dear, that lake, huh?*

She wore so much jewelry on her fingers and wrists that Adam was sure she would sink, were she to enter the waters. But she never would, no one in their right mind would, because to go in there would be to die.

Things are in there, Adam thought. *Shattered aircraft, perhaps? Bodies of passengers I chatted with being ripped and torn and eaten? Where am I now? Where, really, am I?*

"We stand on the shore of bad luck," Amaranth said. "Out there . . . the island, do you see? . . . there live the unlucky ones."

Now that it had been pointed out to him, Adam could see the island, although he was sure it had not been there before. *You never notice a damn thing until it's pointed out to you*, Alison would say to him, and she was right, he was not very observant. But this island was huge—growing larger—and eventually, even though nothing seemed to have actually changed, the lake was a moat and the island filled most of his field of vision.

Sounds reached him then, although they were dulled and weary with distance. Screams, shouts, cries, the rending crunch of buildings collapsing, an explosion, the roar of flames taking hold somewhere out of sight. Adam edged closer to the shore of the moat, straining to see through the hazy air, struggling to make out what was happening on the island. There were signs erected all along its shore. Some of them seemed to be moving. Some of them . . .

They were not signs. They were crucifixes, and most of them were occupied. Heads lolled on shoulders, knees moved weakly as the victims tried to shift their weight, move the pain around their bodies so that it did not burn its way through their flesh.

Beneath some of the crosses, fires had been set.

"It's Hell!" Adam gasped, turning around to glare at the four things with him.

"No," Amaranth said, "we have explained. Those over there are the unlucky ones, but they are not dead. Not yet. Many of them will be soon . . . unlucky ones always die . . . but first, there is pain and suffering."

Adam felt tears burning behind his eyes. He did not understand any of this. Sinking into the Atlantic, dying, being a nameless statistic on an airline's list of victims, that he understood. Losing Alison and Jamie, even—never seeing them again—that he could understand.

But not this.

"I want my family," he said. "If you've saved me like you say, I want my family. I don't want to be here. I don't know where here is."

"Do you ever, truly?"

"Oh, Jesus," Adam gasped in despair, dropping to his knees and noticing as he did that the shore was scattered with pale white bones. Washed up from the island of the unlucky ones, no doubt.

He closed his eyes.

And tumbled into the moat.

He had been expecting fresh water—polluted by refuse perhaps, rancid with death—but inland water nonetheless. His first mouthful was brine.

Beneath him, the aircraft seat. Around his waist the seatbelt, which would ensure that he sank to his death. Above him, the wide blue sky he had fallen from.

Under his arms and around his legs, hands lifting him to safety.

"Here's a live one!" a voice shouted, and it was gruff and excited, not like Amaranth or the people he had heard back there in the land of the lucky. This one held a whole range of experience.

"Unlucky," Adam muttered, spitting out seawater and feeling a dozen pains bite into him at the same instant. "Bad luck . . ."

"No, mate," said a voice with an Irish lilt from somewhere far away. "You're as lucky as fuck. Everyone else is dead."

Adam tried to speak, to ask for Alison and Jamie because he knew he was about to die, he had already visited Heaven and slipped back again for his final breath. But the bright sunlight faded to black and the voices receded. Already, he was leaving once more . . .

As he passed out he fisted his hands so that no one or nothing could hold on to them.

The next time he awakened, Alison was staring down at him. There had been no dreams, no feelings, no sensations. It felt as if a second had passed since he had been in the sea, but he knew instantly that it was much longer. There was a ceiling and fluorescent lights, and the cloying stench of antiseptic, and the metallic grumble of trolley wheels on vinyl flooring.

And there was Alison leaning over him, hair haloed by a bright light.

"Honey," she said. She began to cry.

Adam reached up to her and tried to talk, but his throat was dry and rough. He rasped instead, just making a noise, happy that he could do anything to let her know he was still alive.

"Alive," he croaked eventually. "You're alive."

She looked down at him and frowned, but the tears were too powerful and her face took on the shine of relief once more. "Yes, you're alive. Oh honey, I was so terrified, I saw the news and I knew you were dead, I just *knew* . . . and I came here. Mum didn't want me to, but I just had to be here when they started . . . when they started bringing in the bodies. And the worst thing," she whispered, touching his cheek, ". . . I *wanted* them to find your body. I couldn't live knowing you were still out there, somewhere. In the sea." She buried her face in the sheets covering him and swung her arm across his stomach, hugging him tight, a hug *so* tight that he would never forget it.

This is what love is, he thought to himself. *Never wanting to let go.* He put his hand behind her head and reveled in the feel of her hair between his fingers.

"Come on," he said, "it's all right now. We're both all right now." A terrible thought came out of nowhere. In seconds, it became a certainty. *My leg!*

"I am all right, aren't I? Alison, am I hurt? Am I damaged?"

She looked up and grinned at him, red-rimmed eyes and snotty nose giving her a strange child-like quality. "You're fine! They said it was a miracle, you're hardly touched. Bruises here and there, a few scratches on your face and you bit your tongue quite badly. But you escaped . . . well, you're on the front page of the papers. I kept them! Jamie, he's got a scrapbook!"

"Scrapbook? How long have I been here?"

"Only two days," Alison said. She sat down on the bed, never relinquishing contact with him, eye or hand. He wondered whether she'd ever let go again.

"Two days." He thought of where he had been and the things that had taken him there. As in all particularly vivid dreams, he retained some of the more unusual sensory data from the experience—he could smell the old back-alley, the piss and the refuse . . . he could hear the woman hitting the street, feel the jump in his chest as he realized what had happened. He could taste the strange fear he had experienced every second of that waking dream, even though Amaranth had professed benevolence.

A nightmare, surely? A sleeping, verge-of-death nightmare.

"Where's Jamie?"

Alison started crying again because they were talking about their son, their son who still had his father after all. "He's at home with Mum, waiting for you. Mum's told him you fell out of the sky but were caught by angels. Bless him, he—"

"What does she mean by that?" Adam whispered. His throat was burning and he craved a drink. He felt as if someone was strangling him slowly. *Angels, demons, who can tell?*

Alison shrugged. "Well, you know Mum, she's just telling Jamie stories. Trying to imbue him with her religion without us noticing."

"But she actually said angels?"

His wife frowned and shrugged and nodded at the same time. This was obviously not how she had expected him to react after surviving crashing into the sea in a passenger jet. "Why, hon? You really see some?"

What would you think if I said yes, he thought.

Alison brought him some iced water. Then she kissed him.

Three days later they let him go home.

In the time he had been in hospital, several major newspapers and magazines had contacted Alison and offered her five-figure payments for Adam's exclusive story. He was a star, a survivor among so much death, a miracle man who had lived through a thirty-nine-thousand-feet plunge into the North Atlantic and come out of it with hardly a scratch.

Hardly. The three parallel lines on his cheek had scarred. *You were lucky*, the doctors had said. *Very lucky.*

Lucky to be scarred for life? Adam had almost asked, but thankfully he had refrained. At least he hadn't died.

On his first full day back at home the telephone rang twice before breakfast. Alison answered and calmly but firmly told whoever was on the other end to go away and spend their time more productively. On the third ring she turned the telephone off altogether.

"If anyone wants us badly enough, they can come to see us. And if it's family, they have my cell number."

"Maybe I should do it," Adam said, sipping from a cup of tea. Jamie was playing at his feet, building complex Lego constructions and then gleefully smashing them down again. A child's appetite for creation and destruction never ceased to amaze Adam. His son had refused to move from his feet since they had risen from bed, even when tempted to the breakfast table with the promise of a yogurt. He loved that. He loved that his wife wanted to hold him all the time, he loved that Jamie wanted to be close in his personal space. Even though his son barely looked up at him—he was busy with blocks and cars and imaginary lands—Adam felt himself at the center of Jamie's attention.

"You sure you want to do that?" Alison asked. She sat down and leaned against him, snuggling her head onto his shoulder. He felt her breath on his neck as she spoke. "I mean, they're after sensation, you know that. They're after miracle escapes and white lights at the end of tunnels. They don't want to hear . . . well, what happened to you. The plane fell. You passed out. You woke up in the fishing boat."

Adam shrugged. "Well, I could tell them . . . I could tell them more."

"What more is there?"

He did not elaborate. How could he? *I dreamed of angels. I dreamed of demons scratching my face when I did not believe in them, of a place where good luck and bad luck were distilled into very refined, pure qualities. I dreamed that I gave a pledge.*

"You need time at home. Here, with us. Time to get over it."

"To be honest, honey, I don't feel too bad about it all." And that was shockingly true. He was the sole survivor of a disaster that had killed over three hundred people, but all of the guilt and anger and frustration he thought he should feel were thankfully absent. Perhaps in time . . . but he thought not. After all, he was one of the lucky ones. "Besides," he said quietly, "think of the money. Think what we could do with twenty grand."

Alison did not respond.

He could hear her thinking about it all.

They sat that way for half-an-hour, relishing the contact and loving every sound or motion Jamie made. He joined them on the sofa several times, hugging them and pointing at Adam's ears and eyes, as if he knew what secrets lay within. Then he was back on the floor, back in make-believe. They both loved him dearly and he loved them too, and what more could a family ask? Really, Adam thought, what more?

There *was* more. The ability to pay the mortgage each month without worrying about going overdrawn. The occasional holiday, here and there. Adam's job as a publishing representative paid reasonably well, and he did get to travel, but Alison's previous marriage had damaged her financially, and they were both still paying for her mistakes. Money was not God, but there really was so much more they could ask for.

After lunch, Adam took a look at the numbers and names Alison had been noting down over the past week. He chose a newspaper which he judged to be more serious than most, selling merely glorified news, not outright lies. He rang them, told them who he was, and arranged for a reporter to visit the house.

That afternoon they decided to visit the park. It was only a short stroll from their home, so they held Jamie's hands and let him walk. The buggy was easier, but Adam liked his son walking alongside him, glancing up every now and then to make sure his father was still there. Their neighbors said a friendly hello and greeted Adam with honest joy. Other people they did not know smiled and stared with frank fascination. On that first trip out, Adam truly came to realize just how much he had been the subject of news over the past week. The last time these people had seen him he had been on a television screen, a pixilated victim of a distant disaster, bloodied face stark against the white hospital pillows. Now that he was flesh and blood once more, they did not quite know how to react.

Just before reaching the park, an old stone bridge crossed a stream. Adam loved to sit on the parapet and listen to the water gurgling underneath. Sometimes Alison and Jamie would go on to the park and leave Adam to catch up, but not today. Today Alison refused to leave his side, and she held their son in her arms as they both sat on the cold stone.

"We'll get moss on our arses," she said, glancing over her shoulder.

"I'll lick it off when Jamie's in bed."

"You! Saucy sod."

"You don't know what surviving a fatal air crash does for one's libido," Adam said, and he realized it was true. He could feel the heat of Alison's arm through his shirtsleeve, feel her hip nudging against his. He felt himself growing hard, so he turned away and looked at the opposite parapet. There was a date block set in there, testifying that the bridge had been built over a hundred years ago. He tried to imagine the men who had built it, what they had talked about as they were pointing between the stones, whether they considered who would cross the bridge in the future. Probably not. Most people rarely thought that far ahead.

Something glittered in the compressed leaves at the base of the wall. He frowned, squinted, and leaned forward for a closer look. Something metallic, perhaps, but glass as well. He crossed the quiet road and bent down to see what it was.

"Adam? What have you found, honey?"

Adam could only shake his head.

"Honey, we should go, young rascal's getting restless. He needs his slide and swing fix."

"I'll be damned," Adam gasped.

"What is it?"

He took the watch back to Alison, gently wiping dirt from its face and picking shredded leaves from the expanding metal strap. He showed it to her and watched her face.

"Does it work?"

He looked, tapped it against his palm, looked again. The second hand wavered and then began to move, ticking on from whatever old time it had been stuck in. Strangely, the time was now exactly right.

"Looks quite nice," she said, cringing as Jamie twisted eel-like in her arms.

"Nice? It's priceless. It's Dad's. You remember Dad's old watch, the one he left me, the one we lost in the move?"

Alison nodded and stared at him strangely. "We moved here six years ago."

Adam nodded, too excited to talk.

It told the right time!

"Six years, Adam. It's not your dad's watch, just one that looks a bit—"

"Look." He flipped the strap inside out and showed his wife the back of the watch casing. *For Dear Jack, love from June*, it said. Jack, his father. June, his mother.

"Holy shit."

"Shit, shit, shit," Jamie gurgled, and they looked at each other and laughed because their swearing son took their attention for a moment, stole it away from this near-impossibility.

They walked in silence, Adam studiously cleaning dirt from the watch, checking its face for cracks, winding it, running his fingers over the faded inscription.

At the entrance to the park Alison let Jamie run to the playground and took the timepiece from Adam. "What a stroke of luck," she said. "Oh, you've put it right."

Adam did not say anything. He accepted the watch back and slipped it into his pocket. Maybe this was something that would make a nice end to his interview with the newspaper, but straight away he knew he would never tell them.

With Jamie frolicking on the climbing frame and Alison hugging him, Adam silently began to get his story straight.

Nobody is news forever, even to the ones they love. Stories die down, a newer tragedy or celebrity gossip takes first place, family problems beg attention. It's something to do with time, and how it heals and destroys simultaneously. And luck, perhaps. It has a lot to do with luck.

Three weeks after leaving hospital, Adam's name disappeared from the papers and television news, and he was glad. Those three weeks had exhausted him, not only because he was still aching and sore and emotionally unhinged by the accident—although he did not feel quite as bad as everyone seemed to think he should—but because of the constant, unstinting attention. He had sat through that painful first interview, the paper had run it, he and Alison had been paid. Days later a magazine called and requested one interview per month for the next six months.

The airline wrote to ask him to become involved with the accident investigation, and to perhaps be a patron of the charity hastily being set up to help the victims' families. A local church requested that he make a speech at their next service, discussing how God has been involved in his survival and what it felt like to be cradled in the Lord's hand, while all those around him were filtering through His divine fingers. The suggestion was that Adam was pure and good, and those who had died were tainted in some way. The request disgusted him. He told them so. When they persisted he told them to fuck off, and he did not hear from them again.

His reaction was a little extreme, he knew. But perhaps it was because he did not know exactly what *had* saved him.

He turned down every offer. He had been paid twenty thousand pounds by the newspaper, and nobody else was offering anywhere near as much. Besides, he no longer wanted to be a sideshow freak: *Meet the miracle survivor!*

The telephone rang several times each night—family, friends, well-wishers, people he had not spoken to for so long that he could not truly even call them friends anymore—and eventually he stopped answering. Alison became his buffer, and he gave her *carte blanche* to vet the calls however she considered appropriate.

This was how he came to speak to Philip Howards.

Jamie was in bed. Adam had his feet up on the sofa, a beer in his hand, and a book propped face-down on his lap. He was staring at the ceiling through almost-closed eyes, remembering the crash, his thoughts dipping in and out of dream as he catnapped. On the waking side, there was water and the nudge of dead bodies; when he just edged over into sleep, transparent shapes flitted behind his eyes and showed him miracles. Sometimes the two images mixed and merged. He had been drinking too much that evening.

Alison went straight to the telephone when it rang, sighing, and Adam opened one eye fully to follow her across the room. They had been having a lot of sex since he came home from hospital.

"Hello?" she answered, and then she simply stood there for a full minute, listening.

Adam closed his eyes again and thought of the money. Twenty thousand. And the airline would certainly pay some amount in compensation as well, something to make them appear benevolent in the public eye. He could take a couple of years off work. Finish paying the mortgage. Start work on those paintings he had wanted to do for so long.

He opened his eyes again and appraised his artist's fingers where they were curved around the bottle. He was stronger there, more creative. He felt more of an emotional input to what he was doing. The painting he had started two weeks ago was the best he had ever done.

All in all, facing death in the eye had done wonders for his life.

"Honey, there's a guy on the phone. He says he really has to talk to you."

"Who is it?" The thought of having to stand, to walk, to actually talk to someone almost drove him back to sleep.

"Philip Howards."

Adam shrugged. He didn't know him.

"He says it's urgent. Says it's about the angels." Alison's voice was in neutral, but its timbre told Adam that she was both intrigued, and angry. She did not like things she could not understand. And she hated secrets.

The angels! Adam's near-death hallucination flooded back to him. He reached up to touch the scars on his cheek and Alison saw him do it. He stood quickly to prevent her asking him about it, covering up the movement with motion.

She looked at him strangely as he took the receiver from her. He knew that expression: *We'll talk about it later.* He also knew that she would not forget.

"Can I help you?"

There was nothing to begin with, only a gentle static and the sound of breathing down the line.

"Hello?"

"You're one of the lucky ones," the voice said. "I can tell. I can hear it in your voice. The unlucky ones—poor souls, poor bastards—whatever they're saying, they always sound like they're begging for death. Sometimes they do. One of them asked me to kill her once, but I couldn't do it. Life's too precious for me, you see."

Adam reeled. He recalled his dream again, the island of unlucky souls surrounded by the stinking moat. He even sniffed at the receiver to see whether this caller's voice stank of death.

"Has something happened?" the man continued. "Since you came back, has something happened which you can't explain? Something wonderful?"

"No," Adam spoke at last, but then he thought, *the watch, I found Dad's watch!*

"I'm not here to cause trouble, really. It's just that when this happens to others, I always like to watch. Always like to get in touch, ask about the angels, talk about them. It's my way of making sure I'm not mad."

The conversation dried for a moment, and Adam stood there breathing into the mouthpiece, not knowing what to say, hearing Philip Howards doing the same. They were like two dueling lovers who had lost the words to fight, but who were unwilling to relinquish the argument.

"What do you know about them?" Adam said at last. Alison sat up straight in her chair and stared at him. He diverted his eyes. He could not talk to this man and face her accusing gaze, not at the same time. *What haven't you told me*, her stare said.

The man held his breath. Then, very quietly: "I was right."

"What do you know?"

"Can we meet? Somewhere close to where you live, soon?"

Adam turned to Alison and smiled, trying to reassure her that everything was all right. "Tomorrow," he said.

Howards agreed, they arranged where and when, and the strangest phone call of Adam's life ended.

"What was that?" Alison asked.

He did not know what to say. What could he say? Could he honestly try to explain? Tell Alison that her mother had been right in what she'd told Jamie, that angels really had caught and saved him?

Angels, demons, fairies . . . gods.

"Someone who wants to talk to me," he said.

"About angels?"

Adam nodded.

Alison stared at him. He could see that she was brimming with questions, but her lips pressed together and she narrowed her eyes. She was desperately trying not to ask any more, because she could tell Adam had nothing to say. He loved her for that. He felt a lump in his throat as he stooped down, put his arms around her shoulders, and nuzzled her neck.

"It's all right," he said. Whether she agreed or not, she loved him enough to stay silent. "And besides," he continued, "you and Jamie are coming too."

He never could keep a secret from Alison.

Later than night, after they had made love and his wife drifted into a comfortable slumber with her head resting on his shoulder, Adam had the sudden urge to paint. This had happened to him before but many years ago, an undeniable compulsion to get up in the middle of the night and apply brush to canvas. Then, it had resulted in his best work. Now, it just felt right.

He eased his arm out from beneath Alison, dressed quickly and quietly, and left the room. On the way along the landing he looked in on Jamie for inspiration, then he carried on downstairs and set up his equipment. They had a small house—certainly no room for a dedicated studio, even if he was as serious about his art now as he had been years ago—so the dining room doubled as his workroom when the urge took him.

He began to paint without even knowing what he was going to do.

By morning, he knew that they had lost their dining room for a long, long time.

"You're a very lucky man," Philip Howards said. He was sitting opposite Adam, staring over his shoulder at where Alison was perusing the menu board, Jamie wriggling in her arms.

Adam nodded. "I know."

Howards look at him intently, staring until Adam had to avert his gaze. Shit, the old guy was a spook and a half! Fine clothes, gold weighing down his fingers, a healthy tan, the look of a traveled man about him. His manner also gave this impression, a sort of weary calmness that came with wide and long experience, and displayed a wealth of knowledge. He said he was seventy, but he looked fifty.

"You really are. The angels, they told you that didn't they?"

Adam could not look at him.

"The angels. Maybe you thought they were fairies or demons. But with them, it's all the same thing really. How did you get those scars on your cheek?"

Adam glanced up at him. "You know how or you wouldn't have asked."

Howards raised his head to look through the glasses balanced on the tip of his nose. He was inspecting Adam's face. "You doubted them for a while."

Adam did not nod, did not reply. To answer this man's queries—however calmly they were being put to him—would be to admit to something unreal. They were dreams, that was all, he was sure. Two men could share the same dreams, couldn't they?

"Well, I did the same. I got this for my troubles." He pulled his collar aside to display a knotted lump of scar tissue below his left ear. "One of them bit me."

Adam looked down at his hands in his lap. Alison came back with Jamie, put her hands on his shoulders and whispered into his ear. "Jamie would prefer a burger. We're not used to jazzy places like this. I'll take him to McDonald's—"

"No, stay here with me."

She kissed his ear. "No arguing. I think you want to be alone anyway, yes? I can tell. And later, *you* can tell. Tell me what all this is about."

Adam stood and hugged his wife, ruffled Jamie's hair. "I will," he said. He squatted down and gave his son a bear hug. "You be a good boy for Mummy."

"Gut boy."

"That's right. You look after her. Make sure she doesn't spend too much money!"

"Goodbye, Mr. Howards," Alison said.

Howards stood and shook her hand. "Charmed." He looked sadly at Jamie and sat back down.

Alison and Jamie left. Adam ordered a glass of wine. Howards, he knew, was not taking his eyes from him for a second.

"You'll lose them," he said.

"What?"

Howards nodded at the door, where Alison and Jamie had just disappeared past the front window. "You'll lose them. It's part of the curse. You do well, everyone and everything else goes."

"Don't you talk about my family like that! I don't even know you. Are you threatening me?" He shook his head when the old man did not answer. "I should have fucking known. You're a crank. All this bullshit about angels, you're trying to confuse me. I'm still not totally settled, I was in a disaster, you're trying to confuse me, get money out of me—"

"I have eight million pounds in several bank accounts," Howards said. "More than I can ever spend . . . and the angels call themselves Amaranth."

Adam could only stare open-mouthed. Crank or no crank, there was no way Howards could know that. He had told no one, he had never mentioned it. He had not even hinted at the strange visions he experienced as he waited to die in the sea.

"I'll make it brief," Howards said, stirring his glass of red wine with a finely manicured finger. "And then, when you believe me, I want you to do something for me."

"I don't know—"

"I was on holiday in Cairo with my wife and two children. This was back in '59. Alex was seven. Sarah was nine. There was a fire in the hotel and our room was engulfed. Alex . . . Alex died. Sarah and my wife fled. I could not leave Alex's body, not in the flames, not in all the heat. It just wasn't right. So I stayed there with him, fully expecting rescue. It was only as I was blinded by heat and the smoke filled my lungs that I knew no rescue was going to come.

"Then something fell across me—something clear and solid, heavy and warm—and protected me from the flames. It took the smoke from inside me . . . I can't explain, I've never been able to, not even to myself. It just sucked it out, but without touching me.

"Then I was somewhere else, and Amaranth was there, and they told me what a lucky man I was."

Adam shook his head. "No, I'm not hearing this. You know about me, I've talked in my sleep or . . . or . . ."

"Believe me, I've never been to bed with you." There was no humor in Howards's comment.

How could he know? He could not. Unless . . .

"Amaranth saved you?"

Howards nodded.

"From the fire?"

"Yes."

"And they took you . . . they took you to their place?"

"The streets of Paris and then a small Cornish fishing village. Both filled with people of good fortune."

Adam shook his head again, glad at last that there was something he could deny in this old man's story. "No, no, it was London and Italy and then America somewhere, New York I've always thought."

Howards nodded. "Different places for different people. Never knew why, but I suppose that's just logical really. So where were the damned when you were there?"

"The damned . . ." Adam said quietly. He knew exactly what Howards meant but he did not even want to think about it. If the old man had seen the same thing as he, then it was real, and people truly did suffer like that.

"The unlucky, the place . . . You know what I mean. Please, Adam, be honest with me. You really must if you ever want to understand any of this or help yourself through it. Remember, I've been like this for over forty years."

Adam swirled his wine and stared into its depths, wondering what he could see in there if he concentrated hard. "It was an island," he said, "in a big lake. Or a sea, I'm not sure, it all seemed to change without moving."

Howards nodded.

"And they were crucified. And they were burning them." Adam swallowed his wine in one gulp. "It was horrible."

"For me it was an old prison," Howards said, "on the cliffs above the village. They were throwing them from the high walls. There were hundreds of bodies broken on the rocks, and seagulls and seals and crabs were tearing them apart. Some of them were still alive."

"What does this mean?" Adam said. "I don't know what to do with this. I don't know what to tell Alison."

Howards looked down at his hands where they rested on the table. He twirled his wedding band as he spoke. "I've had no family or friends for thirty years," he said. "I'm unused to dealing with such . . . intimacies."

"But you're one of the lucky ones, like me? Amaranth said so. What happened to your family? What happened to your wife and your daughter Sarah?"

Howards looked up, and for an instant he appeared much older than he had claimed, ancient. It was his eyes, Adam thought. His eyes had seen everything.

"They're all dead," Howards said. "And still those things follow me everywhere."

Adam was stunned into silence. There was chatter around them, the sound of Howards's rings tapping against his glass as he stirred his wine, the sizzle of hot-plates bearing steaks and chicken. He looked at Howards's down-turned face, trying to see if he was crying. "They follow you?" he gasped.

Howards nodded and took a deep breath, steeling himself. "Always. I see them from time to time, but I've known they're always there for years now. I can feel them . . . watching me. From the shadows. From hidden corners. From places just out of sight." His demeanor had changed suddenly, from calm and self-assured to nervous and frightened. His eyes darted left and right like a bird's, his hands closed around his wine glass and his fingers twisted against each other. Someone opened the kitchen door quickly and he sat up, a dreadful look already on his face.

"Are they here now?" Adam asked. He could not help himself.

Howards shrugged. "I can't see them. But they're always somewhere."

"I've not seen them. Not since I dreamed them."

The old man looked up sharply when Adam said *dreamed*. "We're their sport. Their game. I can't think why else they would continue to spy . . ."

"And your family? Sport?"

Howards smiled slightly, calming down. It was as if casting his mind back decades helped him escape the curse he said he lived under in the present. "You ever heard Newton's third law of motion? To every action, there is an equal and opposite reaction."

Adam thought of Alison and Jamie, and without any warning he began to cry. He sobbed out loud and buried his face in his napkin, screwing his fingers into it, pressing it hard against his eyes and nose and mouth. He could sense a lessening in the restaurant's commotion as people turned to look and, soon after, a gradual increase in embarrassed conversation.

"And that's why I have to ask you something," Howards said. "I've been asking people this for many years now, those few I meet by chance or happen to track down. Amaranth doesn't disturb me; they must know that no one will agree to what I ask. My asking increases their sport, I suppose. But I continue to try."

"What?" Adam asked. He remembered the certainty, as he floated in the sea, that Alison was dead. It brought a fresh flow of tears but these were silent, more heartfelt and considered. He could truly imagine nothing worse—except for Jamie.

"Deny them. Take away their sport. They've made you a lucky man, but you can reject that. If you don't . . . your family will be gone."

"Don't you fucking threaten me!" Adam shouted, standing and throwing down his napkin, confused, terrified. The restaurant fell completely silent this time, and people stared. Some had a look in their eyes—a hungry look—as if they knew they were about to witness violence. Adam looked straight at Howards, never losing eye contact, trying to see the madness in his face. But there was none. There was sorrow mixed with contentment, a deep and weary sadness underlying healthy good fortune. "Why don't you do it yourself! Why, if it's such a good idea, don't *you* deny them!"

"It's too late for me," Howards said quietly, glancing around at the other patrons watching him. "They were dead before I knew."

"Fuck you!" Adam shouted. "You freak!" He turned and stormed out of the restaurant, a hundred sets of eyes scoring his skin. He wondered if any of the diners recognized him from his fifteen minutes of fame.

As the restaurant door slammed behind him and he stepped out into the street, the sun struck his tearful eyes, blinding him for a moment. Across the pedestrianized area, sandwiched between a travel agent's and a baker's shop, a green door liquefied for a second and then reformed. Its color changed to deep-sea blue.

Before his sight adjusted, Adam saw something clear and solid pass through the door.

"So?" Alison asked.

"Fruitcake." He slid across the plastic seat and hugged his son to him. Then he leaned over the food-strewn table and planted a kiss squarely on his wife's mouth. She was unresponsive.

"The angels, then?" She was injecting good cheer into her voice but she was angry, she wanted answers, he knew that. He had never been able to lie to his wife. Even white lies turned his face blood-red.

Adam shook his head and sighed, stealing a chip from Jamie's tray and fending off his son's tomato sauce retribution. He looked up, scanned the burger bar, searching for strange faces that he could not explain.

"Adam," Alison said, voice wavering, "I want to know what's going on. I saw the look on your face when you were on the phone to him yesterday. It's like you were suddenly somewhere else, seeing something different, feeling something horrible. You turned white. Remember that time, you tried some pot and couldn't move for two hours and felt sick? You looked worse than you did then."

"Honey, it's just that what he said reminded me of the crash."

Alison nodded and her face softened. She wanted to keep on quizzing, he could tell, but she was also a wonderful wife. She did not want to hurt him, or to inspire thoughts or memories that might hurt him.

"And what your mum said to Jamie about the angels saving me. When Howards mentioned angels, it brought it all back. I was sinking, you know? Sinking into the sea. Bodies around me. Then I floated back up, I saw the sunlight getting closer. And . . . he just reminded me of when I broke the surface." He was lying! He was creating untruths, but he was doing it well. Even so he felt wretched, almost as if he were betraying

Alison, using her supportive nature against her. He looked outside and wondered whether those things were enjoying his lies. He felt sick.

"Park!" Jamie shouted suddenly. "Go to park! Swing, swing!"

"All right tiger, here we go!" Adam said, pleased to be able to change the subject. Tears threatened once more as he wrestled with Jamie and stole his chips and heard his son squeal with delight as he tickled him.

Deny them, Howards had said. *If you don't . . . your family will be gone.*

He thought of the watch, and the interview money, and his painting, and the new-found closeness that surrounded him and Alison and Jamie like a sphere of solid crystal, fending off negative influences from outside, reflecting all the badness that bubbled in the world around them.

How could he give any of this up? Even if it were possible—even if Howards was not the madman Adam knew him to be—how could he possibly turn his back on this?

In the park, he and Alison sat on a bench and hugged each other. Jamie played on a toddler's climbing frame, occasional tumbles making him giggle, not cry. He was an adventurous lad and he wore his grazed knees and bruised elbows as proud testament to this. Adam kissed Alison. It turned from a peck on the lips to a long, lingering kiss, tongues meeting, warmth flooding through him as love made itself so beautifully known.

Then the inevitable shout from Jamie as he saw his parents involved in each other for a moment, instead of him.

"I could have lost you both," Adam said, realizing as he spoke how strange it sounded.

"We could have lost you."

He nodded. "That's what I meant." He looked across to the trees bordering the park, but there were no flitting shadows beneath them.

Nobody was spying on them from the gate. The hairs on the back of his neck stayed down.

They watched Jamie for a while, taking simple but heartfelt enjoyment in every step he climbed, each little victory he won for himself.

"I started a painting this morning," Adam said.

"I know. I saw you leave the room and heard you setting up."

"It's . . . incredible. It's already painted in here," he said, tapping his head, "and it's coming out exactly how I envisaged it. No imperfections. You know the quote from that Welsh writer, *I dream in fire—*"

"*—and work in clay.* Of course I know it, you've spat it out every month since I've known you."

Adam smiled. "Well, this morning I was working in fire. Dreaming and working in fire. I'm alight . . . my fingers and hands are doing the exact work I want of them. I can't explain it, but . . . maybe the crash has given me new insight. New vigor."

"Made you realize how precious life is," Alison mused, watching Jamie slip giggling down the slide.

Adam looked at her and nodded. He kissed her temple. He worshipped her, he realized. She was his bedrock.

He could smell the rich scent of flowers, hear birds chirping in the trees bordering the park, feel the warmth of the wooden bench beneath him, taste the sweetness of summer in the air. He truly was alight.

He finished the painting the following morning. That afternoon he called Maggie, his former art agent, and asked her to come up from London, take a look. Two days later he had placed it in a major exhibition in a London gallery.

The painting was entitled *Dreaming in Fire and Ice.* Only Alison saw it for what it really was: an affirmation of his love, and a determination that nothing—*nothing*—would ever rip their family apart. He was a good man. He would never let that happen.

On the first day of the exhibition he sold the painting for seven thousand pounds. That same evening, Alison's elderly mother, Molly, slipped and fell downstairs, breaking her leg in five places.

"How is she?"

Alison looked up from the magazine she was not reading and Adam's heart sank. Her eyes were dark, her skin pale, nose red from crying. "Not too good. There's a compound fracture, and they're sure her hip's gone as well. She's unconscious. Shock. In someone so old, they said . . . well, I told them she was strong."

He went to his wife and hugged her, wondering whether he was being watched by Amaranth even now. He had seen one of them on the way to the hospital, he was certain, hunkered down on the back of a flatbed truck, raising its liquid head as he motored the other way. He had glanced in the rearview mirror and seen something, but he could not be sure. The car was vibrating, the road surface uneven. It could have been anything. Maybe it was light dancing in his eyes from the panic he felt.

"Oh, honey," he said, "I'm so sorry. I'm sure she'll be all right, she'll pull through. Stubborn old duck wouldn't dream of doing anything otherwise, you know that."

"I just don't want her to meet her god that quickly," Alison said, and she cried into his neck. He felt her warm tears growing cold against his skin, the shuddering as she tried to stop but failed, and he started to cry as well.

"The angels will save her," Adam said without thinking, for something to say more than anything, and because it was what Molly would have said. He didn't mean it. He felt Alison stiffen and held his breath.

They won't, he thought. *They won't save her. They've got their sport in me.*

Something ran a finger down his spine, and he knew that there were eyes fixed upon him. He turned as best he could to look around, but the corridor was empty in both directions. There were two doors half-open, a hose reel coiled behind a glass panel, a junction two dozen steps away, a tile missing from the suspended ceiling grid. Plenty of places to hide.

"I wonder if she's scared," Alison said. "If she's still thinking in there, if she's dreaming. I wonder if she's scared? I mean, if she dies she goes to Heaven. That's what she believes."

"Of course she is, but it doesn't matter. She'll come around. She will." Adam breathed into his wife's hair and kissed her scalp. A door snicked shut behind him. He did not even bother turning around to look.

He knew that Howards was right, purely because his senses told him so.

He was being watched.

Maggie's call came three days later. An influential London gallery wanted to display his paintings. And more than that, they were keen to commission some work for the vestibule of their new wing. They had offered twenty-five thousand for the commission. Maggie had already accepted. They wanted to meet Adam immediately to talk the projects through.

Alison's mother had not woken up, other than for a few brief moments during the second night. No one had been there with her, but a nurse had heard her calling in the dark, shouting what appeared to be a plea: *Don't do it again, don't, please don't!* By the time the nurse reached the room Molly was unconscious once more.

"You have to go," Alison said. "You simply have to. No two ways about it." She was washing a salad while Adam carved some ham. Jamie was playing in their living room, building empires in Lego and then cheerfully aiding their descent.

Adam felt awful. There was nothing he wanted more than to travel to London, meet with the gallery, smile and shake hands—and to see himself living the rest of his life as what he had always dreamed of becoming: an artist. It was so far-fetched, too outlandish. But he was a lucky man now. The faces at distant windows told him so. He was lucky, and he was being watched.

Deny them, Howards had said. *If you don't . . . your family will be gone.*

He could still say no. Maggie had accepted but there was no contract, and she really should have consulted him before even commencing a deal of such magnitude. He could say no thank you, I'm staying here with my family because they need me, and besides, I'm scared of saying yes, I'm scared of all the good luck. Every action has an equal and opposite reaction, you know.

There was still money left from the interview. They didn't really *need* the cash.

And he could always go back to work—they'd been asking for him, after all.

"I'm doing some of the best work of my life," he said, not sure even as he spoke whether he had intended to say it at all. "It's a golden opportunity. I really can't turn it down."

"I know," Alison replied. She was slicing cucumber into very precise, very regular slices. It was something her mother always did. "I don't *want* you to turn it down. You have to go, there's no argument."

Adam popped a chunk of ham into his mouth and chewed. "Yes there is," he said around the succulent mouthful. "The argument is, your mum is ill. She's very poorly. You're upset and you need me here.

And there's no one else who babysits Jamie for us on such a regular schedule. I could ask my parents down from Scotland . . . but, well, you know."

"Not baby types."

"Exactly."

Alison came to him and wrapped her arms around his waist. She nuzzled his ear. When she did that, it made him so glad he had married someone the same height as him. "I know how much you've been aching for this for years," she said. "You remember that time on holiday in Cornwall . . . the time we think we conceived Jamie in the sauna . . . remember what you said to me? *We'll have a big posh car, a huge house with a garden all the way around and a long gravel driveway, a study full of books; you can be my muse and I'll work by day in the rooftop studio, and in the evenings I'll play with my children.*"

"What a memory for words you have," Adam said. He could remember. It used to be the only thing he ever thought of.

"Go," his beautiful wife said. "I'll be fine. Really. Go and make our fortune. Or if you don't, bring a cuddly toy for Jamie and a bottle of something strong for me."

Good fortune, he thought. *That's what I have. Good fortune.*

Deny them, Howards had said. But Howards was a crank. Surely he was.

"Fuck it," he whispered.

"What?"

"I'll go. And I promise I'll be back within two days. And thanks, honey."

Later that night they tried to make love but Alison began to cry, and then the tears worsened because she could not forget about her mother, not even for a moment. Adam held her instead, turning away so that his erection did not nudge against her, thinking she may find it horrible that he was still turned on when she was crying, talking about her injured mother, using his shoulder as a pain-sink.

When she eventually fell asleep he went to look in on Jamie. His son was snoring quietly in the corner of his cot, blankets thrown off, curled into a ball of cuteness. Adam bent over and kissed his forehead. Then he went to visit the bathroom.

Something moved back from the frosted glass window as he turned on the light. It may have been nothing—as substantial as a puff of smoke, there for less than a blink of an eye—but he closed the curtains anyway. And held his breath as he used the toilet. Listening.

In the morning Alison felt better, and Jamie performed so as to draw her attention onto him. He threw his breakfast to the floor, chose a time when he was nappy-less to take a leak, and caused general mayhem throughout the house. And all this before nine o'clock.

Adam took a stroll outside for a cigarette and looked up at the bathroom window. There was no way up there, very little to climb, nothing to hold onto even if someone could reach the window. But then, Amaranth did not consist of someones, but *somethings*. He shivered, took a drag on the cigarette, looked at the garden through a haze of smoke.

He was being watched. Through the conifers bordering the garden and a small public park peered two faces, pale against the evergreens.

Adam caught his breath and let it out slowly from his nose in a puff of smoke. He narrowed his eyes. No, they did not seem to be watching him—seemed not to have even noticed him, in fact—but rather they were looking at the house. They were discussing something, one of them leaning sideways to whisper to the other. A man and a woman, Adam saw now, truly flesh and blood, nothing transparent about them, nothing demonesque.

Maybe they were staking the place out? Wondering when and how to break in, waiting for him to leave so that they could come inside and strip the house, not realizing that Alison and Jamie—

But I'm a lucky man.

Surely Amaranth would never permit that to happen to him.

Adam threw the cigarette away and sprinted across the garden. The grass was still damp with dew—he heard the hiss of the cigarette being extinguished—and it threw up fine pearls of water as he ran. Each footfall matched a heartbeat. He emerged from shadow into sunlight and realized just how hot it already was.

It may have been that their vision was obscured by the trees, but the couple did not see him until he was almost upon them. They wanted to flee, he could see that, but knowing he had noticed them rooted them to the spot. That was surely not the way of thieves.

"What do you want?" Adam shouted as he reached the screen of trees. He stood well back from the fence and spoke to them between the trunks, a hot sense of being family protector flooding his veins. He felt pumped up, ready for anything. He felt strong.

"Oh, I'm so sorry," the woman said, hands raised to her face as if holding in her embarrassment.

"Well, what are you doing? Why are you staring at my house? I should call the police, perhaps?"

"Oh Christ, no," the man said, "don't do that! We're sorry, it's just that . . . well, we love your house. We've been walking through the park on our way to work . . . we've moved into the new estate down the road . . . and we can't help having a look now and then. Just to see . . . well, whether you've put it on the market."

"You love my house. It's just a two-bed semi."

The woman nodded. "But it's so perfect. The garden, the trees, the location. We've got a child on the way, we need a garden. We'd buy it the minute you decided to sell!"

"Not a good way to present ourselves as potential house-buyers, I suppose," the man said, mock-grim-faced.

Adam shook his head. "Especially so keen. I could double the price," he smiled. They seemed genuine. They *were* genuine, he could tell that, and wherever the certainty came from he trusted it. In fact, far from being angry or suspicious, he suddenly felt sorry for them.

"Boy or girl?" he asked.

"I'm sorry?"

"Are you having a boy or a girl?"

"Oh," the woman said, still holding her face, "we haven't a clue. We want it to be a surprise. We just think ourselves lucky we can have children."

"Yes, they're precious," Adam said. He could hear Jamie faintly, giggling as Alison wiped breakfast from his mouth, hands, and face.

"Sorry to have troubled you," the man said. "Really, this is very embarrassing. I hope we haven't upset you, scared you? Here," he fished in his pocket for his wallet and brought out a business card. He offered it through the fence.

Adam stepped forward and took the card. He looked at both of them—just long enough to make them divert their eyes—and thought of his looming trip to London, what it might bring if things went well. He pictured his fantasized country house with the rooftop art studio and the big car and the gym.

"It just so happens," he said, "your dream may come sooner than you think."

"Really?" the woman asked. She was cute. She had big eyes and a trim, athletic figure. Adam suddenly knew, beyond a shadow of a doubt, that she would screw him if he asked. Not because she wanted his house, or thought it may help her in the future. Just because he was who he was.

He shrugged, pocketed the card and bid them farewell. As he turned and walked across the lawn to the back door, he could sense them simmering behind him. They wanted to ask more. They wanted to find out what he had meant by his last comment.

Let them stew. That way, perhaps they would be even more eager if and when the time came.

Saying goodbye at the train station was harder than he had imagined. It was the first trip he had been on without his family since the disastrous plane journey several weeks ago, and that final hug on the platform felt laden with dread. For Adam it was a distant fear, however, as if experienced for someone else in another life, not a disquiet he could truly attribute to himself. However hard he tried, he could not worry. Things were going too well for that.

Amaranth would look after him.

On the way to the station he had seen the things three times: once, a face staring from the back of a bus several cars in front; once, a shape hurrying across the road behind them, seen briefly and fleetingly in the rearview mirror; and finally in the station itself, a misplaced shadow hiding behind the high-level TV monitors that displayed departure and arrival times. Each time he had thought to show Alison, tell her why everything would be all right, that these beings were here to watch over him and bless him—

demon, angel, fairy, god

—but then he thought of her mother lying in a coma. How could he tell her that now? How could he tell her that everything was fine?

So the final hug, the final sweet kiss, and he could hardly look at her face without crying.

"I'll be fine," he said.

"Last time you told me that, ten hours later you were bobbing about in the Atlantic."

"The train's fully equipped with life-jackets and non-flammables."

"Fool." She hugged him again and Jamie snickered from his buggy.

Adam bent down and gave his son a kiss on the nose. He giggled, twisting Adam's heart around his childish finger one more time.

"And you, you little rascal. When your Daddy comes home, he's going to be a living, breathing, working artist."

"Don't get too optimistic and you won't be disappointed," Alison whispered in his ear.

"I won't be disappointed," he whispered back. "I know it."

He boarded the train and waved as it drifted from the station. His wife and son waved back.

The journey was quiet but exciting, not because anything happened, but because Adam felt as though he was approaching some fantastic junction in his life. One road led the way he had been heading for years, and it was littered with stalled dreams and burned-out ambition. The other road—the new road, offered to him since the plane crash and all the strangeness that had followed it—was alight with exciting possibilities and new vistas. He had been given a chance at another life, a newer, better life. It was something most people never had.

He would take that road. This trip was simply the first step to get there.

Howards had been offered the same chance, had taken it, and look at him now! Rich, well-traveled, mad perhaps, but harmless with it. Lonely. No family or friends. Look at him now . . .

But he would not think of that.

The train arrived at Paddington Station and Adam stepped out onto the platform.

Someone screamed: "Look out!"

He turned and his eyes widened, hands raised as if they would hold back the luggage cart careering toward him. It would break his legs at the very least, cast him aside and crumple him between the train and the concrete platform—

Something shimmered in the air beside the panic-stricken driver, like heat haze but more defined, more solid.

A second and the cart would hit him. He was frozen there, not only by the impending impact and the pain that would instantly follow, but also by what he saw.

The driver, yanked to the side.

The ambiguous shape thrusting its hand through the metallic chassis and straight into the vehicle's electric engine.

The cart, jerking suddenly at an impossible right-angle to crunch into the side of the train carriage mere inches from Adam's hip.

He gasped, finding it difficult to draw breath, winded by shock.

The driver had been flung from the cart and now rolled on the platform, clutching his arm and leaving dark, glistening spots of blood on the concrete. People ran to his aid, some of them diverting to Adam to check whether he had been caught in the impact.

"No, no, I'm fine," he told them, waving them away. "The driver . . . he's bleeding, he'll need help. I'm fine, really."

The thing had vanished from the cart. High overhead pigeons took flight, their wings sounding like a pack of cards being thumbed. *Game of luck*, Adam thought, but he did not look up. He did not want to see the shapes hanging from the girders above him.

He walked quickly away, unwilling to become involved in any

discussion or dispute about the accident. He was fine. That was all that mattered. He just wanted to forget about it.

"I saw," a voice croaked behind him as he descended the escalator to the tube station. And then the smell hit him. A grotesque merging of all bad stenches, a white-smell of desperation and decay and hopelessness. There was alcohol mixed in with urine, bad food blended with shit, fresh blood almost driven under by the rancid tang of rot. Adam gagged and bile rose into his mouth, but he grimaced and swallowed it back down.

Then he turned around.

He had seen people like her many times before, but mostly on television. He did not truly believe that a person like this existed, because she was so different from the norm, so unkempt, so wild, so *unreal*. Had she been a dog she would have been caught and put to sleep ages ago. And she knew it. In her eyes, the street person displayed a full knowledge of what had happened to her. And worse than that—they foretold of what *would* happen. There was no hope in her future. No rescue. No stroke of luck to save her.

"I saw," she said again, breathing sickness at his face. "I saw you when you were meant to be run over. I saw your eyes when it didn't happen. I saw that you were looking at one of . . . *them*." She spat the final word, as if expelling a lump of dog turd from her mouth.

Adam reached the foot of the escalator and strode away. His legs felt weak, his vision wavered, his skin tingled with goosebumps. Howards talking about the things he had seen could have been fluke or coincidence. Now, here was someone else saying the same things. Here, for Adam, was confirmation.

He knew the street person was following him; he could hear the shuffle of her disintegrating shoes. A hand fell on his shoulder. The sleeve of her old coat ended frayed and torn and bloodied, as if something had bitten it and dragged her by the arm.

"I said, I saw. You want to talk about it? You want me to tell you what you're doing? You lucky fuck."

Adam turned around and tried to stare the woman down, but he could not. She had nothing to lose, and so she held no fear. "Just leave me alone," he said instead. "I don't know what you're on about. I'll call the police if you don't leave me alone."

The woman smiled, a black-toothed grimace that split her face in two and squeezed a vile, pinkish pus from cracks in her lips. "You know what they did to me? Huh? You want to hear? I'll tell you that first, then I'll let you know what they'll do to you."

Adam turned and fled. There was nothing else to do. People moved out of his way, but none of them seemed willing to help. As confused and doubtful as he was about Amaranth, he still thought: *where are you now?* But maybe they were still watching. Maybe this was all part of their sport.

"They took me from my family," the woman continued. "I was fucking my husband when they came, we were conceiving, it was the time my son was conceived. They said they saved me, but I never knew what from. And they took me away, showed me what was to become of me. And you know what?"

"Leave me alone!" Adam did not mean to shout, but he was unable to prevent the note of panic in his voice. Still, none of his fellow travelers came to his aid. Most looked away. Some watched, fascinated. But none of them intervened.

"They crucified me!" the street person screamed. She grunted with each footstep, punctuating her speech with regular exclamations of pain. "They nailed me up and cut me open, fed my insides to the birds and the rats. Then they left me there for a while. And they let me see over the desert, across to the golden city where pricks like you were eating and screwing and being oh so bloody wonderful."

Adam put on a spurt of speed and sensed the woman falling behind.

"In the end, they took me from my family for good!" she shouted after him. "They're happy now, my family. They're rich and content, and my husband's fucked by an actress every night, and my son's in private school. Happy!"

He turned around; he could not help it. The woman was standing in the center of the wide access tunnel, people flowing by on both sides, giving her a wide berth. She had her hands held out as if feigning the crucifixion she claimed to have suffered. Her dark hair was speckled gray with bird shit. The string holding her skirt up was coming loose. Adam was sure he could see things crawling on the floor around her, tiny black shapes that could have been beetles or wood lice or large ants. They all moved away, spreading outward like living ripples from her death-stinking body.

"It'll happen to you, too!" the bug lady screamed. "This will happen to you! The result is always the same, it's just the route that's different!"

Adam turned a corner and gasped in relief. Straight ahead a tube train stood at a platform. He did not know which line it was on, which way it was going, where it would eventually take him. He slipped between the doors nevertheless, watched them slide shut, fell into a seat, and rested his head back against the glass. He read the poem facing straight down at him.

Wise is he who heeds his foe,
For what will come? You never know.

The bug lady made it onto the platform just as the train pulled away, waving her hands, screaming, fisting the air as if to fight existence itself.

"Bloody Bible bashers," said a woman sitting across from Adam. And he began to laugh.

He was still giggling three stations later. Nerves and fear and an overwhelming sense of unreality brought the laughter from him. His shoulders shook and people began to stare at him, and by the fourth station the laughter was more like sobbing.

It was not the near-accident that had shaken him, nor the continuing sightings of Amaranth, not even the bug lady and what she had been saying. It was her eyes. Such black, hopeless pits of despondency, lacking even the wish to save herself, let alone the ability to try. He had never seen eyes like it before. Or if he had, they had been too distant to make out. Far across a polluted lake. Heat from fires obscuring any characteristics from view.

In the tunnels faces flashed by, pressing out from the century-old brickwork, lit only by borrowed light from the tube train. They strained forward to look in at Adam, catching only the briefest glimpse of him but seeing all. They were Amaranth. Still watching him—still watching *over* him.

And if Howards had been right—and Adam could no longer find any reason to doubt him—still viewing him as sport.

The hotel was a smart four-star within a stone's throw of Leicester Square. His room was spacious and tastefully decorated, with a direct outside telephone, a TV, a luxurious en suite and a minibar charging exorbitant prices for mere dribbles of alcohol. Adam opened three miniatures of whiskey, added some ice he had fetched from the dispenser in the corridor, and sat back on the bed, trying not to see those transparent faces in his mind's eye. Surely they couldn't be in there as well? On the backs of his eyelids, invading his self as they'd invaded his life? He'd never seen them there, at least . . .

And really, even if he had, he could feel no anger toward them.

After he had finished the whiskey and his nerves had settled, he picked up the phone and dialed home. His own voice shocked him for a moment, then he left a message for Alison on the answerphone telling her he had arrived safely, glancing at his watch as he did so. They were usually giving Jamie his dinner around this time. Maybe she was at the hospital with her mother.

He opened a ridiculously priced can of beer from the fridge and went out to stand on the small balcony. Catching sight of the busy streets seemed to draw their noise to him, and he spent the next few minutes taking in the scenery, watching people go about their business unaware that they were being observed; cars snaking along the road as if bad driving could avoid congestion, paper bags floating on the breeze above all this, pigeons huddled on sills and rooftops, an aircraft passing silently high overhead. He wondered who was on the plane, and whether they had any inkling that they were being watched from the ground at that instant. He looked directly across the street into a third-story office window. A woman was kneeling in front of a photocopier, hands buried in its mechanical guts as she tried unsuccessfully to clear a paper jam. Did she know she was being watched, he wondered? Did the hairs on the nape of her neck prickle, her back tingle? She smacked the machine with the palm of her hand, stood and started to delve into her left nostril with one toner-blackened finger. No, she didn't know. None of these people knew, not really. A few of them saw him standing up here and walked on, a little more self-consciously than before, but many were in their own small world.

Most of them did not even know that there was a bigger world out there at all. Much bigger. Way beyond the solid confines of earth, wind, fire, and water.

He took another swig of beer and tried to change the way he was looking. He switched viewpoints from observer to observed, seeking to spy out whoever or whatever was watching him. Down in the street the pedestrians all had destinations in mind, and like most city-dwellers they rarely looked higher than their own eye-level. Nothing above that height was of interest to them. In the hive of the buildings opposite the hotel, office workers sat tapping at computers, stood by coffee machines, huddled around desks or tables, flirted, never imagining that there was anything worth looking at beyond the air-conditioned confines of their domains.

He was being watched. He knew it. He could feel it. It was a feeling he had become more than used to since Howards had forced him, eventually, to entertain the truth of what was happening to him.

The rooftops were populated by pigeons; no strange faces up there. The street down below was a battlefield of business, and if Amaranth were down there, Adam certainly could not pick them out. The small balconies to either side of him were unoccupied. He even turned around and stared back into his own room, fully expecting to find a face pressed through the wall like a waxwork corpse, or the wardrobe door hanging ajar. But he saw nothing. Wherever they were, they were keeping themselves well-hidden for now.

A car hooted angrily and he looked back down over the railing— straight into the eyes of the bug lady. She was standing on the sidewalk outside the building opposite the hotel, staring up at Adam, her gaze unwavering. Even from this distance, Adam could see the hopelessness therein.

There was little he could do. He went back inside and closed and locked the doors behind him, pulled the curtains, grabbed a miniature of gin from the fridge because the whiskey had run out.

He tried calling Alison again, but his own voice greeted him from the past. He had recorded that message before the flight, before the crash, before Amaranth. He was a different person now. He dialed and listened again, knowing how foolish it was: yes, a different person. He had known so little back then.

"Just sign on the dotted line," Maggie said. "Then the deal's done and you'll have to sleep with me for what I've done for you."

"Mags, I'd sleep with you even if you hadn't just closed the biggest deal of my life, you know that." Maggie was close on seventy years old, glamorous in her own way, and Adam was sure she'd never had enough sex in her earlier years. Sometimes, when he really thought about it, he wondered just how serious she was when she joked and flirted.

He picked up the contract and scanned it one more time. Sixth reading now, at least. He hated committing to anything, and there was little as final and binding as signing a contract. True, the gallery had yet to countersign, but once he'd scrawled his name along the bottom there was little chance to change anything.

And besides, this was too good to be true.

He wondered how Alison and Jamie were. And then he wondered *where* they were as well.

It'll happen to you, too, the bug lady had screamed at him, pus dripping from her lips, insects fleeing her body as if they already thought she was dead.

You'll lose them, Howards had stated plainly.

"Mags . . ." he muttered, uncertain of exactly what he was about to say. The alcohol had gone to his head, especially after the celebratory champagne Maggie had brought to his room. His aim had been good. The cork had gone flying through the door and out over the street, and he'd used that as an excuse to take another look. The bug lady had gone, but Adam had been left feeling uncomfortable, unsettled.

That, and his missing wife and son.

The contract wavered on the bed in front of him, uncertain, unreal. He held the pen above the line and imagined signing his name, tried to see what effect it would have. Surely this was his own good fortune, not something thrown his way by Amaranth? But he had only been working in fire since the accident . . .

"Mags, I just need to call Alison." He put the pen down. "I haven't told her I've arrived safely yet."

Maggie nodded, eyebrows raised.

Adam dialed and fully expected to hear his own voice once more, but Alison snapped up the line. "Yes?"

"Honey?"

"Oh Adam, you're there. I got your messages but I was hoping you'd ring . . ."

"Anything the matter?"

"No, no . . . well, Mum's taken a turn for the worse. They think . . . she arrested this afternoon."

"Oh no."

"Look, how's it going? Maggie there with you? Tell her to keep her hands off my husband."

"Honey, I'll come home."

Alison sighed down the phone. "No, you won't. Just call me, okay? Often? Make it feel like you're really here and I'll be fine. But you do what you've got to do to make our damn fortune."

He held the phone between his cheek and shoulder and made small talk with his wife, asked how Jamie was, spoke to his son. And at the same time he signed the three copies of the contract and slid them across the bed to Maggie.

"Love you," he said at last. Alison loved him too. They left it at that.

"Shall we go out to celebrate?" Maggie asked.

Adam shook his head. "Do you mind if we just stay in the hotel? Have a meal in the restaurant, perhaps? I'm tired and a bit drunk, and . . ." *And I don't want to go outside in case the bug lady's there,* he thought. *I don't want to hear what she's telling me.*

In the restaurant an ice sculpture was melting slowly beneath the lights, shedding shards of glittering movement as pearls of water slid down its sides. As they sat down Adam thought he saw it twitch, its face twist to watch him, limbs flex. He glanced away and looked again. Still he could not be sure. Well, if Amaranth chose to sit and watch him eat—celebrate his success, his good luck—what could he do about it?

What could he do?

The alcohol and the buzz of signing the deal and the experience of meeting the bug lady all combined to drive Adam into a sort of dislocated stupor. He heard what Maggie said, he smelled the food, he tasted the wine, but they were all vicarious experiences, as if he were really residing elsewhere for the evening, not inside his own body. Later, he recalled only snippets of conversation, brief glimpses of events. The rest vanished into blankness.

"This will lead onto a lot more work," Maggie said, her words somehow winging their way between the frantic chords of the piano player. "And the gallery says that they normally sell at least half the paintings at any exhibition."

A man coughed and spat his false teeth onto his table. The restaurant bustled with restrained laughter. The shadows of movement seemed to follow seconds behind.

A waiter kept filling his glass with wine, however much he objected.

The ice sculpture reduced, but the shape within it stayed the same size. Over the course of the evening, one of the Amaranth things was revealed to him. Nobody else seemed to notice.

The ice cream tasted rancid.

Maggie touched his knee beneath the table and suggested they go to his room.

Next, he was alone in his bed. He must have said something to her, something definite and final about the way their relationship should work. He hoped he had not been cruel.

Something floated above his bed, a shadow within shadows. "Do not deny us," it said inside his head, a cautionary note in its voice. "Believe in us. Do not deny us."

Then it was morning, and his head thumped with a killer hangover, and although he remembered the words and the sights of last night, he was sure it had all been a dream.

Adam managed to flag down a taxi as soon as he stepped from the hotel. He was dropped off outside the gallery, and as he crossed the pavement he bumped into an old man hurrying along with his head down. They exchanged apologies and turned to continue on their way, but then stopped. They stared at each other for a moment, frowning, all the points of recognition slotting into place almost visibly as their faces relaxed and the tentative smiles came.

"You were on the horse," Adam said. "The unicorn."

"You were the disbeliever. You believe now?" The man's smile was fixed, like a painting overlying his true feelings. There was something in his eyes . . . something about giving in.

"I do," Adam said, "but I've met some people . . . a lucky one, and an unlucky one . . . and I'm beginning to feel scared." Verbalizing it actually brought it home to him; he *was* scared.

The man leaned forward and Adam could smell expensive cologne on his skin. "Don't deny Amaranth," he said. "You can't anyway, nobody ever has. But don't even think about it."

Adam stepped back as if the man had spat at him. He remembered Howards telling him that he would lose his family, and the bug lady spewing promises darker than that.

He wondered how coincidental his meeting these three people was. "How is your family?" he asked.

The unicorn man averted his gaze. "Not as lucky as me."

Adam looked up at the imposing facade of the gallery, the artistically wrought modern gargoyles that were never meant for anything other than ornamentation. Maybe they should have been imbued with a power, he thought. Because there really are demons . . .

He wondered how Molly was, whether she had woken up yet. He should telephone Alison to find out, but if he hesitated here any longer he may just turn around and flee back home. Leave all this behind—all this success, this promise, this hope for a comfortable and long sought-after future . . .

When he looked back down, the man had vanished along the street, disappearing into the crowds. *Don't deny Amaranth,* he had said. Adam shook his head. How could anyone?

He stepped though the circular doors and into the air-conditioned vestibule of the gallery building. Marble solidified the area, with only occasional soft oases of comfortable seating breaking it up here and there. Maggie rose from one of these seats, two men standing behind her. The gallery owners, Adam knew. The men who had signed checks ready to give him.

"Adam!" Maggie called across to him.

His cell phone rang. He flipped it open and answered. "Alison?"

"Adam, your lateness just manages to fall into the league of fashionable," Maggie cooed.

"Honey. Adam, Mum's died. She went a few minutes ago. Oh . . ." Alison broke into tears and Adam wanted to reach through the phone, hug her to him, kiss and squeeze and love her until all of this went away.

He glanced up at the men looking expectantly at him, at Maggie chattering away, and he could hear nothing but his wife crying down the phone to him.

"I'll be home soon," Adam said. "Alison?"

"Yes." Very quietly. A plea as well as a confirmation.

"I'll be home soon. Is Jamie all right?"

A wet laugh. "Watching *Teletubbies*. Bless him."

"Three hours. Give me three hours and I'll be home."

"Adam?" Maggie stood before him now. It had taken her this long to see that something was wrong. "What is it?"

"Alison's mother just died."

"Oh . . . oh shit."

"You got those contracts, Mags?"

She nodded and handed him a paper file.

He looked up at the two men, at their fixed smiles, their moneymaker's suits, the calculating worry-lines around their eyes. "This isn't art," he said, and he tore the contracts in half.

As he left the building, he reflected that it was probably the most artistic thing he had ever done.

There was a train due to leave five minutes after he arrived at the station, as he knew there would be. He was lucky like that. Not so his family, of course, his wife, or his wife's mother. But *he* was lucky.

He should not have taken the train—he should have denied Amaranth and the conditional luck they had bestowed upon him—but he needed to be with Alison. *One more time*, he thought. *Just this one last time.*

They made themselves known in the station. He had been aware of them following him since the gallery, curving in and out of the ground like sea serpents, wending their way through buildings, flying high above him and merging with clouds of pigeons. Sometimes he caught sight of one reflected in a shop window but, whenever he turned around, it was gone.

At the station, the four of them were standing together at the far end of the platform. People passed them by. People walked *through* them, shuddering and glancing around with startled expressions as if someone had just stepped on their graves. Nobody else seemed to see them.

Adam boarded the train at the nearest end. As he stepped up, he saw Amaranth doing the same several carriages along.

He sat in the first seat he found and they were there within seconds.

"Go away," he whispered. "Leave me alone." He hoped nobody could hear or see him mumbling to himself.

"You cannot deny us," their voice said. "Think of what you will lose."

Adam was thinking of what he would gain. His family, safe and sound.

"Not necessarily."

Was that humor there? Was Amaranth laughing at him, enjoying this? And Adam suddenly realized that an emotionless, indifferent Amaranth was not the most frightening thing he could think of. No, an Amaranth possessed of humor—irony—was far more terrifying.

They were sitting at his table. He had a window seat, two sat opposite, a third in the seat beside him. The fourth rested on the table, sometimes halfway through the window glass. The acceleration did not seem to concern the thing, which leaned back with one knee raised and its face pointing at the ceiling, for all the world looking as if it were sunbathing.

So far, thankfully, nobody else had taken the seats.

"Leave me alone," he said again, "and leave my family alone as well." His voice was rising, he could not help it. Anger and fear combined to make a heady brew.

"We are not touching your family," Amaranth soothed. "Whatever happens there simply . . . happens. Our interest is in you."

"But why?"

"That is our business, not yours. But you are in danger . . . in danger of denying us, refuting our existence."

"You're nothing but nightmares." He stared down at the table so that he did not have to look at them, but from the corner of his eye he could see the hand belonging to the one on the table, see it flexing and flowing as it moved.

"Since when did a dream give a man the power to survive?"

He glared up at them then, hating the smug superiority in their voice. "Power of the mind!" he could not help shouting. "Now leave me! I can't see you anymore."

Surprisingly, Amaranth vanished.

Pale faces turned away from him as he scanned along the carriage. Everyone must have heard him—he had been very loud—but this was London, he thought. Strange things happened in London all the time. Strange people. The blessed and the cursed mixed within feet of each other, each cocooned in their own blanket of fate. Maybe he had simply seen beyond his, for a time.

He had been unfaithful to Alison only once. It had been a foolish thing, a one-hour stand, not even bearing the importance to last a night. A woman in a bar—he was drunk with his friends—an instant attraction, a few whiskeys too many, a damp screw against the moldy wall behind the pub. Unsatisfying, dirty more than erotic, frantic rather than tender. He had felt forlorn, but it had taken only days for him to drive it down in his mind, believe it was a fantasy rather than something that had truly happened.

On the surface, at least.

Deep down, in places he only visited in the darkest, most melancholy times, he knew that it was real. He had done it. And there was no escape from that.

Now, he tried to imagine that Amaranth was a product of his imagination, and those people he had met—Howards, the bug lady, the man who had ridden the unicorn—were all coincidental players in a fantasy of his own creation . . .

And all the while, he knew deep down that this was bullshit. He could camouflage the truth with whatever colors he desired, it was all still there, plain as day in the end.

They left him alone until halfway through the journey. He had been watching, trying to see them between the trees rushing by the window, looking for their faces in clouds, behind hedges, in the eyes of the other passengers on the train. Nothing. With no hidden faces to see, he realized just how under siege he had been feeling.

He began to believe they had gone for good. He began to believe his own lies.

And then the woman sat opposite him.

She was beautiful, voluptuous, raven-haired, well-dressed, clothes accentuating rather than revealing her curves. Adam averted his eyes and looked out the window, but he could not help glancing back at her, again and again. Yes. She was truly gorgeous.

"I hate trains," she said. "So boring." Then her unshod foot dug into his crotch.

He gasped, unable to move, all senses focusing on his groin as her toes kneaded, stroked and pressed him to erection. He closed his eyes and thought of Alison, crying while Jamie caused chaos around her. Her father was long dead and there was no close family nearby, so unless she had called one of her friends around to sit with her, she would be there on her own, weeping . . .

And then he imagined himself guiding this woman into the cramped confines of a train toilet, sitting on the seat and letting her impale herself upon him, using the movements of the train to match their rhythms.

He opened his eyes and knew that she was thinking the same thing. Her foot began to work faster. He stared out of the window and saw a plane trail being born high above.

Realized how tentative the other passengers' grips on life were.

Saw just how fortunate he was to still be here.

He reached down, grasped the woman's ankle, and forced her foot away from him. *This isn't luck*, he thought, *not for my family, not even for me. It's fantasy, maybe, but not luck. What's lucky about betraying my wife when she needs me the most?*

They're desperate. Amaranth is desperate to keep me as they want me.

No, he thought.

"No."

"What?" the woman said, frowning, looking around, staring back at him. Her eyes went wide. "Oh Jesus . . . oh, I'm . . ." She stood quickly, hurried along the carriage and disappeared from sight.

Amaranth returned. "Do not deny us," the voice said, deeper than he had ever heard it, stronger.

He closed his eyes. The vision he had was so powerful, quick, and sharp that he almost felt as if he were physically experiencing it then and there. He smelled the vol-au-vents and the caviar and the champagne at the exhibition, he saw Maggie's cheerful face and the gallery owners nodding to him that he had just sold another painting, he tasted the tang of nerves as one of the viewers raved about the painting of his they had just bought, minutes ago, for six thousand pounds.

He forced his eyes open against a stinging tiredness, rubbed his face and pinched his skin to wake himself up. "No," he said. "My wife needs me."

"You will regret it!" Amaranth screeched, and Adam thought he was hearing it for the first time as it really was. The hairs stood on the back of his neck, his balls tingled, his stomach dropped. The things came from out of the table and the seats and reached for him, swiping out with clear, sharp nails, driving their hands into his flesh and grabbing his bones, plucking at him, swirling and screaming and cursing in ways he could never know.

None of them touched him.

They could *not*.

They could not *touch* him.

Adam smiled. "There's a bit of luck," he whispered.

And with one final roar, they disappeared.

Half an hour from the station he called Alison and arranged for her to come and collect him. He knew it was false, but she sounded virtually back to normal, more in control. She said she had already ordered a Chinese takeaway and bought a bottle of wine. He could barely imagine sitting at home, eating and drinking and chatting—one of their favorite times together—with Molly lying dead less than two miles away. He would see her passing in every movement of Alison's head, every twitch of her eyelids. She would be there with them more than ever. He was heading for strange times.

As the train pulled into the station, his cell phone rang. It was Maggie.

"Adam, when are you coming back? Come on, artistic tempers are well and good when you're not getting anywhere, but that was plain rude. These guys really have no time for prima donnas, you know. Are you at your hotel?"

"I'm back home," Adam said, hardly believing her tone of voice. "Didn't you hear what I said, Mags? Alison's Mum is dead."

"Yes, yes . . ." she said, trailing off. "Adam. The guys at the gallery have made another offer. They'll commission the artwork for the same amount, but they'll also—"

"Mags, I'm not interested. This is not . . . me. It'll change me too much."

"One hundred thousand."

Adam did not reply. He could not. His imagination, kicked into some sort of overdrive over the past few weeks, was picturing what that sort of money could do for his family.

He stood from his seat and followed the other passengers toward the exit. "No Mags," he said, shaking his head. He saw the woman who had sat opposite him; it was obvious that she had already spotted him, because her head was down, frantically searching for some unknown item in her handbag. "No. That's not me. I didn't do any of it."

"You didn't do those paintings?"

Adam thought about it for a moment as he shuffled along the aisle: the midnight awakenings when he knew he had to work; the smell of oils and coffee as time went away, and it was just him and the painting; his burning finger and hand and arm muscles after several hours' work; the feeling that he truly was creating in fire.

"No Mags," he said, "I didn't." He turned the phone off and stepped onto the platform.

Alison and Jamie were there to meet him. Alison was the one who had lost her mother, but on seeing them it was Adam who burst into tears. He hugged his wife and son, she crying into his neck in great wracking sobs, Jamie mumbling, "Daddy, Daddy," as he struggled to work his way back into his parents' world.

Adam picked Jamie up, kissing his forehead and unable to stop crying. *You'll lose them*, Howards had said. How dare he? How dare he talk about someone else's family like that?

"I'm so sorry," he said to Alison.

She smiled grimly, a strange sight in combination with her tears and puffy eyes and gray complexion. "Such a bloody stupid way to go," she managed to gasp before her own tears came again.

Adam touched her cheek. "I'll drive us home."

As they walked along the platform toward the bridge to the car park, Adam looked around. Faces stared at him from the train—one of them familiar, the woman who had been rubbing him with her foot—but none of them were Amaranth. Some were pale and distant, others almost transparent in their dissatisfaction with their lot, but all were human.

The open girders of the roof above were lined only with pigeons.

The waste-ground behind the station was home to wild cats and rooks and rusted shopping trolleys. Nothing else.

Around them, humanity went about its toils. Businessmen and travelers and students dodged each other across the platform. None of them looked at Adam and his family, or if they did they glanced quickly away. Everyone knew grief when they saw it, and most people respected its fierce privacy.

In the car park Alison sat in the passenger seat of their car and Adam strapped Jamie into his seat in the back. "You a good boy?" he asked. "You been a good boy for your Mummy?"

"Tiger, tiger!" Jamie hissed. "Daddy, Daddy tiger." He smiled, showing the gap-toothed grin that never failed to melt Adam's heart. Then he giggled.

He was not looking directly at Adam. His gaze was directed slightly to the left, over Adam's shoulder.

Adam spun around.

Nothing.

He scanned the car park. A hundred cars, and Amaranth could be hiding inside any one of them, watching, waiting, until they could touch him once more.

He climbed into the car and locked the doors.

"Why did you do that?" Alison asked.

"Don't know." He shook his head. She was right. Locked doors would be no protection.

They headed away from the station and into town. They lived on the outskirts on the other side. A couple of streets away lay the small restaurant where Adam had talked with Howards. He wondered where the old man was now. Whether he was still here. Whether he remained concerned for Adam's safety, his life, his luck, since Adam had stormed out and told him to mind his own business.

Approaching the traffic lights at the foot of the river-bridge, Adam began to slow down.

A hand reached out of the seat between his legs and clasped onto the wheel. He could feel it, icy-cool where it touched his balls, a burning cold where it actually passed through the meat of his inner thighs.

"No!" he screamed. Jamie screeched and began to cry, Alison looked up in shock.

"What? Adam?"

"Oh no, don't you fucking—" He was already stamping hard on the brakes but it did no good.

"Come see us again," Amaranth said between his ears, and the hand twisted the wheel violently to the left.

Adam fought. A van loomed ahead of them, scaffold poles protruding from its tied-open rear doors. Terrible images of impalement and bloodied, rusted metal leaped into his mind and he pulled harder, muscles burning with the strain of fighting the hand. The windscreen flowed into the face of one of the things, still expressionless but exuding malice all the same. Adam looked straight through its eyes at the van.

The brakes were not working.

"Tiger!" Jamie shouted.

At the last second the wheel turned a fraction to the right and they skimmed the van, metal screeching on metal, the car juddering with the impact.

Thank God, Adam thought.

And then the old woman stepped from the sidewalk directly in front of them.

This time, Amaranth did not need to turn the wheel. Adam did it himself. And he heard the sickening *crump* as the car hit the woman sideways on, and he felt the vehicle tilting as it mounted the pavement, and he saw a lamp-post splitting the windscreen in two. His family screamed.

There was a terrible coldness as eight unseen hands closed around his limbs.

The car gave the lamp-post a welcoming embrace.

"I'm dead," Adam said. "I've been dead for a long time. I'm floating in the Atlantic. I know this because nothing that has happened is possible. I've been dreaming. Maybe the dead can dream." He moved his left hand and felt his father's lost watch chafe his wrist.

A hand grasped his throat and quicksilver nails dug in. "Do the dead hurt?" the familiar voice intoned.

Adam tried to scream, but he could not draw breath.

Around him, the world burned.

"Keep still and you will not die . . . yet."

"Alison!" Adam began to struggle against the hands holding him down. The sky was smudged with greasy black smoke, and the stench reminded him of rotten roadkill he had found in a ditch when he was a boy, a dead creature too decayed to identify. Something wet was dripping on him, wet and warm. One of the things was leaning over him. Its mouth was open and the liquid forming on its lips was transparent, and of the same consistency as its body. It was shedding pieces of itself onto him.

"You will listen to us," Amaranth said.

"Jamie! Alison!"

"You will see them again soon enough. First, listen. You pledged to believe in us and to never deny us. You have reneged. Reaffirm your pledge. We gave you a gift, but without faith we are—"

"I don't want your gift," Adam said, still struggling to stand. He could see more now, as if this world were opening up to him as he came to. Above the heads of the things standing around him, the ragged walls and roofs of shattered buildings stood out against the hazy sky. Flames licked here and there, smoke rolled along the ground, firestorms did their work in some unseen middle-distance. Ash floated down and stuck to his skin like warm snow. He thought of furnaces and ovens, concentration camps, lime pits . . .

"But you have it already. You have the good luck we bestowed upon you. And you have used it . . . we have seen . . . we have observed."

"Good luck? Was that crash good luck?"

"You avoided the van that would have killed you. You survived. We held you back from death."

"You *steered* me!"

Amaranth said nothing.

"What of Alison? Jamie?"

Once more, the things displayed a loathsome hint of emotion. "Who knows?" the voice said slowly, drawing out the last word with relish.

At last Adam managed to stand, but only because the things had moved back and freed him. "Leave me be," he said, wondering if begging would help, or perhaps flattery. "Thank you for saving me, that first time . . . I know you did, and I'm grateful because my wife has a husband, my son has a father. But please leave me be." All he wished for was to see his family again.

Amaranth picked him up slowly, the things using one hand each, lifting and lifting, until he was suspended several feet above the ground. From up there he could see all around, view the devastated landscape surrounding him—and he realized at last where he was.

Through a gap in the buildings to his left, the glint of violent waters. Silhouetted against this, dancing in the flickering flames that were eating at it even now, a small figure hung crucified.

"Oh, no."

"Be honored," Amaranth said, "you are the first to visit both places." They dropped him to the ground and stood back. "Run."

"What? Where?" He was winded, certain he had cracked a rib. It felt like a hot coal in his side.

"Run."

"Why?"

And then he saw why.

Around the corner, where this shattered street met the next, capered a horde of burning people. Some of them had only just caught aflame, beating at clothes and hair as they ran. Others were engulfed, arms waving, flaming pieces of them falling as they made an impossible dash away from the agony. There were smaller shapes among them—children—just as doomed as the rest. Some of them screamed, those who still had vocal chords left to make any sound. Others, those too far gone, sizzled and spat.

Adam staggered, wincing with the pain in his side, and turned to run. Amaranth had moved down the street behind him and stood staring, all their eyes upon him. He sprinted toward them. They receded back along the rubble-strewn street without seeming to walk. Every step he took moved them further away.

He felt heat behind him and a hand closed over his shoulder, the same shoulder the bug lady had grasped. Someone screaming, pleading, a high-pitched sound as the acrid stink of burning clothes scratched at his nostrils. The flames crept across his shoulder and down onto his chest, but they were extinguished almost immediately by something wet splashing across him.

He looked down. There were no burns on his clothing and his chest was dry.

Adam shook the hand from him and ran. He passed a shop where someone lay half-in, half-out of the doorway, a dog chewing on the weeping stump of one of their legs. They were still alive. Their eyes followed him as he dashed by, as if coveting his ability to run. He recognized those eyes. He even knew that face, although when he had first seen her, the bug lady had seemed more alive.

"Let me back!" he shouted at the figures receding along the decimated street ahead of him. From behind, he heard thumps as burning people hit the ground to melt into pools of fat and charred bone. He risked a look over his shoulder and saw even more of them, new victims spewing from dilapidated doorways and side alleys to join in the flaming throng.

Someone walked out into the street ahead of him, limping on crutches, staring at the ground. They looked up and the expression that passed across their face was one of relief. Adam passed her by—he only saw it was a woman when he drew level—and heard the feet of the burning horde trample her into the dirt.

"Let me back, you bastards!" The last time he was here—although he had been on the other side of the lake, of course, staring across and pitying those poor unfortunates on this side—he had not known what was happening to him. Now he did. Now he knew that there was a way back, if only it was granted to him.

"You are really a very interesting one," the voice said as loud as ever, even though Amaranth stood in the distance. "You will be . . . fun."

As Adam tripped over a half-full skull, the burning people fell across him and a voice started shouting again. "Tiger! Tiger!" It went from a shout to a scream, an unconscious, childish exhalation of terror and panic.

The world was on its side, and the legs of the burning people milled beyond the shattered windscreen. One of them was squatting down, reaching in, grasping at his arms even as he tried to push them away.

Something still dripped onto him. He looked up. Alison was suspended above him in the passenger seat, the seatbelt holding her there, holding in the pieces that were still intact. The lamp-post had done something to her. She was no longer whole. She had changed. Adam snapped his eyes shut as something else parted from her and hit his shoulder.

Heat gushed and caressed his face, but then there was a gentle ripping sound above him, and coppery blood washed the flames away from his skin like his wife brushing crumbs from his stubble. The flames could never take him. Not when he was such a lucky man.

You are the first to visit both places, Amaranth's voice echoed like the vague memory of pain. *You will be . . . fun.*

"Tiger!"

Jamie?

"Jamie!"

Flames danced around him once more. Fingers snagged his jacket. A hand reached in bearing a knife and he crunched down into shattered glass as his seatbelt was sliced. Something else fell from above him as he was dragged out, a final present, a last, lasting gift from his Alison. As he was hauled through the windscreen, hands beating at the burning parts of him, his doomed son screaming for him from the doomed car, he wondered whether it was a part of her that he had ever seen before.

He was lying out on the lawn. It had not been cut for a long time, because his sit-on lawnmower had broken down. Besides, he liked the wild appearance it gave the garden. Alison had liked wild. She had loved the countryside; she had been agnostic, but she had said the smells and sounds and sights made her feel closer to God.

Adam felt close to no one, certainly not God. Not with Amaranth peering at him from the woods sometimes, following him on his trips into town, watching as good fortune and bad luck juggled with his life and health.

No, certainly not God.

Alison had been buried alongside her mother over a year ago. He had not been to the cemetery since. He remembered her in his own way—he was still painting—and he did not wish to be reminded of what her ruined body had become beneath the ground. But he was reminded every day. Every morning, on his bus trip into town to visit Jamie in the hospital, he was reminded. Because he so wanted his son to join her.

That was guilt. That was suffering. That was the sickest irony about the whole thing. *He's a lucky lad*, the doctors would still tell him, even after a year. *He's a fighter. He'll wake up soon, you'll see. He'll have scars, yes* . . . And then Adam would ask about infection and the doctors would nod, yes, there has been something over the last week or two, inevitable with burns, but we've got it under control, it's just bad luck that . . .

And so on.

His wife, dead. His son in a coma from which he had only awakened three times, and each time some minor complication had driven him back under. He was growing up dead. And still Adam went to him every day to talk to him, to whisper in his ear, to try and bring him around with favorite nursery rhymes and the secret Dad-voices he had used on him when things were good, when life was normal. When chance was still a factor in his existence, and fate was uncertain.

He looked across at the house. It was big, bought with Alison's life insurance, their old home sold for a good profit to the couple who had wanted it so much. This new property had an acre of land, a glazed rooftop studio with many panes already cracked or missing, a Mercedes in the driveway—a prison. A Hell. His own manufactured Hell, perhaps to deny the idea that such a grand home could be seen as fortunate, lucky to come by. The place was a constant reminder of his lost family because he had made it so. No new start for him.

The walls of the house were lined with his own portraits of Alison and Jamie. Some of them were bright and full of sunshine and light and positive memories. Others contained thoughts that only he could read—bad memories of the crash—and what he had seen of Alison and heard of Jamie before being dragged out from the car. The reddest of these painting hung near the front door for all visitors to see.

Not that he had many visitors. Until yesterday.

Howards had tracked him down. Adam had let him in, knowing it was useless to fight, and knowing also that he truly wanted to hear what the old man had to say.

"I've found a way out," he had whispered. "I tried it last week . . . I injected myself with poison, then used the antidote at the last minute. But I could have done it. I could have gone on. They weren't watching me at the time."

"Why didn't you?"

"Well . . . I've come to terms with it. Life. As it is. I just wanted to test the idea. Prove that I was still in control of myself."

Adam had nodded, but he did not understand.

"I thought it only fair to offer you the chance," Howards had said.

Now, Adam knew that he had to take that chance. Whether Jamie ever returned or not—and his final screams, his shouts of *Tiger! Tiger!*, had convinced Adam that his son had been the twitching shape on the burning cross—he could never be a good father to him. Not with Amaranth following him, watching him. Not when he knew what they had done.

Killed his wife.

Given his son bad luck.

Yesterday afternoon he had been lucky enough to find someone willing to sell him a gun, the weapon with which he would blow his own brains out. And that, he thought, perfectly summed up what his life had become.

"Oh, look," Adam muttered, "a four-leafed clover." He flicked the little plant and sighed, pushing himself to his feet, stretching. He had been lying on the grass for a long time.

He walked across the lawn and onto the graveled driveway, past the Mercedes parked mock-casual. Its tires were flat and the engine rusted through, although it was only a year old. One of a bad batch, he had thought, and he still tried to convince himself of that, even after all this time.

He entered the house and passed into the study.

Two walls were lined with moldy books he had never read, and never would read. The portraits of the people he loved stared down at him and he should have felt at peace, should have felt comforted, but he did not. There was a large map on one wall, a thousand intended destinations marked in red, the half-dozen places he had visited pinned green. Travel was no longer on his agenda, neither was reading. He could go anywhere on his own, because he had the means to do so, but he no longer felt the desire. Not now that his family was lost to him.

He was about to take a journey of a different kind. Somewhere even stranger than the places he had already seen. Stranger than anyone had seen, more terrifying, more—final. After the past year he was keener than ever to find his way there.

And he had a map. It was in the bureau drawer. A .44 Magnum, gleaming snake-like silver, slick to the touch, cold, impersonal. He hugged it between his legs to warm it. May as well feel comfortable for his final seconds.

Outside, the fourth leaf on the clover glowed brightly and then disappeared into a pinprick of light. A transparent finger rose from the ground to scoop it up. Then it was gone.

"Well," Adam said to the house, empty but alive with the memories he had brought here, planted and allowed to grow. "It wasn't bad to begin with . . . but it could have been better."

He heard footsteps approaching along the graveled driveway, frantic footsteps pounding toward the house.

"Adam!" someone shouted, emotion giving their voice an androgynous lilt.

It may have been Howards, regretting the news he had brought.

Or perhaps it was Amaranth? Realizing that he had slipped their attention for just too long. Knowing, finally, that he would defeat them.

Whoever. It was the last sound he would hear.

He placed the barrel of the gun inside his mouth, angled it upward, and pulled the trigger.

The first thing he heard was Howards.

". . . bounced off your skull and shattered your knee. They took your leg off, too. But I suppose that won't really bother you much. The doctors say you were so lucky to survive. But then, they would."

The shuffle of feet, the creak of someone standing from a plastic chair.

"I wish you could hear me. I wish you knew how sorry I am, Adam. I thought perhaps you could defeat them . . ."

He could not turn to see Howards. He saw nothing but the cracked ceiling. A polystyrene tile had shifted in its grid, and a triangle of darkness stared down at him. Perhaps there were eyes hidden within its gloom even now.

"I'm sorry."

Footsteps as Howards left.

With a great effort, one that burned into his muscles and set them aflame, Adam lifted his hands. And he felt what was left of his head.

A face pressed down at him from the ceiling, lifeless, emotionless, transparent but for darker stripes across its chin and cheeks. Another joined it, then two more.

They watched him for quite some time.

For all the world, Adam wished he could look away.

ONE OF US

DENNIS ETCHISON

Dennis Etchison is a three-time winner of both the British Fantasy and World Fantasy Awards. His collections include *The Dark Country, Red Dreams, The Blood Kiss, The Death Artist, Talking in the Dark, Fine Cuts, Got To Kill Them All & Other Stories, A Little Black Book of Horror Tales*, and *It Only Comes Out At Night & Other Stories*.

He is also the author of the novels *Darkside, Shadowman, California Gothic, Double Edge, The Fog, Halloween II* and *III*, and *Videodrome* (the latter three under the pseudonym "Jack Martin"), and the editor of the anthologies *Cutting Edge, Masters of Darkness I–III, MetaHorror, The Museum of Horrors*, and (with Ramsey Campbell and Jack Dann*) Gathering the Bones*.

Etchison has written extensively for film, television, and radio, including more than 150 scripts for *The Twilight Zone Radio Dramas*. He served as President of the Horror Writers Association from 1992–94 and is a recipient of the Bram Stoker Award for Lifetime Achievement.

"My friend Patrick was a professional driver," the author explains. "He owned two limousines, was Ray Bradbury's personal chauffeur (the license plate on that car read F451, naturally), and also provided transportation for some of the motion picture and television studios in Los Angeles. Every year the networks spent two or three busy months publicizing their new shows for the fall season, previewing them for the press and staging various publicity events. Patrick usually had contracts to shuttle stars to and from these events, and when the rush was on it may have been necessary for him to subcontract with other independent drivers in order to guarantee enough cars.

"One day in 2001 he asked me to help him out by driving a TV talk-show host to and from a press junket. When the drive, approximately one-half mile in each direction, netted me a quick fifty-dollar cash tip, I wondered whether Patrick might need help any other time soon. He did, and so over the next couple of months I spent a few hours a week behind the wheel of the F451 Cadillac with its 32-valve Northstar engine, ferrying movie and TV series stars to airports, photo opportunities, studio shoots, and the like—probably the most painless work I have ever done, and a great deal easier than writing.

"The experience was interesting and also turned out to be a research opportunity, the first product being the story you are about to read . . . which, I should emphasize, is fiction."

HEYMAN RANG THE bell one more time, then walked down the driveway to the shade.

The Lincoln was so quiet he had to open the door to be sure it was running. He switched off the engine, pressed the button to pop the trunk, and went around to the back, but before he could reach inside the car the gate behind him buzzed.

A tall boy came up the driveway from the street, dragging his feet through the dry leaves.

"Morning," said Heyman.

The boy had on hiking boots, baggy shorts, and a T-shirt with a distorted logo across the front. He tried to focus his eyes. "Uh. You must be the dude."

Heyman nodded. "I'm the driver."

"Uh, Willy, right?"

"Willy's off today."

"Uh." The boy lost interest and stumbled on toward the house.

Heyman called after him. "Is anybody home?"

"Yih."

"You sure?"

"Dude," said the boy, "it's rilly early."

Now Heyman heard an electric guitar crank up, slashing away at one chord over and over, each time on the downbeat. Heart attack music, he thought. He looked at his watch: 10:30. The boy disappeared along the side of the house. There was the sound of French doors rattling. The music got louder for a moment and then the doors closed.

He started the engine and set the air conditioning on high again, then punched a number into his cell phone.

"It's me," he said. "Yeah, I found it. No problem. They're about ready."

He shut the phone, took a duster out of the trunk, and knocked the dead leaves and haze off the limo until the paint shone like oil. When he saw his reflection sharpen in the black surface he straightened his collar and tie. Then he put the duster away and took the envelope from the trunk, checking to see that everything was there. He lowered the trunk lid.

A few minutes later all three boys came out. One was dressed in old Nikes, jeans, and a ratty T-shirt; the other in leather sandals, pleated slacks, and a silk shirt, carrying a Tumi backpack. The tall boy in the baggy shorts still walked cautiously, as if worried about land mines on the property.

Heyman flashed a smile. "Which one of you is Perry Leyman?"

The boy with the old Nikes hooked a thumb at his friend in the sandals.

The man held out his hand. "I'm Paul."

The well-dressed boy looked through him, went directly to the car, and waited for Heyman to open the passenger door.

The tall one bumped his head getting into the back.

"Watch yourself, there," said Heyman. "I put some chips and sodas in the armrest. If you need anything else, let me know."

"Where's Willy?" asked Perry, climbing into the front seat.

"He couldn't make it."

"Slick Willy." Perry unwound a pair of earplug headphones. "We go way back. My whole life, almost."

"Is that so?"

"Dude," said a voice from the back seat, "did you bring it?"

Perry undid the Velcro on the backpack. Inside were some folded squares of paper, a CD player, and a stack of discs in jewel cases. He passed it all over his shoulder.

"Yih."

"Your brother got the *delivery?*"

In the mirror Heyman saw the tall one elbow him. "Jason, man, try to be cool."

Perry turned to the driver. "You know where you're going?"

Heyman shifted into reverse and rolled down the driveway, waiting for the security gate to slide back. "Irvine. The Bowl."

"Yih."

"When's the concert?"

"Noon."

"We'll make it. Got your tickets?"

"Passes."

"Great." Heyman put it into drive and started the big tires rolling out of the cul-de-sac and down the canyon. "What kind of bands? Punk?"

In the back seat, the tall one laughed. "Punk went underground."

"Yeah," said Jason, "*way* underground."

"New Wave, then," Heyman said. "Or grunge—is that what they call it now?"

"In the day."

"Black metal," Perry explained.

"What label are they on?"

"Lots of different ones. Indies and imports."

"Not your old man's," said Jason.

"I got my dad to sign *Blutvergieben*." Perry spoke the word with a practiced German accent. "But the manager screwed him and kept the advance."

"I think I've heard of them," said Heyman.

"Hang a right."

"I thought we'd take Kester to the freeway . . ."

"We have to pick up Juno." Perry took out a cell phone of his own and hit a programmed number. "Where are you? Stop," he told the driver.

At the next corner a teenage girl with blue streaks in her hair teetered on the curb, about to cross into the cul-de-sac. She had on a black belly shirt with white letters that spelled FUCT. As Heyman pulled over she stashed her phone in a jogger's pouch and squeezed into the back seat.

"Did you call the bitch?" the girl said.

"Nuh," said Perry.

"Thanks!"

"I don't have the number."

"Your dad could get it."

"My dad's in the Caymans."

"Then I'll just have to kick her little ass."

The boys looked out the tinted windows and tried not to laugh.

"You're tripping," Perry told her.

"Is that what you guys think?"

"Nuh."

"Nuh."

"The drummer's pretty big, though," said Perry.

"I could give such a massive shit. Did your brother get the drugs?"

"Later, Juno," Perry told her.

Heyman took the 405 south while she continued to rant. It seemed that she had tried out as lead singer for a band but lost the job to another girl and was royally pissed. They hit a detour after LAX, an overturned truck that forced them onto the surface streets for several miles before he could pick up another freeway. He kept a map book open and followed the jumbled maze of lines that connected through to Orange County and the coast.

After a while she gave it up and put on the earplugs. From the back seat he heard a faint hiss as she sampled one CD after another, jerking her head to the white noise of insect music. The three boys exchanged information about musicians and remixes and club dates. Glancing at the mirror, he decided that they were no more than fifteen. He was responsible for them while they were in the car, at least as far as their parents and the law were concerned. If he saw any drugs come out he would have to pull over. They would love him for that.

The girl took the earphones off and glared at the boy on her right. "Sean, will *you* stand up for me?"

"Yih."

"Don't shit me."

"I'm not."

"What about you, Jason? Do you even have your knife?"

"Sure, but—"

"There's other bands," Perry told her.

"Fine!" she said. "Then you are all so busted. I'll tell Eric what you do with his *good* shit!"

"You don't talk to my brother. Ever."

"And your dad!"

"Try it. We'll see who's busted. My brother just got accepted at Yale."

"Like I care!"

"One word, Juno."

A half-mile from the concert the traffic stopped dead. Dust swirled up. Vendors walked along the side of the road, hawking posters and fake tattoos. Heyman heard guttural lyrics warring between the cars as twin silver-lightning-bolt decals glittered in the sun. With the air conditioner on high the big engine started to overheat. He paid ten dollars to get into the lot and dropped them off in front of the main gate. A poster advertised the German band as the headline act.

"What time?" he asked Perry.

"Eight."

"I'll be here. As close as I can get."

"What's your number?"

The boy meant the cell phone. Heyman wrote it on one of Willy's business cards and gave it to him.

"Call me when you're ready."

"Yih."

He drove on through the parking lot and over the spikes to the street. As soon as he got out of the jam he opened the front console and flipped through Willy's jazz collection. He found a tape of Miles and

Cannonball and looked around for a spot to park for a few hours. Then he dialed Willy.

"I just dropped them off."

"Thanks, man."

"Nice kids."

"You made good time," Willy said. "Did you check the trunk?"

"Yeah."

"All there, right?"

"No sweat."

"I owe you."

"Not you. The dad."

"Sorry," said Willy, "but you know I can't cut that shit anymore."

"I know. You're retired."

"All I want to do now is drive."

"You got it."

He stopped off at the nearest strip mall, loosened his tie, and stretched his legs. Then he ordered a spicy chicken sandwich and a large coffee at Carl's Jr. The fast-food restaurant was full of all kinds. When he finished eating he returned to the limo, popped the trunk again, and took out the padded envelope, but before he could get another look at the photo a panhandler tried to hit him up. He flipped the guy a buck, closed the trunk, got back in the car, and cruised the streets for a better spot.

Everywhere he went people were on their way to the concert. Some had sleeveless shirts and lightning bolts on their biceps but most were normal high school kids in cut-offs and tank tops, college couples in cotton prints and white socks. There were a few old heavy metal fans and even some families, the little ones done up in their best SpongeBob and Powerpuff Girls colors. It had been a while since a rock festival came to town. He drove over to the beachfront and finally found some shade under the palm trees so that he could kick back.

On the jazz album, Cannonball had top billing and most of the time Miles sounded like a sideman. Miles was never greedy. He just laid down his part, got in there and got out of there, and picked up his pay. The man was an inspiration.

Heyman took off his black coat and tried to relax. Whenever he switched tapes he could hear a distant booming, as if a storm were about to roll in even though the air was clear all the way to the horizon. As the day wore on he could feel it inside in the car, pulsing through the ground and the tires like low-frequency electrical waves, coming closer.

At five o'clock he ran a shaver over his chin, straightened his tie, and drove back to the concert site. The throbbing grew deeper as he cruised the perimeter. There were generators beyond the tent, at the rear of the outdoor stage. He could not hear them hammering away but they vibrated and blurred under a floating layer of exhaust. The decibel level from the banked speakers was overpowering, amplifying the lyrics to a hysterical roar. Heyman realized that he could find any pattern at all in the wall of sound, as long as it had to do with anger and rage. The music did not speak to him.

At six o'clock he went back to the fast-food restaurant for more coffee, then gassed up the car and returned to the site. There was a break between sets now and families were already leaving with groggy children on their shoulders. He parked behind a line of limos near the Artists Only entrance, reached under the seat, and found a rolled-up towel. He stuck it under his coat and took it with him to the gate.

A young security guard in a yellow jacket stopped him.

"Who's next?" asked Heyman.

"Last act. Where's your pass?"

A cascade of pyrotechnics lit the night with blue-white lightning. The headline band crouched at the flap of the tent, ready to run up the scaffolding to the stage. The guard looked skyward, shielding his eyes, and Heyman slipped inside the chain-link fence.

In the tent, behind a table full of empty green bottles, exhausted musicians pulled off boots and sweaty shirts. Heyman searched the faces of those around the fringes. The photo in the envelope had been taken with a telephoto lens but it was clear enough. He had it memorized.

At the next round of pyro, a man in butter-soft Italian leather waved the headliners toward the scaffold. The crowd began to stomp, then erupted into thunderous cheers as the band ran up the shaky steps. The phone in Heyman's pocket rang. He covered one ear.

"Dude!" said a frantic voice.

"Perry?"

"He's not here . . ." The voice broke up. "Where are you? We gotta jam!"

"I'm on my way."

Heyman snapped the phone shut and came up behind the man in the leather jacket. He had rings in his ears and the back of his neck was tattooed like a Samoan chief's.

"Brent Jacobson?"

The man glanced over his shoulder.

"Yeah?"

"Those your boys up there?"

He looked Heyman over dismissively, the black sportcoat, the plain white shirt, and tie. "Exclusive," he said.

"I have something for you."

"No demos."

"From a Mr. Leyman."

The man squinted. "Never heard of him."

Heyman had his hand in the towel. He felt his fingers close around metal. His thumb released the safety.

"Sure you have. The record company, on Beverly. You signed a contract. Remember?"

At that moment there was another explosion and a bright burst of sparks in the darkness, as the band up above started slashing away.

He made a U-turn and braked in front of the main gate. The German band was unbelievably loud and the older folks were on their way out. Heyman spotted two of the kids. Sean's knees were scraped raw, Jason's jeans were torn, and both their shirts were wet and stained. Under the mercury vapor lights the stains looked black. He rolled the window down.

"Where's Perry?" he asked as they fumbled the back door open.

"Go!"

"*Where?*"

Now Perry came out, walking calmly through the crowd with his designer backpack, one arm around Juno to support her. His shirt was clean but the front of hers was drenched.

Heyman got out and shoved the girl into the back seat, then opened the front passenger door for Perry. He rolled up the tinted windows, made another U, and fell into line with the other limos.

"Who's hurt?"

"Nobody."

"You sure?"

"Yih," said Perry. His silk shirt was missing a couple of buttons but unspattered.

Heyman flicked on the dome light and twisted around. The letters on the girl's shirt were still white but Sean's and Jason's were smeared with red. So were their hands and arms. Heyman tossed them the towel.

"What happened?"

"Nothing," said Perry.

"What's all the blood?"

"Some dudes started a fight," said Jason.

"Not us," Sean said.

The girl laughed wildly.

Heyman took the side streets for several blocks before he merged onto the boulevard. Ahead was the mall with the fast-food restaurant. He pulled in.

"You can wash up here," he told them.

"Carl's Jr. sucks," said Juno.

"Dude," said Jason frantically, as if it mattered, "she likes McDonald's."

Heyman said, "The head's in back."

While they were gone, he called Willy.

"They stopped for some chow."

"McDonald's?" Willy chuckled. "Got to have their McCrap."

"I'll call the house when we hit LA."

"Don't bother. The dad's out of town."

"I figured."

"And the mother's never there." A pause on the line. "How did it go?"

"Done."

"Just like that?"

"No problem."

"Pretty slick," said Willy. "Now you're the man."

"No, you are. Take it easy."

Jason came out of the restroom without his T-shirt and motioned for Heyman to lower the window.

"She wants to eat. Is that okay?"

Heyman waited while they sat at a round table and dipped fries and sipped Cokes. He folded the towel and wiped the back seat, then wrapped it around the gun and dropped it into a dumpster full of grease and flies. When they were finished they came back to the car.

On the freeway, in the dark, each of them took out a cell phone and made nervous calls to friends and family, three silhouettes waving their antennae like alien insects. The boys in the back talked to their mothers with the voices of sweet, dutiful sons while the girl giggled and slurred her words. When the calls were over she put her feet up.

"Whoo!"

"How much did you take?" asked Jason.

"All gone." She opened her mouth, pointed down her throat, lifted the bottom of her belly shirt and rubbed her tummy. "See?"

"Yih."

"You really did it," she said.

The boys said nothing.

"The bitch was all ready to sing. But you cut her good. Didn't you."

"It's done," said Perry. "Forget about it."

"You see her face? Sean takes out his lockback and her eyes are all—"

"It's over, Juno."

Sean and Jason looked out the windows, their eyes large and white in the headlights, their sunburned skin a washed-out red in the passing taillights. The girl took her feet down and sprawled across them, about to pass out. In the mirror Heyman saw her head in their laps, first one and then the other, as they continued to stare with blank, stark expressions. After a while she began to snore.

"You like Bush?" said Perry.

It took a few seconds for Heyman to realize that Perry was talking to him.

"I think I've heard of them. They made that video, what was it called?"

"Not the band. George W. The leader of our country."

Heyman considered. "Do you?"

"My dad does. He says he's a patriot."

There was no percentage in lying. "As a matter of fact," Heyman said, "I don't."

"Good." Perry gazed out at the lights as though trying to find a pattern, his eyes empty. "Then I guess that means you can."

"Can what?"

"Be one of us."

He drove on. They carried Juno to a porch and used her key to open the door. Then they went to Perry's house.

"Thank you for waiting," said Sean politely.

"Thanks a lot," added Jason, "sir."

As the others went up the driveway, Perry lingered by the driver's side. He reached into his backpack. It was stuffed with bills now. He handed some over.

"Here's your tip."

"That's okay," said Heyman. "I'm covered."

"You sure?"

"One question, though. What did they do with the knife?"

"Why?"

"Knives are messy. I hope they wiped it before they threw it away. You have to watch those things. The details."

Perry looked off into the darkness, the trees and the bushes inside and outside the security gate, as if listening for something, the movement of unseen creatures that crawled the canyon at night.

"How'd you like to be my driver next time?"

"When?"

"I don't know yet."

"Where are you going?"

Perry thought about it. "The mountains."

"With Juno?"

"Maybe."

"Angeles Crest is good. Nobody ever goes there."

Perry nodded. "I have your number."

"If you're serious."

"How much?"

"Same as Willy."

"I can get it."

"I know."

Heyman waited to see that they were all in safely before he started backing down.

At the side of the house, Perry turned and waved.

"Say hello to Slick Willy for me."

"You got it."

Perry grinned, his teeth small and straight and sharp in the moonlight.

Heyman put a jazz tape on as he came to the freeway, ready to take the car back to Willy's. It was *Workin'*, another famous set with Miles. A classic.

"Slick Paulie," he said to himself in the dark, trying out the sound of it. He liked it. "You the man, dude."

He looked into the mirror, adjusting his collar and tie. If he wanted to be a regular driver from now on he would need business cards, an Italian suit, black and shiny, and a big car of his own, a Lincoln or a Caddy, at least, with low mileage. Willy could help him find one. No problem. "The man," he said again and smiled, as taillights streamed past him like blood cells rushing in or out through the arteries of the city. "*Yih.*"

IS THERE ANYBODY THERE?

KIM NEWMAN

Kim Newman is a novelist, critic, and broadcaster. He is the author of *The Night Mayor, Bad Dreams, Jago, The Quorum, The Original Dr. Shade and Other Stories, Famous Monsters, Seven Stars, Unforgivable Stories, Dead Travel Fast, Life's Lottery, Back in the USSA* (with Eugene Byrne), *Where the Bodies Are Buried, Doctor Who: Time and Relative, The Man from the Diogenes Club, Secret Files of the Diogenes Club, Mysteries of the Diogenes Club, Professor Moriarty: The Hound of the D'Urbervilles, An English Ghost Story, The Secrets of Drearcliff Grange School,* and *Angels of Music* under his own name, and *The Vampire Genevieve* and *Orgy of the Blood Parasites* as "Jack Yeovil."

Newman's acclaimed Anno Dracula vampire series comprises *Anno Dracula, The Bloody Red Baron, Dracula Cha Cha Cha,* and *Johnny Alucard,* while *Anno Dracula 1895: Seven Days in Mayhem* was a recent five-issue graphic serial. His most recent collection is *Anno Dracula 1899 and Other Stories,* and his short story "Week Woman" was adapted for the Canadian TV series *The Hunger.*

The author's nonfiction titles include *Ghastly Beyond Belief* (with Neil Gaiman); *Horror: 100 Best Books* and *Horror: Another 100 Best*

Books (both with Stephen Jones); and *Wild West Movies, The BFI Companion to Horror, Millennium Movies, Nightmare Movies: Horror on Screen Since the 1960s, Kim Newman's Video Dungeon: The Collected Reviews*, and BFI Classics studies of *Cat People, Doctor Who,* and *Quatermass and the Pit.*

He has won the Bram Stoker Award, the International Horror Critics Award, the British Science Fiction Award, the British Fantasy Award, The Children of the Night Award, and the Annual Rondo Hatton Classic Horror Award.

"The similarities between the spiritualist table-rapping craze of the early twentieth century and the Internet obsessions of today are fairly obvious," observes Newman. "Except, at least spiritualists sat around holding hands as opposed to sitting alone in a room staring at a screen."

"IS THERE A presence?" asked Irene.

The parlor was darker and chillier than it had been moments ago. At the bottoms of the heavy curtains, tassels stirred like the fronds of a deep-sea plant. Irene Dobson—Madame Irena, to her sitters—was alert to tiny changes in a room that might preface the arrival of a visitor from beyond the veil. The fizzing and dimming of still-untrusted electric lamps, so much less impressive than the shrinking and bluing of gaslight flames she remembered from her earliest seances. A clamminess in the draught, as fog-like cold rose from the carpeted floor. The minute crackle of static electricity, making hair lift and pores prickle. The tart taste of pennies in her mouth.

"Is there a traveler from afar?" she asked, opening her inner eye.

The planchette twitched. Miss Walter-David's fingers withdrew in a flinch; she had felt the definite movement. Irene glanced at the no-longer-young woman in the chair beside hers, shrinking away for the moment. The fear-light in the sitter's eyes was the beginning of true belief. To Irene, it was like a tug on a fishing line, the satisfying twinge of the hook going in. This was a familiar stage on the typical sitter's journey from skepticism to fanaticism. This woman was wealthy; soon, Irene would taste not copper but silver, eventually gold.

Wordlessly, she encouraged Miss Walter-David to place her fingertips on the planchette again, to restore balance. Open on the round table before them was a thin sheet of wood, hinged like an oversized chessboard. Upon the board's smoothly papered and polished surface was a circle, the letters of the alphabet picked out in curlicue. Corners were marked for yes—"*oui*," "*ja*"—and no. The planchette, a pointer on marble castors, was a triangular arrowhead-shape. Irene and Miss Walter-David lightly touched fingers to the lower points of the planchette, and the tip quivered.

"Is there anybody there?" Miss Walter-David asked.

This sitter was bereft of a fiancé, an officer who had come through the trenches but succumbed to influenza upon return to civilian life. Miss Walter-David was searching for balm to soothe her sense of hideous unfairness and had come at last to Madame Irena's parlor.

"Is there—"

The planchette moved, sharply. Miss Walter-David hissed in surprise. Irene felt the presence, stronger than usual, and knew it could be tamed. She was no fraud, relying on conjuring tricks, but her understanding of the world beyond the veil was very different than that which she wished her sitters to have. All spirits could be made to do what she wished them to do. If they thought themselves grown beyond hurt, they were sorely in error. The planchette, genuinely independent of the light touches of medium and sitter, stabbed toward a corner of the board, but stopped surprisingly short.

Y

Not YES, but the Y of the circular alphabet. The spirits often used initials to express themselves, but Madame had never encountered one who neglected the convenience of the YES and NO corners. She did not let Miss Walter-David see her surprise.

"Have you a name?"

Y again. Not YES. Was Y the beginning of a name: Youngman, Yoko-Hama, Ysrael?

"What is it?" she was almost impatient.

The planchette began a circular movement, darting at letters, using the lower tips of the planchette as well as the pointer. That also was unusual and took an instant or two to digest.

M S T R M N D

"Msstrrmnnd," said Miss Walter-David.

Irene understood. "Have you a message for anyone here, Master Mind?"

Y

"For whom?"

U

"For Ursula?" Miss Walter-David's Christian name was Ursula.

N U

"U?"

"You," said Miss Walter-David. "You."

This was not a development Irene liked a bit.

There were two prospects in his Chat Room. Women, or at least they said they were. Boyd didn't necessarily believe them. Some users thought they were clever.

Boyd was primarily MstrMnd but had other log-in names, some male, some female, some neutral. For each ISDN line, he had a different code name and e-address, none traceable to his physical address. He lived online, really; this flat in Highgate was just a place to store the meat. There was nothing he couldn't get by playing the web, which responded to his touch like a harpsichord to a master's fingers. There were always backdoors.

His major female ident was Caress, aggressively sexual; he imagined her as a porn-site Cleopatra Jones, a black model with dom tendencies. He kept a more puritanical, shockable ident—SchlGrl—as back-up, to cut in when Caress became too outrageous.

These two users weren't tricky, though. They were clear. Virgins, just the way he liked them. He guessed they were showing themselves nakedly to the Room, with no deception.

IRENE D.

URSULA W-D.

Their messages typed out laboriously, appearing on his master monitor a word at a time. He initiated searches, to cough up more on their handles. His system was smart enough to come up with a birth name, a physical address, financial details, and, more often than not, a JPEG image from even the most casually assumed one-use log-on name. Virgins never realized that their presences always left ripples. Boyd knew how to piggyback any one of a dozen official and unofficial trackers, and routinely pulled up information on anyone with whom he had even the most casual, wary dealings.

IRENE D: Have you a message for anyone here, Master Mind?

Boyd stabbed a key.

Y

IRENE D: For whom?

U

IRENE D: For Ursula?

N U

IRENE D: U?

URSULA W-D: You.

At least one of them got it. IRENE D—why didn't she tag herself ID or I-D?—was just slow. That didn't matter. She was the one Boyd had spotted as a natural. Something about her blank words gave her away. She had confidence and ignorance, while her friend—they were in contact, maybe even in the same physical room—at least understood she knew nothing, that she had stepped into deep space and all the rules were changed. IRENE D—her log-on was probably a variant on the poor girl's real name—thought she was in control. She would unravel very easily, almost no challenge at all.

A MESSAGE FOR U I-D, he typed.

He sat on a reinforced swivel chair with optimum back support and buttock-spread, surveying a semicircle of keyboards and monitors all hooked up to separate lines and accounts, all feeding into the master-monitor. When using two or more idents, he could swivel or roll from board to board, taking seconds to chameleon-shift. He could be five or six people in any given minute, dazzle a solo into thinking she—and it almost always was a she—was in a buzzing Chat Room with a lively crowd when she was actually alone with him, growing more vulnerable with each stroke and line, more open to his hooks and grapples, her backdoors flapping in the wind.

I KNOW WHO U ARE

Always a classic. Always went to the heart.

He glanced at the leftmost screen. Still searching. No details yet. His system was usually much faster than this. Nothing on either of them, on IRENE or URSULA. They couldn't be smart enough to cover their traces in the web, not if they were really as newbie as they seemed.

Even a netshark ace would have been caught by now. And these girls were fighting nowhere near his weight. Must be a glitch. It didn't matter.

I KNOW WHAT U DO

Not DID, but DO. DID is good for specifics, but DO suggests something ongoing, some hidden current in an ordinary life, perhaps unknown even to the user.

U R NOT WHAT U CLAIM 2 B

That was for sure.

U R NOT WHAT U CLAIM 2 B

"You are not what you claim to be?" interpreted Miss Walter-David. She had become quickly skilled at picking out the spirit's peculiar, abbreviated language. It was rather irritating, thought Irene. She was in danger of losing this sitter, of becoming the one in need of guidance.

There was something odd about "Master Mind." He—it was surely a he—was unlike other spirits, who were mostly vague children. Everything they spelled out was simplistic, yet ambiguous. She had to help them along, to tease out from the morass of waffle whatever it was they wanted to communicate with those left behind, or more often to intuit what it was her sitters wanted or needed most to hear and to shape her reading of the messages to fit. Her fortune was built not on reaching the other world, but in manipulating it so that the right communications came across. No sitter really wanted to hear a loved one had died a meaningless death and drifted in limbo, gradually losing personality like a cloud breaking up. Though, occasionally, she had sitters who wanted to know that those they had hated in life were suffering properly in the beyond and that their miserable post-mortem apologies were not accepted. Such transactions disturbed even her, though they often proved among the most rewarding financially.

Now, Irene sensed a concrete personality. Even through almost-coded, curt phrases, "Master Mind" was a someone, not a something. For the first time, she was close to being afraid of what she had touched.

"Master Mind" was ambiguous, but through intent rather than fumble-thinking. She had a powerful impression of him, from his self-chosen title: a man on a throne, head swollen and limbs atrophied, belly bloated like a balloon, framing vast schemes, manipulating lesser beings like chess pieces. She was warier of him than even of the rare angry spirit she had called into her circle. There were defenses against him, though. She had been careful to make sure of that.

"Ugly Hell gapes," she remembered from *Doctor Faustus*. Well, not for her.

She thought "Master Mind" was not a spirit at all.

U R ALLONE

"You are all one," interpreted Miss Walter-David. "Whatever can that mean?"

U R ALONE

That was not a cryptic statement from the beyond. Before discovering her "gift," Irene Dobson had toiled in an insurance office. She knew a type-writing mistake when she saw one.

U R AFRAID

"You are af—"

"Yes, Miss Walter-David, I understand."

"And are you?"

"Not any more. Master Mind, you are a most interesting fellow, yet I cannot but feel you conceal more than you reveal. We are all, at our worst, alone and afraid. That is scarcely a great insight."

It was the secret of her profession, after all.

"Are you not also alone and afraid?"

Nothing.

"Let me put it another way."

She pressed down on the planchette, and manipulated it, spelling out in his own language.

R U NOT ALSO ALONE AND AFRAID

She would have added a question mark, but the Ouija-board had none. Spirits never asked questions, just supplied answers.

IRENE D was sharper than he had first guessed. And he still knew no more about her. No matter.

Boyd rolled over to the next keyboard.

U TELL HIM GRRL BCK OFF CREEP

IRENE D: Another presence? How refreshing. And you might be?

CARESS SISTA.

IRENE D: Another spirit?

Presence? Spirit? Was she taking the piss?

UH HUH SPIRT THAT'S THE STUFF SHOW THAT PIG U CAN STAND UP 4 YRSELF

IRENE D: Another presence, but the same mode of address. I think your name might be Legion.

Boyd knew of another netshark who used Legion as a log-on. IRENE D must have come across him too. Not the virgin she seemed, then. Damn.

His search still couldn't penetrate further than her simple log-on. By now, he should have her mother's maiden name, her menstrual calendar, the full name of the first boy she snogged at school, and a list of all the porn sites she had accessed in the last week.

He should close down the Room, seal it up forever and scuttle away. But he was being challenged, which didn't happen often. Usually, he was content to play a while with those he snared, scrambling their heads with what he had found out about them as his net-noose drew tauter around them. Part of the game was to siphon a little from their bank accounts: someone had to pay his phone and access bills, and he was damned if he should cough up by direct debit like some silly little newbie. But mostly it was for the sport.

In the early days, he had been fond of coopting idents and flooding his playmates' systems with extreme porn or placing orders in their names for expensive but embarrassing goods and services. That now seemed crude. His current craze was doctoring and posting images. If IRENE D was married, it would be interesting to direct her husband to, say, a goat sex site where her face was convincingly overlaid upon an enthusiastic animal-lover's body. And it was so easy to mock up mugshots, complete with guilty looks and serial numbers, to reveal an ineptly suppressed criminal past (complete with court records and other supporting documentation) that would make an employer think twice about keeping someone on the books. No one ever bothered to double-check by going back to the paper archives before they downsized a job.

Always, he would leave memories to cherish; months later, he would check up on his net-pals—his score so far was five institutionalizations and two suicides—just to see that the experience was still vivid. He was determined to crawl into IRENE D's skull and stay there, replicating like a virus, wiping her hard drive.

URSULA W-D: Do you know Frank? Frank Conynghame-Mars.

Where did that come from? Still, there couldn't be many people floating around with a name like that. Boyd shut off the fruitless backdoor search and copied the double-barrel into an engine. It came up instantly with a handful of matches. The first was an obituary from 1919, scanned into a newspaper database. A foolish virgin had purchased unlimited access to a great many similar archives, which was now open to Boyd. A local newspaper, the *Ham & High*. He was surprised. It was the world wide web after all. This hit was close to home—maybe only streets away— if eighty years back. He looked over the obit and took a flyer.

DEAD OF FLU

URSULA W-D: Yes. She knows Frank, Madame Irena. A miracle. Have you a message from Frank? For Ursula?

Boyd speed-read the obit. Frank Conynghame-Mars, "decorated in the late conflict," etc. etc. Dead at thirty-eight. Engaged to a Miss Ursula Walter-David, of this parish. Could the woman be still alive? She would have to be well over a hundred.

He launched another search. Ursula Walter-David.

Three matches. One the Conynghame-Mars obit he already had up. Second, an article from something called *The Temple*, from 1924—a publication of the Spiritualist Church. Third, also from the *Ham & High* archive, her own obit, from 1952.

Zoiks, Scooby—a ghost!

This was an elaborate sting. Had to be.

He would string it along, to give him time to think.

U WIL BE 2GETHER AGAIN 1952

The article from *The Temple* was too long and close-printed to read in full while his formidable attention was divided into three or four windows. It had been scanned in badly, and not all of it was legible. The gist was a testimonial for a spiritualist medium called Madame Irena (no last name given). Among her "sitters," satisfied customers evidently, was Ursula Walter-David.

Weird. Boyd suspected he was being set up. He didn't trust the matches. They must be plants. Though he couldn't see the joins, he knew that with enough work he could run something like this—had indeed done so, feeding prospects their own mocked-up obits with full gruesome details—to get to someone. Was this a vengeance crusade? If so, he couldn't see where it was going.

He tried a search on "Madame Irena" and came up with hundreds of matches, mostly French and porn sites. A BD/SM video titled *The Lash of Madame Irena* accounted for most of the matches. He tried pairing "+Madame Irena" with "+spiritualist" and had a more manageable fifteen matches, including several more articles from *The Temple*.

URSULA W-D: Is Frank at peace?

He had to subdivide his concentration, again. He wasn't quite ambidextrous, but could pump a keyboard with either hand, working shift keys with his thumbs and splitting his mind into segments, eyes rolling independently like a lizard's, to follow several lines.

FRANK IS OVER HIS SNIFFLES

Among the "Madame Irena"/"medium" matches was a *Journal of the Society of Psychical Research* piece from 1926, shout-lined Fraudulence Alleged. He opened it up and found from a news-in-brief snippet that a court case was being prepared against one "Irene Dobson," known professionally as "Madame Irena," for various malpractices in connection with her work as a spirit medium. One Catriona Kaye, a "serious researcher," was quoted as being "in no doubt of the woman's genuine psychical abilities but also sure she had employed them in an unethical, indeed dangerous, manner."

Another match was a court record. He opened it: a declaration of the suit against Irene Dobson. Scrolling down, he found it frustratingly incomplete. The document set out what was being tried, but didn't say how the case came out. A lot of old records were like that, incompletely scanned. Usually, he only had current files to open and process. He looked again at the legal rigmarole, and his eye was caught by Irene Dobson's address.

The Laburnums, Feldspar Road, Highgate.

This was 26 Feldspar Road. There were big bushes outside. If he ran a search for laburnum.jpg, he was sure he'd get a visual match.

Irene Dobson lived in this house.

No, she *had* lived in this house. In the 1920s, before it was converted into flats. When it had a name, not a number.

Now she was dead.

Whoever was running this on Boyd knew where he lived. He was not going to take that.

"This new presence," said Miss Walter-David. "It's quite remarkable."

There was no new presence, no "Caress." Irene would have felt a change, and hadn't. This was one presence with several voices. She had heard of such. Invariably malign. She should call an end to the séance, plead fatigue. But Ursula Walter-David would never come back, and the husbandless woman had a private income and nothing to spend it on but the beyond. At the moment, she was satisfied enough to pay heavily for Irene's service. She decided to stay with it, despite the dangers. Rewards were within reach. She was determined, however, to treat this cunning spirit with extreme caution. He was a tiger, posing as a pussycat. She focused on the center of the board and was careful with the planchette, never letting its points stray beyond the ring of letters.

"Caress," said Miss Walter-David, a-tremble, "may I speak with Frank?"

"Caress" was supposed to be a woman, but Irene thought the first voice—"Master Mind"—closer to the true personality.

IN 52

"Why 1952? It seems a terribly long way off."

WHEN U DIE

That did it. Miss Walter-David pulled away as if bitten. Irene considered: it seemed only too likely that the sitter had been given the real year of her death. That was a cruel stroke, typical of the malign spirit.

The presence was a prophet. Irene had heard of a few such spirits—one of the historical reasons for consulting mediums was to discern the future—but never come across one. Could it be that the spirits had true foreknowledge of what was to come? Or did they inhabit a realm outside time and could look in at any point in human history, future as well as past, and pass on what they saw?

Miss Walter-David was still impressed. But less pleased.

The planchette circled, almost entirely of its own accord. Irene could have withdrawn her fingers, but the spirit was probably strong enough to move the pointer without her. It certainly raced ahead of her push. She had to keep the planchette in the circle.

IRENE

Not Irena.

DOBSON

Now she was frightened, but also annoyed. A private part of her person had been exposed. This was an insult and an attack.

"Who's Dobson?" asked Miss Walter-David.

SHE IS

"It is my name," Irene admitted. "That's no secret."

ISNT IT

"Where are you?" she asked.

HERE THERE EVERYWHERE

"No, here and there perhaps. But not everywhere."

This was a strange spirit. He had aspirations to omnipotence, but something about him was overreaching. He called himself "Master

Mind," which suggested a streak of self-deluding vanity. Knowledge wasn't wisdom. She had a notion that if she asked him to name this year's Derby winner, he would be able to furnish the correct answer

(an idea with possibilities)

but that he could reveal precious little of what came after death. An insight struck her: this was not a departed spirit, this was a living man.

Living. But where?

No.

When?

"What date is it?" she asked.

GOOD QUESTION.

Since this must be a sting, there was no harm in the truth.

JAN 20 01

IRENE D: 1901?

N 2001

URSULA W-D: I thought time had no meaning in the world beyond.

IRENE D: That depends which world beyond our guest might inhabit.

Boyd had run searches on "Irene Dobson" and his own address, independent and cross-matching. Too many matches were coming up. He wished more people had names like "Frank Conynghame-Mars" and fewer like "Irene Dobson." "Boyd Waylo," his birth-name, was a deep secret; his accounts were all in names like "John Barrett" and "Andrew Lee."

Beyond the ring of monitors, his den was dark. This was the largest room in what had once been a Victorian townhouse and was now divided into three flats. Was this where "Madame Irena" had held her séances? His raised ground-floor flat might encompass the old parlor.

He was supposed to believe he was in touch with the past.

One of the "Irene Dobson" matches was a JPEG. He opened the picture file and looked into a small, determined face. Not his type, but surprising and striking. Her hair was covered by a turban and she wore a Chinese-style jacket, buttoned up to the throat. She looked rather prosperous and was smoking a black cigarette in a long white holder. The image was from 1927. Was that when she was supposed to be talking to him from?

WHAT DATE 4 U

IRENE D: January 13, 1923. Of course.

Maybe he was supposed to bombard her with questions about the period, to try and catch her out in an anachronism. But he had only general knowledge: Prohibition in America, a General Strike in Britain, talking pictures in 1927, the Lindbergh flight somewhere earlier, the stock market crash a year or two later, *Thoroughly Modern Millie*, and P. G. Wodehouse. Not a lot of use. He couldn't even remember who was Prime Minister in January 1923. He could get answers from the net in moments, though; knowing things was pointless compared with knowing how to find things out. At the moment, that didn't help him.

Whoever these women were—or rather, whoever this IRENE D was, for URSULA W-D plainly didn't count—he was sure that they'd have the answers for any questions he came up with.

What was the point of this?

He could get to IRENE D. Despite everything, he had her. She was in his Room; she was his prey and meat and he would not let her challenge him.

I C U

I C U

I see you.

Irene thought that was a lie, but "Master Mind" could almost certainly hear her. Though, as with real spirits, she wondered if the words came to him as human sounds or in some other manner.

The parlor was almost completely dark, save for a cone of light about the table.

Miss Walter-David was terrified, on the point of fleeing. That was for the best, but there was a service Irene needed of her.

She did not say it out loud, for "Master Mind" would hear.

He said he could see, but she thought she could conceal her hand from him.

It was an awkward move. She put the fingers of her left hand on the shivering planchette, which was racing inside the circle, darting at the letters, trying to break free.

I C U ID

I C U R FRIT

She slipped a pocketbook out of her cardigan, opened it one-handed, and pressed it to her thigh with the heel of her hand while extracting the pencil from the spine with her fingernails. It was not an easy thing to manage.

U R FRIT AND FRAUD

This was just raving. She wrote a note, blind. She was trusting Miss Walter-David to read her scrawl. It was strange what mattered.

"This is no longer Caress," she said, trying to keep her voice steady. "Have we another visitor?"

2TRU IM SNAKE

"Im? Ah-ha, 'I'm.' Snake? Yet another speaker of this peculiar dialect, with unconventional ideas about spelling."

Miss Walter-David was backing away. She was out of her seat, retreating into darkness. Irene offered her the pocketbook, opened to the message. The sitter didn't want to take it. She opened her mouth. Irene shook her head, shushing her. Miss Walter-David took the book, and peered in the dark. Irene was afraid the silly goose would read out loud, but she at least half-understood.

On a dresser nearby was a tea tray, with four glasses of distilled water and four curls of chain. Bicycle chain, as it happened. Irene had asked Miss Walter-David to bring the tray to the Ouija table.

"Snake, do you know things? Things yet to happen?"

2TRU

"A useful accomplishment."

NDD

"Indeed?"

2RIT

There was a clatter. Miss Walter-David had withdrawn. Irene wondered if she would pay for the séance. She might. After all, there had been results. She had learned something, though nothing to make her happy.

"Miss Walter-David will die in 1952?"

Y

Back to Y. She preferred that to 2TRU and 2RIT.

"Of what?"

A pause.

PNEU

"Pneumonia, thank you."

Her arm was getting worn out, dragged around the circle. Her shoulder ached. Doing this one-handed was not easy. She had already set out the glasses at the four points of the compass, and was working on the chains. It was important that the ends be dipped in the glasses to make the connections, but that the two ends in each glass not touch. This was more like physics than spiritualism, but she understood it made sense.

"What else do you know?"

U·R FRAUD

"I don't think so. Tell me about the future. Not 2001. The useful future, within the next five or ten years."

STOK MRKT CRSH 29

"That's worth knowing. You can tell me about stocks and shares?"

Y

It was a subject of which she knew nothing, but she could learn. She had an idea that there were easier and less obtrusive fortunes to be made there than in Derby winners. But she would get the names out of him, too.

"Horse races?"

A hesitation.

Y

The presence was less frisky, sliding easily about the circle, not trying to break free.

"This year's Derby?"

A simple search ("+Epsom" "+Derby" "+winner" "+1923" "-Kentucky") had no matches; he took out "-Kentucky" and had a few hits and an explanation. Papyrus, the 1923 winner, was the first horse to run in both the Epsom and Kentucky Derby races, though the nag lost in the States, scuppering a possible chance for a nice long-shot accumulator bet if he really was giving a woman from the past a hot tip on the future. Boyd fed that all to IRENE D, still playing along, still not seeing the point. She received slowly, as if her system were taking one letter at a time.

Click. It wasn't a monitor. It was a Ouija-board.

That was what he was supposed to think.

IRENE D: I'm going to give you another name. I should like you to tell me what you know of this man.

OK

IRENE D: Anthony Tallgarth. Also, Basil and Florence Tallgarth.

He ran multiple searches and got a cluster of matches, mostly from the '20s—though there were birth and death announcements from the 1860s through to 1968—and, again, mostly from the *Ham & High*. He picked one dated February 2, 1923, and opened the article.

TYCOON FINDS LOST SON.

IRENE D: Where is Anthony? Now.

According to the article, Anthony was enlisted in the Royal Navy as an Able Seaman, under the name of T. A. Meredith, stationed at Portsmouth and due to ship out aboard the H.M.S. *Duckett*. He had parted from his wealthy parents after a scandal and a quarrel—since the brat had gone into the Navy, Boyd bet he was gay—but had been discovered through the efforts of a "noted local spiritualist and seeress." A reconciliation was effected.

He'd had enough of this game. He wasn't going to play anymore.

He rolled back in his chair, and hit an invisible wall.

IRENE D: I should tell you, Master Mind, that you are bound. With iron and holy water. I shall extend your circle, if you cooperate.

He tried reaching out, through the wall, and his hand was bathed with pain.

IRENE D: I do not know how you feel, if you can feel, but I will wager that you do not care for that.

It was as if she was watching him. Him!

IRENE D: Now, be a good little ghostie and tell me what I wish to know.

With his right hand lodged in his left armpit as the pain went away, he made keystrokes with his left hand, transferring the information she needed. It took a long time, a letter at a time.

IRENE D: There must be a way of replacing this board with a typewriter. That would be more comfortable for you, would it not?

FO, he typed.

A lash at his back, as the wall constricted. She had understood that. Was that a very 1923 womanly quality?

IRENE D: Manners, manners. If you are good to me, I shall let you have the freedom of this room, maybe this floor. I can procure longer chains.

He was a shark in a play-pool, furious and humiliated and in pain. And he knew it would last.

Mr. and Mrs. Tallgarth had been most generous. She could afford to give "Master Mind" the run of the parlor, and took care to refresh his water-bindings each day. This was not a task she would ever entrust to the new maid. The key to the parlor was about Irene's person at all times.

People would pay to be in contact with the dead, but they would pay more for other services, information of more use in the here and now. And she had a good line on all manner of things. She had been testing "Master Mind," and found him a useful source about a wide variety of subjects, from the minutiae of any common person's life to the great matters which were to come in the rest of the century.

Actually, knowing which horse would win any year's Derby was a comparatively minor advantage. Papyrus was bound to be the favorite, and the race too famous for any fortune to be made. She had her genie working on long-shot winners of lesser races, and was sparing in her use of the trick. Bookmakers were the sort of sharp people she understood only too well, and they would soon tumble to any streak of unnatural luck. From now on, for a great many reasons, she intended to be as unobtrusive as possible.

This morning, she had been making a will. She had no interest in the disposal of her assets after death, when she herself ventured beyond the veil, for she intended to make the most of them while alive. The entirety of her estate was left to her firm of solicitors on the unusual condition that, when she passed, no record or announcement of her death be made, even on her gravestone. It was not beyond possibility that she mightn't make it to 2001, though she knew she would be gone from this house by then. From now on, she would be careful about official mentions of her name; to be nameless, she understood, was to be invisible to "Master Mind," and she needed her life to be shielded from him as his was from hers.

The man had intended her harm, but he was her genie now, in her bottle.

She sat at the table and put her hands on the planchette, feeling the familiar press of resistance against her.

"Is there anybody there?"

YYYYYYYYYYYYYYYYYYYYYY

"Temper temper, Master Mind. Today, I should like to know more about stocks and shares . . ."

Food was brought to him from the online grocery, handed over at the front door. He was a shut-in forever now. He couldn't remember the last time he had stepped outside his flat; it had been days before IRENE D, maybe weeks. It wasn't like he had ever needed to post a letter or go to a bank.

Boyd had found the chains. They were still here, fixed into the skirting boards, running under the doorway, rusted at the ends, where the water traps had been. It didn't matter that the water had run out years ago. He was still bound.

Searches told him little more of Irene Dobson. At least he knew someone would have her in court in four years' time—a surprise he would let her have—but he had no hopes that she would be impeded. He had found traces of her well into the 1960s, lastly a piece from 1968 that didn't use her name but did mention her guiding spirit, "Master Mind," to whom she owed so much over the course of her long and successful career as a medium, seer, and psychic sleuth.

From 1923 to 1968. Forty-five years. Realtime. Their link was constant, and he moved forward as she did, a day for a day.

Irene Dobson's spirit guide had stayed with her at least that long.

Not forever. Forty-five years.

He had tried false information, hoping to ruin her—if she was cast out of her house (though she was still in it in 1927, he remembered) he would be free—but she always saw through it and could punish him.

He had tried going silent, shutting everything down. But he always had to boot up again, to be online. It was more than a compulsion. It was a need. In theory, he could stop paying electricity and phone bills—rather, stop other people paying his—and be cut off eventually, but in theory he could stop himself breathing and suffocate. It just wasn't in him. His meat had rarely left the house anyway, and as a reward for telling her about the extra-marital private habits of a husband whose avaricious wife was one of her sitters, she had extended his bindings to the hallway and—thank heavens—the toilet.

She had his full attention.

IRENE D: Is there anybody there?

Y DAMNIT Y

DEAR ALISON

MICHAEL MARSHALL SMITH

Michael Marshall Smith is a novelist and screenwriter. He has published more than ninety short stories and five novels—*Only Forward*, *Spares*, *One of Us*, *The Servants*, and *Hannah Green and her Unfeasibly Mundane Existence*—winning the Philip K. Dick, International Horror Guild, and August Derleth Awards, along with the Prix Bob-Morane in France. He has also received the British Fantasy Award for Best Short Fiction four times, more than any other author.

Writing as "Michael Marshall" he has published seven internationally best-selling thrillers, including The Straw Men series (currently in development for television), *The Intruders*—recently a BBC America series starring John Simm, Mira Sorvino, and Millie Bobby Brown—and *Killer Move*. His most recent novel under this byline is *We Are Here*.

"Stories start in different ways," explains the author. "Sometimes you begin with the beginning, and sometimes it's the end that comes to you first. Others present their middle to you, the underlying idea, and leave you to work out the best way in. 'Dear Alison' was one of these, and I can remember the small event which finally gave me the impetus to start writing it.

"It was looking out of the window in the house in Kentish Town, London, we were living in, and seeing a small, quiet eddy of leaves in the pavement below. One of the great things about computers is the covert records they keep, and I see by looking at the original file of the story that the day it was started was October 25th. That feels about right—an autumnal day for a melancholy tale.

"This is a slightly different (and later) version of the story to the one previously published. When I was putting together my collection *What You Make It*, there were originally going to be many more stories in it—until we realized that it would produce a book about three inches thick. 'Dear Alison' was one of the ones I regretfully removed, but by then I'd done a little editing and cutting on it. In the time-honored fashion, that means this version is very slightly longer."

IT IS FRIDAY, the 25th of October, and beginning to turn cold. I'll put the heating on before I go.

I'm leaving in about half an hour. I've been building up to it all day, kept telling myself that I'd leave any minute now and spend the day waiting in the airport. But I always knew that I'd wait until this time, until the light was going. London is at its best in the autumn, and four o'clock is the autumn time. Four o'clock is when autumn is.

An eddy of leaves is turning hectically in the street outside my study window, flecks of green and brown lively against the tarmac. Earlier the sky was clear and blue, bright white clouds periodically changing the light which fell into the room; but now that light is fading, painting everything with a layer of gray dust. Smaller, drier leaves are falling on the other side of the street, collecting in a drift around the metal fence in front of Number 12.

I'll remember this sight. I remember most things. Everything goes in, and stays there, not tarnishing but bright like freshly cut glass. An attic of experience to remind me what it is I've lost. The years will soften with their own dust, but dust is never that hard to brush away.

I'll post the keys back through the door, so you'll know there is no need to look for me. And a spare set's always useful. I'm not sure what I'm going to do with this letter. I could print it out and put it somewhere, or take it with me and post it later. Or perhaps I should just leave it on the computer, hidden deep in a subfolder, leaving it to chance whether it will ever be discovered. But if I do that then one of the children will find it first, and it's you I should be explaining this to, not Richard or Maddy; you to whom the primary apology is due.

I can't explain in person, because there wouldn't be any point. Either you wouldn't believe me, or you would: neither would change the facts or make them any better. In your heart of hearts, buried too firmly to ever reach conscious thought, you may already have begun to suspect. You've given no sign, but we've stopped communicating on those subtler levels and I can't really tell what you think any more. Telling you what you in some sense already know would just make you reject it, and me. And where would we go from there?

My desk is tidy. All of my outstanding work has been completed. All the bills are paid.

I'm going to walk. Not all the way—just our part. Down to Oxford Street.

I'll cross the road in front of our house, then turn down that alley you've always been scared of (I can never remember what it's called; but I do remember an evening when you forgot your fear long enough for it to be rather interesting). Then off down Kentish Town Road, past the Woolworths and the Vulture's Perch pub, the mediocre sandwich bars and that shop the size of a football pitch which is filled only with spectacles. I remember ranting against the waste of space when you and I first met, and you finding it funny. I suppose the joke's grown old.

It's not an especially lovely area, and Falkland Road is hardly Bel Air. But we've lived here fifteen years, and we've always liked it, haven't we? At least until the last couple of years, when it all started to curdle; when I realized what was going to happen. Before that Kentish Town suited us well enough. We liked Café Renoir, where you could get a reasonable breakfast when the staff weren't feeling too cool to serve it to you. The Assembly House pub, with its wall-to-wall Victorian mirrors and a comprehensive selection of Irish folk on the jukebox. The corner store, where they always know what we want before we ask for it. All of that.

It was our place.

I couldn't talk to you about it when it started, because of how it happened. Even if it had come about some other way, I would probably have kept silent: by the time I realized what it meant there wasn't much I could do. I hope I'm right in thinking it's only the last two years which have been strained, that you were happy until then. I've covered my tracks as well as I could, kept it hidden. So many little lies, all of them unsaid.

It was actually ten years ago, when we had only been in this house a few years and the children were still young and ours. I'm sure you remember John and Suzy's party—the one just after they'd moved into the new house? Or maybe not: it was just one of many, after all, and perhaps it is only my mind in which it retains a peculiar luminosity.

You'd just started working at Elders & Peterson, and weren't very keen on going out. You wanted a weekend with a clear head, to tidy up the house, do some shopping, to hang out without a hangover. But we decided we ought to go, and I promised I wouldn't get too drunk, and you gave me that sweet, affectionate smile which said you believed I'd try but that you'd still move the aspirin to beside the bed. We engaged our dippy babysitter, spruced ourselves up, and went out hand-in-hand, feeling for once as if we were in our twenties again. I think we even splashed out on a cab.

Nice house, in its way, though we both thought it was rather big for just the two of them. John was just getting successful around then, and the size of the property looked like some kind of a statement. We arrived early, having agreed we wouldn't stay too late, and stood talking in the kitchen with Suzy as she chopped vegetables for the dips. She was wearing the Whistles dress which you both owned, and you and I winked secretly to each other: after much deliberation you were wearing something different. The brown Jigsaw suit, with earrings from Monsoon that looked like little leaves. Do you still have those earrings somewhere? I suppose you must, though I haven't seen you wearing them in a while. I looked for them this morning, thinking that you wouldn't miss them and that I might take them with me. But they're buried somewhere.

By ten the house was full and I was pretty drunk, talking hard and loud with John and Howard in the living room. I glanced around to check if you were having a good enough time and saw you leaning back against a table, a plastic cup of red wine hovering around your lips. You were listening to Jan bang on about something—her rubbish ex-boyfriend, probably. With your other hand you were fumbling in your bag for your cigarettes, wanting one pretty soon but trying not to let Jan see you weren't giving her familiar tale of woe your full attention. You are wonderful like that. Always doing the right thing, and in the right way. Always eager to be good, and not just so that people would admire you. Just because.

You finally found your packet and offered it to Jan, and she took a cigarette and lit it without even pausing for breath, a particular skill of hers. As you raised your Zippo to light your own you caught me looking at you. You gave a tiny wink, to let me know you'd seen me, and an infinitesimal roll of the eyes—but not enough to derail Jan. Your hand crept up to tuck your hair behind your ear—you'd just had it cut, and only I knew you weren't sure about the shorter style. In that moment I loved you so much, felt both lucky and charmed.

And then, just behind you, she walked into the room, and everything went wrong.

Remember Auntie's Kitchen, that West Indian café between Kentish Town and Camden? Whenever we passed it we'd peer inside at the cheerful checked tablecloths and say to each other that we must try it someday. We never did. We were always on the way somewhere else, usually to Camden market to munch on noodles and browse at furniture we couldn't afford, and it never made sense to stop. I don't even know if it's still there anymore. After we started going everywhere by car we stopped noticing things like that. I'll check tonight, on the way down into town, but either way it's too late. We should have done everything, while we had the chance. You never know how much things may change.

Then, over the crossroads and down past the site where the big Sainsbury's used to be. I remember the first time we shopped there together—Christ, must be twenty-five years ago—both of us discovering what the other liked to eat, giggling over the frozen goods, and getting home to discover that despite spending forty pounds we hadn't really bought a single proper meal. It's become a nest of *bijou* little shops now, of course, but we never really took to them: we'd liked the way things were when we started seeing each other, and there's a limit to how many little ceramic pots anyone can buy.

By a coincidence I ate my first new meal just round the back of Sainsbury's, a week after the party. It was gone midnight, and I knew you'd be wondering where I was, but I was desperate. Four days of the chills, of half-delirious hungers. Of feeling nauseous every time I looked at food, yet knowing I needed something. A young girl in her early twenties, staggering slightly, having reeled out of the Electric Ballroom still baked on e. I know that because I could taste it in her blood. She noticed me in the empty street, and giggled, and I suddenly knew what I needed. She didn't run away as I walked toward her.

I only took a little.

You and I went to Kentish Town Library one morning, quite soon after we'd got the first flat together. You were interested in finding out a little more about the area, and found a couple of books by the Camden Historical Society. We discovered that no one was very interested in Kentish Town, despite the fact it's actually older than Camden, and you were grumpy about that because we liked where we lived. But we found out some interesting snippets—like the fact that the area in front of Camden Town tube station, the part which juts out into the crossroads, had once housed a tiny jail and a stocks. Today the derelicts and drunks still collect there, as if there is something in that patch of ground which draws society's misfits and miscreants even now.

I'll cross that area on my way down, avoiding one of those tramps— who I think recognizes something in me, and may be one of us—and head off down Camden Road toward Mornington Crescent.

I don't understand why it happened. You and I loved each other, we had the kids, and had just finished redecorating. We were happy. There was no reason for what I did. No sense to it. No excuse, unless there was something about her which simply drew me. But why me, and not somebody else?

She was very tall, and extremely slim. She had short blonde hair and nothing in her head except cheekbones. She came into the room alone, and John immediately signaled to her. Drunkenly he introduced her to Howard and I, telling us her name was Vanessa, and that she worked in publishing. I caught you glancing over, and then looking away again, unconcerned. John burbled on at us for a while about some project or other he was working on, and then set off for more drinks, pulling Howard in his wake.

By then I was pretty drunk, but still able to function on the level of "What do you do, blah, this is what I do, blah." I talked with Vanessa for a while. She had very blue eyes, a little curl of hair in front of each ear, and the way her neck met her shoulders was pleasing. That was all I noticed. She wasn't really my type.

After ten minutes she darted to one side to greet someone else, a noisy drama of squeals and cheek-kisses. No great loss: I've never found publishing interesting. I revolved slowly about the vertical plane until I saw someone I knew, and then went and talked to them.

This person was an old friend I hadn't seen in some time—Roger, the one who got divorced last year—and the conversation took a while and involved several drinks. As I was returning from fetching one of these I noticed the Vanessa woman standing in the corner, holding a bottle of wine by the neck and listening patiently to someone complaining about babysitters. I suffered a brief moment of disquiet about ours—we suspected her of knowing where our stash of elderly dope was—and then made myself forget about it. When you're thirty all your friends can talk about are houses and marriage; by a few years later babies and their sitters become the talk of the town. It's as if everyone collectively forgets that there's a real world out there with interesting things in it, and becomes progressively more obsessed with what happens behind their own front doors.

I muttered something to this effect to Roger, glancing back across at the corner as I did so. The woman was swigging wine straight from the bottle, her body curved into a swan's neck of relaxed poise. I couldn't help wondering why she was here alone. Someone like that had to have a boyfriend.

Then I noticed that she was looking at me, the mouth of the bottle an inch from her wet lips. I smiled, uncertainly.

We never really spent much time in Mornington Crescent. Nothing to take us there, I suppose. Not even really a proper district as such, more a blur between Camden and the top of Tottenham Court Road. I remember once, when Maddy was small, telling her that the red two-story building we were driving past had once been a station like Kentish Town's, and that in fact there were many other disused stations dotted over London. Mornington Crescent tube was shut and supposed to be being renovated, but I told Maddy I didn't believe them. She didn't believe *me* at first, but I showed her an old map, and after that she was always fascinated by the idea of abandoned stations. York Road, Down Street, and South Kentish Town—which you can see when you pass it underground, if you know when to look. Places which had once meant something to the people who lived there, and which were now nothing but scar tissue in a city that had moved forward in time. Mornington Crescent opened again, in time, proving me wrong and providing both of us with a lesson in parental fallibility.

Then down toward the Euston Road, the part of the walk you never liked. It's a bit boring, I'll admit. Nothing but towering council blocks and busy roads, and by then you'd be complaining about your feet. But I'll walk it anyway. It's part of the trip, and by the time I come back it will all have changed. Maybe it'll be less boring. But it won't be the same.

One in the morning. The party was going strong—had, if anything, surged up to a new level. I saw that you were still okay, sitting cross-legged on the floor in the living room and happily arguing with Suzy about something.

By then I was very drunk, and on something like my seven billionth trip to the toilet. I reached down with my hand as I passed you, and you squeezed it for a moment. Then I flailed up two flights to the nearest unoccupied bathroom, cursing John for having so many stairs. The top floor of the house was darker than the rest, but I'd worn a channel in the new carpet by then and found my way easily enough.

Afterward I washed my hands with expensive soap for a while, standing weaving in front of the mirror, giggling at my reflection and chuntering cheerfully at myself.

Back outside again and I seemed to have got more drunk. I tripped down the small flight of steps which led to the landing, and reached out to steady myself. Suddenly my mouth was filled with saliva and I had a horrible suspicion I was about to christen the house, but a minute of deep breathing and compulsive swallowing convinced me I'd survive to drink another drink.

I heard a rustling sound, and turned to peer through a nearby doorway. I recognized the room—it was one John had shown us earlier, destined to become his study. "Where you'll sit becoming more and more successful," I'd thought churlishly to myself. At that stage it didn't seem very likely he would commit suicide six years later.

"Hello," she said.

The woman called Vanessa was standing in the empty room, over by the window. Cold moonlight made her features look as if they'd been molded in glass, but whoever'd done it must have been pretty good.

Without really knowing why, I stumbled into the room, pulling the door shut behind me. As she walked toward me her dress rustled again, the sound like a shiver of leaves outside a window in the night.

We met in the middle. I don't remember her pulling her dress up, just the long white stretch of her thighs. I don't remember undoing my trousers, but someone must have done. All I remember is saying, "But you must have a boyfriend," and her just smiling at me.

It was insane. Someone could have come in at any moment.

But it happened.

Tottenham Court Road. Home of cut-price technology, and recipient of many an impulse buy on my part. When we walked down it toward Oxford Street you used to grab my arm and try to pull me past the stores, or throw yourself in front of the window displays to hide them from me. Then later I'd end up standing in Marks & Spencer for hours, while you dithered over underwear. I moaned, and said it was unfair, but I didn't really mind.

Past the *Time Out* building, where Howard used to work, and then the walk will be over. At the junction of Oxford Street and Tottenham Court Road I'll turn around and look back the way I've come, and say goodbye to it all. Sentimental, perhaps: but that walk means a lot to me.

Then I'll go down into Oxford Street tube and sit on the Piccadilly Line to Heathrow.

I have a ticket, my passport, and some dollars, but not very many. I'm going to have to find a way of earning more sooner or later, so it may as well be sooner. I've left the rest of our money for you. If you're stuck for a present for Maddy's birthday I've heard her mention the new Asylum Fields album a couple of times. Though probably she'll have bought it herself, I suppose. I keep forgetting how old they've gotten.

After those ten minutes in John's study I came downstairs again, suddenly shocked into sobriety. You were sitting exactly where I had left you, but it felt like everything else in the world had changed. I was terrified that you'd read something from my face, realize what I had done, but you just reached up and yanked me down to sit next to you. Everybody smiled, apparently glad to see me. Howard passed a joint. My friends, and I felt like I didn't deserve them. Or you.

Especially not you.

We left an hour later. I sat a little apart from you in the cab, convinced you'd smell Vanessa on me, but I clutched your hand and you seemed happy enough. We got home, and I had a shower while you clanked around in the kitchen making tea. Then we went to bed, and I held you tightly until you drifted off. I stared at the ceiling for an hour, chilled with self-loathing, and then surprised myself by falling asleep.

Within a few days I was calmer. A drunken mistake: these things happen. I elected not to tell you about it—partly through self-serving cowardice, but more out of a genuine knowledge of how little it meant, and how much it would hurt you to know. The ratio between the two was too steep for me to say anything. After a fortnight it had sunk to the level of vague memory, the only lasting effect an increased realization of how much I wanted to be with you. That was the only time, in all our years together, that anything like that happened. I promise you.

It should all have been okay, a cautionary lesson learned, but then the first hunger pangs came and everything changed for me. If anything, I feel lucky that we've had ten years, that I was able to hide it for that long. I developed the habit of occasional solitary walks in the evening, a cover that no one seemed to question. I started going to the gym and eating healthily, and maybe that also helped to hide what was happening. At first you didn't notice, and then I think you were even a little proud that your husband was staying in such good shape.

But a couple of years ago that pride faded, around about the time the kids started looking at me curiously. Not very often, and maybe not even consciously, but just as you started making unflattering remarks about your figure, how your body was not lasting out compared to mine, I think at some level the children noticed something, too. Maddy had always been daddy's girl. You said so yourself. She isn't any more, and I don't think that's just because she's growing up and going out with that dickhead. She's uncomfortable with me. Richard's overly polite too, these days, and so are you. It's like I've done something which none of us can remember, something small which nonetheless set me apart from you. As if we're all tip-toeing carefully around something we don't understand.

You'll work out some consensus among you. An affair. Depression. Something. I know you all care for me, and that it won't be easy, but it has to be this way. I'm not telling you where I'm going. It won't be one of the places we've been on holiday together, that's for sure. The memories would hurt too much.

After a while, a new identity. And then a new life, for what it's worth. New places, new things, new people: and none of them will be you.

I've never seen Vanessa since that night, incidentally. If anything, what I feel for her is hate. Not even for what she did to me, for that little bite disguised as passion. More just because, on that night ten years ago, I did something small and normal and stupid which would have hurt you had you known. The kind of mistake anyone can make, not just people like me.

I regret that more than anything: the last human mistake I made, on the last night I was still your husband and nothing else. That I was unfaithful to the only woman I've ever really loved, and with someone who didn't matter to me, and who only did it because she had to.

I knew she must have had a boyfriend—I just didn't realize what kind of man he would be.

I can't send this letter, can I? Not now, and probably not even later. Perhaps it's been nothing more than an attempt to make myself feel better; a selfish confession for my own peace of mind. But I've been thinking of you while I've been writing it, so in that sense at least it is written to you. Maybe I'll find some way of keeping track of your lives, and send this when you're near the end. When it won't matter so much, and you may be asking yourself what exactly it was that happened.

But probably that's not fair either, and by then you won't want to know. Perhaps if I'd told you earlier, when things were still good between us, we could have worked out a way of dealing with it. It's too late now.

It's nearly four o'clock.

I'll come back some day, when it's safe, when no one who could recognize me is still alive. It will be a long wait, but I will come. That day's already planned.

I'll start walking at Oxford Street, and walk all the way back up, seeing what remains and what has changed. The distance at least will stay the same, and maybe I'll be able to pretend you're walking it with me, taking me home again. I could point out the differences, and we'd remember the way it was: and maybe, if I can recall it clearly enough, it will be like I never went away.

But I'll reach Falkland Road eventually, and stand outside looking up at this window; not knowing who lives here now, only that it isn't us. Perhaps if I shut my eyes I'll be able to hear your voice, imagine you sitting inside, conjure up the life that could have been.

I hope so. And I will always love you.

But it's time to go.

THE GOSSIPS

BASIL COPPER

Basil Copper (1924–2013) worked for thirty years as a journalist and editor of a local newspaper before becoming a full-time writer in 1970.

His first story in the horror field, "The Spider," was published in 1964 in *The Fifth Pan Book of Horror Stories*. Since then his short fiction has appeared in numerous anthologies and collected in *Not After Nightfall, Here Be Daemons, From Evil's Pillow, And Afterward the Dark, Voices of Doom, When Footsteps Echo, Whispers in the Night, Cold Hand on My Shoulder*, and *Knife in the Back*.

Besides publishing two nonfiction studies of the vampire and werewolf legends, his other books include the novels *The Great White Space, Necropolis, House of the Wolf*, and *The Black Death*. He also wrote more than fifty hardboiled thrillers about Los Angeles private detective Mike Faraday.

More recently, PS Publishing collected all the author's horror and supernatural fiction in the retrospective two-volume set *Darkness, Mist & Shadow: The Collected Macabre Tales of Basil Copper*; issued a restored version of Copper's 1976 novel *The Curse of the Fleers*; and brought together his continuations of the adventures of

August Derleth's Holmes-like consulting detective Solar Pons in the definitive *The Complete Adventures of Solar Pons. Basil Copper: A Life in Books* is a nonfiction study from the same publisher.

One of the author's most reprinted stories, "Camera Obscura," was adapted for a 1971 episode of the NBC-TV series *Rod Serling's Night Gallery*, and "The Recompensing of Albano Pizar" was dramatized for BBC Radio 4's *Fear on Four* series in 1991 as "Invitation to the Vaults."

"Like most authors," explained Copper, "one's ideas seem to come naturally, by a strange process—rather like osmosis—whereby fragmentary images surface in one's consciousness. Many years ago, during World War II, when I was on the communications staff on a huge depot ship in Alexandria harbor, I went ashore one day and met a chap I knew in the bar of the Fleet Club. He was a fellow radio operator and had been stationed on a wireless station in Sicily, after the war had passed on.

"He mentioned that it was an extremely strange place away from the towns—baking heat, oppressive silences, hidden villages where no one seemed to stir, half-ruined *palazzos* in certain areas; the only sound the buzzing and chirping of insects where there was grass and foliage.

"This, combined with the remembrance of Canova's statue 'The Three Graces,' came back into my mind when I was compiling a collection of macabre tales years ago, which I intended to call *The Gossips and Other Queer Tales*. I thought it might be interesting if the narrator heard whispering going on, as though emanating from the statues, and things progressed from there.

"Such stuff as dreams are made of, of course, but none the worse for that. Anyway, I hope the resurfacing of this story will give some pleasure to readers, along with the occasional chill . . ."

I

IT HAPPENED A long time ago, in Sicily—something like twenty-five years, in fact. Though many intervening events have grown dim, the extraordinary episodes which I myself witnessed and which I later pieced together through Arthur Jordan, are still present in my mind with unusual clarity.

I was on holiday and had found my way to this wild and remote corner without anything special in mind. At Messina, I had fallen in with Grisson, an Englishman who had lived in Italy for many years. He was at that time Director of the Museum of Antiquities at Naples and was currently traveling on leave in pursuit of acquisitions for his foundation.

I gladly acceded to his suggestion that we should travel together and some days later we found ourselves in a wild and savage landscape, almost lunar in aspect, that only the farthest districts of old Sicily can produce. The sun beat down with fierce intensity on stunted trees, sparse vegetation, rocks that seemed to writhe in the heat and undulate with the haze that shimmered about them, while the chirping of thousands of insects only emphasized the brooding silence of this ancient land.

It was some time after midday and an inadequate lunch in the shade of a remote village when we set out to see something which I gathered my companion considered of special interest. We had traveling with us a guide from Messina, whom Grisson had found it necessary to engage, for, as he said, he sometimes had to deal with noble old Sicilian families who spoke no language other than their own difficult dialect. This made things tedious, for though Grisson spoke fluent Italian, even the people of the mainland often could not understand the local Sicilian tongues, and these were many.

It seemed to me that the guide appeared somewhat startled, almost nervous, when he learned our destination; but he said nothing, and at about 1:00 in the afternoon we had left the village far behind and were making our way in single-file along a rough track through the scrubland.

It was the hottest moment of the day, the sky like beaten bronze and the heat bouncing back off the rocks so that one walked as though through an incinerator. My enthusiasm had ebbed noticeably, and it was almost two o'clock when Grisson's attitude showed unmistakably that we were near our journey's end. It seemed suddenly as though we were in a garden, with formal hedges of cypress, and statues dotted about.

Then there was the glint of a lake through the trees and welcome shade. We sat thankfully upon a stone bench and though I still felt too hot and exhausted to begin a conversation, I was once again myself and began to revive my spirits. But Grisson seemed impervious to either heat or atmosphere and began to speak with enthusiasm and wide scholarship of our destination. I did not at first pay much attention, but I gradually became aware of a charged tension that seemed to play around our little group among the somber trees. I noticed that our guide had remained standing, despite his evident fatigue, and continued to glance around him in an uneasy manner.

A few minutes passed, and we continued walking. It was then, for the first time, that I became aware that we were not exactly within a garden. A fountain began to sparkle in the sunlight, there were even plots of what appeared to be dusty lawn and more statues. I do not recall at which point I realized that we had left the garden—if it had ever been a garden—and that we were within some sort of private cemetery, or perhaps public graveyard. There were great slabbed tombs with inscriptions in the ancient Sicilian language, evidently immensely old, and Grisson, who seemed to know his way about, led us forward with evident enthusiasm, taking photographs at intervals and silently flourishing his notebook.

We had gone on in this way for perhaps half-an-hour, Grisson with the dedicated purpose of the specialist, myself as a half-bemused spectator, and the guide with distinct unease, when the character of the landscape changed. We were still within the cemetery, with its white and brown stone sepulchers gleaming in the harsh light—the bounds of the place must have stretched for an immense distance—and the lake was behind us now, when we entered a sort of valley.

On one side there rose a high cliff of perhaps two hundred feet, which was composed of what I should have said was a pink granite, except that there was no such stone in these parts. It may have been that the limestone had become permeated by the action of damp and lichens, as a small trickle of water made its way down the face.

Standing on an eminence as we were at the other side of the valley, we could see on to the plateau opposite. There seemed to be more hedges and formal gardens, and, farther back, the white facade of a *château* or *palazzo* could be seen above the tops of the trees.

But what took my attention and that of my companions was a group of statuary which stood at the edge of the cliff, almost facing us. There were three figures, which appeared to be inclined inward. At that distance it was difficult to make out detail, but they seemed to be females, clad in flowing robes. They must have been of immense weight and bulk, and I judged each to be about fifteen feet high to stand out in such a manner at the height we were viewing them.

Grisson saw my curiosity had been roused but said nothing. Other than a quiet smile of satisfaction he took no visible notice of the statuary, but continued his examination of the ancient, lichen-covered tombs we continued among. For some minutes he worked on, and as we two walked behind him, I gradually became aware that we were not alone in the garden. I do not know at what stage this impinged itself on my consciousness.

Grisson did not seem to notice, but I sensed, though I did not look behind me, that the guide had also heard it. There was a quick, sly murmuring, little chuckles and snickerings, which seemed to come and go in the light wind which had sprung up. I strained my ears but could not make out what language was being spoken, and my first thought was that some children were playing in another part of the cemetery. I mentioned as much to Grisson, whose smile only deepened. But the effect on the guide was most unfortunate. He turned deathly pale under his tan and began to tremble violently. I followed his gaze upward, and though the great statues were now partly hidden from us by the overhang, it seemed to me that the murmur of voices came from the region of their edge of the plateau.

The remark of mine, once uttered, seemed a silly one, but what other explanation could there be? Children do play in stranger places than graveyards, but the remoteness of this region from the town and its company escaped me.

Grisson explained, "There are no people here nowadays, except for the people of the *palazzo*," and here he mentioned the name of a famous and celebrated duke, one of the last of a noble family.

"There was a town here once, which was served by this lower graveyard, but the people went away many years ago. All that is left now is the estate on the plateau above."

It was evidently there we were going, and most probably the voices belonged to servants' gossip in the garden. As I had difficulty in restraining my curiosity any longer, I asked Grisson about the statues. I gathered they were one of the principal reasons for his expedition.

Their proper name in the Sicilian I have forgotten, but I learned they were something on the lines of the "Three Graces" and were reputed to be over five hundred years old, though the estimate, as is so often the case with folklore, was about three hundred years too early as I later came to decide.

"Some people call them 'The Gossips'," he said, referring to a savage joke, the significance of which escaped me. We were going up a flimsy wooden staircase let into the face of the cliff as he spoke, and I shall never forget the look of fear on the guide's face, as he stumbled against me in the temporary gloom, when he caught the gist of Grisson's remarks.

Nevertheless, we continued in silence. Nothing further was said, and a few minutes later we emerged from the overhanging outcrops of rock into a blinding world of sunshine and greenery again. We were now on the plateau and leaving the staircase, which ended in a sort of ornamental bridge spanning a fissure. We passed through a rustic gate and found ourselves in the extensive gardens of the *palazzo*.

Below us, the enormous area of the cemetery lay dazzling in the sun, with the lake piercing the middle-distance and throwing back the burnished image of the sky, while the white and brown tombstones and monuments, shifting and undulating in the heat haze, crawled into the far distance and were lost among the trees.

Here, for a few minutes, I no longer heard the voices which were apparently muffled by a bluff, but as we threaded a white gravel path among well-trimmed lawns, the mumbling began again, but gradually faded as we approached the palace. This was very much larger than I had expected and was built on grand classical lines, evidently for a very ancient and wealthy family. Great stone griffins flanked an enormous marble terrace, and beyond the semi-Greek facade I could see more lawns and peacocks preening themselves.

A *majordomo* appeared with silent efficiency from beyond the terrace and greeted Grisson as an old friend. Moments later, motioning the guide to follow him to the kitchen quarters in due course, he said the Duke would see us at once and led the way through a maze of apartments to a very grand study, decorated chiefly in pale blue and gold.

Our host was a very tall man, in his late fifties I should have said, who exhibited nothing remarkable either in his features or demeanor which would have distinguished him as of noble lineage in Western society; other than—and this is a major differentiation—his exquisite manners, which were carried to such extremes that one eventually imagined he would rather suffer hardships and indignities himself, than that a friend or guest should be inconvenienced.

He evidently knew all about Grisson's errand and it became obvious later—despite my slight grasp of Italian—that the conversation concerned the large group of statues in the grounds. Presently, when the discussion turned to more general matters regarding the antiquities of the villa, the guide was called in. After exaggerated obeisance to the Duke—he remained standing despite the latter's injunction to seat himself—he was asked to translate from the Sicilian for Grisson, as I gathered the Duke was more familiar with that tongue and the conversation could proceed with greater speed.

At some stage, my attention slackened and I amused myself with wandering up and down and perusing the exquisitely tooled leather-bound volumes that lined one of the walls of the great study. Some were undoubtedly records of the Duke's family, for they bore a great crest with armorial bearings tooled in gold on the brown bindings, and stretched away for shelf after shelf. Others, from the titles on the spines, were historical records related to Sicily, while yet others were concerned with theology and divinity.

Presently, we were served with a delightful-tasting liqueur, of a warm amber color, the derivation of which was strange to me, and small, sweet cakes and biscuits. The coolness of the room and the abundance of our refreshment were so welcome after our long and heated trek that I had quite recovered my spirits and lolled back at my ease when a sudden crash jerked me from my reverie.

The Duke, with customary courtesy, had asked the guide to accept a glass of wine, and I was now startled to see a scarlet splash irradiating from the splintered fragments of wine glass scattered about the study carpet. The guide was full of apologies, the Duke made light of the matter, but as a servant hastened to clear up the mess, I could see that the guide was white and badly frightened.

I could surmise, from what I had heard in both English and Italian— for Grisson had addressed me occasionally—that the later conversation had concerned the statues, which Grisson wished to photograph and include in a coming book. The Duke had no particular objection but had warned my companion, in a semi-jocular way, that he would not advise him doing so. The guide had added his objection also, pointing out that this part of the garden had been walled-off for many years, and had included an unfortunate gesture of his arm— the cause of the wine glass accident—when Grisson had asked him to accompany us.

During the next few minutes the guide was banished to the kitchen, still muttering to himself, to await our return. Grisson and the Duke withdrew, amid many apologies on the latter's part, to one corner of the room where there was a huge marble-topped desk. Here their council continued in Italian, and I soon saw that the couple had before them various volumes bound in morocco, which Grisson was consulting and copying down portions in his notebook.

When he rejoined me he looked satisfied, as though his journey had been well worthwhile.

"Sorry about that," he remarked. "This must all have been very boring for you."

"Not at all," I answered. "I've been most interested, but somewhat puzzled by the difficulties with the guide."

Grisson laughed, quite shortly, and then added something to the Duke, *sotto voce*. That gentleman hurried forward to bid us goodbye temporarily, and then said, to my great surprise, that he would see us on our return from the garden—in perfect English.

I was still more intrigued at this singular turn in the situation but I could not, of course, pursue it in the Duke's presence. He evidently had no intention of accompanying us, but disappeared into another part of the palace. And I had no opportunity of speaking to Grisson alone, as another servant—middle-aged and of dour aspect, wearing a leather apron—met us on the terrace and led the way to the garden with a great, rusty bunch of keys.

I was again surprised at this—though by now, I suppose, I shouldn't have been—the whole atmosphere of the place was so extraordinary.

So I noticed little of the splendid grounds through which we were hurrying. Presently, we came to a huge stone wall, about fifteen feet in height, and evidently quite old, which completely cut off the garden from the plateau, so far as I could make out.

It was pierced by a large, thick wooden door, reinforced with metal, and I noticed that the footman, or whoever he was, scraped the lock several times in his hurry to get the door open or—as I afterward realized—in his eagerness to be gone.

He handed Grisson a duplicate key and, another curious procedure, relocked the door behind us. His footsteps died away up the path, and we were alone in the walled-off portion of the garden.

This itself appeared to be of considerable size, and the wall against which we were now standing was thickly hemmed-in with vegetation. Indeed, we had to force our way through and could faintly make out a stone path—a continuation of the one which ended the other side of the wall—which had been overgrown by weeds, moss, and vegetation a considerable time ago.

It may have been imagination, but the air seemed to have grown colder here. It was positively damp, and I saw that the ground under foot inclined to lichen and gave off a nauseous odor.

At the same time that I heard the tinkling of water, the sun burst into our faces again, and through a tangle of grass which had once been a lawn we could make out the terrace and part of one of the stone figures facing toward the valley below. It was all on a much bigger scale than I had expected. And then, above the noise of the water, I once again became aware of voices.

I am not an imaginative man or given to undue nervousness, but I must confess there was something about these sounds—reminiscent of whispered confidences, half-heard in sleep—that gave me distinct unease. That, combined with the chill air, despite the evident heat of the sun which poured on us, made me consciously slacken my pace, but my companion pressed on stoutly, apparently impervious to atmosphere.

After this lapse of time, I find it difficult to recollect my impressions. The coldness in the air continued and the whispering increased, then died away and increased again, according to which direction we seemed to be facing. And how shall I describe the statues? I do not know what I had been prepared for when Grisson asked me to accompany him into that accursed garden. My impression was one of dampness, stench, and nauseous decay.

The surface of the circular, tessellated pavement on to which we presently ventured was covered with some slippery form of moss that gave off a most appalling odor.

And the statues themselves: great heaven, they haunt me still . . . the three vast figures rearing toward the bronze sky seemed to writhe and undulate in the heat haze, and the veined brownish rock from which they were carved was split through with shards of scarlet.

At the same time I seemed to be mysteriously affected by the heat. I grew dizzy, hot and cold by turn, and the statues themselves seemed to change shape in some strange, unknown manner. How can I convey those faces of nightmare: carved from some weird, brown-stained basaltic material, with crooked teeth, lank-seeming hair, and yellow eyes that appeared to glow as though human?

And the stench! My stomach turned at that stagnant miasma which exuded or emanated from the statues themselves, smeared with those scarlet-brown stains. Along the plinth, as I staggered and stumbled my way with Grisson impassive beside me, was carved huge lettering in an unknown character. I reeled toward the railings, away from this bestial group, and attempted to focus my throbbing eyes on what would normally have been an impressive and even delightful view. I was conscious that Grisson was still carrying out his functions, translating the inscription, even photographing the group.

As I turned toward him, that obscene, unnerving whispering and tittering began again. I was sure now, with what fevered insanity I knew not, that the statues themselves were talking—discussing us in the most insidious way. As I strained my eyes in the sun, I became convinced that they were moving: the heads seemed to change shape and expression; the eyes now glowed, now lifted, now dosed; the lips writhed and the dreadful stone teeth chattered on. Even the arms, the very draperies as well as the heads, seemed to shift effortlessly, change position, move again, freeze, coalesce. All the while those ghastly voices seemed to be bursting my eardrums.

Now, I know the reader will say that I was the sudden victim of a fever, induced by the heat, or even that the supposed movement of rigid stone objects was an optical illusion, brought about by the combined reaction on my eyes of heat and light. There is something in that, well enough, but my senses were not so addled as to imagine the appalling suggestive power of those vile voices that echoed so unmistakably in the evil stillness of that accursed garden.

My legs were trembling as though in fever, and I pressed my nails into the palms of my hands and attempted to look out across the valley, to where the distant panorama was undulating and rippling like an agitated film developed in a dish. I was not at all conscious of my next movements. I seemed to hear a shout from Grisson. The voices boiled up and crackled in my brain, my hands were on the railings at the edge of the plateau, and in another instant I should have been over and into the cool and blessed peace of the valley below.

But Grisson's iron hand was on my shoulder, his voice reassuring in my ears as he half-dragged, half-carried me through the heat and rotted vegetation into the sane quietude of the green trees and undergrowth that fringed the wall. I waited until we had regained the Duke's garden and a secluded corner of the lakeside, before I began to retch and collapse.

II

IT WAS QUITE an hour before I was myself again. Grisson was all solicitude. He brushed away a servant who came to inquire too pressingly after us, bathed my forehead in icy water from a fountain, and, gradually, I regained my senses. We eventually found ourselves back in the presence of an alarmed Duke. Grisson was, of course, all apologies, but he had asked me to make light of the affair to our host, who speedily produced a stiff whiskey and begged us to stay to dinner.

"It will not be dark until very late, and you will be able to get well clear during daylight," he said, with an emphasis that revealed he knew all too clearly what was the matter.

As for Grisson, he soon plunged himself into further study of the massive books in the Duke's library, and that gentleman himself, though obviously concerned, did not press any inquiries regarding our experiences.

"A touch of the sun and nerves," was Grisson's own explanation to the Duke and the servants, and by *sotto voce* comments and gestures he asked me particularly not to say anything to the guide.

As for myself, youth and a good dinner rapidly restored my spirits, and as the wine went round, I even began to wonder whether I had not, in fact, dreamed my experiences. As the aftertaste of the adventure began to fade away, I became ashamed of my panic on the bluff where the statues stood, and even hoped that Grisson himself would not refer to it.

It was past eight in the evening and the light was still bright in the western sky when Grisson and I, after many thanks and repeated goodbyes to the courteous Duke, made our way once again past the lake and through the valley. My last glimpse was of the statues, high on their plateau brooding over the bluff; but the sunset tinged the whole place with such beauty and melancholy that even then I said nothing and thought—fool that I was—that the group even looked beautiful against the sky, ablaze with greens and blues, reds and golds.

Grisson made only one more direct reference to the episode when he spoke shortly of the celebrated "mirage effect" which, combined with vertigo, had brought on my attack, as he called it. I said nothing further, but later came a little incident which led me to believe that Grisson had not played fair over my ordeal. But he made handsome amends eventually, though I had to wait over three years for the explanation.

We were fairly on our way back to the village, and the light was still strong enough to see clearly, when Grisson drew some papers out of his pocket to consult them. We were walking abreast, and something brushed against my arm and fell onto the white dust of the path. It had evidently been carried from Grisson's pocket with the documents.

My first instinct was to draw his attention to it, but something held me back. Instead, on pretence of tying my shoelace, I dropped behind and picked up the small object. It was unidentifiable to my immediate glance, and did not appear to be of any value.

However, I said nothing and placed it carefully in my pocket, stuffing down my handkerchief on top of it. Later that night, back in a well-lit hotel room and my adventure receding into limbo, I picked up the small, round object and examined it carefully under the glare of a table-lamp. It took me some while to identify it and then, afterward, when I had thought things over, I did not sleep so well. The article Grisson had dropped appeared to be, so far as I could make out, one of a pair of rubber earplugs.

III

SOME YEARS LATER, as I indicated earlier, I met Grisson again; this time, fortunately, under less frightening circumstances. I had maintained correspondence with him, on and off, in the interim, and though neither of us had made reference to our extraordinary adventure, the question marks it had raised in my mind seemed to hang cloudily between the lines of the occasional letters we exchanged. So something in a letter he wrote me long afterward raised my expectations, and I was not disappointed in the sequel.

I had run into Grisson one afternoon of a hot July, when I was shopping on the Canebière in Marseilles. I had only half-an-hour or so to get to St. Charles to catch my train on to Nice, but we exchanged addresses and he promised to write. I thought little more of it until a letter, heavily stamped and addressed and readdressed in multi-colored inks, reached me some ten days and three hotels later in Genoa.

Grisson was in Florence, attending some sort of congress of museum curators. He knew I intended to visit there. He had a friend, Arthur Jordan, he would like me to meet. Would I join them for a day or two? They were sharing a villa. There was room for me, and I would not have to put up with their company for too long, as they had to attend morning and afternoon sessions of the congress and would only be able to see me in the late afternoons.

The idea was attractive, but what decided me was a curious postscript, which Grisson had heavily underlined, not once, but three times: *Please come. Most important. Jordan has the Sicilian explanation.* The last two words were again underscored.

To say that I was interested would be an understatement. Genoa was palling in the heat, despite the breeze off the sea, and I knew no one in the city. I telegraphed the same afternoon, made an inquiry about trains, and little more than two days later was comfortably settled in at a small but delightful villa in the hills outside Florence.

I had haunted the Uffizi, duly admired once again the incomparable cathedral, and it was not until the second night of my stay that Grisson had broached the subject which had brought me to the city. A moon like an orange was pasted to the hilly backcloth as we passed through the square, past the massive portals then thought to be bronze, now known to be gold, and my companions selected a pavement café not far from the Ponte Vecchio.

There is nothing like a summer evening in Florence, with its scent of flowers and all the atmosphere of a Tuscan night, with a thousand years of history pressing on one, for a story. But such a story as I heard then made me feel doubly glad that I was in such delightful surroundings, with the reassuring river sounds of the Arno only a few yards distant from my comfortable cane chair.

I had come to like Arthur Jordan immensely, in the few hours I had known him. Still young—in his late forties, I believe—with prematurely white hair crowning a boyish face, the most predominant feature being square white teeth which flashed attractively into a smile, startling in the dark brown of his face. He was a born adventurer.

He too, like Grisson, was a curator. Not of a famous museum like his companion, but I gathered that his duties left him time in the summer months for a number of roving commissions, in which he not only brought himself up-to-date on the more important Continental collections, but from time to time had been responsible for staging unusual exhibitions of statuary, pottery, and mediaeval glass of many ages and periods, in halls, galleries, and museums in Paris and London.

It was on such an errand that he had gone to Sicily, and to the scene of our startling adventure, a year or two before. He was hunting this time principally for statuary and sculpture of the seventeenth century, mostly from gardens and parks, to be exhibited on loan, as part of a gigantic presentation of the art of that period in London.

As he spoke, I gained something of his enthusiasm and remembered reading newspaper reports of that time. The exhibition had been unusual in that it represented complete rooms, looking on to "gardens" of various palaces, each one illustrative of a particular facet of the seventeenth century; each complete down to the smallest detail of the art of its period. Jordan's purpose in his Sicilian visit was to secure the loan of "The

Gossips," as I continued to call them, for the show, in one of the biggest halls in London, which was to last three months. I then remembered that one of the exhibition halls had been closed after three or four days, under dramatic circumstances, and had then reopened, but with part of it barred to the public.

I was trying to bring my mind to bear on the hazy details Jordan's remarks had evoked in my mind, when his narrative was interrupted by the arrival of the waiter and the renewal of drinks. I took the opportunity to ask Grisson about the photographs he had taken for his book.

In reply, he handed me a small cardboard wallet, with a wry smile. As our drinks were placed on the table, I examined it.

I found I was holding several pieces of white, glossy paper. I could just make out hazy details of what appeared to be foliage. I was completely baffled, and asked Grisson what he meant by it.

"These are the photographs I took with you," he explained, his smile widening.

I did not realize the import of his remark for a moment and added stupidly, "Were they overexposed?"

"Quite impossible," Grisson retorted dryly. "My books are noted for the quality of the photography. I always take my own photos, and I developed and printed these myself. I could see the negatives were almost blank, but I wanted to make completely sure, so I printed up what I could. As you see, there is only the faintest suspicion of the foliage in the *palazzo* garden."

I was bewildered and turned to Jordan.

"They never have been photographed, you see," he explained, almost apologetically. "'The Gossips,' I mean. Nothing ever comes out."

I was still trying to get my bearings but before I could go on, Grisson asked me to be patient and said that all would be explained when Jordan had told his story. It took some little while for our companion to take up the thread of his remarks again. He said he had first to explain to me what "The Gossips" represented in artistic terms, something of their history, and why he required them for the London show.

"You might think," he said, "that it would be an enormously expensive and cumbersome job to ship all that masonry to England. I offered the Duke, of course, complete *carte blanche* in the matter of expenses connected with the venture. In fact, it cost the old boy nothing, as we were covered by a British Government grant, only part of the shipping costs being borne by the exhibition organizers. And the inclusion of this group in the exhibition would be a sort of *coup* which seldom occurs.

"The statues are masterpieces of their kind, and had never been seen outside their Sicilian setting. In fact, few people had seen them at all, which I thought at the time was a pity, in view of their antecedents.

"The exhibition as a whole, packed as it would be with so many rare and extraordinary things, would not only bring an international cachet to the museum authorities and bodies connected with it in England, but would be worth an enormous sum of money.

"This would arise, not only through entrance money to the exhibition itself, but via the many articles, broadcasts, magazines, and newspaper and photographic rights in journals and other media throughout the world. A film had been planned to cover the whole field, and also colored lantern-slides, which were to form the basis of lectures by eminent men in their various spheres.

"My securing 'The Gossips' would set the seal on all this, in view of its extraordinary history, and my hopes were high when I went on my momentous errand to the Sicilian hinterland."

Jordan said he had not warned the Duke of his intentions, only of his arrival, and though he had expected at first a flat refusal, in view of the many difficulties to be overcome in connection with transporting the statues to England, he did not at all realize that he would receive such a cordial reception as the Duke gave him.

But in fact, there was little objection on the latter's part to loaning the statues when Jordan had explained the situation, and the Duke was enthusiastically cooperative, going into great detail on the technical problems involved. Jordan had broached his errand a full six months before the exhibition was due to begin in London, so there was plenty of time to put the scheme in train.

I must emphasize, at this point, that Jordan, though he was fully conversant with the evil history of the statuary as it appeared in histories and books of various periods, had himself heard little or nothing of their unsavory reputation in the Sicilian countryside in modern times; and as he had no opportunity of discussing it with the local inhabitants, who are, in any case, reticent before strangers, it was hardly surprising.

Jordan at first confined his researches to the books in the Duke's library and, having been pressed to stay a day or two, delayed an examination of the statues *in situ* until the following day.

I was disappointed to hear from the man's own lips that, though he was fascinated and delighted with the group, which he thought well worth his time and long journey, nothing unusual had occurred in those early days. He had not, being a sensible man, seen anything extraordinary in the lichen, the vile stench (he had traveled too widely in South American jungles for that), or the sinister, red-streaked statues themselves. The troubles began later, and in a different form from those I had experienced.

"If I may interrupt a moment," said Grisson, waving for another round of drinks. "I think I ought to put our friend more in the picture by telling him something of the history of the *palazzo* and of the statues in particular. Have you ever heard of Caravallo?"

I shook my head. Try as I would, the name meant nothing to me, and there was no reason why it should, for the man had been a minor Italian sculptor of the seventeenth century. His work stood really on the threshold of genius, but was marred by an evil way of life and a demoniac method of expressing his artistic impulses that came more and more to make his work looked on askance by the patrons and nobles who commissioned the artworks of the time.

But he had apparently found a kindred soul in Leonardo, the then master of our Sicilian *palazzo*, Grisson told me. As he went on talking, I began to piece together a bizarre story, and much that had been dark and obscure to me before began slowly to fit into place, like the well-oiled tumblers in a lock.

Leonardo was an authority on demonology and other blasphemous arts, and his thoroughly dissolute way of life had made him shunned by the local people quite early in his career.

He had succeeded to the title at the age of nineteen, on the death of his father, and within only a few years the *palazzo* had become the scene of epic orgies indulged in by the local women and Leonardo and his friends.

The evil fame of the man spread far afield, and beautiful women of all classes were guests for weeks at a time, from towns as far afield as Naples and Rome, as well as places on the island itself.

Legend even had it that Leonardo's mother was made to witness and take part in unspeakable ceremonies herself—she was a beautiful woman, only in her late thirties at the time of which Grisson was speaking—and when she was found dead one morning by a servant before attaining her fiftieth year, even uglier rumors began to gather.

So it was at the height of Leonardo's notoriety that people began to leave the immediate vicinity of the *palazzo*. There had been a small

224 / Basil Copper

town there originally, as I think I mentioned earlier, but bands of young bloods were out at night, abducting eligible young women from local families whenever they got the opportunity, so that the young duke and his estate were the scandal of Sicily.

It was at this stage in his wicked career that Leonardo came into contact with Caravallo. The two were greatly alike in many ways, and the duke had been delighted with the acquisition of a number of obscene but exquisitely wrought carvings, created by Caravallo as parodies in the Greek style. And it was also then that Caravallo had the notion which crowned his blasphemous fancy. Leonardo had currently three beautiful mistresses, three young sisters, each of whom seemed to outshine the azure sea in beauty. It was Leonardo's custom to indulge with them mutually in indescribable orgies that, for lust and ingenious frenzy, far outdid the spectacles of ancient Rome. And when the moon was in certain quarters, ritual acts of sex magic took place between Leonardo and the three young girls in an ornately equipped "throne room" in the palace, in which other young men and women unashamedly took part—to the number of fifty or sixty persons, according to one old chronicle.

Caravallo had often painted the women and his young friend in the most erotic and abandoned of acts, and his sketchbook was crammed with hundreds and hundreds of vile and shameful drawings that today, said Grisson, still existed in thirty or forty locked volumes of erotica in a sealed-off and almost permanently locked section of the present Duke's library.

It was Caravallo's idea to compose a large group of statuary to perpetuate Leonardo and his coven of three young women. The original form of this had been of a nature which had blanched even Leonardo's shameless cheeks, but he pointed out to his erratic genius that statuary could not be hidden as could smaller *objets d'art*, and as the statue would have to be more or less public. Because of its huge size, the form would have to take a semi-classical theme and the hidden, secret, and perverse meanings could be read into the public statuary by those "in the know."

The three young women were given, it might be added, said Grisson almost superfluously, to endless conversations and laughter among themselves. And their disporting in a pavilion in the grounds, long since burned down in a fire, their shrill chatter, sniggerings and mutterings, had earned them the nickname—the Sicilian equivalent—of "The Gossips" among the local people of the time.

That their intentions and discussions were malicious there can be no doubt, and it would be interesting to discover, if it were possible, just who were the personalities, public and private, that formed the subject of their scandalous talk in those far-off days.

At all events, Caravallo plunged eagerly into the new commission given him by the young duke, and for a time all went well. The statues were taking shape, when suddenly a bigger scandal than ever broke out. No records came down of it, but the story is that some incorruptible nobleman suddenly descended on the villa at the height of an orgy. At all events, the coven was broken, questions were asked in government circles, and the three young women, the center—with Leonardo—of the sensation, were hurriedly and secretly packed off to their own remote hometown.

Leonardo lingered on in his villa, but his drive and energy were gone with the departure of his three "brides," and though he was consoled by the dark genius and wit of Caravallo, the old days were over. Caravallo completed his group of statuary—his "masterpiece," he ever afterward called it—though it had been left for a time only half-finished—using other women in place of the original models. But it is believed that he fashioned the heads from original drawings of the duke's three mistresses.

The duke had by then abandoned his original idea of his own effigy appearing in the middle of the group, as the master of ceremonies, and the finished creation was as Grisson and I had seen it on that unforgettable day: as a circle of dancing women in flowing draperies, with an inscription running around the outer pedestal.

I was deeply interested in this strange story, and was convinced that I had been asked to Florence for a denouement. So interested, in fact, that our glasses had long been empty and the crowds at the nearby tables were beginning to thin out when I called for another round.

The rest of the tale grows dim and shadowy (Grisson presently continued), and his next words gripped my attention with undeniable impact, as no doubt they were meant to do. Some years after the commissioning of the statues, Leonardo was found dead at the foot of the cliffs leading to the upper garden, in the most tragic and horrifying circumstances.

His body appeared to have been reduced to a jelly, though the cliff was not high enough to have inflicted such damage by a simple fall, and the expression on what remained of his face was enough to cause a fainting fit in the first manservant on the scene.

There were uglier rumors and, amid wild stories and further scandal, the great house was closed for a time and Caravallo left the district, the death of his old friend having apparently shattered him. He eventually died in Padua a few years afterward, and little more is known of him, other than what I have told you this evening, though minor works of his continue to come to light even today, Grisson added.

The reputation of "The Gossips" apparently stems from the period immediately after the strange death of Leonardo and, as was said earlier, the people gradually drifted away from the area. New dukes continued to inhabit the ancient palace, but parts of the library were sealed, and, after a particularly bad fright, a descendant of the bad young duke had part of the garden walled-off, as I had seen on the occasion of my ill-fated visit with Grisson.

The latter leaned back after completing his story, and looked moodily out over the water. Despite the warmth of the still air, and the delights of the ancient city surrounding us, I had become aware that this was not the end of the affair and that there was a great deal more to come. Grisson had been speaking for upward of half an hour and, at a sign from him, Jordan looked up with a smile. It was his turn to continue the tale.

IV

HE FIRST WENT back to the thread of his original remarks, which had been so lengthily interrupted by our companion. Arthur Jordan smiled even more broadly as he recollected this, and Grisson stirred uneasily in his chair as if to comment obliquely that he hadn't meant to take so long.

Jordan had completed his arrangements with the Duke to exhibit "The Gossips" in London, and all had apparently gone very well until the time came to move the statues.

Jordan was, of course, extremely anxious that no damage should come to the group while it was in his care, and he had gone to considerable trouble in getting up one of the best firms in Naples to undertake the job. I did not understand the technicalities as Jordan explained them, but I gathered that the whole group of statuary and the plinth on which they stood had first to be jacked up most carefully, and then edged on to a sort of lift which had been constructed of strong steel scaffolding up the face of the cliff.

When they had been lowered to the valley below, they were to be crated and transported by stages in a large, wheeled cradle to Palermo for shipment to England. This was the plan which Jordan explained to me, but unfortunately, things didn't work out like that. The first stages of the dismantling of the statues went smoothly and without incident. Workmen from the Italian mainland had been brought in—specialists to a man—and they had laughed at the local tales and legends.

Nothing odd occurred regarding the statues: there were no voices, and nothing untoward about their appearance. In fact, Jordan regarded the whole thing as a straightforward civil engineering operation and, apart from perfunctory supervision, his mind was on other affairs: the shipment from Palermo, general details of the exhibition, his researches in the Duke's library, and so on.

It seemed that the statues could be removed separately, and that the granite plinth on which they rested was also a separate entity. This would mean that the figures could be removed one by one for crating, and a larger crate would contain the plinth. As a start, the three figures were lifted and removed to one side. They were left for the time being, until the lifting gear would be ready to lower them down the face of the cliff.

Then the experts examined the plinth, and professed themselves satisfied with what they found.

The plinth could be lifted in one section with the equipment available, and would not crack. This work occupied all of the first day and part of the following morning, and it was then that the troubles had begun.

Perhaps Jordan had been trapped into a position of false security by the tranquil atmosphere and the deepening interest of his task. Whatever the reason, the disaster which afterward befell came with stunning suddenness.

During the latter part of the morning, the plinth had first been lowered to the ground. This operation was not without its hazards. The plinth was the bulkiest single item of the group, though it was not the heaviest, and it called for delicate maneuvering. Some of the workmen had anxious looks as the great mass was lowered, inch-by-inch almost, with much rattling of chains in the blocks, down the face of the cliff. A gantry had been erected on top of the scaffolding and a flat steel platform, with chains around it, was to be used for the operation.

But all had gone well, and by the end of the morning the great mass had been cradled and was already out of sight along the lower road through the old cemetery. In the afternoon, though the heat was intense, Jordan was surprised to see that the workmen intended to stick to their task. Unlike most Italians, they took only an hour for their *siesta*, though the sun was cruel, and soon after 2:00 the sound of the winch warned him that their labors were about to begin again.

Excusing himself from his host, Jordan hurried back to the platform of rock to superintend operations, and was once again impressed with the efficiency and hard work put in, both by the principals and laborers of the firm which had been engaged. Perhaps they were being paid a bonus or special rates if they finished the job in a certain time. Whatever the reason, Jordan mentally resolved to invite them as his guests to a celebration dinner when he met them again in Palermo in a few days' time. Jordan had remarked at the Duke's lack of interest in such an unusual operation, but if he had known the real history of the statuary, he would have thought it remarkable if the Duke had felt otherwise.

Jordan was idly mulling these and other thoughts over in his mind as the winch chains rattled away, and the statues I had found so repellent, but which merely excited his keenest antiquarian interest, were lowered slowly down to the cemetery level with infinite care and precision.

A highly skilled contracting engineer was in charge, and it was the fact that he had established close contact with him and had been so impressed with the quality of his mind that made Jordan refuse to accept an obvious explanation which occurred to some other people after the tragic events of the later afternoon.

Two of the statues had been lowered safely, and the third was being jacked on to the lift-like platform. The cradle crew had not yet returned from their task of conveying the plinth, and one would not have expected them to, with the weight and the distance they had to traverse. So the first two statues were simply left in the shade at the cliff bottom while the engineers and laborers concentrated on the remainder of the task.

Jordan does not yet know why he came to find himself on the lift platform. The man who performed the delicate and dangerous task of directing the operation from the platform itself during the hazardous descent had been called to the bottom of the cliff on some errand or other, and had not yet returned. The laborers, directed by the engineer, had levered the third statue into position on the platform, and were awaiting their instructions to lower away.

And so it happened that Arthur Jordan found himself the only qualified person, and the nearest to the platform, when the signal was about to be given. The engineer in charge, looking about for his key man, saw him at the foot of the cliff.

He himself had to direct the winching operations, and the man on the platform transmitted his instructions to a third man at the cliff-edge, who passed them on to the engineer. They were quite simple signals, and Jordan had fully understood their use during the morning's work. Rather than hold up the proceedings, he waved to the engineer, exchanged a few shouted words and, at the former's nodded assent, jumped lightly on to the platform and hooked up the securing chains.

Down below, another team of men gripped steadying cables and, as they also noted his signals, held the platform to prevent it bumping against out-jutting rocks. Jordan gave his first signal, the machinery clanked, chains ran snittering through blocks, and the platform swung gently away from the rock-face.

It descended an infinitesimal fraction and then steadied, keeping to a strictly controlled procedure. The sun baked Jordan, the rock face seemed to throw back the heat like a blast furnace, and he was suddenly afraid. He could not, to this day, ascribe any rational cause for his alarm. It was just a "feeling." He looked down at the brown, oval faces of the men below, and then up over the stretch of cemetery, blinding in that fierce sun. Everything began to shimmer in the haze, and the platform started to vibrate in an odd manner.

I put down my wine glass as Jordan leaned forward. In my short acquaintance with the man he had not been demonstrative, but I could swear I saw moisture exuding from the skin of his forehead and rolling down his cheek as he came to what was obviously the most harrowing part of his story.

Jordan had gripped one of the side-chains—a simple movement which subsequently saved his life—and had braced himself to give his second series of signals. He felt better, and the platform again descended a minute distance. It was then that he became aware of the faint, insidious mumbling that I had heard in that self-same garden so long ago: an undertone of sibilant, nauseous whispering, mingled with obscene titters, that tingled the skin of his scalp in an electric fashion. The next thing that happened was a confusion of noise and motions: he heard a sharp crack, at the same time as a shout of alarm or terror—which, he couldn't tell. Similarly, he didn't know whether it came from above or below.

Then the platform suddenly tipped, and tilted, throwing him against the chains. There was the harsh scream of metal against rock and it was this, with the pain of contact with the chain, that convulsed him into action. Something had broken in the main bearings of the winch, or perhaps it was a cable. The platform was tipping at an impossible angle, and then Jordan saw what he will never forget: the tons of statue sliding inexorably toward him to crush him down, and on the carved face a sardonic sneer.

Jordan was against the retaining chains. Instantaneously it flickered across his brain that if the statue once caught against the chains, it must inevitably tear everything with it and dash cradle and man to destruction below. As he saw the workmen scattering in panic at the cliff floor, Jordan, with the quickness inspired by terror, swiftly unhooked the two massive chains from their retaining cradles and hurled himself upward into the cables above his head.

There was a noise like an avalanche, a boiling dust of stone and chippings, and the flimsy platform bucked about like a cork. But Jordan was precariously safe. The monstrous statue had gone over the platform edge as it tipped, and had fallen clear. It, and the two other statues, were ground to fragments and the dust, like smoke from artillery fire, was lapping at the heels of the frantically running workmen, while boulders, perhaps weighing half-a-ton, bounded excitedly among them like playful terriers. Jordan clung to the cable, half-dazed, the strength of his arms almost gone, borne up by the calm instructions of the engineer above him, who, with pipe securely jammed in his mouth, was testing the winch, his band of shaken colleagues only just beginning to stir themselves.

Jordan had first to be lowered, so that the gear could be freed. Then a rope had to be got out, so that the platform could be pulled back to the safety of the cliff-top, for many of the fittings had been torn away. This epic would make a story in itself, as would the courage of the workman who volunteered to lower himself down from the shattered jib gear and lash Jordan securely to the remaining cables, so that it was impossible for him to fall. Later, it was found that the chain on which this admirable man had relied for this long and complicated operation had been almost sheared through, and was hanging by a few strands.

When Jordan regained the safety of the ground, worse was to come. The loss of the statues was bad enough—that was his responsibility, and to him would fall the heavy task of explaining to the Duke. But a small boy, an especial favorite of the workmen, had been standing beneath when the great statue fell. He had been unnoticed by many of the men who swarmed about him and, though repeatedly ordered away, had insisted on returning.

The operation had some fascination for him. The statues had been conceived in blood and cruelty, and in their destruction they demanded a human sacrifice. The death of this small boy, Tonio, whose pitiful remains were eventually found beneath the biggest single intact piece of rock, had a profound effect on Jordan and all who were there that afternoon. It was a dazed and demoralized party that prepared to quit the ground on which they had started out so well in the morning.

And there was another, a final horror, of which few could ever be induced to talk again. Jordan, sipping at a new drink set before him, with a manner more like himself now that this portion of his story was over, promised that he would allude to this again before the end.

I must confess that I had been considerably shaken at the events described by Jordan so far. Compared with his experiences, my own had been trifling. Yet, though the way Jordan had described the happenings of that afternoon of recent times it had seemed quite a normal industrial accident, I was convinced he would have some more *outré* explanation, in view of my own strong feelings.

And so it proved. But first, Jordan had the painful duty of informing the Duke of what had happened. To his surprise, though deeply shocked and moved at the death of the child and Jordan's narrow escape, the loss of the statues worried him not at all. In fact, when the effect of the tragedy had worn off, he seemed relieved rather than otherwise. He hastily prevented any further discussion of details of the affair, and asked Jordan to deal with the workmen. He himself took on the responsibility of interviewing the child's father, and though the boy should not have been where he was when the accident occurred, he insisted on paying the funeral expenses and substantial compensation to the bereaved parents.

While all this was going on, Jordan and the engineer made a thorough examination of the equipment used to lower the statuary down the cliff. What they found completely exonerated the company, but caused pale faces among the workmen. In fact, there was no explanation of the disaster in material terms. The only solution was of so monstrous a nature that Jordan and his associates refused to accept this, and the cause of the accident was put down to the equivalent of an "act of God," which Jordan felt was a tremendous irony under the circumstances.

The representative of the Milan insurance company who traveled up to the site was at first inclined to blame some fault of the equipment used, but after he had been shown the evidence and had examined the area of the plateau, he rapidly came to the same conclusion as the others.

He departed, lips compressed and shaking his head. His last words to Jordan and the engineer were that, fortunately, such happenings occurred only once in a lifetime—otherwise, nothing would be insurable.

The engineering firm, with many expressions of regret, packed up their gear and departed. Jordan and the Duke were undecided what to do about the plinth. It had already been crated and was sealed in a warehouse in Palermo, awaiting shipment to London. They left it there for the moment, while they debated more weighty matters. Jordan cabled news of the disaster to London, and remained on as the Duke's guest until the insurance problems had been sorted out.

Eventually, there came a cable to say that the company would bear the full loss. This, together with the compensation which the British government had decided to pay instead of the exhibition grant, more than covered the material and artistic loss sustained by the Duke. In fact, he was most effusive over this turn of the affair, and his handshake was extremely cordial when Jordan eventually left, a week later.

The inquest on the child, in a nearby village, had revealed nothing, as Jordan had anticipated. After a perfunctory judicial inquiry by the local police, the affair died down and was written off as an unfortunate accident, though coroner and police alike were hard-put to it to explain away the manner of the accident in natural terms.

Jordan contented himself with certain documents, drawings, and other material the Duke had lent him from his library, and this would have to represent the statuary in the London exhibition. Jordan took these away with him in a locked valise, and after other business had been completed on the Italian mainland, he made his way back to London just over a fortnight afterward, a slightly different man from the one who had made the outward journey.

He duly reported to his foundation, conferred with the Chairman of the Exhibition Committee, and went on with his other preparations for the opening, which was now about four months away. This work absorbed him so continuously that, combined with the trips he was obliged to make from London to other parts of England, the whole business gradually faded from his mind.

But some weeks later, it was again in the forefront. He had received an urgent message from the Chairman of the Exhibition Committee when spending a weekend at the Kent coast. It asked him to return to London at once.

Sir Portman Ackroyd was a solid, red-faced man, whose claret features seemed even more suffused as he passed a buff message from across his desk to a confused Jordan. The message read: sicilian statuary crated arrived london docks today stop bonded warehouse for clearance stop awaiting instructions stop ross.

Jordan's feelings, as he read this extraordinary message, can perhaps be imagined rather than felt. His first instincts, as he discussed the matter with Ackroyd, were that a mistake had been made. Then his face lightened. There had evidently been some confusion at Palermo. No doubt the plinth alone had arrived.

Sir Portman's brow cleared, and he got on the telephone. Ross could not be reached, but inquiries would be made at the docks. In half-an-hour the phone rang again. There were definitely four crates, three of them upright and one horizontal.

To say that the room turned black, Jordan explained to his two friends, would be a slight exaggeration, but the receipt of this stupefying message had something of that effect.

In fact, he looked so queer that Sir Portman solicitously led him to a deep easy-chair and poured him a liberal brandy. Then the two men debated the curious mystery, and Jordan decided that he would leave for the docks himself, and investigate. Sir Portman insisted that he would come also. In the meantime, he left his secretary with the task of checking with the Italian shipping company which had handled the transportation of the crates. They could do little else, without appearing foolish, until they had personally inspected the contents.

At this point Jordan fell silent, and the quiet atmosphere of the Florentine café again came back to my ears. Far away there was the thin, high note of a violin and this, mingled with the occasional clink of glasses and the splash of the river at our front, gave an agreeable touch of sanity after hearing this nightmare tale.

Grisson leaned toward me as Jordan stopped speaking. "To give Arthur a chance to catch his breath," he said, "I feel I owe you an apology. As you may have guessed, I didn't make my visit with you totally unprepared."

"I gathered that," I said. "I picked up one of your earplugs after we left the site. I kept it all these years."

And I handed him a small scrap of tissue paper. Grisson reddened, and then joined in the laughter of Arthur Jordan and myself. Jordan evidently knew this story, and he continued amused for some minutes as Grisson drew out the earplug from the twist of paper.

"I was really sorry about that," he told me. "But I had to have a neutral observer who knew nothing of the area or of the history of "The Gossips." I wore these to see whether or not I would be affected, and also to ensure there would be someone on the spot who could act freely in case of emergency."

He broke off awkwardly as he finished his sentence, but was reassured by the smile I gave him. All the same, I was glad he had offered his explanation, which cleared up many things. As Jordan prepared to take up the story again, Grisson shifted his position in his chair and said something whose significance escaped me until later.

"You will not have overlooked two curious facts, I presume? One is that the statues are of women and that, so far as is known, all the victims were males."

I had not much time to ponder on this cryptic announcement when Arthur Jordan, who was already beginning to display impatience, recommenced his story.

He and Sir Portman had driven to the docks. There, in a vast shed, backed by cranes and all the maritime activities of a great port, were the four enormous crates, plainly labeled for their destination. Ross led the two men into the stone-floored shed, where a crowd of dockers had gathered.

As Sir Portman gave the order, several of them began to carefully pry back the stout boards on the top of one box which Jordan had indicated. In about a quarter of an hour, after boards, straw, and packing had been removed, the unmistakable features of one of the hideous stone trio was revealed.

Even some of the hard-bitten dock workers were shaken at the savage expression on that vile face, and Sir Portman's rubicund features turned a shade whiter. Arthur Jordan did not shriek, neither did he faint away, but he felt the shed whirl around him and had to be helped back to the taxi.

All the way back into central London, as the mean streets of the docks fled past the windows, he said, over and over to Sir Portman, "How could such a thing be? With my own eyes I saw them smashed to fragments. With my own eyes!"

As for Sir Portman, who had never experienced the appalling atmosphere of their Sicilian setting, he no longer debated whether devilry or science was at the bottom of the things' arrival in London. He knew he had the statues for his exhibition, and that was the principal matter which concerned him. Jordan turned paler than ever when he learned that Ackroyd intended to go ahead with the display of the statuary as planned, but all his pleading to the contrary was in vain. Sir Portman advised him to rest for several days, and in the meantime he would have inquiries put in train.

Jordan turned over to him such documents as were necessary for this purpose. Once arrived at his flat near the museum, where he usually worked, he went to bed for three days with a raging fever. At the end of this time, his housekeeper, who had tended his wants during his illness, admitted an excited Sir Portman and a fellow colleague from the museum. The Exhibition Committee Chairman had seldom been so enthusiastic about an exhibit.

"The Gossips" had been uncrated and reassembled, and in a month's time would be set up on their exhibition site in the hall. Designers were fashioning a miniature cliff, so that they could be displayed in something of their original setting. Sir Portman thought they would be the sensation of the entire show and congratulated the unfortunate Jordan on all he had done to secure them.

As for the mystery, he confessed himself as baffled as anyone else, but what did it really matter—the great thing was that they were available for display. Sir Portman had cabled the Duke immediately, but had a reply from his steward to say he had gone abroad for a protracted tour. He had then cabled again, asking for an examination to be made at the foot of the cliff at the *palazzo*. This cable had gone to one of the museum's agents in Palermo, a man who Jordan had originally contacted, and he had personally visited the site.

He had replied that the figures had disappeared, but there were boulders and crushed stone at the foot of the cliff, as though there had been a bad rock fall. Further inquiries at the Palermo docks had revealed that the crates had arrived for loading shortly after Jordan left for London.

The orders for the shipping of the consignment to London had never been cancelled. Jordan had been too upset to remember this, and no doubt the crated plinth had given the impression to the shippers that things were proceeding normally.

Records of the Italian shipping line engaged had confirmed afterward, continued Jordan, that the crates had arrived in the normal manner: local labor had brought them to the docks on large lorries. But the greater mystery remained.

Had it been possible, asked Sir Portman, for the Duke's agents to have reconstructed the figures in time for them to have been forwarded? It would have been a colossal task, but skilled savants from one of the Italian museums could have achieved this.

Jordan had to admit that it was barely possible, but the job would have taken months. He would like to examine the group himself, he said, when he felt up to it. Sir Portman, the antiquarian in him still intensely excited by the whole affair, and far more enthusiastic than Jordan ever felt likely to be again over this particular exhibit, said the whole surface of the group was cracked and pitted, and it could well have been pieced together from fragments. He felt the effect added to the *diablerie* of the group.

A few days later Jordan, quite recovered, visited the warehouse in the City where the group was being prepared. Despite his fears, the figures seemed quite normal, and no one who had been concerned in their erection had noticed anything untoward. Indeed, beneath the prosaic electric light, and in the close company of other groups of figures and statues from the same period, they seemed to have lost something of their diabolical quality. To Jordan's relief, after a close examination of the stone, he felt they could have been reassembled after fragmentation. The granite-like, brownish-stone from which they were carved was split and fissured from end to end—that was apparently a quality of it. But if the group had been reassembled—and it had to be, for no other theory would account for it—then the job had been done with tremendous cunning and skill.

What dark shadows hovered around the fringes of Jordan's mind, he no longer confided to Sir Portman. With the exhibition fast coming upon them, it would have done no good. So he kept his forebodings to himself, with the mental reservation that the responsibility was no longer his. The whole affair had been discussed in camera at a full meeting of Sir Portman's Committee, all distinguished men in their various fields, and they had decided to go ahead with this once-in-a-lifetime *coup*.

What mainly troubled Jordan still was that no one had yet heard anything from the Duke, though they had sent him at least three cables, asking for the messages to be forwarded. Also, further diligent inquiries both in Sicily and on the mainland of Italy had failed to unearth any more information on the reassembling of the figures, or who had given the orders for their crating and forwarding.

But as the weeks went by, and with the exhibition work mounting up, he found less and less time for his wilder imaginings and was content to leave the affair of "The Gossips" to more stolid spirits who had not accompanied him on the Sicilian expedition, and who knew nothing of their wild history.

No less than five of London's largest halls were to be utilized for this biggest exhibition of its kind ever staged in the capital, and almost a month beforehand the three female figures and their plinth were moved to their final position in one of the most prominent positions in the Steinway Hall.

This vast auditorium had been chosen for a number of reasons. The principal one was that it featured a huge balcony, supported by enormous iron trusses of Victorian manufacture, which together provided the tremendous strength necessary for the support of such a heavy group.

Engineers had calculated the stress and had told the exhibition organizers there was a large safety margin. The balcony railings were then dismantled, slabs of stone laid down, and eventually a most realistic artificial cliff was erected to give "The Gossips" the most impressive setting of the entire exhibition.

Skillful lighting, with sky effects at the rear, gave a day and night cycle of dawn, daylight, sunset, and night, which lasted twenty minutes and was destined to be a most memorable sight for the crowds who witnessed it.

Even Jordan, who viewed the progress of the work with understandable interest, had to admit that the effect was splendid. But for the lamentable tragedy of a month or two before, which he could not erase from his mind, it would have been a triumphant climax in his career. As it was, the matter brought many congratulations from distinguished colleagues, and he was the subject of a number of articles in the press.

Curiously enough, those pressmen and photographers who were given a preview a week before the exhibition opened to the public, though delighted, like the laymen, with the group's fantastic qualities, saw nothing extraordinary in it. Neither was there anything wrong with their photographs.

"But," said Jordan, looking at me with expressive eyes across the café table, "within six months after the exhibition, every single photograph or photographic block had faded and disappeared, even to the individual images in newspaper files.

"But by that time World War II had broken out, and people had other things to think about. The scientists had theories about the fading, too. They argued that dampness and storage conditions may have been responsible—as if that could have affected zinc and lead blocks, not to mention the countless thousands of newspaper file copies stored under dry, perfect conditions."

He was silent again for a moment, and the noise of the river a few yards away from our chairs appeared suddenly to intrude with its compelling murmur.

Grisson seemed to awake with a start from a trance-like pose— evidently he had been deeply stirred by Jordan's fantastic story.

However, all he said, in a mild voice, was, "My round, I think," and another tray of drinks presently appeared.

The night before the exhibition was due to be opened to the public, Arthur Jordan was invited to a celebration dinner by Sir Portman and the Exhibition Committee. This started at 7:00 p.m. and was attended by many distinguished guests. Later, a fleet of cars toured the five halls to view the exhibits. Everything went well, and those present enjoyed a memorable evening.

Some genius had thought up a selection of recordings of genuine medieval Sicilian folk-tunes as a background for "The Gossips" tableau, and when the day and night lighting cycle had finished, and the last quavering note died in the gallery, the large audience of invited guests broke into furious and spontaneous applause.

Arthur Jordan found himself, unwillingly, the center of all eyes, and his introduction was sought by many of these distinguished people. Some of their questions he found embarrassing in the extreme—the music in fact was out of period, but few of the guests seemed to realize this—and it was with gratitude that he was able to excuse himself, over an hour later, and sought a side-exit to make his way home.

He had to pass near the gallery in which the group of statues was exhibited, and as he made his way through the now empty, echoing building, someone began to extinguish the lights, one by one. His foot-steps sounded unnaturally loudly along the deserted stairs and corridors, and to Jordan's nerves, strained as they were by his recent experiences, the sounds were unpleasantly evocative.

Some light yet lingered in the galleries and he was descending a spiral staircase, whose metallic clangor gave back a somber echo from the gallery beyond, when he heard the sharp, staccato steps of a man in the gloom below him. He clung to the staircase, as the noise came nearer, and then saw a miniature flashlight bobbing uncertainly about beneath.

"Who's there?" he called out, in unnecessarily loud tones, clamping down a rising wave of hysteria.

The light swerved in an alarming manner, and then came toward him, picking him out on the staircase like an acrobat pinpointed in the spot lamp of a circus.

"Thank God it's you, sir."

With relief Jordan saw the uniform and peaked cap of one of the museum attendants.

"Hullo, Hoskins," he said. "Anything wrong?"

He had reached the ground floor by this time and was not prepared for the answer which came. In the dim light of the lamp Hoskins's face looked pale and strained.

"I can't help telling you, Mr. Jordan, I nearly lost my head when someone switched out the lights just now. I was up on top there, near those ugly big statues, and I heard the most horrible whispering coming from the gallery."

Jordan had started and put his hand on the other's arm.

"Let's find a light-switch before you go any further," he said, with all the strength of mind he could command. As light sprang out in the nearby galleries, he reflected that his face probably looked just as pallid and unnatural as the gallery attendant's. "Right, now . . ." he went on.

"Well," said Hoskins, switching off his lamp, his tones more normal as the atmosphere was restored to everyday. "I was on the Somme in the last war and I've seen some things in my time, but that whispering fair gave me the creeps. I thought someone had got in the gallery, or perhaps some of the guests were playing a joke, so I shone my flashlight up and went along to see what was up. Well, I didn't like it at all.

"To tell you the truth, I didn't dare go in among those statues. They were all in silhouette, and I know it sounds daft, but I could have sworn the faces were moving. I expect it was the effect of the shadow, God knows my hand was trembling enough. Anyway, I was just debating what to do when some fool put the main lights out. I couldn't face that, not in the darkness, sir, and I turned and ran."

"Quite understandable," said Jordan in a kindly manner, laying his hand on the other man's shoulder. "I don't mind telling you that I've had quite an experience with these statues myself, one way or another."

"Ah, of course, you brought 'em over, didn't you, sir, now I remember," said Hoskins, in evident relief. "So you know what I'm talking about."

"I do indeed, Hoskins," said Jordan. "I can assure you it's a mere aural trick, caused by natural draught and their clever method of construction."

He had decided to take this attitude, for the success of the exhibition meant a lot to him and the organizers, and he could not afford to let an attendant's panic—though how he sympathized with the poor devil!—prejudice the opening and spread a lot of dark rumors about.

"Let's go and have a look, shall we?" he continued to Hoskins, walking easily and naturally forward, though what this effort cost him, no one would ever know.

The attendant, his confidence restored, went back into the main hall with him and in the full light of the flood-lamps self-respect slowly oozed back.

The statues glared malevolently in the strong lighting, but the silence was absolute. For once, Jordan understood the meaning of the phrase "not a whisper," and he was profoundly thankful for it.

"You see, all well," he said, with what he felt was nonchalance in his voice, hoping to God that nothing untoward would occur. And after this brief inspection the pair moved off, Jordan to find his car and Hoskins to continue his round. As he drove off, Jordan looked in his mirror, and saw the lights in the great exhibition hall dying in the night, one by one.

V

I HAD BOUGHT another round of drinks, and the first infusion of late night theatre-goers and those coming out of cinemas had enlivened the terrace tables around us, before Jordan went on with the next part of his story. Though the chattering and the laughter from the nearer tables at first put him off his stride, I myself was glad to have this lively background to the somberness of the main tapestry, and while he said nothing, I felt Grisson was of the same mind.

The next incident was very simple and very terrible, and it must have come with an appalling effect on Jordan, being in possession of all the facts as he was. He was awakened the following morning by the relentless tones of his telephone bell, to find Sir Portman on the line. Had he seen the morning paper? Something unfortunate had happened at the Steinway Hall the previous evening. Jordan said he would come round to see Sir Portman at nine o'clock and rang off.

He hadn't asked his caller what the matter was, but it must be pretty serious to warrant such an early call. It was curious, too, that Sir Portman had not volunteered any information but had merely asked him to look at the paper. If Jordan expected sensational headlines on the front page, he was mistaken. He went for his *Daily Post* on the hall mat in trepidation, but it took him almost ten minutes to find the item.

It was a small piece on page three, under a single column heading which said: Gallery Attendant Dies in Fall. The text ran:

Albert Hoskins, 54, gallery attendant at the Steinway Hall, S.W., was found dead on the floor by a colleague early this morning, just a few hours before London's biggest-ever 17th century exhibition was due to begin. Mr. Hoskins, who had been employed by the Hall authorities for about seven years, had apparently slipped from an unfenced balcony containing the group of Sicilian statuary, "The Gossips." The accident had happened at about 12:30 a.m., a doctor's report established, and Mr. Hoskins had fallen head-first nearly twenty feet on to a newly-laid rocky area, representing a cliff face.

There was a bit more, but Jordan was too sick to read it. Hoskins had died—he hardly dared say to himself, had been killed—only about twenty minutes after his conversation with Jordan. He must have been on his way back through the gallery, after letting the latter out.

It was a trembling Jordan who downed a large whiskey—at breakfast of all times—and faced Sir Portman and the Exhibition Committee an hour or two later. They had braced themselves, in view of opening day, and though the accident was unfortunate, they had to repress any morbid thoughts when the first members of the public would be coming in through the turnstiles at 11:00 a.m.

Eventually, Jordan saw that it would be of little use to tell them of his talk with the gallery attendant. He did stress the desirability, though, of fencing the ledge on which the group rested, to prevent any repetition of the accident. The Committee saw his point, but were of the opinion that it would greatly reduce the effectiveness of the set-piece and place it on a level with something out of a public park. And in any case, no members of the public would be allowed on the ledge.

Jordan could not but agree with them, and went to his office to prepare for the opening, fervently praying that nothing further would happen to mar the long-awaited triumph. It was at this point that Grisson again entered the story. He had known Arthur Jordan for some years, and had followed the occasional newspaper stories of the exhibition with interest. It was when he learned that "The Gossips" were to be exhibited that he contacted Jordan, and the two men pooled their knowledge. Grisson did not at first reveal all that he knew, particularly of the unfortunate visit he and I had paid to the *palazzo* some years before, but he had said enough to make Jordan realize that here he had an expert and initiated ally.

So it was naturally to Grisson that he again turned in his current predicament. Fortunately, his colleague was in London for the express purpose of attending the exhibition, though he had been unable to be present at the preview the previous evening. He hadn't seen the newspaper item when Jordan phoned his hotel, but agreed to come round to the Steinway Hall at once.

He found Jordan in a very ragged state of nerves, which was hardly surprising. The two men spoke for an hour, and after a very full and frank comparison of notes, while realizing the strange and unnatural nature of "The Gossips," neither of them felt justified in interfering with the course of the exhibition.

Hoskins's death could have been an accident, and who would have believed such a story? Certainly not the Exhibition Committee, or any other person in his right mind. With their special knowledge, and particularly Arthur Jordan's agonizing responsibility as the person who had secured the statues for London and as a principal organizer of the exhibition, the two men could only agree to act together and keep a keen supervisory eye on things.

In the event, it was agreed that whenever possible, one or other of the two men would be on duty in the gallery. At the first sign of any out-of-the-way manifestations, that part of the gallery would be closed. As a double precaution, Sir Portman was persuaded to have the immediate area at the foot of the simulated cliff roped off, to prevent any spectators from crowding underneath during the performances. With this much achieved, the two men felt they had done all that was humanly possible to prevent any further tragedy.

As if to reinforce this view, the exhibition was a tremendous success—certainly, beyond anything that the organizers could have suspected. People in the thousands flocked to the five halls every day, and for every one who had heard of the death of the gallery attendant, there were at least five hundred who hadn't. Even Jordan's wan face relaxed, and Sir Portman's features expanded like a sunrise in the blaze of publicity which surrounded such an unusual exhibition.

As was to be expected, "The Gossips" tableau was the biggest single "draw" at the Steinway Hall and extra performances had to be laid on every day, so many people wanted to see the dawn and sunset effects.

Press and radio were no less enthusiastic, and the first week saw both record crowds and record profits for the various antiquarian funds to which the exhibition was devoted.

But it was on the Saturday night that the incident occurred which provided the last shock for the harassed Jordan, caused a furore and agitated speculation in the press, and was finally responsible for the partial closure of the exhibition at Steinway Hall. No one could be blamed for what occurred, really. The last performance of the sky effects around the statuary was taking place at about 10:00 p.m., prior to the exhibition closing for the night.

A large crowd gathered, had heard an exposition on their history from a distinguished professor, and Grisson, who was on duty, had taken the opportunity to slip out for a few minutes to the buffet for a sandwich and a cup of coffee. It was as the sunset effects were at their most splendid, that a rippled murmur made itself audible among the crowd, a murmur which rapidly changed to cries of horror. A middle-aged man was seen climbing over the rocky terrain around the base of the statues. He was reeling about as though drunk, and as the helpless crowd watched, horrified, he stepped forward and plunged from the edge of the platform upon the rocks beneath.

Spectators rushed to his assistance and a doctor was soon on the scene, but the man had broken his neck and died a few minutes afterward. There was no rational explanation. He was a retired tailor, named Matthews, who lived at Streatham. Of impeccable antecedents and habits, he most certainly had not been drunk. No attendants had seen him approach any parts of the building closed to the general public, and the doors leading to the terrace on which the statues were situated were locked, as was the custom.

This time the morning papers took a lot of notice, and after a hurried conference of his Committee the next day, Sir Portman and his colleagues decided to close down the gallery and make arrangements to ship back the statues to their place of origin. Although the Committee members were far from believing that the two deaths, coming so closely, were anything more than unconnected accidents, the information Grisson and Jordan were able to give them produced some raised eyebrows and blown cheeks in the committee room.

The fact that an inquest would also have to be held tipped the scales. Reluctant as they were to lose such a fine asset as "The Gossips" for the exhibition, they simply could not afford any more adverse publicity. Jordan—and to a lesser extent, Grisson—was relieved at the Committee's decision. The malevolent group was removed from the Steinway Hall, while that portion of the gallery remained closed for a couple of days.

The statues were then crated to await transport to the docks, and a further cable was sent to the Duke. This, too, remained unanswered.

Jordan remained silent for a moment, as he reached this point in his story. He fumbled in his wallet and eventually produced an envelope which contained some scraps of faded newspaper clippings. He selected one of these, and passed it over to me. It merely said that while the S.S. *Janine* was loading at London Docks, Albert Williams, docker, thirty-five, was crushed to death between a crate and the ship's side. I looked up at Arthur Jordan.

"This time the press hadn't done all their homework," he said. "The crate contained one of the statues, of course, but fortunately that didn't get out. Again, no one could prove that it was anything other than an accident."

He had informed Sir Portman of the latest incident, as the exhibition went on from triumph to triumph, and the Chairman had remarked succinctly that the Sicilians were welcome to the statues. The next development was almost the most curious of all. Jordan had eventually received a letter from the Duke, apologizing for his absence from home during the arrival of the various cables.

He went elaborately around the ground, and without actually admitting that the statues had been broken, he did go so far as to say that the estate workers had done their best to ensure that the statuary would be in condition for presentation at the exhibition. He expressed regret at the London incidents, and acknowledged receipt of the messages regarding the shipment.

The letter covered a mere two pages of flowing handwriting, and left Jordan more puzzled and disgruntled than ever. He showed the documents to Sir Portman, who was equally mystified at the contents. But the matter didn't seem worth following up and was gradually dropped.

Three weeks later, Jordan happened to pick up a newspaper dated two or three days earlier, and his attention was arrested by a small paragraph on the front page. This he passed to me to read also.

It was only about six lines and said that the Italian steamship *Janine*, of so many thousand tons, had foundered in a terrific storm in the Gulf of Lions, and had been lost with all cargo. There were no casualties among the crew, who had been landed at Marseilles by a Swedish freighter, which had picked them up.

Even then, it was not quite the end of the story. Jordan smiled quizzically, as he looked back over his experiences with those cursed stones. The biggest surprise of all came at the end. Jordan was engaged in the clearing up of the exhibition, after its closure, when he received another telegram from the Duke. This merely acknowledged receipt of the crated statues at Palermo, in good order, and thanked him for his cooperation.

This time Jordan showed the cable to no one except Grisson. The two met in an obscure London pub and thrashed the thing out between them. Wild horses would not have dragged either of them back to that haunted bluff in Sicily, if they had the time or the money, but they just had to know what had happened to those crates.

Jordan went as far as to search the records at Lloyds. It was true that the *Janine* had foundered: all cargo had been lost and Lloyds made full settlement. It was not possible that four crates containing tons of stone could have been washed hundreds of miles farther south. After debating a while longer, Jordan cabled his agent in Palermo and asked him to inspect the site again. A fortnight later, he received a letter from the agent to say that the statues were once more *in situ* on the bluff in the Duke's *palazzo* gardens. So far as the man could make out with field glasses, they appeared as they were before the accident.

Even then Jordan did not quite give up. In the hope that there might be some more rational explanation, he again wrote to the Duke, asking him, as a matter of urgency, for the full details to which he felt entitled.

In reply he did get a long letter this time, and after he had read it, he wished, for his own peace of mind, that the Duke hadn't been quite so loquacious. Some of the information Grisson had already told me earlier in the evening, but much was for Jordan's ear only, and he was asked to burn the letter after he had read it.

Regarding the reappearance of "The Gossips," the Duke had written, in what appeared to be a frantically scrawled hand, *there is no explanation; think what you will, but do not ask for one.* His text had then gone into Sicilian. This, Jordan had translated by a colleague at his museum.

"It was something on the lines of the old English saw about the female of the species being more deadly," he said to me, with an apologetic smile.

The Duke did reveal that his own grandfather had been skeptical of the legend, and had actually started to have a smaller wall, which then existed to separate the statues from the house, taken down. No one knew exactly what happened, but he had such a bad fright one evening that the young man, as he then was, had the larger wall erected as I had seen it on the occasion of my memorable visit.

Jordan stopped again, and played a little tune on the marble-topped table with the handle of his coffee spoon.

"That wasn't what frightened us in the garden," he said, with a sort of slow defiance. "I'd been pretty steady-nerved until then."

"He's saving the best till last, like all good storytellers," said Grisson, in a vain attempt to lighten the atmosphere. The café lights were beginning to go out along the Arno, though a few lamps still reflected back its brilliant surface.

"You see," said Jordan with a deep sigh. "The explanation was in the nature of the statues. Caravallo's masterpiece had been created from life."

From the shattered horror of the stonework in the garden, after the accident to the lift, had poured the raw materials on which he had based his devilish art—mingled with the brownish-red basaltic stone were the teeth, bones, and hair of three young girls.

IN THE FOURTH YEAR
OF THE WAR

HARLAN ELLISON®

Harlan Ellison (1934–2018) won the Hugo Award eight-and-a-half times, the Nebula Award four times, the Bram Stoker Award five times (including Lifetime Achievement in 1996), and the Mystery Writers of America Edgar Allan Poe Award twice.

He was also the recipient of the Silver Pen for Journalism by International P.E.N., the World Fantasy Award, the Georges Méliès fantasy film award, an unprecedented four Writers Guild of America awards for Most Outstanding Teleplay, and the International Horror Guild's Living Legend Award. In 2006, he was made a Grand Master by the Science Fiction and Fantasy Writers of America (SFWA).

Ellison moved to New York in his early twenties to pursue a writing career, and over the next two years he published more than one hundred stories and articles. Relocating to California in 1962, he began selling to Hollywood, coscripting the 1966 movie *The Oscar* and contributing two dozen scripts to such shows as *Star Trek*, *The Outer Limits*, *The Man from U.N.C.L.E.*, *The Alfred*

Hitchcock Hour, Cimarron Strip, Route 66, Burke's Law, and *The Flying Nun*. His story "A Boy and His Dog" was filmed in 1975, starring Don Johnson, and he was a creative consultant on the 1980s revival of *The Twilight Zone* TV series.

His books include *Rumble* (aka *Web of the City*), *Rockabilly* (aka *Spider Kiss*), *All the Lies That Are My Life*, and *Mefisto in Onyx*, while some of his almost two thousand short stories have been collected in *The Juvies* (aka *Children of the Street*), *Ellison Wonderland, Paingod and Other Delusions, I Have No Mouth and I Must Scream, Love Ain't Nothing But Sex Misspelled, The Beast That Shouted Love at the Heart of the World, Deathbird Stories, Strange Wine, Shatterday, Stalking the Nightmare, Angry Candy, Slippage*, and *The Essential Ellison: A 50-Year Retrospective* edited by Terry Dowling.

Ellison also edited the influential science fiction anthology *Dangerous Visions* in 1967, and followed it with a sequel, *Again Dangerous Visions*, in 1972.

More recently, he was the subject of Erik Nelson's revelatory feature-length documentary *Dreams with Sharp Teeth* (2008), chronicling the author's life and work, which was made over a period of twenty-seven years.

"When I was a very little boy in Painesville, Ohio, at age five" recalled Ellison, "a woman who lived up the street had my dog, Puddles, picked up by the dog-catcher and gassed while I was away at summer camp. I've never forgotten her. I think I hate her as much today, almost eighty years after the fact, as I did the day I came back from camp and my father took me in his arms and explained that Puddles was dead. That old woman is no doubt long gone, but hate lives on.

"Each of us moves through life shadowed by childhood memories. We never forget. We are bent and shaped and changed by those ancient fears and hatreds. They are the mortal dreads that in a million small ways block us off or drive us toward our destiny.

"Is it impossible to realize that those memories are merely the dead, ineffectual past; that they need not chain us?

"A fine writer named Meyer Levin once wrote, 'Three evils plague the writer's world: suppression, plagiarism, and falsification.'

"The first two are obvious. They are monstrous and must be fought at whatever cost, wherever they surface.

"The last is more insidious. It makes writers lie in their work. Not because they want to, but because the truth is so terribly clouded by insubstantial wraiths, personal traumas, the detritus of adolescent impressions. Who amongst us can deny that within every adult is caged a frightened child?

"This is a horror story. It speaks to the death of my father.

"There are no ghosts or slimy monsters or antichrist omens. At least none that can physically reach out and muss the hair. The horrors are the ones we create for ourselves; and they are the ones we all share.

"This is also a cautionary tale, intended to say 'You are not alone.' We all carry the past with us like the chambered nautilus; and we all must find ways to exorcise it at peril of our destiny."

> The King grew vain;
> Fought all his battles o'er again;
> And thrice he routed all his foes,
> And thrice he slew the slain.

> —JOHN DRYDEN, *ALEXANDER'S FEAST* (1697)

IN THE FOURTH year of the war with the despicable personage that had come to live in my brain, the utterly vile tenant who called himself Jerry Olander, I was ordered to kill for the first time.

It came as no surprise. It had taken Jerry Olander four years, plus or minus a couple of months, to get sufficient control over my motor responses. He had been working toward just such a program of monstrous actions, and though I never knew till the moment he ordered the hit that the form of his evil was to be murder, that was one of the few possibilities. Even though I wasn't surprised, I was sickened, and refused. It didn't do me any good, of course. Jerry was strong enough after four years of constant warfare within my brain; I was just weak enough, weary enough, just enough filled with battle fatigue, to put up a losing argument.

The target was to be my mother's older brother, my Uncle Carl. Had Jerry Olander suggested the Pope, or the President of the United States, or some notorious public figure, I might have grasped a thin edge of rationality in the order. But Uncle Carl? A man in his late sixties, a retired jeweler whose wife had died of cancer fifteen years earlier, who lived quietly and inoffensively in a suburb of Chicago. Carl? Why should the unwanted roommate of my brain want to see old Uncle Carl dead?

"Don't *you* want to see him dead?" Jerry replied, when I put the question to him.

"Who, Carl?" I didn't mean to sound stupid; but I was nonplussed; and sounded stupid.

Jerry laughed. I had come to know that miserable sound. In the dead of night, when I was hovering on the lip between wakefulness and whatever was strobing across the face of my bedside television set, and the abyss of thankful sleep, he would begin laughing. It was the sound I'm certain was made when the broken-handled claw hammer wrenched out the rusty spikes from Jesus's crucified wrists.

He laughed that rusty laugh and mimicked me. "Who, Carl? Yes, Carl. Old Uncle Carl, who killed your father's dreams. Don't begin to tell me, don't even *begin* to tell me that you've forgotten all that, chum."

"Don't call me chum."

"Well, then, using the short form: yes, Uncle Carl."

"You're crazy. I can't do it . . . *won't* do it!"

"Oh, you'll *do it*, all right. We have no problem on that score. As for my being crazy, I won't argue the point. One would have to be a bit crazy to share a mind with you."

"Carl never did anything to my father," I said.

"Think about it," Jerry said. I hated his smugness.

But I thought about it. And from the quicklime pit of forgotten memories something dead but still moving rose from corruption and dragged itself into my consciousness. A zombie recollection, a foulness from childhood, half-understood, miserable, something that intellectually I knew was a lie, yet a thing I believed true with that trapped child's refusal to abandon the terrors of the past.

Jerry laughed. "Yeah, that's it, chum. Remember now?"

"That isn't true. I know it isn't. I only thought that was the way it was . . . because I was a kid. I didn't know any better."

"Nobody's evil, right? No black and white. Just a shitload world of grays. Right? Then how come you still believe it?" He was really gnawing at me now. I tried to send that shambling awfulness back to its quicklime grave, but it stalked through my mind, led forward by Jerry's voice. "Look at it, chum. Consider Uncle Carl and what he did to your old man."

The memory grew larger in my mind. I found myself unable to turn away from its rotted flesh and stinking breath, the dead eyes covered with a gray film. I found myself remembering my father . . .

He had managed Carl's jewelry store during the war, when Carl had gone off to the navy. My father had been too old, had had a heart condition; so he had worked in the store instead of serving. Carl had pulled strings and wound up on the West Coast, at one of the supply terminals. And my father had worked twelve, fifteen, eighteen hours a day building up the clientele. He had always wanted his own store, to be in business for himself, to go to Tucson or San Francisco, a warm and wonderful place away from the snow and the biting Lake Michigan winds. But my mother had insisted that family was more important than self-realization. "Stay with family," she had said. "Carl told you he'd make you a partner. The family always keeps its promises."

So my father had let his dreams fade, and had stayed on with the store.

When the war was over, and Carl came home, and my father finally summoned up the courage to call in the promise, Carl had thrown him out of the store.

I never knew why, really. I was a child. Children are never told the whys of family disasters. They just happen. You wouldn't understand, children are told; and then, in the next breath, they are told, You mustn't hate your Uncle Carl for this, he has his reasons.

But my father had to start all over again. At the age of fifty. He rented a small apartment on the second floor in a business district close to the Loop, and he opened a jewelry shop. It was two long flights up, one steep set of stairs, a landing, and a switchback flight half as long but just as steep. And the drive from Evanston, back and forth, each day. Working far into the evening to catch the late foot traffic; on the phone with customers, trying to hustle an extra sale, even at night when he was home and should have been relaxing. A grinding, terrible schedule without break or release, to keep my mother and myself fed and clothed, not to lose the house.

One year. He lasted one year, almost to the week of opening the new store. And on a Sunday morning, sitting in his big chair by the old

Philco radio, he had a sudden smash of a coronary thrombosis and he died. In a moment, as I watched, he went pale and his eyes popped open so I could see how blue they were, and his mouth drooped at one side, and he died. He had no last words.

The zombie memory would not free me. I saw things I never could have imagined as a child. My father's blue eyes, with the realization in them that all the dreams had been stolen from him, that he had lived his life and it had come to nothing, that he was dead and had never made his mark, had been here and was gone, and no one would remember or care. I saw, I remembered, I cared.

My child's memories were of hatred, and revenge. Carl.

"My father did it to himself," I said, walking upstairs. "He allowed his dreams to die. If he'd really had the courage to break loose and go to the Coast he would have done it," I said, entering my bedroom and going to the closet. "Carl had nothing to do with it. If it hadn't been Carl, it would have been someone else in whom my father placed his trust. I can't hate a man for not keeping a promise twenty-five years ago," I said, pulling down my overnight case. "This is crazy. You can't get me to do this." I began packing for the flight to Chicago. I heard the sound of spikes being twisted out of wormwood.

It took Carl a long time to answer the door. He had a serious arthritic condition, and it was late. Highland Park was silent and sleeping. I stood under the porch light and saw Carl's pale, tired eyes peering at me through the open-weave curtain behind the door's glass panes. He blinked many times, and finally seemed to recognize me. He opened the door.

"You didn't tell me you were coming," he said. I put my hand against the half-opened door and pushed it slowly inward. Carl moved back and

I walked in. My overnight case was still lying on the back seat of the rental compact at the curb. "Why didn't you call me and tell me you were coming? How's your mother?"

"Mom died three years ago."

He blinked again. His liver-spotted forehead drew down and he thought about it. "Yes. I'd forgotten. Why didn't you call me up on the phone and tell me you were coming?"

He closed and locked the door behind me. I walked into the darkened living room, only faintly outlined by the hall light. He followed me. He was wearing something I had seen only in period movies, a long night-gown that reached to his thin calves, white with blue veins prominent. The fabric was rough cotton, and like his calves was veined with blue pinstriping. I turned around to look at him. In my head I said, "This is crazy. Look at him. He's an old man. He won't even remember. What's the point of this?"

And Jerry Olander said, "It doesn't matter if *he* doesn't remember. *You* remember. But if it makes you feel any better, tell him why you've come to kill him."

"What are you doing here in the dead of night, I wish you'd called me up on the phone and told me," Carl said.

I couldn't see his face. He was standing with the hall light behind him. It was a black circle without feature. I said to him, "Do you remember a night a long time ago, in the red brick house you had on Maple Street, when Lillian was alive?"

"I remember the house. It was a small house. We had much bigger houses. Maybe you called and I was asleep."

I moved toward him till he could see *my* face, lit along the sharp planes of cheeks and nose by the light over his shoulder. "I see it all now the way a little boy would see it, Uncle Carl. I'm looking out from under a dining room table, through the legs and cross-braces of chairs,

262 / *Harlan Ellison*

watching you and my father on the screened back porch. You're arguing. It was the first time I ever heard my father swear or raise his voice. I remember it very clearly, even if it isn't true, because he was such a quiet person. You know that. He never raised his voice or got angry. He should have. He might not have died when he did, or died so miserably, if he'd raised his voice a few times."

"What are you talking about?" Carl said. He was beginning to realize he wanted to be annoyed at his nephew barging in on him at three o'clock in the morning while he was still half-asleep. "Do you want something to eat? What are you doing here in Chicago? Don't you live out there in California now?"

He hadn't seen me in years. We had no contact. And here I stood before him, dragging him back through the dead years to a night he didn't even remember. "Then you stood up and yelled at him, and he pushed back his chair till it fell over, and he yelled at you, and then you swung at him, and he hit you with a cushion off one of the chairs. And the next day he didn't go down at seven-thirty to open the store while you stayed in and slept late and had a nice breakfast with Lillian. Do you remember all that, Uncle Carl?"

"Lillian is dead. She's been gone a long time."

I walked to the sofa and looked down. Then I walked back to him and took him by the arm. He resisted for a moment, but he was very old, and I wasn't, and he came with me to the sofa, and I forced him to sit down. Then I took the pillow with the fringe, and I held it in one hand as I shoved him down, and held it over his face while he thrust himself up against it, until he stopped. It was over much more quickly than I'd thought. I'd always thought people struggle much harder to cling to life. But he was old, and his memories were gone.

And all the while I was begging Jerry Olander to stop. But he had spent four full years of wresting control from me, and in those four years of the war I had come to know he would win a battle or two. This was the first battle. And he had won. "Very efficient," Jerry Olander said.

In the fourth year of the war with the homicidal maniac that had come to nest in my brain, a second hit was ordered. A woman I wasn't even certain was still alive. She had had my dog gassed, *put to sleep* as they tell it to children, one summer when I was away at camp. Her name was Mrs. Corley, and she had lived down at the end of our street in Evanston.

I argued with Jerry Olander. "Why did you pick me to live in?" I had asked that question surely more than a hundred and fifty thousand times in four years.

"No particular reason. You haven't got a wife, or many friends. You work at home most of the time—though I still can't see how you make any kind of a living with that mail order catalog—and nobody's going to put you away too quickly because you talk to yourself."

"Who *are* you?" I screamed, because I couldn't get him out of me. He was like the eardrums refusing to pop when a plane lands. I couldn't break his hold on me, no matter how hard I swallowed or held my nose and blew.

"The name is Jerry Olander," he said, lightly, adding in an uncannily accurate imitation of Bogart, "and somebody's always gotta take the fall, shweetheart."

Then he made me go to the main branch of the public library, to look at all the telephone books. He didn't have control of my vocal cords, couldn't make my brain call the 312-555-1212 information operator in Chicago, to establish if Mrs. Corley still lived in Evanston. But he *could* make my legs carry me to my car, make my hands place themselves at 11:50 and 12:05 on the steering wheel, make my eyes run down the columns of names and phone numbers in the Evanston telephone directory in the library's stacks.

She lived in the same house, at the same address, in the same world I had shared with her as a child.

Jerry Olander made my body drive to the savings and loan where I had my small account, made my right hand ink in the withdrawal slip, made my mouth smile as the teller handed me my last five hundred dollars.

And Jerry Olander made me tape the basement window of Mrs. Corley's house before I broke it with a rock. Fighting him every step of the way, I was nonetheless made to walk silently through the basement to the steps, was made to climb them to the kitchen where I found old Mrs. Corley fixing herself a vegetarian dinner, and was made to tie and gag her.

But when I refused to go farther, Jerry Olander's voice played Pied Piper to the living dead in the quicklime pit of memory, and another shambling, rotted thing dragged itself up onto the landscape of my mind, and I saw myself as a child, coming home from a ghastly month at some nameless summer camp. And, of course, the name was right there, unremembered for thirty years, just as fresh as if I had come home yesterday. Camp Bellefaire. On Lake Belle. I had hated it, had pleaded with my mother and father every Sunday when they had come to visit me—like seeing a Death Row resident during visitation hours—"Please take me home, Momma, Poppa, *please,* I don't like it here!" But they had never understood that there are some children for whom organized activities in which they can *never* distinguish themselves is a special sort of debasement.

And I had come home gladly, to see Charlie, my dog; to move around freely in my room with the Erector set and the comic books and my very own radio; to build Stukas and Lightnings and Grumman seaplanes, and smell TesTor's cement once again.

And Charlie was dead. "Do you remember that summer, Mrs. Corley?" I heard myself saying, and Jerry Olander wasn't making me say it. "Do you remember how you told the man at the pound that the dog was running loose for a week? Do you remember how you found Charlie's tags caught on your bush in the backyard, and didn't turn them in? I remember, Mrs. Corley, because you told Mrs. Abrams next door, and she told my Momma, and I overheard my Momma telling my Poppa. You knew who Charlie belonged to, Mrs. Corley; he'd lived here for ten years, so you *had* to know."

And then I pushed Mrs. Corley to her knees, and turned on all four jets of the gas range, and opened the oven and put her head inside while she struggled, and hit her once sharply behind the left ear, and laid her head down on the open door of the oven, left her kneeling there in prayer, final prayer, ultimate prayer . . . and went away.

"I liked the part about the dog tags best," Jerry Olander said, on the plane back to California.

In the fourth year of the war with that evil intelligence in my brain, I was ordered to kill, and *did* kill, seven people, including my Uncle Carl and old Mrs. Corley. And each one made me sick to think about it. I had no idea if Jerry Olander was merely the product of my own mind, a sick and twisted, deranged and malevolent phantom of a personality that had finally split, or if he was a disembodied spirit, an astral projection, a *dybbuk* or poltergeist or alien from the center of the Earth that had come to wreak murder on the race of humans, using me as his unwitting tool. I have seen enough motion pictures, read enough mystery stories, seen enough television programs in which a man's evil nature takes him over, to know that is the most rational answer.

There is no reason to believe me, but I *swear*, Jerry Olander never came from within me. He was from outside, a rejected thing. And he inhabited me without my consent. It had been war, and he had won battle after battle, and I knew if those killings were ever traced to me I would spend the rest of my life in a home for the criminally insane . . . but further than saying, as quietly and as miserably as I can . . . I was not Jerry Olander . . . what can I say to convince . . .

And finally, it came the time I had known would arrive, from the moment he ordered the death of my Uncle Carl.

Jerry Olander said to me, as the fourth year of the war drew to an end, "Now it's time to kill Nancy."

"No!" I screamed. "No. I won't do it. I'll kill myself first. You can't make me, there's no way you can make me, I'll fight you, you're not going to make me do *that!*"

Nancy was my ex-wife. She had left me, but there wasn't the faintest vestige of bad feeling in me about it. She had made her reasons for wanting a divorce plain to me, and they were good and sound reasons. We had been married when we were too young to know better, and through the years we had loved each other. But Nancy had learned she was more than a wife, that she had never been provided the opportunity to know herself, to expand herself, to fulfil the dreams she had had. And we had parted with love.

Now she lived in Pasadena, working with an orthopedic shoe company that had designed a special footgear for those who suffered with Hansen's disease. Her life was full, she was responsible and settled, mature and wonderful. We talked from time to time, occasionally had dinner together.

I meant her no harm.

"There's no sense to this!" I said, pleading with Jerry Olander. "There's no sense to any of this. Please let me alone, let me kill myself if that'll give you some satisfaction! But don't try to make me do this!"

"It all makes sense," he said, getting nastily quiet. "Everything you do is colored by those memories. How many nights have you lain awake in pain from a toothache, rather than going to a dentist because the family sent you to Cousin Franklyn to save a few dollars on dental bills? How many of your teeth that might have been saved did he pull because he was no damned good, should have been a butcher instead of a dentist? You're afraid of dentists to this day because of Cousin Franklyn. And how many women who might have loved you have you walked away from, picked fights with, ignored, considered better or worse than you, not your 'type,' because of Peggy Mantle and the way she laughed at you when you were fifteen? How many times have you walked past a store where you needed to buy something, because you remembered the way old man Clareborne threw you out of his department store when you were a little boy? How much of what you think is free will is just a programmed reaction to things you've buried, memories you don't want to remember, pains and slights and affronts you suffered as a child? How many, chum? How goddam many? Oh, there's sense here!"

Jerry Olander had me walk across the room. To the telephone. "But I'm all alone now. I have no one. No wife, no children, no mother, no father, not even too many people I can call friends. I'm all alone; won't you leave me Nancy!"

I began to dial a number.

The phone began to ring.

"You're not alone, chum," Jerry Olander said softly. "I'm right here with you. And I've got a long, long memory."

The receiver was picked up at the other end and a voice said, "Hello."

Zombie things from the quicklime pit began emerging, one after another of them; dozens of them, summoned by Jerry Olander's long, long memory. I wanted to shout, to make a terrible dying sound, to clarion a warning, and found I could not even do that. In the fourth year of our war, Jerry Olander had even gained control of my words, and I had lost, I had lost, I had lost!

"Hi, Nancy," I heard myself saying, "what are you doing for dinner tonight?"

> Life is too short to occupy oneself with the slaying
> of the slain more than once.
>
> —THOMAS HENRY HUXLEY, CIRCA 1861

INVASION FROM INFERNO

HUGH B. CAVE

Time for some pulp thrills. Hugh Barnett Cave (1910–2014) had the distinction of having been one of the original authors published in Christine Campbell Thompson's Not at Night series, with stories in *Keep on the Light*, *Terror By Night*, and *The "Not at Night" Omnibus*.

Born in Chester, England, he emigrated with his family to America when he was five. From the late 1920s onward Cave's stories began appearing in such legendary pulp magazines as *Weird Tales*, *Strange Tales*, *Ghost Stories*, *Black Book Detective Magazine*, *Spicy Mystery Stories*, and the infamous "weird menace" or "shudder pulps," *Horror Stories* and *Terror Tales*.

After leaving the horror field in the early 1940s for almost three decades, a volume of the author's best horror tales, *Murgunstrumm and Others*, was published by Karl Edward Wagner in 1977. Cave subsequently returned to the genre with new stories and a string of modern horror novels: *Legion of the Dead*, *The Nebulon Horror*, *The Evil*, *Shades of Evil*, *Disciples of Dread*, *The Lower Deep*, *Lucifer's Eye*, *Isle of the Whisperers*, *The Dawning*, *The Evil Returns*, and *The Restless Dead*. His short stories were also collected in a number of volumes, including *The Corpse Maker, Death Stalks the Night, The Dagger of Tsiang, Long Live the Dead: Tales from Black Mask, Come Into My Parlor, The Door Below*, and *Bottled in Blonde*. Milt Thomas's biography, *Cave of a Thousand Tales: The Life & Times of Hugh B. Cave*, was published by Arkham House a week after the author's death.

During his lifetime, Cave received Life Achievement Awards from the Horror Writers Association, the International Horror Guild, and the World Fantasy Convention. He was also presented with the Special Convention Award at the 1997 World Fantasy gathering in London, where he was a Special Guest of Honor.

"I long ago lost most of my pulp stories in a fire," he lamented. "A few years back, a friend urged me to try finding copies of them, and helped me in many ways to do so.

"As these stories arrived in the mail, my wife Peggy and I read them aloud to each other at bedtime and rated them from 1 to 10. I have her comment attached to my file-copy of the story: *'Invasion from Inferno' is one of the best shudder stories you've written. It's exciting, different, and full of surprises. Definitely a 10!*"

I: THE SPIDER WOMAN

THE LITTLE GIRL'S mouth opened and her brown eyes filled with terror. On her knees beside the berry bush, she leaned backward with a convulsive jerk and upset her pail of picked berries.

"Spiders!" she screamed. "*Spiders!* Oh-h-h-h, help, help!"

She was alone in the forest clearing, and the shadows of gathering dusk had crept in upon her without her knowing it. Screaming wildly, she staggered to her feet and looked frantically for the road. Weak from fright, she ran toward it.

"HERS WAS A HORRIBLE SORT OF BEAUTY."

She had been told not to go into the woods. She had been told about the spiders, and how they might devour her. And now . . .

Now the clearing seemed to be wriggling after her like some huge, hungry monster. The woods were alive with crawling things. The child's shrieks had no effect whatever on the living wave of red horror that pursued her. She tripped, fell flat on her face. The undulating wave caught up to her and slithered over her. Her last scream was like a siren wail wandering out over the purple countryside.

Andy Gale heard the screams and slammed his foot down on the brake-pedal. The car stopped with a spine-jarring jerk and he flung himself out of it, stood staring, doubting his senses. Then he rushed forward.

A wall of trees and heavy underbrush blinded him to the horror until he was in the midst of it. He could have whirled then and raced back to the road, could have fled before the things attacked him. But he saw the child lying there and heard her ghastly sobs.

A sea of red death rolled over her. Hundreds of tiny red horrors were fighting among themselves for possession of her body.

Gale stumbled forward and ground the hideous creatures under his feet, staining the earth red with their mangled bodies. He beat at them with his hands, then tore off his coat and swung it as he advanced. Horror iced his blood and swelled in his brain, but he fought his way to the girl's side and pulled her to her feet.

"God!" he groaned.

The spiders were like a thick red blanket enveloping her. They were in her hair. They covered her little arms and legs and were under her dress, swarming over her flesh. They were feeding!

He wiped them off with frantic sweeps of his hands, as the little girl clung to him and cried her heart out. He kicked them aside as they rushed forward to climb her trembling body. Lifting her in his arms, he staggered back toward the road.

Twice he had to stop, because the awful things leaped upon him from every scraping bush. They attacked his eyes, and he fell to his knees, clawing at his face with his free hand. It was impossible to fight so many of them. For everyone he killed, there were hundreds more rushing to attack!

On fire with pain, he reached the car and dropped his limp burden on the seat, flung himself behind the wheel. The machine roared ahead. The little girl had stopped moaning.

Half a mile down the road, Gale braked the car and bent over the child. Some of the things were still crawling on her dress and in her hair. He plucked them off and killed them, and killed others that were wriggling over the upholstery.

They were tiny, eight-legged creatures with crab-like legs. Prickly, spine-like clusters of hair grew out of their potato-bug bodies. "Red spider" was the common name for them. Hideous little things, non-poisonous, but capable of breeding with frightful rapidity, they were notorious in the farm-belt for the depredations they committed.

The little girl had regained consciousness and dazedly watched him as he worked over her. Suffering from shock, she moaned timidly:

"Who—who are you? Do—do you live—near here?"

"I'm Andy Gale," he said. "I'm on my way to visit Nicklus Brukner."

The little girl nodded weakly. Like a person coming out of ether, she seemed to be struggling to orient herself, and the pain of her wounds would not let her. She badly needed medical attention, but first Gale had to make sure no more of those voracious little red devils were feeding on her.

"Nicklus Brukner," she whispered, "lives in the next house. At the foot of the hill. Why—why are you going there?"

"I'm going there," Gale said, "to marry Miss Reid, the schoolteacher. She's my sweetheart."

His casual words, instead of soothing her, produced an effect startlingly opposite! The child cringed as if he had struck her. Her small body trembling violently, she gazed at him with terrified eyes.

"You—you're the *Spider Woman's* sweetheart?" she sobbed. "Then you're as wicked as she is! Let me go! Oh, please let me go! I'm afraid!" Amazement put a scowl on Gale's face as he leaned toward her. The Spider Woman's sweetheart? In God's name what was the child talking about? In her terror, she struck at him, and the exertion was too much for her. She slumped down in the seat . . .

With the unconscious girl in his arms, Andy Gale climbed the weather-worn steps of Nicklus Brukner's enormous house and rang the bell. It was an old, rambling house, flanked by acres of drought-seared farmland. It looked mean and dismal. He wondered how Arachne had stood it all these months.

Even while teaching school she must have hated to board here. And since the end of the school term she had been patiently waiting here for him to get his vacation and take her away. The door opened and a thick-set, bearded man glared out at him.

"What you want?"

"I'm a friend of Miss Reid's," Gale said quickly. "This child is hurt."

The man, Gale knew, was Nicklus Brukner. Arachne had described him in her letters as being an ugly, morose individual with a violent temper, and the description seemed to fit. Hunching closer, Brukner peered into the child's face.

"Bring her in!"

Gale trailed him into a musty, shadow-ridden parlor and placed the girl on a divan. He knew how she must be suffering, for he himself was on fire from the bites of the spiders. Non-poisonous the tiny spiders might be, but their bites were like the stings of wasps, driving agony through tortured flesh.

He started to explain what had happened, but Brukner had turned and was shouting harshly: "Fada! Fada! Come here quickly!"

Over the threshold came the girl who had promised to become Andy Gale's wife.

"Arachne!" He strode forward, took her in his arms. For a moment the child on the divan was forgotten, and he thought only of the months he had waited, of Arachne's wonderful letter saying she would marry him.

But she was trembling now. Her lips, whispering his name, were pale, and her wide eyes refused to look into his. Something was wrong.

"What is it, Arachne? Aren't you glad to see me?"

"Of course, Andy." And suddenly she saw the girl on the divan. "Why, it's little Hope Wiggin! She's hurt!"

"She was attacked by spiders," Gale muttered.

As if conjured up by his mention of the word, a strange, deformed creature came limping into the room. Involuntarily Gale fell back a step. This, he knew, was Fada, the crippled daughter of Nicklus Brukner.

The lame girl stopped short and rudely stared at him. He stared back. Horror and pity welled up inside him as he gazed at her thin, twisted legs, her humped body, her amazingly beautiful, sensuous face. How could any living thing be such a combination of ugliness and rare beauty?

"Spiders?" Fada said stiffly, limping to the divan. "Spiders, did you say? Let me look at her!"

Evidently she was accustomed to having her own way. Nicklus Brukner and Arachne stepped back to make room. No one spoke as the crippled girl went to her knees and pawed at the little girl's frail body.

A scowl twisted Andy's face. He remembered what the child had said to him in the car. *You—you're the Spider Woman's Sweetheart!* Evidently in her agony she had been confused, had really been thinking of the deformed Fada. Fada, kneeling there beside the divan, did resemble a spider. Her thin limbs and malshaped back created a frightening illusion.

Gale suddenly wanted to lurch forward and drag her away, but she was already laboriously rising to her feet. Staring straight at Arachne, the crippled girl said in a low, threatening voice: "The youngster is dead. The pain and shock have killed her. For this, my dear, the farmers will tear you into small, bloody bits, as you deserve! *Spider Woman!*"

Andy Gale gazed mutely at the girl he loved. For an instant he doubted that he had really heard those ghastly words hissing from Fada's lips. But he *had* heard them, and so had the others.

Arachne's face was as gray as the room's high ceiling. She fell back, pressing a hand to her breast. The crippled girl slowly advanced, then stopped and glared at Nicklus Brukner. "Take the child home," she snapped, "and tell the people what has happened!"

Brukner gathered the lifeless body in his arms and strode from the room. "Nothing can save you now," the crippled girl snarled at Arachne. "Not even your handsome lover!"

"Damn you, shut up!" Gale said angrily.

Fada's dark eyes threw hate at him as he thrust himself forward and put his hands on Arachne's shoulders. He could feel that hate eating into him, a tangible, chilling force that was somehow foul and unclean.

"Let's get out of here," he said to Arachne huskily.

The crippled girl threw a harsh, bitter laugh after them but made no attempt to interfere. Slamming the door, Gale led Arachne out to the front porch where the air seemed cooler, cleaner. There he forced her gently into a chair. "Now tell me what this is all about," he said.

She shuddered. Almost inaudibly she replied: "They're calling me the Spider Woman, Andy. They blame me for what's happened."

"Well, what *has* happened?"

"Flood River Valley is overrun with red spiders, whole armies of them. The horrible things have destroyed the crops and attacked livestock. The damage they've done is frightful. Now—now they are attacking human beings."

Gale stood still and stared at her. "And the people blame you?" he said, unbelievingly. "Why?"

"Red spiders are not native to this region, Andy. The farmers say *I* brought them here. My name—you know what my name means, and how I've always hated it."

Yes, he knew what her name meant. To him it was the loveliest name on Earth. Greek legend told of a maiden named Arachne who, in a contest of spinning and weaving, won a victory over the goddess Athena. To punish the maiden for daring to defeat a goddess, Athena had transformed her into a spider and ordered her to spin webs throughout eternity.

The scientific name *Arachnida*, as applied to the spider and all its kin, owed its origin to that ancient fable. But surely that was no reason for calling Arachne Reid a spider woman!

He suddenly wanted to laugh, but the death of little Hope Wiggin had destroyed all the laughter within him. "Is it just because of your name that—" he began dully.

"No, Andy. We had a sort of insect zoo at the schoolhouse. For weeks the children brought all kinds of insects, and we kept them alive and studied them. There were fifty or more spiders, including a few red ones. When school closed, I turned them all loose, and now the people are saying that I—I—"

Gale nodded, scowling. There was something darkly sinister here, something ugly and mysterious. The significance of Arachne's name and the fact that she had liberated a few spiders were mere scratches on the surface. Below the surface, a hateful sort of hell was brewing. Fada, the crippled girl, perhaps knew more about it than anyone else.

"So they claim you started the plague by turning loose a handful of spiders," he said grimly. "Ignorant, superstitious fools, that's what they are, and I'd like a chance to tell them so!"

Trembling with rage, Gale gripped the rotted porch railing so fiercely that his strong hands threatened to pulverize it.

"Well, we're getting out of here," he snorted. "They can think what they like."

"No, Andy. I can't go yet."

He stared at her. Something tightened inside him.

"But you said in your letter—" he whispered.

"I'm sorry. I'm terribly sorry, Andy. Please don't be angry."

"You mean—you've changed your mind? You don't love me?"

Her trembling lips told of the torment in her heart as she returned his stare of stunned amazement.

"I love you, Andy," she said steadily, "but I can't marry you. Not yet. Please don't ask me to explain. I can't go away with you. I've got to stay here."

"But you *can't* stay here!" he said hoarsely. "You mustn't! You heard what Fada said."

She didn't answer immediately. Staring out into the darkness, she shuddered, then lowered her face into her hands, as if the thought of what might happen to her were more than she could bear. Gale stumbled forward and knelt beside her, put his arms around her.

"You've got to go away with me!" he pleaded. "Even if you no longer love me or want to marry me, you've got to let me take you away from here."

He wanted her to say, "I do love you, Andy." If only she would whisper those few simple words, the iron bands around his heart would relax and he could breathe again. Instead, she raised her head and looked at him with dead, dull eyes. "No. I can't leave," she said. "I've got to stay."

Half an hour later, they came.

They were a rough, ugly lot, the farmers of Flood River Valley. Led by a great hulk of a man who carried a lantern in one hand and a shotgun in the other, they stormed along the road and marched into Nicklus Brukner's yard. Gale and Arachne were on the porch when they arrived.

One look at that angry, muttering mob convinced Gale that the danger threatening Arachne was appallingly real.

"Get inside!" he whispered. "Hurry!" And as she closed the door behind her, he advanced to the steps and stood there, gazing down into a sea of sinister faces.

"What do you want?"

Suddenly the door behind him opened again, and Fada, the crippled girl, was beside him.

"You know what they want," she laid shrilly. "They've come for the Spider Woman, and they can have her! They're welcome to her!"

With one sweep of his arm, Gale thrust her aside.

"What do you want?" he demanded again.

"We want the Spider Woman!"

"Why? What has she done?"

One of them strode up the steps and looked Gale over. That man never knew how close he came to getting a fist in the mouth as he thrust his head forward and poked a gnarled forefinger into Gale's stomach.

"Who might you be?" he snarled.

"Never mind who I am. I'm here to protect Miss Reid."

"You're here to protect her, are ye? Well, *we* aim to run her out of Flood River Valley! She's workin' with the Devil, she is. With her gone, the spiders'll leave too, and we'll be able to live in peace again. Where is she?"

"She's in the house!" Fada screamed. "Go in and drag her out, Clem!"

The fellow she called Clem put a hand on Andy Gale's chest.

"One side, you!" he ordered. "We aim to get the Spider Woman!"

He never knew what struck him. Gale's fist, backed by a seething volcano of rage, exploded in the fellow's sneering mouth and sent him sprawling. He fell in a gurgling heap at the foot of the steps. The others surged forward, filling the night with the din of their voices.

At that moment, as Gale faced annihilation, two things happened simultaneously. Arachne Reid appeared suddenly at Gale's side, with the obvious intention of giving herself up to protect him from harm; and, from the rear of the mob, a commanding voice rang out like a tocsin, halting the farmers in their tracks.

Gale stared in amazement as a tall, broad-shouldered man strode forward, opening a lane with his voice. All other voices had died until there was a weird silence. The man climbed to the porch and calmly faced the mob.

"What's the meaning of this?" he demanded.

They told him. He turned to look at Arachne, and there was something in that look, something in the flush of color that climbed suddenly into Arachne's face, that thrust a knife-point into Andy Gale's heart. He knew at that moment why Arachne had refused to go away with him.

The broad-shouldered man gazed down at the crowd.

"You're wrong," he said sternly. "Miss Reid had nothing to do with the death of that little girl. Go home, all of you!"

To Gale it looked like a daring bluff, because he was close enough to see signs of turmoil in the fellow's face. Would it work? Would those sullen, superstitious farmers obey the command?

They did. None of them, not even the man Clem, had nerve enough to advance. With a mutter of sound the mob broke up. The handsome young man turned and took both of Arachne's hands in his, and said fervently: "Thank God!"

Pale and trembling, Arachne beckoned to Gale. "This is John Slayton, Andy. He came here a few days ago to interest the farmers in a cooperative packing plant."

Gale took the man's hand.

"You seem to have quite a hold over them, Mr. Slayton," he said dully.

"No. But I've talked with most of them, and they evidently trust me."

Someone else trusted him, too. Gale could see it in her eyes—in Arachne's eyes. Mumbling excuses, he turned and walked back into the house, his own eyes glazed with torment, his feet heavy. Five minutes later, Fada found him sitting on an old piano bench in the parlor.

"Your sweetheart and Mr. Slayton, they are still talking together," the crippled girl murmured cruelly. "You're no fool. I guess you can see they're in love."

Gale raised his head and stared without answering. She moved closer.

"Are you thinking of going away?"

"Yes."

"You mustn't. There is something dishonest about John Slayton. Why would any man come to this drought-stricken area to talk to the farmers about a packing plant? The farmers are desperate. They have no crops. The red spiders have ruined everything. If you go away now, like a beaten dog, there's no telling what may happen. Arachne should be protected."

The words bored deep into Andy's brain. He saw the wisdom behind them. Strange, that this deformed creature should one minute wish to turn Arachne over to a mob of mad beasts, and then suddenly, with an amazing change of heart, seek to protect her. But so many things here were strange and bewildering.

"You must not go away," Fada whispered. "You must stay! There is a vacant bedroom upstairs, next to mine . . ."

II: Night Calls

A SPIDER CRAWLED over the patchwork quilt and dropped onto Andy Gale's twitching face. Without waking, he stirred restlessly and uttered mumbling sounds of torment.

He was dreaming, and there were spiders in the dream—hideous red armies of them, stalking him.

The red spider on his face crept across his mouth and bit him. He waked with a convulsive jerk and sat up in bed. A clock on the antique bureau said 2:00 a.m., and the room was weirdly aglow with moonlight.

The door, which he had carefully closed before retiring, was creaking as someone inched it open. Gale turned to stare at it. The sledging of his own heart startled him. Then he stifled a grunt of amazement as his unexpected visitor came limping into view.

"You are awake—darling?"

The moonlight was kind to Fada as she stood there. It lessened the horror of her shriveled limbs and deformed back, and glorified the amazing beauty of her face. Hers was a frightening sort of beauty, unearthly and savagely sensual. Gale swung his feet clear of the bedclothes and scowled at her.

"What do you want?" His scowl deepened, and he pushed himself erect. There was something unholy about this woman.

"You—you think I should not have come here to talk to you a little while—when I'm lonely?" she asked. Her red lips ceased smiling and writhed back to reveal a curled tongue and white, gleaming teeth. "Am I—so ugly as that?"

"It isn't that, Fada. It's just that I—Arachne . . . I'm sorry."

"You are sorry?" Her bitter laugh chilled his blood. "Yes, you are sorry for *me*! All men are. I am hideous. It hurts you to look at me!" Her snarling outburst smothered Gale's feeble word, of protest. "And I thought you were different!"

A look of helplessness was in Gale's tired face. "You'd better go now," he said dully.

"Yes, I'd better go now." Bitterly she mocked the tone of his voice. "But some day you'll look at me without that loathing in your eyes, Andrew Gale! Some day you'll go on your knees to me, and beg me—"

He shuddered. Never before in the eyes of a human being had he seen hate smoldering so fiercely. In a daze he stood by the bed and watched her as she limped to the door. She did not look back. The door creaked shut behind her.

Sleep was impossible then. With an unlit cigarette clamped in his teeth, he paced the floor. The hate from Fada's warped soul hung like a foul miasma in the room, stifling him. Outside, the moon was high and full, spilling a cold, blue light through the windows.

Suddenly there were voices.

Rigid at an open window, Gale stared down into the yard. The white fence, newly painted, gleamed like a row of giant teeth against the grayness of the road. A man and a woman stood near the gate.

A thick, strangling mass gathered in Gale's throat as he watched. The words of the crippled girl whispered again in his brain. *You're no fool. I guess you can see they're in love.*

Yes, he could see. How long Arachne and John Slayton had been out there, he had no way of knowing; but evidently they had been there some time. Slayton's hands were on Arachne's shoulders. He was holding her close to him.

Their conversation reached Gale only as a low murmuring in which words were indistinguishable. They separated. Slayton, tall and straight, strode down the road toward the village. Arachne, without even a glance at the windows of Gale's room, glided swiftly toward the rear door.

With a dull, glazed look in his half-shut eyes, Gale sprawled on the bed . . .

At breakfast the next morning a red spider, crawling over the table, died under the descending fist of Nicklus Brukner.

"Damned spiders!" Brukner grumbled. "They've ruined every farm in the valley!"

His crippled daughter leered at him. "Why should *you* worry? You hold mortgages on nearly every acre of land within thirty miles. If the farmers can't pay what they owe you, you can take their land."

"And what do I want with their land? It's money I need! Money to buy food!"

Nicklus Brukner looked tired. Shadows of exhaustion darkened the pouches under his eyes. His hands trembled as he poured coffee.

"You worked in the laboratory all night, Nicklus?" Arachne asked him.

"Yes, all night again. There'll be no rest now. I've *got* to find a poison that will kill those hellish things; if I don't, they'll keep right on breeding and there will be millions of them. They'll drive us out of our homes and take possession of the whole valley!"

"But why do you work alone? Why don't you get help?"

"Because I daren't trust anyone—that's why!"

"Perhaps John Slayton would help," Arachne suggested softly.

"Slayton? Him I trust least of all! Him and his cooperative packing plant! He's here for no good reason!"

Andy Gale glanced at Arachne and saw a dull red flush ascending from her throat. Across from her, Fada leaned forward, elbows denting the tablecloth.

"Whatever John Slayton is," the crippled girl said viciously, "you are, too." With her knife she pointed at Arachne. "Don't deny it! You're in love with him! Last night I saw you in his arms!"

Arachne's flush faded. Her face went white for an instant, and seemed to be made of wax. She stared straight at Fada, then turned, looked at Gale. Andy Gale thought he saw a mute, frantic appeal in her eyes, as if she were begging him not to believe Fada.

Then, pushing back her chair, she thrust herself up from the table and left the room. There was silence for a moment. Fada shattered it by uttering a harsh, brutal laugh.

"Spider woman!" she snarled. "That's what she is—a spider woman!"

No longer hungry, Gale excused himself. Nicklus Brukner went right on eating, as if nothing had occurred. Half an hour later, while Gale was reading a newspaper in the parlor, the doorbell rang. Fada limped down the hall to answer it. Gale lowered his paper and listened.

"You're not goin' to cause trouble in this house, Clem Degnan!" Fada was saying. "I don't care how you feel about him hittin' you."

The "Clem" part of that name was familiar, and Gale guessed the fellow's mission. Striding into the hall, he pushed Fada aside and confronted the caller.

"You're looking for me?"

Clem Degnan glared at him. A large purple bruise disfigured the man's face. "I come here," Degnan said, "to settle a score with you. No one ever struck Clem Degnan yet without payin' for it!"

"And I say," declared Fada, "that I won't have any disturbance here!"

Gale's mouth wore a grim smile. The prospect of a good fight was a relief. It would keep him from thinking of other things which, unfortunately, could not be settled so easily.

"We'll go outside," he said to Degnan.

They went outside. It was a good fight. When it was over, Gale wiped a trickle of blood from bruised knuckles and smiled down at his beaten opponent who swayed groggily on hands and knees.

Degnan did not smile back. Staggering erect, he backed away, his battered face livid with rage.

"I'll get you for this!" he promised. "I'll get even, Gale! Don't think you're done with me!"

Snarling, he went away. And when Gale reentered the house, Fada was waiting in the parlor.

"I'm glad you did it," she whispered. "I hate that man."

"Do you? Who is he?"

"Oh—just one of the valley farmers." Suddenly she saw the blood on his knuckles. "You're hurt!"

She painted his hand with iodine while he sat on the piano bench. It took her a long time, and her heady perfume crept through him like a drug as she bent over him.

"Are you angry with me for what I did last night?" she whispered.

He shook his head. "No, of course not."

"Then—you don't hate me? You might even—in time—learn to love me?"

He was slow in answering. His first impulse was to tell her bluntly that he loved someone else; but after all, there was something uniquely attractive about this girl, despite her deformity. She was like a creature of some other world, ugly when judged by the standards of this world, but savagely beautiful in her own right.

Such thoughts frightened him. He shook them loose and pushed himself erect. "I'm sorry," he mumbled. "I think I'll take a walk."

Later he reached a decision. He would face Arachne and demand that she tell him the truth about John Slayton. If she loved Slayton, that would be the end, and he would go back to his job in the city.

Returning to the house, he found Fada asleep in the parlor. Nicklus Brukner was nowhere around. In the kitchen a door was open, and a sound of footsteps in the cellar led Gale down a flight of steep, dark stairs. Someone—Brukner, probably—was in the little laboratory at the end of the cellar.

A sudden desire to see the inside of that laboratory sent Gale forward on the balls of his feet. It was dark here. If he were quiet, he could remain hidden and watch Brukner at work. The laboratory door was open.

Silently approaching the aperture, he reached a vantage point and stood motionless. His eyes widened. His brows drew into a frown.

For it was not Nicklus Brukner who stood there at the wooden workbench. It was Arachne.

Four earthenware crocks stood on the bench. From one of them, Arachne was ladling a dark, oily liquid into a bottle. Even at a distance, Gale's nostrils quivered in protest as the strangling odor of the liquid attacked him.

It was a small, dirty room, and the dangling lamp bulb threw a pale glow over the array of paraphernalia that loomed there. Two huge vats of well water stood on the floor. Crude shelves supported bottles of vari-colored liquids. A three-burner gasoline stove occupied half the bench space.

Arachne had finished her task. Replacing the crock, she thrust a stopper into the pint bottle of oily liquid and, with a soiled rag, wiped away the few drops she had spilled on the bench. Gale stepped back as she hurried from the room.

Without seeing him, she ascended the stairs to the kitchen.

Gale followed. Hearing a door click shut, he knew she had gone out into the yard; and from a kitchen window he watched her. With a furtive backward glance at the house, she hurried along a path that skirted the lower section of Brukner's farm. The nearby woods swallowed her.

Hating himself for his suspicions, Gale went after her.

It was weirdly quiet in the woods, even though at times the girl ahead of him disturbed the silence by walking through brush or stepping on dead limbs. The hush was somehow menacing, like the frightening stillness before a storm. And there were crawling things everywhere.

Spiders! A dozen times he had to leave the path and circle around, because the little red spiders had taken possession. They dropped down on him from low-hanging branches, wriggled over his hands and face and neck. He thought of little Hope Wiggin, and shuddered.

Then, as the winding path led him into a weed-grown clearing, he caught sight of Arachne again.

A house had stood here once. Its foundation loomed among the weeds, and Arachne was hiding the bottle of oily liquid beneath the rusted hulk of an old wheelbarrow. Rising, she looked around before retracing her steps.

This time, Gale resisted the temptation to follow her. In all probability, he told himself, she would go straight back to Brukner's house.

He waited half an hour, angrily brushing away the spiders that discovered and attacked him. What, he wondered, would be the fate of

Flood River Valley if these nonpoisonous red spiders should suddenly become poisonous, or grow to the size of tarantulas? The fantastic thought chilled him.

Then suddenly he was not alone. From the far side of the clearing emerged the tall, athletic figure of John Slayton.

Gale stiffened, forgot the spiders for a moment and watched Slayton's movements. The man walked straight to the place where the bottle was hidden. Thrusting the bottle into his coat pocket, he turned and strode back the way he had come.

III: ATTACK IN THE HIDEAWAY

AN HOUR LATER, in his own room at the Brukner farmhouse, Andy Gale finished packing. He had resolved to go away quietly, without saying goodbye. The heaviness in his heart did not alter that resolve as he swung his suitcase off the bed and opened the door.

Fada, limping along the hall, stopped him by whispering his name.

"You are—going?"

"This time, yes."

"And if I prove to you," Fada said softly, "that your Arachne is in love with a man who is wicked, and that she is in grave danger—what then?"

Gale lowered his suitcase to the floor and stared at her. The hope that surged through him was like a swift, hot pain. "You have proof that John Slayton is not what she thinks he is?" he demanded.

"Come with me."

She led him downstairs and out of the house. Without a word of explanation, but with a strange twist to her face, she limped along the hot, dusty road that led to the village.

"Where are you taking me?" he demanded.

"You'll see."

It was not far. At the top of the bill, near the berry patch where little Hope Wiggin had been attacked by the red spiders, she pointed and said: "There!"

"Why, that's a schoolhouse!"

"The schoolhouse where your sweetheart taught the children of this district. But the school term is over now, and what better place could John Slayton find for the brewing of his evil schemes?"

She led him forward again, this time along a path that terminated in the school yard. It was quiet here, almost too quiet, and the squat little building with its boarded windows exuded an air of desolation. The road was at least a hundred yards distant, hidden by trees and brush. A perfect hideout indeed! And who would be likely to come here snooping?

Cautioning Gale to make no noise, Fada paced stealthily to the rear door and opened it. The empty building amplified her footbeats as she entered. In a moment she was on the threshold again, beckoning.

"You'll find proof enough in here!" she said bitterly, as Gale crossed the sill. "Look for yourself, and be quick about it. If Slayton finds us here—"

She was pointing to a five-gallon milk can that stood near the door. It was the only thing in the room that seemed the least unusual. The rest of the room was bare. Desks and benches were stacked against the walls. A pot-bellied wood stove loomed in one corner.

Gale paced forward, frowning. It was dark here. The boarded windows admitted no light, and Fada had cautiously closed the door. The little room seemed more like some dark, heathen temple than like a schoolhouse. The wailing importunities of a black-robed temple priest would have been more appropriate here than would the shrill voices of school children.

He bent over the milk can and wondered what evil thing it contained.

Fada, moving up behind him, whispered fearfully: "Listen! You can hear them crawling in there! Ugh!"

He *could* hear something crawling inside the can. When he tapped the metal with his foot, the hollow reverberation was accompanied by a sudden slithering sound, as if hundreds of imprisoned insects had been disturbed from sleep and were frantically seeking to escape.

Was the can full of spiders? Red spiders?

Gale gripped the top of the milk can and turned it. Uneasiness had conquered his curiosity, and he acutely wanted to get the job over and get out of this gloomy place. The darkness was stifling him. The air had a musty, unpleasant odor that made breathing difficult.

Suddenly, with a hoarse cry, he put both hands to his throat and could not breathe at all.

The thing had happened with uncanny quickness. His attention had been focused on the task of opening the can. Fada, slipping a wire noose from under her dress, had attacked without warning!

The noose bit deep into Andy Gale's neck as he staggered back. It strangled him. He slid to his knees, gasping and choking, and fought frantically to tear the thing loose.

But Fada's hands were at the back of his neck, twisting the wire tighter. Despite her deformity, she was agile as a cat, and those bony wrists possessed amazing strength. He could not reach her with his hands. She kept behind him, forced him backward.

When he ceased struggling at last, she stood over him and uttered a low, gurgling laugh of triumph.

"You were a fool," she said, "to trust me. You should have known better, darling."

Gale did not lose consciousness, but hovered on the brink of oblivion for at least five minutes, his face purple, his body laden with sickness. There was nothing gentle about her treatment of him. Loosening the noose only enough to let him breathe, she gripped his arms and dragged him across the floor, propped him in a sitting position against the wood stove.

There, with rope enough to hold a dozen men, she bound him. And the last coil of rope went around his mouth, holding in place a wad of unclean cloth that gagged him.

"You won't escape, darling," she told him. "In the first place, I lied to you about John Slayton. This is *my* little hideout, not his. It was *I* who brought the milk can here."

He stared, trying to analyze the odd look in her eyes as she gloated over him. It was not a look of hate, but rather one of anticipation. He wondered if she were insane.

"You won't escape," she said again. "I won't be gone that long." Then, turning, she limped to the door and was gone.

Gale worked feverishly for half an hour to free himself. At the end of that half hour, his wrists and ankles were bleeding and his lame body was drenched with sweat. But, by rubbing a double section of rope against the stove's iron door, he had worn the strands almost to the breaking point. He had one foot free when he heard the tell-tale limp of Fada's returning footsteps.

A groan welled into his throat and he ceased struggling, stared dully at the door. He heard voices then and realized that Fada was not alone. The door opened. Arachne Reid stepped over the threshold. Fada was behind her.

At that moment the sweat on Gale's body turned ice cold, and he tried mightily to shout a warning. Arachne stared at him and uttered a muffled cry of horror. The warning yell went no further than the gag in Gale's mouth, and died there. To Arachne it must have sounded like a moan of pain.

She rushed forward. "You were right!" she sobbed to Fada. "Oh, why did I doubt you? Help me!"

On her knees, she clawed at Gale's bonds. And he, powerless to intervene, saw the whole ghastly routine as Fada leaped to the attack.

The wire noose encircled Arachne's slender throat. It bit into soft, tender flesh and yanked her over backward. Arachne screamed, but the noose smothered the scream and drew blood. And then, while Gale raged like a madman at his bonds and Arachne writhed in agony on the floor, Fada knelt beside the stricken girl and calmly twisted the noose until the job was finished.

Arachne lay unconscious. Rising, Fada limped to the far wall and seized a heavy wooden bench. Piled-up chairs fell with a crash as the bench shuddered out from under them, but with the same unholy fixation of purpose Fada dragged the bench across the room, upended it, and bound Arachne to it.

Deliberately she tore the front of Arachne's dress, exposing the soft, creamy flesh of molded breasts. Then, limping over to Gale, she removed his gag, inspected his bonds and reinforced the frayed sections. And then, rolling the five-gallon milk can from the corner, she set it upright near the stove and said softly: "Now, darling, we begin!"

Gale's eyes bulged in their sockets as the girl came closer. Her hands were outstretched, and he shrank from the touch of them. In her eyes glowed an unholy menace, a flame of dark, evil desire.

She flung herself upon him, forced her twisted body against his. Her lips fastened on his mouth; her hands pawed at him.

"You are mine!" she whispered. "Mine! You're going to marry me!"

"You're mad!" Gale gasped.

"Mad? What if I am? You're going to marry me and love me! If you refuse—" She backed away, leering at him. "If you refuse," she said, "Arachne dies horribly, and you die with her."

Mad or not, the crippled girl evidently knew exactly what she meant to do. There was no hesitation, no indecision. Bending over the milk can, she tugged the top loose and held it just above the opening; held it there until a hideous, hairy thing crawled over the lip of the aperture and escaped. Before others could follow, she thrust the top back again.

The hairy, eight-legged horror dropped to the floor and became motionless. A dew of cold sweat formed on Gale's face as he watched it. He had been wrong! The crawling things imprisoned in the can were not red spiders; they were another variety of a far more terrible breed.

Tarantulas!

"Kill it!" he gasped. "Step on it, you fool! Those things are deadly poisonous!"

Retreating to a safe distance, Fada gazed at the tarantula and began chuckling. "Of course they're poisonous," she said, nodding. "And this is only one of them. There are half a hundred more in the can. Now—will you promise to make me your wife?"

The tarantula had apparently oriented itself to its new surroundings. It turned, crept sluggishly toward Gale's bound legs. A swelling mass of terror threatened to explode in the man's heaving chest, and he strove frantically to twist himself out of the way.

The crippled girl limped forward. Her foot came down on the huge spider, crushing it. The smile still lingered on her lips as she halted beside Arachne Reid and gently caressed the unconscious girl's bare shoulder.

"You saw what the little red spiders did to Hope Wiggin," she murmured. "Think of what these things would do to this poor girl. It would be horrible, wouldn't it?" And she turned, calmly awaiting Gale's answer.

"You can't do it!" he groaned. "You can't!"

"Oh, but I can. And I will unless you promise to marry me."

She was enjoying herself. Every word she spoke was tainted with sadistic triumph, and she tasted each syllable before uttering it. She was mad; but she knew what she wanted, and knew she could not fail. Patiently she awaited Gale's decision.

His heart filled with revulsion, he stared at her, stared past her at the limp, lovely figure of Arachne. God, how different were the two! And he loved Arachne, had loved, worshipped her for years. He had come to Flood River Valley to make her his wife, after an eternity of waiting.

And now . . .

"Don't forget," Fada whispered, "that you will die, too. If you refuse me, I shall release the spiders, all of them, and go away from here, locking the door after me. The tarantulas will destroy both of you."

Gale shuddered. Already he could feel the hideous things crawling over him; could see them climbing Arachne's legs to reach the alabaster flesh of her uncovered breasts. His gaze strayed to the milk can, and a cold, constricting wave of terror crept through him, thinning his blood, forcing an icy dew through his pores.

"Well?" Fada demanded.

"You can't do it!"

"Can't I?" Again she pulled the milk can top, this time gripping the handle of the container and tipping it so that the great spiders could escape more easily. "Can't I?" she murmured. "You'll see!"

"No, no! Wait!"

"Wait? What for?"

"Give me time!" he groaned.

She replaced the lid and shrugged her shoulders. Evidently she was in no hurry. She could wait. She was sure of herself.

His eyes glazed with torment, Gale stared again at Arachne. Silently he prayed for courage enough to do what had to be done. Arachne did not love him; she loved John Slayton. Of that he was positive.

By sacrificing himself—by dooming himself to a hell-union with a woman who was both mad and deformed—he could give Arachne to the man she loved. Otherwise, both he and she would die horribly.

"Well?" Fada said again.

"I—I'll marry you," he groaned.

"You swear it?"

"Yes, I swear it."

"Good!" she whispered.

Suddenly she was like a child delighted with a new toy. Limping forward, she draped her arms about his neck and embraced him, kissed his mouth, his eyes, his bloodless cheeks. "You'll learn to love me," she said, gleefully. "We'll be so happy together!"

The transformation was amazing. No longer a leering, maddened woman, she clung to him in a frenzy of childish delight and then made haste to unbind him. Apparently it had not occurred to her that he might refuse to keep his promise. Her warped mind had not wandered that far from its original fixation.

He shook himself loose and strode forward to free Arachne. Fada went with him, hugging him. Even when he placed Arachne's limp body on the floor and worked over it, Fada continued her idiotic chuckling and kept annoying him with kisses.

"Get some water," he ordered. "Help me."

She brought water, and he bathed Arachne's face. Before long, the eyes in that white face were open, staring up at him.

"What—what happened, Andy?" Arachne asked weakly.

"Nothing," he said dully. "Nothing—much. Fada lost her head and attacked you."

Arachne gazed, bewildered, at the milk can. "What's that for?"

"That," he muttered, "is full of Fada's pets. Spiders." Suddenly he turned, gripped the arms of the crippled girl and glared at her. "Fada! Where did those spiders come from?"

"Why, from my father's laboratory."

"You're lying! There were no spiders in that laboratory! I looked!"

She snuggled close to him. "You didn't look in the right room," she said simply. "There are two rooms, you know. If you'd looked in the little one, you'd have seen ever so many boxes and containers, all filled with different kinds of spiders. My father has some black widow spiders, and tarantulas, and some wolf spiders—oh, all kinds. He breeds them."

Gale stood still, staring at her. The significance of her words beat like a sledge-hammer into his brain. For a moment his tongue refused to form words.

"How long have you known this?" he suddenly flung out.

"Oh, a long time," she admitted. "He never told me about the room, but I found it for myself and went there often."

"Then your father is responsible for the plague of red spiders! He turned them loose to destroy the farms!"

It was hellishly clear, all of it. Nicklus Brukner had released a plague of death and destruction upon Flood River Valley in order to bankrupt the farmers. He held mortgages on most of the valley farms. He had lied in declaring that he didn't want the land. He did want it; and this was his way of getting it!

Not content with the havoc already wrought by his crawling red armies, he was now experimenting with all the poisonous great spiders themselves, breeding them, assembling new hordes!

Andy Gale seized the woman he had sworn to marry, and dragged her close to him.

"Listen to me, Fada," he said hoarsely. "I want you to take me to that room. Do you understand? I want to see what it looks like."

"You want to see the spiders?"

"Yes!"

"And does she want to come, too?" Fada frowned, indicating Arachne.

"Yes," Arachne said almost inaudibly.

"Well—all right. Come on. Only don't forget you are to be *my* husband, not hers!"

IV: Poison Brew

THE FARMHOUSE OF Nicklus Brukner loomed gray and gaunt at the foot of the hill, and seemed deserted as Andy Gale pushed open the gate. Red spiders, crawling like ants over the front steps and the veranda, had apparently taken possession.

"Nicklus," Arachne said fearfully, "must be in his laboratory."

The crippled girl pulled Gale back as he put a foot on the steps. Clinging to his arm, she steered him around the house to the rear door. He opened the door and entered, stared across the kitchen and saw that the door at the head of the cellar stairs was open. Arachne and Fada followed him as he paced forward. In the strange silence that seemed to have taken possession here, it was impossible to muffle the thud of his feet as he advanced.

He wondered dully what he would do after discovering Brukner's secret laboratory. Go to the state troopers? As for his promise to marry Brukner's mad daughter, he had not dared think about it. It was too horrible.

"Show me," he muttered, pausing at the foot of the stairs, "where the spiders are!"

Fada led the way. Oblivious to any possible danger, she hurried to the far end of the cellar and entered the room where Arachne, not long ago, had stolen a pint of Brukner's poison. And with a sudden low cry she stepped back, colliding with Gale as he entered behind her.

On the floor in front of the work-bench lay a sprawled, contorted shape—Nicklus Brukner!

Gale strode forward, stared down at the man. There was nothing much left to stare at. An earthenware crock lay shattered on the floor, and the oily liquid had eaten away Brukner's hair and clothes and most of his flesh. The liquid, gurgling and bubbling even now with an uncanny life of its own, was still feeding on the man's remains.

"Dead," Gale mumbled, shuddering. "Yes—dead. He must have upset the crock while working here and—"

"It wasn't an accident," Arachne said dully, horror in her staring eyes.

"What?"

"The liquid in that crock wouldn't have killed him. It wasn't even a strong poison—certainly not strong enough to—to eat into him like that." Her face was chalk-white as she whispered the words. Twin smears of rouge stood out like bloodstains on her waxy-white cheeks.

"You see," she said, "I—know. I took some of that liquid to John Slayton, and he tested it."

Gale glanced at Fada. Apparently the crippled girl had not realized that the dead man was her father. Rather stupidly she was staring at the corpse, and the expression on her face was bewilderment, not horror.

"Where are the spiders?" Gale demanded. "We might as well see this thing through to the finish!"

Fada limped to the opposite end of the room and pushed aside a crudely built cabinet. A door loomed behind it.

"It may be locked," she said. "If it is, we can't get in. I have no key."

The door creaked open when she turned the knob.

It was dark in there—dark as the interior of a vault. Leading the way, Gale fumbled for matches and struck one against the wall. The sputtering flare showed him a room only half the size of the chamber where Brukner lay dead.

Boxes and wooden barrels, some of them carelessly covered with ill-fitting boards, occupied two-thirds of the floor space. A pool of blood gleamed red and wet at Gale's feet.

He turned slowly, his gaze stiffly following the rivulet of blood which had formed the pool. The match expired in his fingers as he lurched forward. Striking another, he went to his knees beside the inert figure of John Slayton. Arachne saw, and uttered a shrill scream of horror.

"John! Oh, God! Darling!"

Gale closed his eyes and moved aside. He had no desire to do any staring as Arachne gathered that bloody shape in her arms. Her pitiful sobs tore through Andy Gale, hurting him almost as much as the assailant's knife must have hurt Slayton. Even Fada seemed to realize the intensity of Arachne's anguish, and stayed at a distance.

"Andy!" Arachne cried suddenly. "He's not dead! He's breathing!"

Gale swayed forward again, saw that she was right. Slayton's blood-smeared body was twitching; some strange force inside him was fighting its way back, through a mist of dark agony, to consciousness. Gale pushed the hysterical girl aside and lifted the man to a sitting position.

"We've got to get him out of here," he muttered. The answer to that came not from Arachne but from the doorway, in a guttural voice that was vaguely familiar.

"You ain't goin' out of here, mister! You're stayin'—for keeps."

Andy Gale whirled. The menacing muzzle of a small-bore rifle jerked to a level with his chest and stopped him. He took a faltering backward step and stood rigid.

Arachne stifled a scream. Fada, stupidly staring, said nothing.

The man in the doorway was Clem Degnan, his battered face still swollen and discolored from the beating Andy had given him.

"This," Degnan said, slowly advancing, "is a real pleasure. I told you I'd get even."

Gale stood quite still, blood ebbing slowly from his taut face. If he leaped, that gnarled finger would tighten on the trigger; and at that range the bullet would shred his chest to pulp.

"What do you want, Degnan?" he asked, almost inaudibly.

"You."

"Then let the women go."

"Let 'em go?" Degnan's wide mouth curled in a leer. "Let 'em run to the state troopers and tell what they found in this room of mine? I ain't that big a fool!"

It was a chance to stall for time. Gale seized it rapaciously. "*Your* room? You're crazy! This is Brukner's laboratory."

"It ain't Brukner's laboratory, and Brukner never had the faintest idea of what was goin' on in here, mister. It's *my* laboratory, this is. It was me that brought the first load of red spiders here and turned 'em loose to ruin the crops; and it's me that's breedin' more and bigger spiders to make sure the farmers clear out of Flood River Valley and turn their land over to Brukner. *I* want that land—see? Soon as it's mine, I'll get rid of the spiders in short order, and the land'll make me rich."

With an effort, Gale pretended to be unafraid. The man behind that menacing rifle was of low mentality—not low enough to be classed as a moron, but still not blessed with any great intelligence. Unless he suddenly became enraged, there was a feeble chance of talking him out of his obvious intent to murder his three prisoners in cold blood.

"How do you figure you'll get the land?" Andy scowled.

"Don't worry. I'll get it."

"But if the farmers can't pay their debts, the land will belong to Brukner, won't it?"

"Brukner's dead. I killed him."

"You shot him?"

"No, I killed him the same way I'm fixin' to kill you." Degnan took a step forward. "It ain't lawful to shoot people Gale. They'd put me in jail for doin' that. So I made it look like Brukner died accidental—and that's how they'll think you died—you and Fada and Miss Reid. You see that tank there?"

He pointed, and Gale's gaze wandered to a large metal tank in a corner of the room. A length of black hose lay curled on the floor beside it.

"That," Degnan said, grinning, "is full of poison. I worked in a chemical plant before I come here and married—before I come here to be a farmer. I learned plenty about poisons, and that stuff was all mixed up, ready for use, even before I brought the spiders here. I wouldn't be fool enough to turn an army of spiders loose unless I knew how to destroy 'em. Not me! That stuff is real powerful—as you're about to find out!"

A series of slow backward steps carried Degnan to the tank. Helpless to stop him, Andy Gale clenched both hands and stood stricken. A thick, viscous volcano of fear erupted inside him.

"You can't do it, Degnan! My God, you can't kill helpless women!"

"It'll be an accident," Degnan declared, grinning again.

Stooping, he seized the black hose and slid his hand along to the gleaming nozzle. There was a gleam of unholy triumph in his narrowed eyes as he straightened. He was remembering the beating he had received.

"Go on—crawl," he said, glaring at Gale. "Get down on your knees and beg for your life. See what good it does you!"

Gale stayed erect, fists clenched and body swaying slightly on stiff legs. The room was slowly turning. He didn't want to die. Even though he had sworn to marry a mad woman, he didn't want . . . to . . . die. God!

Through the mist, Arachne moved to his side. Strangely calm, she put her head on his shoulder.

"I love you Andy," she said dully. "I know you don't believe it, and there isn't time to explain now; but I do love you. Hold me. I—I'm terribly afraid."

He took her in his arms. Clem Degnan leered at them and put down the rifle. He didn't need the rifle anymore; his right hand gripped the gleaming nozzle of the hose.

Fada, the mad one, neither moved nor spoke, but stared straight at Gale.

"Well," Degnan said shrugging, "here goes!"

A hissing sound filled the room as he turned the nozzle, The black hose writhed on the floor, uncoiling like a sleek snake. Oily liquid dripped from the lip of the nozzle but failed to spew forth under pressure.

Degnan, his back to the wall, did not see what had happened; did not know that John Slayton, conscious from the beginning, had wriggled slowly forward like a great human slug and seized a section of hose in his hands, squeezing it to prevent the flow of liquid.

Degnan, snarling, thought something was wrong with the nozzle. Frantically he twisted it, trying to make it work.

Andy Gale flung Arachne aside and hurtled forward.

There was a prayer in Gale's heart as he lunged. Death had been horribly close, and the nearness of it had twisted something in his brain, made a mumbling madman of him. He struck with the force of a battering ram. Both he and Degnan fell over John Slayton's sprawled body and crashed into the wall—but Degnan still clung to the hose.

John Slayton's hands lost their grip. The hissing sound became a shrill, whining voice of horror, and the nozzle vomited forth a dark stream of liquid.

Gale writhed away from that hellish torrent as it fumed toward him. He seized Degnan's wrist, twisted with all his strength. A bone snapped, and Degnan shrieked in agony. The serpent of horror seethed wildly about the room, soaking walls and floor and ceiling. Once—just once—it leaped into the startled, bewildered face of Fada, the mad woman.

Fada sank to her knees, moaning. With both hands she clawed at her eyes. Arachne, stumbling forward to help her, fell back when Gale bellowed a warning.

The hose, unchecked by human hands, writhed and slithered on the floor while Gale fought a life-and-death battle with the pain-crazed Clem Degnan. He had defeated Degnan before; defeated him easily. But the man was no longer human!

Hooked fingers tore at Andy Gale's eyes. An upthrust knee sought for his groin. Like a jungle beast gone amuck, Degnan fought with insane fury.

A blinding fist hurled Gale against the wall and stunned him. Blood trickled from his nose, bubbled at the corners of his mouth. He fought for breath, but the room seemed empty of air, and the stifling stench of the poison brew strangled him as it burned through his lungs.

Dazed, he saw Degnan reach with both hands for the death hose; saw the man's twitching fingers wrap themselves around the nozzle. Terror gave Andy Gale the needed strength for one last lunge.

He hurled himself at Degnan's bent body, buried an elbow in the man's twisted face. Degnan sprawled sideward, off-balance, and the weight of Gale's body slammed him to the floor.

Gale's right hand shot out and down, seizing the hose. The seething stream of liquid described a ghastly semicircle, spraying the ceiling, and then, at close range, centered its full fury on Degnan's face.

When Degnan's mouth opened to scream, Gale rammed the nozzle into it, breaking teeth. The hose writhed. Degnan's death shriek was smothered under a roaring rush of oily liquid.

For one hideous moment the man squirmed as if endowed with some strange, inhuman form of life. Then the life subsided. Horribly bloated, he rolled over, pawed feebly at his rigid face, and died.

Shutting off that ghastly river of death, Andy Gale staggered erect.

Fada, the mad one, was dead. By some blessed miracle, Arachne was still on her feet, still unhurt, and stumbled forward to put her arms around Gale as he swayed and would have fallen. John Slayton was able to stand when they helped him.

"Dead, is he?" Slayton muttered, staring at Degnan. "Dead? Well, he deserved it. His was a fiendish plan—to ruin the farmers and murder Nicklus Brukner, so he could take over all the land. A clever monster if ever there was one!"

"But how would *he* take over the land?" Gale demanded, scowling.

"This man was Fada's husband. Only this morning I talked with the minister who married them. Degnan never lived here, because he and

Brukner hated each other. But he knew that with Brukner dead, everything would belong to Fada—and to him."

Arachne, clinging to Gale, looked at the acid-eaten body of the crippled girl and shuddered. Andy stared, too.

"Lord, she *must* have been mad," he whispered, "wanting me when she already had a husband! Just—just a child, playing with toys."

"I'm through here now," Slayton said. "I can take a sample of Degnan's poison brew to Headquarters and have enough of the stuff made to clean the spiders out of Flood River Valley. Degnan knew what he was doing when he imported his horde of red spiders. The things breed so rapidly it's almost impossible to control them."

"Did you say—Headquarters?"

Slayton and Arachne exchanged glances and then, with a shrug, Slayton nodded.

"I pledged Arachne to secrecy because this job looked mean and dirty," he said simply. "Now that it's over I don't mind telling you I'm an inspector in the Government Quarantine Service. And"—he smiled—"I'm also your future brother-in-law, old man." He thrust out his hand. "Mighty glad to know you, Gale. We met under strange circumstances, but I knew all along that my sister would pick the right sort of man—and you're certainly that."

"You," Gale choked, "are Arachne's brother?"

"That's what I'm trying to tell you. My name's John Reid, not John Slayton."

Tears gleamed in Andy Gale's eyes. Trembling, he turned to Arachne and knew that he had been wrong, dead wrong, in all his suspicions.

"I'll clean up this mess," John Reid said gently. "You two had better get started on your wedding trip."

THE ART NOUVEAU FIREPLACE

CHRISTOPHER FOWLER

Christopher Fowler is the award-winning author of a number of story collections and more than thirty novels, including the popular Bryant & May series of mysteries.

He has fulfilled several schoolboy fantasies—releasing a terrible Christmas pop single, becoming a male model, posing as the villain in a Batman graphic novel, running a night club, appearing in *The Pan Books of Horror Stories*, and standing in for James Bond. His work divides into black comedy, horror, mystery, and tales unclassifiable enough to have publishers tearing their hair out.

His often hilarious and moving autobiography, *Paperboy*, was about growing up in London in the 1950s and '60s, while *The Book of Forgotten Authors*, featuring insightful mini-essays on ninety-nine forgotten authors and their forgotten books, was based on a series of columns he wrote for the *Independent on Sunday* newspaper.

"I wanted to write a timeless ghost story of the kind I had been so fond of as a youth," reveals the author. "I was a fan of the Not at Night books, as well as other volumes like *Tales My Mother Never Told Me* and *Not at Bedtime*. Such collections often contained novellas that would have made great Alfred Hitchcock movies.

"The traditional tales are challenging because of the rules one must follow to construct them correctly. I collect a lot of arcane facts, and the one which forms the lynchpin of this story is quite true. This story comes from a period when I was obsessed with punishing guilty characters. Now I'm happy to punish the innocent—it's more like real life!"

AT NINE THIRTY-FIVE on a wet Monday morning a man telephoned Brockton & Shipley about a house. There was nothing odd in that. After all, Linnea Shipley was an estate agent. No, it was the manner of the man that was strange. He sounded vague and disinterested, as if he hardly cared about the house at all. He wanted it valued, today if possible, and as the property was situated in an extremely desirable location, Linnea decided to attend to the matter personally. She had already been at work for two hours, and felt like stretching her legs.

It was a very rare thing for a building in Rathbone Terrace to come on to the market. Usually a For Sale board only appeared there if an owner had died. Linnea brought the car to a stop and ricked up the handbrake, dipping her head to look through the windscreen as she did so. It was a curving, leafy road of pleasantly terraced red-brick houses. They had been built in a style which dated from the turn of the present century. The decorative scrollwork around the doorways, the carefully rendered window surrounds showed a craftsmanship rarely found these days, one which evoked memories of a forgotten era. Linnea was aware that every house in the street was a potential goldmine, and that their proximity to the new railway station added further to their value. In fact, she and Simon had been wanting to move to this particular part of North London for quite some time.

The front garden of number 35 was wild and overgrown with

"THEN SUDDENLY SHE WAS LOOKING INTO ANOTHER PAIR OF EYES
STARING BACK AT HER FROM WITHIN THE CAVITY."

enormous nettles. Linnea stung her hand on them as she edged her way up the half-hidden path. The windows were dark and coated with grime, but the brickwork appeared to be in sound condition. And at least the bell seemed to work. She quickly checked her appearance, then unbuttoned the top of her blouse. Every little helped when it came to impressing a future client.

The man who opened the door was indeed as strange as he had sounded on the telephone. He was tall and dark and thin, all angles and elbows, and walked with a shuffle as he beckoned Linnea in. He wore spectacles with black plastic frames, and an old nylon shirt that was buttoned right up to the collar. As he showed the estate agent from room to room he threw out odd little gestures, as if suffering a minor affliction. Linnea had seen plenty of people like this on valuation trips, but they were normally old and had lived too long alone. This man could scarcely have been more than thirty-five.

The house was decorated in the worst excesses of mid-1960s taste. Orange-patterned wallpaper in the lounge, op-art swirls in the bedrooms, cheap fitted cupboards in white Formica, all showed signs of long-term neglect. Linnea smiled to herself. The owner was obviously penniless, and could be beaten into the ground when it came to settling the price. What little furniture there was appeared damaged and worn. There was also a very unpleasant smell emanating from the ancient carpet . . . but the walls were sound and dry, the floorboards strong, the ceilings unbowed.

And there was the fireplace.

She had noticed it the second she walked into the lounge: an art nouveau fireplace with curling, fluted columns, and long-gowned women standing on either side of the bricked-in grate. It was sculpted in the style of Alphonse Mucha—indeed, it could have been created by him. The women stood facing each other with their hands demurely folded together and their hair piled high. They were exquisitely detailed, with budding roses and climbing vines entwined about them in a complex Parisian motif. The fireplace had been sloppily painted over a number of times and was currently a sickly pea-green, but it was easy to see how extraordinary the thing would look cleaned up. It had to be worth a fortune.

Linnea studied the vendor, who was now drifting into the kitchen, muttering about having to sell up quickly and get out. The man obviously inhabited his own private world and knew nothing at all about selling a house. She asked her new client, whose name was Mr. Myson or at least something which sounded very much like it, how he had come to pick Brockton & Shipley as his estate agent. Myson pointed to the circular that Linnea's company dropped through letterboxes in the area, then resumed mumbling on about his reasons for wanting a quick sale—something to do with a dream he'd had recently.

It was then that Linnea knew she could undervalue the house, buy it for herself and make a killing.

She was quick to exaggerate the building's faults—the lack of central heating, the dangerous electrics, the medieval plumbing—and she invented a few new drawbacks of her own. She played down the good features and pointed out the bad, and finally, with much heart-searching and shaking of her undeniably attractive head, produced a selling figure so low that she shocked even herself. But the owner seemed unsurprised, and half-heartedly agreed to the terms, and Linnea shook his hand and left with a promise to draw up the details immediately and send them on.

She couldn't wait to tell Simon the news, but it was better not to mention anything until the sale had gone through. Linnea stuck to her original low valuation, typed out the description sheet within an hour of returning to the office, and then delivered it to Rathbone Terrace by hand. The sale that followed was one of the fastest she had ever made. She handled the documentation by using her maiden name on the forms. Naturally, it was important for Mr. Myson not to discover that she was buying the place for herself.

Seller and purchaser met just once more, on the day that Linnea arranged to collect the keys. Mr. Myson looked as if he had not slept for a week. He promised to collect the few remaining sticks of furniture, which had been carelessly stacked at the back of the hall, then passed the keys to Linnea as if the ring to which they were attached had suddenly grown red hot in his hand.

It began to rain just as Linnea reached her car, but the young estate agent failed to notice. She was already thinking about the bottle of champagne she would open in celebration as soon as she returned to the office.

Two weeks later the builders moved into the now vacant house at number 35 Rathbone Terrace. A month after that, Linnea and Simon Shipley arrived and began to decorate.

They concentrated on finishing one room at a time, starting with the bedroom, and then the kitchen. Surprisingly, Linnea had trouble adjusting to the new house. Her sleep was disturbed by bad dreams, but she was never able to remember them when morning came.

One windswept autumn afternoon she stood in front of the fireplace and scraped at the curving mantelpiece with a pocketknife.

"God, Simon, it's gold underneath the pea, then purple, can you believe that?" She scraped a little more and checked the blade. "Then it's black, and underneath that it's finally marble. White marble or alabaster, I think. But the figures are made out of inlaid bronze. Do you suppose we can take the paint off without scratching the metal?"

"There are all kinds of solvents. It shouldn't be too difficult." Simon knelt down and examined the floor. "These boards are in good enough condition to varnish."

"Then let's do it. I hate carpets, especially the one that was down in here. It smelled like someone had died on it." Linnea stepped back from the fireplace and admired it, her head on one side. The lounge had been painted white but still seemed cold and gloomy. The only way to make the place brighter would be to cut down the overgrown laburnum in the front garden.

"Perhaps we shouldn't sell the house once it's finished," said Simon, rising from the floorboards and dusting down his jeans. "It's in such a great area."

"I know," agreed Linnea, "but we could make fifty grand on it, at least. I'll find us another one around here." She gathered her long red hair at the back of her neck and tied it up. "Of course, we'll never find another fireplace like this so we'll have to take it with us."

"Do you think that's fair?"

"Of course it's fair. Anyway, who cares? You've no business sense, Simon. It's not part of the original house, anyway. Someone imported it and installed it in the wall. Pity it's bricked up, though." Linnea ran her hand over the blocks which had been amateurishly cemented into place between the supporting pillars. "I wonder why he did that?"

"Who knows?" replied Simon. "It sounds like he was a loony. It shouldn't be too hard to open up. Hang on a minute."

He disappeared upstairs and returned with a hammer and chisel. After tapping at the mortar which surrounded the bricks for a few minutes, he rocked back on his heels and wiped his forehead with the cuff of his shirt.

"There wasn't much sand in this cement, I can tell you. I've barely left a mark, look."

Linnea examined the wall of bricks and stepped back, worrying a nail with her teeth. "Perhaps the whole cavity is filled in."

"I don't think so. Listen." He banged the wall with the head of the hammer. The sound reverberated up the chimney. "I'll get to it at the weekend, but right now I'm going to take a shower."

As Simon left the lounge, shucking his shirt as he went, his wife crouched down against the fireplace wall and listened. It seemed to her there was a scratching from within, as if a bird had blundered down the chimney and was now flapping about in the darkness of the cavity, bloodying itself in a desperate frenzy to find the narrow passageway back to the light . . . She rose quickly, shivering, and ran from the room.

That night she remembered her dreams for the first time since they had moved into the house. She saw a man, tall and thin, dragging a woman's body across the floor of the lounge. The man pulled the corpse away to the side of the room, then darkness closed around them as he stepped through the wall, heaving his human burden in with him.

"Well, it's obvious, isn't it?" said Simon when she described her dream to him the next morning. He pointed to the small portable television, which stood on a pile of books at the end of the bed. "You were watching that ridiculous horror film when you fell asleep. You know how susceptible you are. How many times does Doctor Hammond have to warn you about being influenced by such rubbish before you take notice of him? The last thing we want is for you to have a relapse."

He slammed the hall door on his way out of the house, angry with her for revealing this glimpse of her former self.

Although her husband asked her not to, Linnea worked late the rest of the week. There was a big auction coming up, and the new office was due to open in a fortnight's time. That meant a lot of extra paperwork, and as Linnea had recently been made a partner she was now expected to shoulder more of the responsibility. Besides, she made more money than Simon ever did in his teaching post, so who was he to tell her when she should and shouldn't work?

Most nights when she returned home he could be found asleep on the couch cradling an empty wine bottle. He had always been a heavy sleeper after a few drinks, so she got into the habit of going to bed alone rather than trying to wake him. She turned off the portable lounge heater as she went, so that he would inevitably join her upstairs at some point before dawn, when the chill of the night finally penetrated his bones and forced him to wakefulness.

One night, letting herself in and finding Simon in his usual unconscious state, she did not go straight to bed but sat sipping the last of the Chablis bottle as she stared at the art nouveau fireplace, wondering if he would ever manage to finish the job he had started. Much of the paint had now been removed from the surround, revealing tantalizing portions of the lustrous bronze figures beneath. The grate was still blocked up. There were heavy scratch-marks over the brickwork, as if Simon had half-heartedly attempted to break through the wall to the cavity beyond. He would need a power drill, she thought, making a mental note to buy one tomorrow. God, how he hated her being in control of the purse strings. But, she thought bitterly as she drained the glass, he had no choice in the matter. She was the one with the buying power.

Half-asleep, she rose and walked over to the electric radiator to unplug it from the wall. As she bent down she heard the scraping sound again, as if something was trapped behind the fireplace bricks. Tucking her unruly hair behind her ear and pressing her head against the cool stone, she listened intently. There it was again. Faint and repetitive, a tapping and scratching, like the claws of a squirrel, or the dragging fingertips of a slowly reviving corpse . . .

That night she firmly locked the bedroom door.

"It's always the same thing," she said, pulling the dressing gown tightly around her as she entered the kitchen. "He's dragging a body through the lounge. It's in this house, and the room is decorated the way it was before we moved in, when Myson lived here."

"That's how you first saw it," said Simon, following her. "The scene left a strong impression on you, so you dream about it."

"He drags the body over to the fireplace with great difficulty."

"Why's that?"

"I'm not sure. I can't see too clearly. I think his victim is just stunned, or maybe drugged. Anyway, she's resisting. Then he pulls her into the fireplace and steps over her body, out of the hole."

"Then what?"

She looked at him as if the answer was obvious. "He bricks it up, of course," she replied.

She had to work through most of the weekend, but managed to find time to buy Simon the drill. When she presented it to him, however, he was reluctant to use it. "Unsealing the hearth can wait until I've cleared away all the paintwork," he said. "I'm not going to rush things just because you're convinced you're going to find a body behind there. You've been warned God knows how many times about your overactive imagination." He sighed, exasperated with her. "Try to remember the way you felt before your breakdown. All the things you imagined were happening to us. Just keep that in mind, okay?" And with that he resumed rubbing a small patch of the mantelpiece, carefully removing layer after layer of the paint.

Upset, Linnea left the house and went for a walk to clear her head. At times she found the house stuffy and claustrophobic. And she was starting to feel uncomfortable when left alone in the lounge. Alone in the room with the fireplace, and its odd little scratching sounds that nobody else seemed to hear . . .

The next evening she came home from work at nine o'clock and found that he had finished removing the paint from one side of the fireplace. The effect was startling. The women were carved in glistening bronze, with sashes of inlaid copper strip tied around their waists. The stems of the twining lilies and roses were fashioned in green metal, the color of the deepest part of the sea. The piece was an extraordinary work of art, most likely unique. Linnea thought of what it was worth and her excitement overcame her growing fear of the object.

"I think we're going to find that it's signed somewhere," said Simon, wiping his brush clean on a rag. "Nobody could fashion this and not put their signature to it. Now do you see how silly your imaginings were?"

"What do you mean?" asked Linnea coldly.

"Well . . ." He sat down on the floor and crossed his legs. "Ask yourself, how could something as beautiful as this be hiding a corpse?"

"There are a great many beautiful tombs," she said, turning on her heel and leaving the room.

Simon sighed and threw down the brush. He would not go after her. Showing sympathy had no effect. He still remembered the time before. Linnea had been working until all hours, growing increasingly neurotic, and becoming so convinced that he was having an affair while she worked late that she managed to smash up the flat before the doctor finally arrived. One way or another he would have to see to it that the events of the past did not repeat themselves.

At Brockton & Shipley the auction was due to take place in three days' time, the new office was about to open and several members of staff were off sick with the flu. Linnea was the only member of staff who had a clue about the company's ongoing sales, and was consequently working harder than ever.

Halfway through the week she returned home late to find the house closed and dark. There was no sign of Simon. Angry, she let herself in, went straight to the lounge and poured out a whiskey. Then she flopped down on to the couch to gather her thoughts. It took another few moments for her to notice the sheet that had been draped over the fireplace.

Standing her drink down, she rose and moved closer. Why had Simon covered the damned thing up? Two cans of paint pinned the sheet to the ends of the mantelpiece. Gingerly she reached out and touched the cloth, but could not bring herself to remove it. A cold draught seemed to move through the room, as if someone had opened the door to the garden. And there was a strange sour-sweet smell, reminiscent of rotting vegetables. Strengthening her resolve, she raised one of the paint pots and let the sheet pull out from beneath it.

Simon had succeeded in removing a large area of paint from the remaining covered column of the fireplace. Now the other woman stood revealed in magnificent detail, from the delicate tracery of her burnished hair to the tiny scrolled stitchwork of her bodice. And he had managed to remove one of the center bricks from the blocked cavity between the columns.

Linnea felt the draught brush her legs again and realized that it was coming from the neatly chiseled hole. She badly wanted to look into the wall beyond, but lacked the courage to do so. Obviously, there was nothing inside the fireplace. Simon had presumably removed the brick in daylight, and would never have left it open for her to stumble upon if there was anything unpleasant to be found beyond. Slowly, she bent her legs and brought her eyes close to the opening. Cool air fanned her face. *So*, she thought, *the chimney* is *open.*

There was a muted sound from within, the light tapping she had heard before. It's the wind, she thought, lifting and dropping a desic-cated, ancient piece of paper, or perhaps dry leaves, fallen from the blackened tunnel above. Moving closer, she peered into the dark oblong hole. For a few moments her eyes failed to adjust to the gloom. Then, in the faint light which filtered from the distant chimney opening, she found that she could just discern the soot-caked far wall of the fireplace. All was quiet as she stared in, save for her own hesitant breath and the continuous faint scratching behind the brickwork.

Then suddenly she was looking into another pair of eyes, staring back at her from within the cavity, eyes in an ancient corpse-black face, rolling eyes, glittering and mad. She screamed and fell backward, knocking over the paint pot of turpentine, scattering the brushes and scrapers as she fought to her feet and fled the room, terror still shrilling in her throat.

Simon did not return at all that night. Linnea ran to her room and stayed there, breast heaving, locked in with the lights on and the radio playing, until exhaustion robbed her of consciousness in the cold hour of dawn-light.

She heard him come in. He went straight to the kitchen and boiled water for tea, barely acknowledging the rumpled figure in the dressing gown who stood in the doorway and stared at him in silent accusation.

"I know what you're thinking," he said casually, filling the teapot, "but you're wrong. I got drunk last night and stayed at the school. The staff party—I warned you about it, remember?"

"I remember nothing of the kind," said Linnea icily. "I know you. I could see this coming, as soon as I began working late again. I've always been able to tell what you're about to do."

"Well, you were wrong last time, and you're wrong again," he replied with a sigh. "Call the school if you don't believe me. My energies are all taken up here, with you. I haven't the strength to see anyone else, believe me." He held out a cup of milky tea to her.

"Believe you!" she repeated, knocking the cup from his hand and storming out.

In the office later she considered the rashness of her behavior. She had accused him of starting an affair. The pattern was repeating itself. She had been wrong before. As the telephones rang around her, she buried her head in her hands and thought carefully. She would find a way of letting him know that there would be no repetition of last time. This was just an isolated incident. She was still a sane, rational person. She would apologize for flying off the handle. She would even leave the office a little early tonight and take Simon to dinner somewhere smart, just to show him that she was still in control.

Then she remembered the fireplace. How could she describe what she had seen without him thinking her mad? Of course there had been nothing within the wall. Her mind had provided an apparition because it knew she would be perversely disappointed if there was nothing to be found. She decided to treat the incident as if it had never happened.

She called Simon, then booked the restaurant. The rest of the day followed smoothly, until she opened the evening newspaper.

"It's not the same man," said Simon finally. "This one's name is Parsons, not Myson."

"And I'm telling you that it is," said Linnea, her voice rising. "He may have changed his name, but that is definitely the man I bought the house from. I'd know his face anywhere." She tapped the photograph with a bitten nail. "He's lying to the police about his identity."

"Come on, they don't even know if they've got the right person." Simon pushed the folded newspaper back across the table. "All it says here is that he's helping the police with their inquiries. Besides, that photograph's so blurred that it could be anyone."

"For God's sake, don't you see?" Several other diners at nearby tables looked up from their meals at her. Noticing their alarm, she lowered her voice. "It all fits. He's wanted in connection with the murder of a woman."

"The body was found in a railway siding, not a house," said Simon patiently.

"Who knows how many others he's murdered? He could be like that man who killed all those teenagers and buried them beneath his floorboards. He was scared when I met him, anxious to sell up and get out." She tried to recall the occasion of her meeting with Mr. Myson. She had been so intent on reducing the value of the house that she'd missed parts of his mumbled conversation.

"He said he'd been having bad dreams. He kept looking at the fireplace. I've been having the same dreams, only it's *him* I see!"

Simon pushed his glasses back up his nose and thought for a moment. "You can't possibly know that you've been having the same dream as him. You're building a case out of nothing. A few nightmares, a blurry photograph, it makes no sense." He reached across the table and took her hand. "Please, darling, listen to yourself."

"There's a body behind the fireplace," she said quietly. "I looked in, I could see it. I know it's there, I could smell it. He killed someone in our house, then he killed again and the police caught him. You took the brick out. Didn't you see anything?"

"No, I didn't," he admitted. "But I was in a hurry. I wanted to get through the cavity wall, just to make a start on the removal of the bricks. Then I remembered I had the staff function to get ready for, so I left everything where it was."

"I want to go to the police, Simon." She drained the Chablis from her glass and refilled it, finishing the bottle. "I'll take the morning off and we'll go first thing."

"That's stupid. We'll open the fireplace first, completely. We'll see that there's nothing inside and we'll be able to forget the whole ridiculous incident." He shook his head. "I'm beginning to sound as . . ." He changed the sentence. "Like you."

In the car on the way home she could feel him watching her as she drove. He had been about to say "as crazy as," but had caught himself. Could she be crazy, concocting conspiracies where there were none to be found?

That night he tried to hold her in bed, but she rejected his attentions, pushing him away to the far side of the mattress. She slept fitfully, winding stickily in the sheets until she became trapped by them. The fireplace and its grisly secret burdened her dreams until the nightmare once more replayed itself in full, as if the corpse in the wall below was forcing the images of its death upon her.

She saw the man again, dragging his stunned victim across the threadbare carpet to the fireplace, but this time she saw the details clearly. The room was different, brighter, as if the laburnum beyond the lounge window no longer obstructed the sunlight. The fireplace was unveiled now, and stood free of paint in full magnificence. Indeed, there was a fire burning fiercely in its bright copper grate. This was not her dream but a variation on it, a bizarre off-kilter version where details were subtly altered. The light source in the room was different, the victim seemed much plumper than before, the room itself more gaily decorated. What was happening here? The murderer was dressed in clothes from an earlier era. Now he stooped over the sleeping body and slipped his hands beneath her broad, bare arms. Slowly he dragged her nearer to the blazing log fire. Decorative tiles were inlaid about the hearth. A coal scuttle stood to one side, an extravagantly designed poker and brush set to the other. She could even read the lettering on the side of the scuttle: vulcain. The murderer raised his victim to a sitting position. The lace on her ample bosom rose and fell as he gently lowered her face into the searing flames . . .

Linnea awoke in a gasping fit, unable to catch her breath, the sheet twisted about her. Her head throbbed with the aftereffects of the wine she had consumed at dinner. She turned to wake Simon but found herself alone in the bed. From downstairs came the rhythmic sound of metal on brick. The luminous hands of the wall clock stood at 3:35. Linnea swung her legs from the mattress, untangling the sheet as she did so, and reached for her dressing gown.

The lights were on in the lounge. She came down the stairs and pushed the door open. Simon was kneeling before the fireplace, his forehead beaded with sweat. He was wearing a short-sleeved sweater over his pajamas. He lowered the hammer and chisel, and twisted around to face his wife.

"I couldn't sleep," he said with a shrug. "You were tossing and turning so much. Anyway, I knew I wouldn't get any peace until I opened the damned thing up . . ." He turned back to the brickwork and continued striking at it with the chisel. The second brick was loose now, nearly ready to come out.

"I know about the fireplace," she said, her mind still heavy with sleep.

"What do you mean?" He hammered at the brickwork. A shower of cement fell to the newspaper which wreathed the hearth.

"I know who built it." She raised her hand to her head, feeling dizzy once more. Already, the nightmare was fading.

"You've been dreaming again. You were talking in your sleep." He checked the cynicism in his voice. "So who built it?"

"Henri . . . Henri Désiré . . . something . . ." The name blurred and vanished, erased from her slumber-ridden mind. "I can't remember any more."

The chisel bit deep into stone and dislodged the second brick. Simon carefully removed it and began on the third. Outside, rain began to spatter the windows.

"Simon, don't take any more out," she cried suddenly. "I'm afraid."

"Look at it from a logical viewpoint," he replied, hammering rhythmically at the brickwork as he spoke. "If there *was* a corpse behind here, it couldn't hurt us now. It would hardly be likely to leap out, would it?"

"There is danger here. The most terrible danger."

She barely recognized her own voice. Behind her, the rain fell hard against the glass. She could hear it falling on the roof, drumming distantly at the top of the chimney. As she inched closer to Simon he removed the third brick and started on the fourth. The rest came away easily, and soon a pile of bricks had formed on the newspaper beside the fireplace. The black hole which gaped before them was ready for investigation.

"Pass me the flashlight." Simon held out his hand, not once removing his eyes from the terrible dark space between the engraved pillars.

"Don't go in there. Please, Simon, listen to me." She stood behind him as he switched on the flashlight and shone its beam into the cavity. Linnea could not bring herself to look.

"Well, there's your corpse all right." He turned and gently removed her hands from her face. "Take a look."

Slowly, Linnea raised her eyes to the spot where the flashlight shone. The cavity within the fireplace was completely empty, save for a large dead rat. The plump meatiness of the rodent's body suggested that it had died not long before.

"It was probably what you heard scratching at the wall. It may even have been what you saw. No ghosts, no murder victims, just a poor bedraggled old rat."

"Oh, Simon." She felt like crying with relief—and yet the feeling of dread was still there. After a moment or two, it began to grow again, stronger and stronger.

He took her hand and brought her close to the fireplace. "Such a beautiful object." His voice sounded far away, lost in dreams. She looked down at the carvings of the women who posed resplendent in bronze and copper raiments, at the delicately curved roses and lilies which grew in profusion about their feet, and at the small patch of pea-green paint-work still to be removed at the base of the column.

"You've forgotten a bit," she heard herself saying, as if she had intoned the same remark a hundred times before. She pointed a wavering finger at the patch.

"If I'm not mistaken," said Simon jovially, "that will provide us with the last piece of the puzzle."

He switched off the flashlight and the soot-covered corpse of the rat jumped back into darkness. Removing a palette knife from a tin filled with methylated spirit, he wiped the blade and began to gently lift the paint away in small strips.

She leaned forward, her curiosity overcoming her fear. Inlaid letters were appearing beneath the paint. Simon picked delicately with the knife, gradually revealing an extravagantly scrolled signature. Linnea's hand flew to her mouth as she read the name with mounting horror. The room dipped beneath her and tendrils of darkness swam across her vision, removing the scene from view and thrusting her into a void of blackest night. She fell heavily to the floor.

The dream closed in again, but this time she was a part of it, cast in the role of the murderer's victim. She felt herself being dragged across the carpet, then pulled upright into a sitting position, in preparation for her interment within the wall. The dream grew dark as all sensation faded.

She awoke from the nightmare to find herself crouched in a tight, dark space with her hands tied painfully behind her back. It took a few moments for her to realize that she was inside the fireplace. Her worst fear realized, she tried to scream but the cotton rag tied across her mouth prevented her. She was still wearing her nightgown, which had somehow become hitched up about her thighs. At her back, the cold furry body of the rat pressed against her bare buttocks. Far above, a dim luminescence showed at the top of the soot-encrusted chimney. Droplets of rain lightly touched her face.

Before her terrified eyes, Simon was patiently cementing the bricks back into place. His face appeared sheened in sweat through the shrinking gap in the wall. Behind his spectacles, his eyes were blank and unseeing as he labored at his task, fulfilling his prophesied role. She longed to tell him of her mistake, of how she had confused past, present, and future to arrive at this inevitable conclusion.

Henri Désiré Landru, the signature had read, the signature of Bluebeard himself. The insane mass murderer had spent his childhood years at the Vulcain ironworks in Paris, where his father was a fireman. He had disposed of at least ten women in his fireplace, macerating them in flame and destroying them so thoroughly that no trace of their bodies could ever be found. Even after his capture, he had remained silent and unrepentant.

Myson had been aware of the fireplace's influence, had grown fearful for his sanity, and although he was able to escape the house, had eventually succumbed to his terrible destiny.

As Simon eased the final brick into position and patted the surrounding mortar into a smooth finish, she knew that it was now too late for either of them to break the unending pattern.

Alone in final darkness, she provided appeasement to the stone and metal thing which made up her prison. The fireplace fed on her terror, just as it would eventually rob her of her life.

THESE BEASTS

TANITH LEE
from an idea by John Kaiine

Tanith Lee (1947–2015) did not learn to read—she was dyslectic—until almost age eight, and then only because her father taught her. This opened the world of books to her, and by the following year she was writing stories. She worked in various jobs, including shop assistant, waitress, librarian, and clerk, before Donald A. Wollheim's DAW Books issued her novel *The Birthgrave* in 1975.

The imprint went on to publish a further twenty-six of her novels and collections. Since then, she published more than one hundred novels and collections, including *Death's Master, The Silver Metal Lover, Red as Blood,* and the Arkham House volume *Dreams of Dark and Light.* She also scripted two episodes of the BBC series *Blakes 7,* and her story "Nunc Dimittis" was adapted as an episode of the TV series *The Hunger.*

She was a winner of the World Fantasy Award and the British Fantasy Award, and she received Life Achievement Awards from the World Horror Convention, the World Fantasy Convention, and the Horror Writers Association.

"Like a lot of my plots," recalled the author, "this one was coined by my partner, John Kaiine, in fact many years before we met. Tomb robbers seem to fascinate us both, and his idea of the liquid map (yes, it's John's invention, not mine) provided a final element for this nasty, nasty tale."

HE WAS A tomb robber.

Well, when you were dead, you were dead. All came to it. The mighty in their gold and gems, the impoverished unknown, wrapped in rags, their legs broken to fit the grave. And even he, Carem, would one day die. He did not mind if someone robbed him, after death. Welcome, my friend.

It was this life that counted.

Oh, he had been born as no one in the splendid city among the pink rocks. Noom Dargh, once the seat of kings, but no longer. He had been a whore's son, sold at three months to be another whore. At ten, evading the man who was his owner—spuriously charming, as Carem had learned to be, they all trusted him—he made off with traders. He was quick as fire. Handsome too.

Among the traders he learned his profession.

The caravan routes went all ways. And in the yellow deserts, stood up strange bulbous stones, caught forever in mid-topple. "What is that place?" "Ah, we will show him." It was a place of tombs.

They went by night. No moon. Things howled in the desert, but he was not afraid. No, not until they breached the stinking hotness of the rock, and the bats, which laired there, poured outward—then the man who liked Carem consoled him. "There's nothing here to hurt you. But look—what's that which shines?" What shone was gold, contrary to so many proverbs.

By the time he was a man, Carem had gained much knowledge, and some wealth. Let it be said, the wealth came from others and the knowledge was all to do with thievery. But Carem did not harm the living. No, he was kind to them. He gave to beggars in the street, and was generous with the girls he dighted.

By his twenty-eighth year, he had a house on the edge of Noom Dargh, a house with gardens and channels of water, a house with courtyards and dovecotes, and awnings embroidered by gold.

He had also two wives, Bisint, who was rich, and Zulmia, who was beautiful.

In the city they spoke of him with respect. No one publicly remembered anymore what he did. Indeed, he did not do it, for now other men worked on his behalf, and brought him treasures by night through a secret walk in the starry garden.

Lucky Carem. A life from death.

One sunset as, half a mile away below his mansion, the city turned blood-red and the desert scarlet, someone came seeking Carem; would speak only to him.

They met on a shady terrace and drank fig wine.

"I hurried straight to you, sir," said the visitor, a traveler from antique lands. "You alone could do it."

"Do what?"

"Get in, get out. It needs skill and wisdom. It needs *knowledge* of such things."

"What things are they?"

The traveler smiled. "They call yours a bestial career, but I say one does what one is good at."

"You mean my shares in merchant enterprise."

"No. Your tomb-robbery."

Carem said, smiling too, "Have I been insulted?"

"Not at all. You're known as a master. And this, believe me, who would not dare it, needs a master's touch."

"You may explain. For purposes of amusement. If I laugh enough, you shall have gold to fill one hand, and sufficient silver to fill two."

"Treble that. You will find you'll laugh your head off, Lord Carem." Then the traveler spoke of an ancient country, once astride the world, and now come down to ruination. Its great obsession, this land, had been the burial of its kings and princes—of whom there were many—in the most sumptuous and enduring manner. And, too, in deepest secret. Now and then one of these burial spots would be thought to have been discovered. Then everyone went mad. And, often as not, since they were usually also wrong, venturers came back with nothing but sore bones and empty wallets.

"This *I* have, however," said the traveler, "is not only sure—and I can give you proof—it is infallible. Besides which, it is known. Spoken and dreamed of, a thing of sparkle and nightmare."

"Is there the normal curse, then, on the tomb?" asked Carem, indolently. Had he been a fox, his ears would have stood up high enough to touch the awning overhead.

"A curse known as familiarly as the tomb. Indeed, the tomb is named for it. There in the waste beyond the pastures of the River Khenemy."

"Oh, is it Stone-Beard's Palace? That was pillaged three years ago. So I've been led to believe."

"Not there."

"The Garden of Arches, then? That too. And only a wisp of gold got from it."

"Not there."

"More wine?" inquired Carem. "A cake?"

"Yes, I will take more wine. The burial place I offer you is the Tomb of the Black Dog."

Then Carem, despite the last trace of the sunset, paled. His eyes opened and closed, and opened. He said, "Surely that is only a story."

"Till now. Now it can be yours."

"And your proof?"

Then the traveler took a purse out of his clothing and out of the purse he drew a narrow gleaming snake. This he set on the terrace, where, after two or three convulsive movements, it brought up out of its jaws a small black egg.

The egg sat on the paving.

The traveler spoke a word that fell like a raw, hot drop of unseasonal rain.

The egg burst, and there lay a tiny black figure of a dog at rest, its head erect, and its throat rimmed by gold.

"A copy of the image that guards the tomb?"

"Found in the sand not twenty paces from the area."

Muttering a protective charm, Carem picked up the figurine and held it. It was unearthly cold. He put it down. It cast no shadow, turn it as he would.

"Tell me all you know," said Carem.

The traveler did so. Presently much gold and silver were given over in handfuls.

At midnight they parted, the traveler and Carem, and Carem went prudently to sleep with his plain wife, Bisint, for in the morning he would be going away.

The journey to Khenemy took several months, longer than was ordinarily needful, since Carem undertook the end of it in disguise, as a poor lame pilgrim, seeker of the shrines of the holy river.

Many tiresome days Carem spent, smothered by dust and ringing his irritating little pilgrim's bell at the gates of collapsed temples, until at last, moved apparently by that mystic urge which drives prophets and seers, he wandered out into the desert waste.

The desert of Khenemy was like no other.

Where the River was, emerald pastures swelled, with cows and cameloids feeding beneath palms heavy with dates, and lime-green banana trees. Then there lay the strips of fields, and sacred groves, and thereafter the first of the waste, brown as an egg, where, in caves, the former inhabitants of old fallen cities lived, lighting at night their fires and lamps of horn, like yellow stars felled to the land.

After this, a place opened that was like Hell.

The land was white, and blistered the soles through your boots, the sun was a ball of white matter, and the sky white, and here and there rose monuments of the race of Khenemy, which had passed away. Statue men a hundred feet tall, wielding swords of stone, towers and gateways that led nowhere, all blasted by a hot moistureless wind, the breath of something long dead.

Carem, though, had a map. Not to hand, but written accurately in his head.

So he trekked by day the burning waste, and slept by night under the suns of other indifferent worlds. And on the second evening he reached a sort of cliff. And in the eastern front of it was a mark, that looked only natural, but not to him. It was like the face of a dog.

No time like the present.

Carem went to the cliff and stared hard, and saw how the rock was.

Then he put up his agile right "lame" foot, and lifted himself. From the first step he discovered the second. They were set oddly, and were not safe. He negotiated them all, with only a little powdering of dust to show his passage.

Above, far up, the cliff was flat as a stone table.

Once there, it was possible to look for miles, and see nothing but the nighttime desert, with here and there, one of its ghastly monuments.

Instead Carem looked and saw a hag seated by a round hole in the stone.

"Stay," said the hag. "Let me tell you what you risk."

"Very well," said Carem.

"Once I was very young," said the hag.

"That might be said of all of us."

"I traveled here," continued the hag, humorlessly. "I sought to enter the Tomb of the Black Dog. Aiece! I did not know. I thought it the burial place of some great king, guarded by that fearsome guardian, Anubar, the Biter of Souls."

Carem nodded.

The hag said, "Know, it is the Tomb of the Black Dog Himself. So we discovered to our cost. He Himself lies buried here, that guardian invoked in so many other places."

Carem shivered, but it was only the heat.

"Thus all of you died, granny, and you're a ghost."

"Nay," said granny, "me alone He let live. But see," and she opened her robe with her left hand to reveal horrid scars and omissions. "He tore off my right arm and my right breast. I am His warning."

"Thank you," said Carem. "Now you have warned me you may be off."

The hag got up and walked away. She cast no shadow. That too the Black Dog had torn from her. She went down the cliff by another way, invisible to ordinary persons.

Oh, he was not alarmed. Not Carem.

He sat by the black hole in the stone and took a pipe from his garments. On this he blew. It made no noise.

It would sound however a few hours' journey away, at the spot to which he had earlier sent the men who would help him at the tomb. He had now merely to wait.

He first anointed himself from a phial, then stretched out in the hot night. The dead breath of the wind lulled him. He slept.

When the moon rose, the jingle of harness conveniently roused him again, and sitting up, he beheld the twenty men he had hired, who had gathered at the foot of the cliff.

Carem rose and poured onto the stone of the tomb some wine and oil.

"What are you doing?" demanded one of the men below among the cameloids.

"Making the first offering," said Carem. "Come up now, as I will direct you."

Up they came. A mixed bag they were. Some aristocratic and anxious, others pure fresh scum. They crowded around him, and Carem pointed to the hole.

"The rope I have readied. Who will be first down into the tomb?"

No one thrilled at the chance.

Carem said, "This gold piece to the first."

After this there were some offers.

Presently three men climbed down, one after the other.

"What do you see?"

"Darkness."

"Yes that's as it should be."

Then Carem went down and the others followed him.

In the tomb, Carem struck a light, and lit a torch.

It was very hot, as Carem was well used to, but no bats l1aired there. Nothing lived in that enclosure. Not even a spider or a beetle. Bones there were, however, on the floor.

The walls were brown, and painted dimly by a massive figure that had the head of a long-nosed black dog. At this the crew pointed uneasily.

Carem drew from his clothes a small dark bottle. He spilled out its contents on the stone floor. Fluid ran, and formed a pattern. It was a map, in liquid, of the tomb.

Just at that moment came a low, soft growl.

The hired men, most of them, bleated with alarm.

But, "It's only magic," said one.

"Exactly so," said Carem. "You are meant to fear it and run away empty-handed. Think of the treasures that lie in the inner chambers."

The men were somewhat consoled. They rubbed their amulets and muttered.

"Do you see that door," said Carem, consulting his liquid map, "who will go through first?"

There was great rivalry as to who would not.

While they argued, something came rushing.

It was like a wind, or five hundred hounds, packed close as fish in a shoal, running after game.

The man nearest the door was one minute there, and then his head was off. It was wrenched from his shoulders. Next the fellow beside him was disemboweled, and another split from throat to crotch. All this was done by an agency invisible.

With quick screams, and sometimes so swift there was no time for that either, the twenty men of Carem's hire landed in pieces and bits on the floor, where the bones of previous victims lay.

But Carem, who had anointed himself with a certain thing repellent to all dogs, was not touched.

When the last man had had his throat torn out, a low satisfied growl rang round the space.

"Thus I make the second offering," said Carem.

Then he walked through the dark door without being molested, and through thirteen passages, right up to the farthest wall. There he kneeled and felt with his hands by the light of his torch.

Soon he made out a round door no higher than a child of three, and no wider than said child lying sideways.

Through that Carem crawled, and so entered the treasure vault.

There was just enough light to behold.

The room was stuffed with gold, and jewels, green and crimson, blue and white. But everything was on a little scale, even the emeralds no larger than a thumbnail, and the golden effigies of dogs and wolves, foxes and jackals, were the size of acorns and peach-stones.

Carem filled the bags inside his clothes, his boots, his loin-pouch. He opened the ready purses at his neck and waist. He put things into his mouth, and up his nostrils, and in his ears, and elsewhere, which shall be nameless.

Take as you find.

On the wall of this last room, which was a sort of kennel, was painted no dog, but a black eye. Carem took no obvious notice of it as he screwed a ruby into his navel. Sucking a last golden standing jackal with diamond eyes between his lips, Carem crawled back out of the inner place.

He had accrued a great amount, yet a greater was left. Let that, then, be the third offering, his temperance. For the rest, he would have reputation. That was worth a vaster amount than the stones themselves.

Back through the thirteen passages he waddled. In the outer passage he waddled. In the outer place, he stepped fastidiously over the bones.

He stood a moment listening.

Somewhere something howled, but it was, as usual, on the desert outside.

Carem climbed the rope, awkwardly, and emerged into the boiling air, which was itself like the interior of a grave.

On the table-top of the tomb, huge black paw marks were apparent in the moonlight, and overhead the mass of stars seemed to describe, for a moment, the skull of a dog.

Carem pulled up the rope, and spoke a word. The entry to the tomb, the hole, vanished.

Below the cliff most of the cameloids had run off. But a few remained, trembling and farting with fear. He would sell them at a handy village. Well, a shame to waste.

When he got down from the cliff, Carem turned about on the sand, clanking and clinking from his weight of jewels and gold.

There on the smooth ground lay something black, pointing from him and away from the moon. He had kept his shadow. All was well.

On his return home, plain Bisint tactfully sent word that she was out of sorts, and beautiful Zulmia met Carem in the garden, plump as a white plum and garlanded with blue-black hair. Much joy he had of her, under the roses and lemon trees, while bees buzzed and the honeyed sun slowly set into the uncomplicated pink desert of Noom Dargh.

He did not tell Zulmia, or even Bisint, anything of his exploits, nor did he give them anything from his robbery. Instead he brought Zulmia a rope of pearls and sapphires to match her skin and eyes, and Bisint a rope of topaz to match her teeth.

The treasure of the tomb Carem sold carefully and meagerly. Soon nobles and lords sent word to him, and later might come the words of kings. He would be famous now. He would be feared as well as praised.

Zulmia approached her husband modestly. She told him, as if he, not she, had been clever, that she was with child.

"I am sure it's a boy, masterful husband. Only a male would spring from your loins."

Carem was pleased, for never before, to his knowledge, had he reproduced himself.

He looked delightedly at his lovely wife, plumper than ever, her hair like silk, and at her feet her jet-black shadow. All was wonderfully well.

How charmingly the days and nights passed then. Even Bisint was helpful, often ailing, and keeping to her rooms. If she should die, all her wealth would come to Carem.

He would think now, upon sunny evenings, watching the final noose of light about the towers of the city below, how he might give up for good his profession. How he might turn to other things, from which none would dare refuse him entry. His son, after all, should inherit a business, not merely an empire of robbery.

On the night of the full moon, eight months later, Bisint peacefully passed away.

In a generous spirit, Carem left her her topazes to be buried in.

It was midday, and beautiful Zulmia had gone into labor. From the arbor where Carem sat drinking pomegranate wine, the house was closely visible, and her screams of pain might now and then be heard.

They were good, rounded, healthy screams. It seemed the birth was going perfectly.

Carem saw a woman approaching through his gardens. He took her for a servant bringing roast lamb and date leaves. He smiled and poured a little wine on the ground, an old custom, for the child to be.

Something caught Carem's eye then. It was his fine dark shadow. How bold it was. How black.

Carem studied this. He noticed, oh yes, that some curious arrangement of the awning, or the arbor trees, had caused his shadow to take on a peculiar shape. It had two upright ears. Its nose was very long.

As Carem was pondering this, the servant woman came up to him. She was not his servant, but a squat female, veiled, with the sun shining through her. Around her neck gleamed faintly a rope of yellow stones.

"I am your dead wife," said Bisint's uncomely ghost, unnecessarily. "I have arrived to warn you."

"That was most kind. Of what?"

"Hark."

Carem hearkened, and heard another loud scream from the house.

"Yes," said Carem. "That is Zulmia."

"Indeed," said Bisint, "and she does well to scream. O stupid Carem, what did you bring away from the Tomb of the Black Dog?"

It was random to lie to or upbraid a ghost. "Some trinkets," he replied.

"What else, O stupid Carem?"

"Nothing."

"Yes."

"Only I, myself."

"Stupid, *stupid* Carem," emphasized Bisint, and disappeared.

Carem looked down for his shadow, that had pointed ears and a snout. It too had vanished.

A particularly awful scream rocked through the air.

Carem glanced at his mansion.

Zulmia's windows, which were hung with crystal-clear cloth, turned suddenly violently red. More, they appeared wet.

Then came other screams, the shrieks of women and the bawling of men.

A noted physician sprang suddenly out of the window. He fell down among the lemon trees.

Carem rose and went toward him.

"What, pray, goes on?"

"Your wife is delivered," said the physician. He had broken both legs, but paid them no heed. His robe, like the window hangings, was soaked by blood.

"A boy or a girl?" asked Carem.

"Neither. I will tell you," said the physician, "since I cannot run away. Something tore itself from the womb of your wife, up out of her belly. It burst her like an orange. It was dark. It had a pointed snout."

Carem turned from the physician and gazed at the doorway of his house.

From the golden inner walk, something black was coming. It was tall and lean and moved lightly on its hind limbs.

Nothing had he brought from the Tomb of the Black Dog, save his loot and his body, with every aperture blocked. But one. One too small indeed to fill. And the shadow had gone with him. The shadow had run out of him, there among the roses.

From Carem's doorway stepped Anubar, Biter of Souls. He was black as night, in the mid of day. His ears stood up, His snout was long. In His clawed paws lay the remains of Zulmia's womb and round His feet, like bracelets, were wrapped the entrails of others. He ripped the physician's body in half, in passing. Then stared at Carem, who bowed low and waited for death.

As well he might.

TIGHT LITTLE STITCHES IN A DEAD MAN'S BACK

JOE R. LANSDALE

Joe R. Lansdale has published more than forty-five novels, dozens of novellas, and over four hundred short stories and articles. He has written for *Batman: The Animated Series* and *Superman: The Animated Series*; his novella *Bubba Hotep* was filmed by director Don Coscarelli and starred Bruce Campbell, and his novel *Cold in July* was made into a movie starring Michael C. Hall, Don Johnson, and the late Sam Shepard. More recently, his series of books about the eponymous oddball couple has been adapted for the Sundance Channel as *Hap and Leonard*, featuring James Purefoy and Michael Kenneth Williams.

Lansdale has been named a Grand Master by the World Horror Convention and has received the Lifetime Achievement Award from the Horror Writers Association. His other awards include ten Bram Stoker Awards from the HWA, an Edgar Award from the Mystery Writers of America for his novel *The Bottoms*, and a Spur Award from The Western Writers of America for his novel *Paradise Sky*.

"'Tight Little Stitches . . .' was written in response to an anthology request," the author recalls. "An after-the-bomb anthology titled *Nukes*. I have always been interested in 'after the bomb' or 'after the disease' or 'what happens after' type of stories, but frankly, I didn't have an idea for one. Then, for whatever reason, the idea of a man with his back tattooed (maybe I recalled Ray Bradbury's *The Illustrated Man?*) came to me and the rest of the story filled itself in with dollops of *The Day of the Triffids* and other novels of that ilk, and it became its own thing, I'm glad to say.

"I hated writing it at the time and thought I had a total disaster. It was the first story I wrote that actually got attention and was a nominee for the World Fantasy Award. To this day people surprise me by thinking it won the award. It's nice the story is remembered, and I think, though it's somewhat atypical of my style, that it's one of my best."

FROM THE JOURNAL OF PAUL MARDER

(BOOM!)

That's a little scientist joke, and the proper way to begin this. As for the purpose of this notebook, I'm uncertain. Perhaps to organize my thoughts and not go insane.

No. Probably so I can read it and feel as if I'm being spoken to. Maybe neither of those reasons. It doesn't matter. I just want to do it, and that is enough.

What's new?

Well, Mr. Journal, after all these years I've taken up martial arts again—or at least the forms and calisthenics of Tae Kwon Do. There is no one to spar with here in the lighthouse, so the forms have to do.

"ALL AROUND IT LITTLE WORMY THINGS SQUIRMED."

There is Mary, of course, but she keeps all her sparring verbal. And as of late, there is not even that. I long for her to call me a sonofabitch. Anything. Her hatred of me has cured to 100 percent perfection and she no longer finds it necessary to speak. The tight lines around her eyes and mouth, the emotional heat that radiates from her body like a dreadful cold sore looking for a place to lie down is voice enough for her. She lives only for the moment when she (the cold sore) can attach herself to me with her needles, ink, and thread. She lives only for the design on my back.

That's all I live for as well. Mary adds to it nightly and I enjoy the pain. The tattoo is of a great, blue mushroom cloud, and in the cloud, etched ghost-like, is the face of our daughter, Rae. Her lips are drawn tight, eyes are closed, and there are stitches deeply pulled to simulate the lashes. When I move fast and hard they rip slightly and Rae cries bloody tears.

That's one reason for the martial arts. The hard practice of them helps me to tear the stitches so my daughter can cry. Tears are the only thing I can give her.

Each night I bare my back eagerly to Mary and her needles. She pokes deep and I moan in pain as she moans in ecstasy and hatred. She adds more color to the design, works with brutal precision to bring Rae's face out in sharper relief. After ten minutes she tires and will work no more. She puts the tools away and I go to the full-length mirror on the wall. The lantern on the shelf flickers like a jack-o'-lantern in a high wind, but there is enough light for me to look over my shoulder and examine the tattoo. And it is beautiful. Better each night as Rae's face becomes more and more defined.

Rae.

Rae. God. Can you forgive me, sweetheart?

But the pain of the needles, wonderful and cleansing as they are, is not enough. So I go sliding, kicking, and punching along the walkway around the lighthouse, feeling Rae's red tears running down my spine, gathering in the wasteband of my much-stained canvas pants.

Winded, unable to punch and kick anymore, I walk over to the railing and call down into the dark, "Hungry?"

In response to my voice a chorus of moans rises up to greet me.

Later, I lie on my pallet, hands behind my head, examine the ceiling and try to think of something worthy to write in you, Mr. Journal. So seldom is there anything. Nothing seems truly worthwhile.

Bored of this, I roll on my side and look at the great light that once shone out to the ships, but is now forever snuffed. Then I turn the other direction and look at my wife sleeping on her bunk, her naked ass turned toward me. I try to remember what it was like to make love to her, but it is difficult. I only remember that I miss it. For a long moment I stare at my wife's ass as if it is a mean mouth about to open and reveal teeth. Then I roll on my back again, stare at the ceiling, and continue this routine until daybreak.

Mornings I greet the flowers, their bright red and yellow blooms bursting from the heads of long-dead bodies that will not rot. The flowers open wide to reveal their little black brains and their feathery feelers, and they lift their blooms upward and moan. I get a wild pleasure out of this. For one crazed moment I feel like a rock singer appearing before his starry-eyed audience.

When I tire of the game I get the binoculars, Mr. Journal, and examine the eastern plains with them, as if I expect a city to materialize there. The most interesting thing I have seen on those plains is a herd of large lizards thundering north. For a moment, I considered calling Mary to see them, but I didn't. The sound of my voice, the sight of my face, upsets her. She loves only the tattoo and is interested in nothing more.

When I finish looking at the plains, I walk to the other side. To the west, where the ocean was, there is now nothing but miles and miles of cracked, black sea-bottom. Its only resemblance to a great body of water is the occasional dust storms that blow out of the west like dark tidal waves and wash the windows black at midday. And the creatures. Mostly mutated whales. Monstrously large, sluggish things. Abundant now where once they were near extinction. (Perhaps the whales should form some sort of Greenpeace organization for humans now. What do you think, Mr. Journal? No need to answer. Just another one of those little scientist jokes.)

These whales crawl across the sea-bottom near the lighthouse from time to time, and if the mood strikes them, they rise on their tails and push their heads near the tower and examine it. I keep expecting one to flop down on us, crushing us like bugs. But no such luck. For some unknown reason the whales never leave the cracked seabed to venture onto what we formerly called the shore. It's as if they live in invisible water and are bound by it. A racial memory perhaps. Or maybe there's something in that cracked black soil they need. I don't know.

Besides the whales I suppose I should mention I saw a shark once. It was slithering along at a great distance and the tip of its fin was winking in the sunlight. I've also seen some strange, legged fish and some things I could not put a name to. I'll just call them whale food since I saw one of the whales dragging his bottom jaw along the ground one day, scooping up the creatures as they tried to beat a hasty retreat.

Exciting, huh? Well, that's how I spend my day, Mr. Journal. Roaming about the tower with my glasses, coming in to write in you, waiting anxiously for Mary to take hold of that kit and give me the signal. The mere thought of it excites me to erection. I suppose you could call that our sex act together.

And what was I doing the day they dropped The Big One?
Glad you asked that Mr. Journal, really I am.

I was doing the usual. Up at six, did the shit, shower, and shave routine. Had breakfast. Got dressed. Tied my tie. I remember doing the latter, and not very well, in front of the bedroom mirror, and noticing that I had shaved poorly. A hunk of dark beard decorated my chin like a bruise.

Rushing to the bathroom to remedy that, I opened the door as Rae, naked as the day of her birth, was stepping from the tub.

Surprised, she turned to look at me. An arm went over her breasts, and a hand, like a dove settling into a fiery bush, covered her pubic area.

Embarrassed, I closed the door with an "excuse me" and went about my business—unshaved. It was an innocent thing. An accident. Nothing sexual. But when I think of her now, more often than not, that is the first image that comes to mind. I guess it was the moment I realized my baby had grown into a beautiful woman.

That was also the day she went off to her first day of college and got to see, ever so briefly, the end of the world.

And it was the day the triangle—Mary, Rae, and myself—shattered.

If my first memory of Rae alone is that day, naked in the bathroom, my foremost memory of us as a family is when Rae was six. We used to go to the park and she would ride the merry-go-round, swing, teeter-totter, and finally my back. ("I want to piggy Daddy.") We would gallop about until my legs were rubber, then we would stop at the bench where Mary sat waiting. I would turn my back to the bench so Mary could take Rae down, but always before she did, she would reach around from behind, caressing Rae, pushing her tight against my back, and Mary's hands would touch my chest.

God, but if I could describe those hands. She still has hands like that, after all these years. I feel them fluttering against my back when she works. They are long and sleek and artistic. Naturally soft, like the belly of a baby rabbit. And when she held Rae and me that way, I felt that no matter what happened in the world, we three could stand against it and conquer.

But now the triangle is broken and the geometry gone away.

So the day Rae went off to college and was fucked into oblivion by the dark, pelvic thrust of the bomb, Mary drove me to work. Me, Paul Marder, big shot with The Crew. One of the finest, brightest young minds in the industry. Always teaching, inventing, and improving on our nuclear threat, because, as we often joked, "We cared enough to send only the very best."

When we arrived at the guard booth, I had out my pass, but there was no one to take it. Beyond the chain-link gate there was a wild mêlée of people running, screaming, falling down.

I got out of the car and ran to the gate. I called out to a man I knew as he ran by. When he turned his eyes were wild and his lips were flecked with foam. "The missiles are flying," he said, then he was gone, running madly.

I jumped in the car, pushed Mary aside and stomped the gas. The Buick leaped into the fence, knocking it asunder. The car spun, slammed into the edge of a building and went dead. I grabbed Mary's hand, pulled her from the car, and we ran toward the great elevators. We made one just in time. There were others running for it as the door closed, and the elevator went down. I still remember the echo of their fists on the metal just as it began to drop. It was like the rapid heartbeat of something dying.

And so the elevator took us to the world of Down Under and we locked it off. There we were in a five-mile layered city designed not only as a massive office and laboratory, but as an impenetrable shelter. It was our special reward for creating the poisons of war. There was food, water, medical supplies, films, books, you name it. Enough to last two thousand people for a hundred years. Of the two thousand it was designed for, perhaps eleven hundred made it. The others didn't run fast enough from the parking lot or the other buildings, or they were late for work, or maybe they had called in sick.

Perhaps they were the lucky ones. They might have died in their sleep. Or while they were having a morning quickie with the spouse. Or perhaps as they lingered over that last cup of coffee.

Because you see, Mr. Journal, Down Under was no paradise. Before long suicides were epidemic. I considered it myself from time to time. People slashed their throats, drank acid, took pills. It was not unusual to come out of your cubicle in the morning and find people dangling from pipes and rafters like ripe fruit. There were also the murders. Most of them performed by a crazed group who lived in the deeper recesses of the unit and called themselves the Shit Faces. From time to time they smeared dung on themselves and ran amok, clubbing men, women, and children born down under, to death. It was rumored they ate human flesh.

We had a police force of sorts, but it didn't do much. It didn't have much sense of authority. Worse, we all viewed ourselves as deserving victims. Except for Mary, we had all helped to blow up the world.

Mary came to hate me. She came to the conclusion I had killed Rae. It was a realization that grew in her like a drip growing and growing until it became a gushing flood of hate. She seldom talked to me. She tacked up a picture of Rae and looked at it most of the time.

Topside she had been an artist, and she took that up again. She rigged a kit of tools and inks and became a tattooist. Everyone came to her for a mark. And though each was different, they all seemed to indicate one thing: I fucked up. I blew up the world. Brand me.

Day in and day out she did her tattoos, having less and less to do with me, pushing herself more and more into this work until she was as skilled with skin and needles as she had been Topside with brush and canvas. And one night, as we lay on our separate pallets, feigning sleep, she said to me, "I just want you to know how much I hate you."

"I know," I said.

"You killed Rae."

"I know."

"You say you killed her, you bastard. Say it."

"I killed her," I said, and meant it.

Next day I asked for my tattoo. I told her of this dream that came to me nightly. There would be darkness, and out of this darkness would come a swirl of glowing clouds, and the clouds would meld into a mushroom shape, and out of that—torpedo-shaped, nose pointing skyward, striding on ridiculous cartoon legs—would step The Bomb.

There was a face painted on The Bomb, and it was my face. And suddenly the dream's point of view would change, and I would be looking out of the eyes of that painted face. Before me was my daughter. Naked. Lying on the ground. Her legs wide apart. Her sex glazed like a wet canyon.

And I/The Bomb, would dive into her, pulling those silly feet after me, and she would scream. I could hear it echo as I plunged through her belly, finally driving myself out of the top of her head, then blowing to terminal orgasm. And the dream would end where it began. A mushroom cloud. Darkness.

When I told Mary the dream and asked her to interpret it in her art, she said, "Bare your back," and that's how the design began. An inch of work at a time—a painful inch. She made sure of that.

Never once did I complain. She'd send the needles home as hard and deep as she could, and though I might moan or cry out, I never asked her to stop. I could feel those fine hands touching my back and I loved it. The needles. The hands. The needles. The hands.

And if that was so much fun, you ask, why did I come Topside?

You ask such probing questions, Mr. Journal. Really you do, and I'm glad you asked that. My telling you will be like a laxative, I hope. Maybe if I just let the shit flow I'll wake up tomorrow and feel a lot better about myself.

Sure. And it will be the dawning of a new Pepsi generation as well. It will have all been a bad dream. The alarm clock will ring, I'll get up, have my bowl of Rice Krispies, and tie my tie.

Okay, Mr. Journal. The answer. Twenty years or so after we went Down Under, a fistful of us decided it couldn't be any worse Topside than it was below. We made plans to go see. Simple as that. Mary and I even talked a little. We both entertained the crazed belief Rae might have survived. She would be thirty-eight. We might have been hiding below like vermin for no reason. It could be a brave new world up there.

I remember thinking these things, Mr. Journal, and half-believing them.

We outfitted two sixty-foot crafts that were used as part of our transportation system Down Under, plugged in the half-remembered codes that opened the elevators, and drove the vehicles inside. The elevator lasers cut through the debris above them and before long we were Topside. The doors opened to sunlight muted by gray-green clouds and a desert-like landscape. Immediately I knew there was no brave new world over the horizon. It had all gone to hell in a fiery handbasket, and all that was left of man's millions of years of development were a few pathetic humans living Down Under like worms, and a few others crawling Topside like the same.

We cruised about a week and finally came to what had once been the Pacific Ocean. Only there wasn't any water now, just that cracked blackness.

We drove along the shore for another week and finally saw life. A whale. Jacobs immediately got the idea to shoot one and taste its meat.

Using a high-powered rifle he killed it, and he and seven others cut slabs off it, brought the meat back to cook. They invited all of us to eat, but the meat looked greenish and there wasn't much blood and we warned him against it. But Jacobs and the others ate it anyway. As Jacobs said, "It's something to do."

A little later on Jacobs threw up blood and his intestines boiled out of his mouth, and not long after those who had shared the meat had the same thing happen to them. They died crawling on their bellies like gutted dogs. There wasn't a thing we could do for them. We couldn't even bury them. The ground was too hard. We stacked them like cord-wood along the shoreline and moved camp down a way, tried to remember how remorse felt.

And that night, while we slept as best we could, the roses came.

Now, let me admit, Mr. Journal, I do not actually know how the roses survive, but I have an idea. And since you've agreed to hear my story—and even if you haven't, you're going to anyway—I'm going to put logic and fantasy together and hope to arrive at the truth.

These roses lived in the ocean bed, underground, and at night they came out. Up until then they had survived as parasites of reptiles and animals, but a new food had arrived from Down Under. Humans. Their creators actually. Looking at it that way, you might say we were the gods who conceived them, and their partaking of our flesh and blood was but a new version of wine and wafer.

I can imagine the pulsating brains pushing up through the sea bottom on thick stalks, extending feathery feelers and tasting the air out there beneath the light of the moon—which through those odd clouds gave the impression of a pus-filled boil—and I can imagine them uprooting and dragging their vines across the ground toward the shore where the corpses lay.

Thick vines sprouted little, thorny vines, and these moved up the bank and touched the corpses. Then, with a lashing motion, the thorns tore into the flesh, and the vines, like snakes, slithered through the wounds and inside. Secreting a dissolving fluid that turned the innards to the consistency of watery oatmeal, they slurped up the mess, and the vines grew and grew at amazing speed, moved and coiled throughout the bodies, replacing nerves and shaping into the symmetry of the muscles they had devoured, and lastly they pushed up through the necks, into the skulls, ate tongues and eyeballs and sucked up the mouse-gray brains like soggy gruel. With an explosion of skull shrapnel, the roses bloomed, their tooth-hard petals expanding into beautiful red and yellow flowers, hunks of human heads dangling from them like shattered watermelon rinds.

In the center of these blooms a fresh, black brain pulsed and feathery feelers once again tasted air for food and breeding grounds. Energy waves from the floral brains shot through the miles and miles of vines that were knotted inside the bodies, and as they had replaced nerves, muscles and vital organs, they made the bodies stand. Then those corpses turned their flowered heads toward the tents where we slept, and the blooming corpses (another little scientist joke there if you're into English idiom, Mr. Journal) walked, eager to add the rest of us to their animated bouquet.

I saw my first rose-head while I was taking a leak.

I had left the tent and gone down by the shoreline to relieve myself, when I caught sight of it out of the corner of my eye. Because of the bloom I first thought it was Susan Myers. She wore a thick, woolly Afro that surrounded her head like a lion's mane, and the shape of the thing struck me as her silhouette. But when I zipped and turned, it wasn't an Afro. It was a flower blooming out of Jacobs. I recognized him by his clothes and the hunk of his face that hung off one of the petals like a worn-out hat on a peg.

In the center of the blood-red flower was a pulsating sack, and all around it little wormy things squirmed. Directly below the brain was a thin proboscis. It extended toward me like an erect penis. At its tip, just inside the opening, were a number of large thorns.

A sound like a moan came out of that proboscis, and I stumbled back. Jacobs's body quivered briefly, as if he had been besieged by a sudden chill, and ripping through his flesh and clothes, from neck to foot, was a mass of thorny, wagging vines that shot out to five feet in length.

With an almost invisible motion, they waved from west to east, slashed my clothes, tore my hide, knocked my feet out from beneath me. It was like being hit by a cat-o'-nine-tails.

Dazed, I rolled onto my hands and knees, bear-walked away from it. The vines whipped against my back and butt, cut deep.

Every time I got to my feet, they tripped me. The thorns not only cut, they burned like hot ice picks. I finally twisted away from a net of vines, slammed through one last shoot, and made a break for it.

Without realizing it, I was running back to the tent. My body felt as if I had been lying on a bed of nails and razor blades. My forearm hurt something terrible where I had used it to lash the thorns away from me. I glanced down at it as I ran. It was covered in blood. A strand of vine about two feet in length was coiled around it like a garter snake. A thorn had torn a deep wound in my arm, and the vine was sliding an end into the wound.

Screaming, I held my forearm in front of me like I had just discovered it. The flesh, where the vine had entered, rippled and made a bulge that looked like a junkie's favorite vein. The pain was nauseating. I snatched at the vine, ripped it free. The thorns turned against me like fishhooks.

The pain was so much I fell to my knees, but I had the vine out of me. It squirmed in my hand, and I felt a thorn gouge my palm. I threw the vine into the dark. Then I was up and running for the tent again.

The roses must have been at work for quite some time before I saw Jacobs, because when I broke back into camp yelling, I saw Susan, Ralph, Casey, and some others, and already their heads were blooming, skulls cracking away like broken model kits.

Jane Calloway was facing a rose-possessed corpse, and the dead body had its hands on her shoulders, and the vines were jetting out of the corpse, weaving around her like a web, tearing, sliding inside her, breaking off. The proboscis poked into her mouth and extended down her throat, forced her head back. The scream she started came out a gurgle.

I tried to help her, but when I got close, the vines whipped at me and I had to jump back. I looked for something to grab, to hit the damn thing with, but there was nothing. When next I looked at Jane, vines were stabbing out of her eyes and her tongue, now nothing more than lava-thick blood, was dripping out of her mouth onto her breasts, which, like the rest of her body, were riddled with stabbing vines.

I ran away then. There was nothing I could do for Jane. I saw others embraced by corpse hands and tangles of vines, but now my only thought was Mary. Our tent was to the rear of the campsite, and I ran there as fast as I could.

She was lumbering out of our tent when I arrived. The sound of screams had awakened her. When she saw me running she froze. By the time I got to her, two vine-riddled corpses were coming up on the tent from the left side. Grabbing her hand I half-pulled, half-dragged her away from there. I got to one of the vehicles and pushed her inside.

I locked the doors just as Jacobs, Susan, Jane, and others appeared at the windshield, leaning over the rocket-nose hood, the feelers around the brain-sacks vibrating like streamers in a high wind. Hands slid greasily down the windshield. Vines flopped and scratched and cracked against it like thin bicycle chains.

I got the vehicle started, stomped the accelerator, and the rose-heads went flying. One of them, Jacobs, bounced over the hood and splattered into a spray of flesh, ichor, and petals.

I had never driven the vehicle, so my maneuvering was rusty. But it didn't matter. There wasn't exactly a traffic rush to worry about.

After an hour or so, I turned to look at Mary. She was staring at me, her eyes like the twin barrels of a double-barreled shotgun. They seemed to say, "More of your doing," and in a way she was right. I drove on.

Daybreak we came to the lighthouse. I don't know how it survived. One of those quirks. Even the glass was unbroken. It looked like a great stone finger shooting us the bird.

The vehicle's tank was near empty, so I assumed here was as good a place to stop as any. At least there was shelter, something we could fortify. Going on until the vehicle was empty of fuel didn't make much sense. There wouldn't be any more fill-ups, and there might not be any more shelter like this.

Mary and I (in our usual silence) unloaded the supplies from the vehicle and put them in the lighthouse. There was enough food, water, chemicals for the chemical toilet, odds and ends, extra clothes, to last us a year. There were also some guns. A Colt .45 revolver, two twelve-gauge shotguns, and a .38, and enough shells to fight a small war.

When everything was unloaded, I found some old furniture downstairs, and using tools from the vehicle tried to barricade the bottom door and the one at the top of the stairs. When I finished, I thought of a line from a story I had once read, a line that always disturbed me. It went something like, "Now we're shut in for the night."

Days. Nights. All the same. Shut in with one another, our memories and the fine tattoo.

A few days later I spotted the roses. It was as if they had smelled us out. And maybe they had. From a distance, through the binoculars, they reminded me of old women in bright sun hats.

It took them the rest of the day to reach the lighthouse, and they immediately surrounded it, and when I appeared at the railing they would lift their heads and moan.

And that, Mr. Journal, brings us up to now.

I thought I had written myself out, Mr. Journal. Told the only part of my life story I would ever tell, but now I'm back. You can't keep a good world-destroyer down.

I saw my daughter last night and she's been dead for years. But I saw her, I did, naked, smiling at me, calling to ride piggyback.

Here's what happened.

It was cold last night. Must be getting along winter. I had rolled off my pallet onto the cold floor. Maybe that's what brought me awake. The cold. Or maybe it was just gut instinct. It had been a particularly wonderful night with the tattoo. The face had been made so clear it seemed to stand out from my back. It had finally become more defined than the mushroom cloud. The needles went in hard and deep, but I've had them in me so much now I barely feel the pain. After looking in the mirror at the beauty of the design, I went to bed happy, or as happy as I can get.

During the night the eyes ripped open. The stitches came out and I didn't know it until I tried to rise from the cold, stone floor and my back puckered against it where the blood had dried.

I pulled myself free and got up. It was dark, but we had a good moon-spill that night and I went to the mirror to look. It was bright enough that I could see Rae's reflection clearly, the color of her face, the color of the cloud. The stitches had fallen away and now the wounds were spread wide, and inside the wounds were eyes. Oh God, Rae's blue eyes. Her mouth smiled at me and her teeth were very white.

Oh, I hear you, Mr. Journal. I hear what you're saying. And I thought of that. My first impression was that I was about six bricks shy a load, gone around the old bend. But I know better now. You see, I lit a candle and held it over my shoulder, and with the candle and the moonlight, I could see even more clearly. It was Rae all right, not just a tattoo.

I looked over at my wife on the bunk, her back to me, as always. She had not moved.

I turned back to the reflection. I could hardly see the outline of myself, just Rae's face smiling out of that cloud.

"Rae," I whispered, "is that you?"

"Come on, Daddy," said the mouth in the mirror, "that's a stupid question. Of course, it's me."

"But . . . You're . . . you're . . ."

"Dead?"

"Yes . . . Did . . . did it hurt much?"

She cackled so loudly the mirror shook. I could feel the hairs on my neck rising. I thought for sure Mary would wake up, but she slept on.

"It was instantaneous, Daddy, and even then, it was the greatest pain imaginable. Let me show you how it hurt."

The candle blew out and I dropped it. I didn't need it anyway. The mirror grew bright and Rae's smile went from ear to ear literally—and the flesh on her bones seemed like crêpe paper before a powerful fan, and that fan blew the hair off her head, the skin off her skull, and melted those beautiful, blue eyes and those shiny white teeth of hers to a putrescent goo the color and consistency of fresh bird shit. Then there was only the skull, and it heaved in half and flew backward into the dark world of the mirror and there was no reflection now, only the hurtling fragments of a life that once was and was now nothing more than swirling cosmic dust.

I closed my eyes and looked away.

"Daddy?"

I opened them, looked over my shoulder into the mirror. There was Rae again, smiling out of my back.

"Darling," I said, "I'm so sorry."

"So are we," she said, and there were faces floating past her in the mirror. Teenagers, children, men and women, babies, little embryos swirling around her head like planets around the sun. I closed my eyes again, but I could not keep them closed. When I opened them the multitudes of swirling dead, and those who had never had a chance to live, were gone. Only Rae was there. "Come close to the mirror, Daddy."

I backed up to it. I backed until the hot wounds that were Rae's eyes touched the cold glass and the wounds became hotter and hotter and Rae called out, "Ride me piggy, Daddy," and then I felt her weight on my back, not the weight of a six-year-old child or a teenage girl, but a great weight, like the world was on my shoulders and bearing down.

Leaping away from the mirror I went hopping and whooping about the room, same as I used to in the park. Around and around I went, and as I did, I glanced in the mirror. Astride me was Rae, lithe and naked, her red hair fanning around her as I spun. And when I whirled by the mirror again, I saw that she was six years old. Another spin and there was a skeleton with red hair, one hand held high, the jaws open and yelling, "Ride 'em, cowboy."

"How?" I managed, still bucking and leaping, giving Rae the ride of her life. She bent to my ear and I could feel her warm breath. "You want to know how I'm here, Daddy-dear? I'm here because you created me. Once you laid between Mother's legs and thrust me into existence, the two of you, with all the love there was in you. This time you thrust me into existence with your guilt and Mother's hate. Her thrusting needles, your arching back. And now I've come back for one last ride, Daddy-o. Ride, you bastard, ride."

All the while I had been spinning, and now as I glimpsed the mirror, I saw wall-to-wall faces, weaving in, weaving out, like smiling stars, and all those smiles opened wide and words came out in chorus, "Where were you when they dropped The Big One?"

Each time I spun and saw the mirror again, it was a new scene. Great flaming winds scorching across the world, babies turning to fleshy jello, heaps of charred bones, brains boiling out of the heads of men and women like backed-up toilets overflowing, The Almighty, Glory Hallelujah, Ours is Bigger Than Yours Bomb hurtling forward, the mirror going mushroom white, then clear, and me, spinning, Rae pressed tight against my back, melting like butter on a griddle, evaporating into the eye-wounds on my back, and finally me alone, collapsing to the floor beneath the weight of the world.

Mary never awoke.

The vines outsmarted me.

A single strand found a crack downstairs somewhere and wound up the steps and slipped beneath the door that led into the tower. Mary's bunk was not far from the door, and in the night, while I slept and later while I spun in front of the mirror and lay on the floor before it, it made its way to Mary's bunk, up between her legs, and entered her sex effortlessly.

I suppose I should give the vine credit for doing what I had not been able to do in years, Mr. Journal, and that's enter Mary. Oh God, that's a funny one, Mr. Journal. Real funny. Another little scientist joke. Let's make that a mad scientist joke, what say? Who but a madman would play with the lives of human beings by constantly trying to build the bigger and better boom machine?

So what of Rae, you ask?

I'll tell you. She is inside me. My back feels the weight. She twists in my guts like a corkscrew. I went to the mirror a moment ago, and the tattoo no longer looks like it did. The eyes have turned to crusty sores and the entire face looks like a scab. It's as if the bile that made up my soul, the unthinking, nearsightedness, the guilt that I am, has festered from inside and spoiled the picture with pustule bumps, knots and scabs.

To put it in layman's terms, Mr. Journal, my back is infected. Infected with what I am. A blind, senseless fool.

The wife?

Ah, the wife. God, how I loved that woman. I have not really touched her in years, merely felt those wonderful hands on my back as she jabbed the needles home, but I never stopped loving her. It was not a love that glowed anymore, but it was there, though hers for me was long gone and wasted.

This morning when I got up from the floor, the weight of Rae and the world on my back, I saw the vine coming up from beneath the door and stretching over to her. I yelled her name. She did not move. I ran to her and saw it was too late. Before I could put a hand on her, I saw her flesh ripple and bump up, like a den of mice were nesting under a quilt. The vines were at work. (Out goes the old guts, in goes the new vines.)

There was nothing I could do for her.

I made a torch out of a chair leg and an old quilt, set fire to it, burned the vine from between her legs, watched it retreat, smoking, under the door. Then I got a board, nailed it along the bottom, hoping it would keep others out for at least a little while. I got one of the twelve-gauges and loaded it. It's on the desk beside me, Mr. Journal, but even I know I'll never use it. It was just something to do, as Jacobs said when he killed and ate the whale. Something to do.

I can hardly write anymore. My back and shoulders hurt so bad. It's the weight of Rae and the world.

I've just come back from the mirror and there is very little left of the tattoo. Some blue and black ink, a touch of red that was Rae's hair. It looks like an abstract painting now. Collapsed design, running colors. It's real swollen. I look like the hunchback of Notre Dame.

What am I going to do, Mr. Journal?

Well, as always, I'm glad you asked that. You see, I've thought this out.

I could throw Mary's body over the railing before it blooms. I could do that. Then I could doctor my back. It might even heal, though I doubt it. Rae wouldn't let that happen, I can tell you now. And I don't blame her. I'm on her side. I'm just a walking dead man and have been for years.

I could put the shotgun under my chin and work the trigger with my toe, or maybe push it with the very pen I'm using to create you, Mr. Journal. Wouldn't that be neat? Blow my brains to the ceiling and sprinkle you with my blood.

But as I said, I loaded the gun because it was something to do. I'd never use it on myself or Mary.

You see, I want Mary. I want her to hold Rae and me one last time like she used to in the park. And she can. There's a way.

I've drawn all the curtains and made curtains out of blankets for those spots where there aren't any. It'll be sunup soon and I don't want that kind of light in here. I'm writing this by candlelight and it gives the entire room a warm glow. I wish I had wine. I want the atmosphere to be just right.

Over on Mary's bunk she's starting to twitch. Her neck is swollen where the vines have congested and are writhing toward their favorite morsel, the brain. Pretty soon the rose will bloom (I hope she's one of the bright yellow ones, yellow was her favorite color and she wore it well) and Mary will come for me.

When she does, I'll stand with my naked back to her. The vines will whip out and cut me before she reaches me, but I can stand it. I'm used to pain. I'll pretend the thorns are Mary's needles. I'll stand that way until she folds her dead arms around me and her body pushes up against the wound she made in my back, the wound that is our daughter Rae. She'll hold me so the vines and the proboscis can do their work. And while she holds me, I'll grab her fine hands and push them against my chest, and it will be we three again, standing against the world, and I'll close my eyes and delight in her soft, soft hands one last time.

For Ardath Mayhar

NEEDING GHOSTS

RAMSEY CAMPBELL

The *Oxford Companion to English Literature* describes Ramsey Campbell as "Britain's most respected living horror writer." He has received more awards than any other writer in the field, including the Grand Master Award of the World Horror Convention, the Lifetime Achievement Award of the Horror Writers Association, the Living Legend Award of the International Horror Guild, and the World Fantasy Lifetime Achievement Award. In 2015 he was made an Honorary Fellow of Liverpool John Moores University for outstanding services to literature.

Among his novels are *The Face That Must Die*, *Incarnate*, *Midnight Sun*, *The Count of Eleven*, *Silent Children*, *The Darkest Part of the Woods*, *The Overnight*, *Secret Story*, *The Grin of the Dark*, *Thieving Fear*, *Creatures of the Pool*, *The Seven Days of Cain*, *Ghosts Know*, *The Kind Folk*, *Think Yourself Lucky*, and *Thirteen Days by Sunset Beach*. His most recent title, *The Way of the Worm*, concludes "The Three Births of Daoloth" trilogy, which also comprises *The Searching Dead* and *Born to the Dark*.

Campbell's short fiction is collected in *Waking Nightmares*, *Alone with the Horrors*, *Ghosts and Grisly Things*, *Told by the Dead*, *Just*

Behind You, *Holes for Faces*, and *By the Light of My Skull*, while *Needing Ghosts*, *The Last Revelation of Gla'aki*, *The Pretence*, and *The Booking* are novellas.

His novels *The Nameless* and *Pact of the Fathers* have been filmed in Spain, where a movie of *The Influence* is in production.

"*Needing Ghosts* rather crept up on me," recalls the author. "Immediately before it I'd written *Midnight Sun* and had the hardest time I've ever had with the first draft of a novel. In the midst of this, Deborah Beale at Legend did her best to persuade me to write a novella that would appear in a series she was publishing. I'd never previously tried to write one, and I resisted until I came upon a suggestion by Brian Aldiss that the form should cover the events of a short period—a day, perhaps. This helped awaken a couple of ideas that had been lying dormant in one of my notebooks, and I amassed material while I rewrote *Midnight Sun*.

"I wasn't prepared for how *Needing Ghosts* would take off. From the point where Mottershead arrives at the bus terminal, it became so much stranger than I'd expected that I was delighted to follow. The rest of it was more like dreaming onto the page than anything else I've written, and I went up to my desk every morning eager to find out what new surprises were in store. In a way I think it's the dark dwarfish twin of *Midnight Sun*, owning up to themes the novel can't quite handle, but it also released the comedy underlying much of my earlier fiction, and the next novel I wrote was the overtly comic *Count of Eleven*. I hope the reader has as much deranged fun with it as I did."

HE KNOWS THIS dark. Though it feels piled against his eyes, it doesn't mean he's blind. He only has to lie there until he can tell where he is. As soon as his sense of his body returns he'll know which way he's lying.

He feels as though he has forgotten how to close his eyes and how to breathe. Perhaps he could shout and gain some idea of the extent of his surroundings from whatever happens to his voice, but he can't think of anything to say. The notion of shouting without words dismays him, and so does the possibility that he mightn't know what he means to shout until he hears himself.

In any case, his sense of himself is beginning to gather. His arms are stretched out parallel to his body, his hands lie palms downward by his sides. How thin they are! He's disinclined to raise them to his eyes in case he's unable to see them. The darkness must relent eventually, and meanwhile there's no call for him to move; didn't he take some trouble to achieve this peace? Now that he's aware of the remainder of his body—the outstretched legs, the upturned toes, the tight skin over the ribs—he ought to be able to enjoy lying still.

But the darkness is no longer absolute. It has begun to betray hints of shapes standing tall and immobile as if they're waiting to be seen. Those directly ahead of him appear to be draped in robes, and can't he hear voices whispering? He thinks of judges watching him with eyes that pierce the blackness, judges waiting for the dawn to reveal them and himself.

To his right he can just distinguish the profile of an open box at least as tall as himself. Hovering within it is an object which looks too oddly proportioned to be complete. To his left is an open horizontal box, from which shapes dangle as though exhausted by their struggle to emerge. He very much hopes that the whispers aren't coming from either box.

His clenched fists spread their fingers and reach out shakily on either side of him. By stretching his arms to their limit he can grasp the edges of the lumpy creaking mattress, and the action gives him some

"THE THIN WHITE FINGERS ARE VISIBLY LENGTHENING."

awareness of the room. Those aren't robed figures ahead of him, they're heavy curtains, and he's almost sure that if he parts them to admit more light he'll see that the figure hovering in the wardrobe, the stumps of its legs drawn up towards its handless monkey arms, is nothing of the kind.

He drags his hands over the mattress, the twang and contour and inclination of each buried spring reviving that much of his memory. He digs his knuckles into the frayed canvas and lifts himself into a sitting position, then he swings his legs into the dark and inches them downward until his feet touch the floor. The carpet is so worn he can distinguish the outlines of the floorboards. Pushing himself away from the bed, he pads to the curtains, beyond which he can hear the whispering. He pokes his fingers through the gap in the musty velvet and heaves the curtains back.

The night is dancing just beyond the grimy window. Poplars whose foliage the dark has transmuted into coal toss their long heads in the wind. Several yards below him, wind ploughs through the grass of an unkempt garden hemmed in by trees. Inside the window, at the bottom left-hand corner of the lower sash, a draught plucks at a stray leaf caught in a spider's glimmering web.

So much for the whispering, however nearly articulate it sounds. He turns to the room. His suit is on a single hanger in the wardrobe, other clothes of his spill out of the chest of drawers. He isn't used to waking by himself in the dark, that's all. Now that he has risen he'll stay up and be on his way by dawn.

He trots out of the room and along the threadbare corridor without switching on the light above the stairs. When he tugs the cord in the bathroom, the light bulb greets its own reflection in the mirror full of white tiles, and something disappears into the plughole of the bruised bath. It must be a drip from the taps whose marble eyeballs bulge above their brass snout; he sees the movement glisten as it vanishes. He crosses the knotted floor and confronts himself in the mirror.

"There you are, old thinface. Nothing wrong with you that a blade can't put right." He's being deliberately cheerful, because he has never cared for the way electric light looks at this hour—too bright, as if its glare is straining to fend off the dark, and yet too feeble. His face resembles a paper mask, the skin almost smooth except for furrows underlining the sparse shock of grey hair and almost white save for touches of pink in the twin hollows of the pinched cheeks, in the large nostrils of the long nose, on the pursed lips. The stubble on the pointed chin makes him feel grimy, and he ransacks the clutter by the sink for a razor.

Most of the stuff there seems to have nothing to do with him. At last he finds a razor folded into its handle among the sticky jars. He digs his thumbnail into the crescent-shaped nick in the blade, which springs out so readily that he can't help flinching. What's become of his electric razor? It's posing as another jar, its heads clogged by talcum powder. On second thoughts, his chin can stay as it is. He stoops to the sink and wets his face with water from the right-hand tap, which grumbles like a sleeping animal, then he dries himself on a towel with a hole in it the size of his face. He lets down the dark with the cord and hurries to his room.

This time he switches on the light above the bed. The walls absorb much of the glow of the dim unshaded bulb, as their blurred surface seems already to have assimilated the pattern and the colours of the paper. Though the room is spacious, it contains little furniture: the open wardrobe, the overflowing chest of drawers, the double bed with the bare mattress whose stripes trace the unevenness of the springs—just enough, he thinks, to show that it's a bedroom. He lifts his suit from the hanger and picks up the shoes which stand beneath it as though they've fallen from the legs. Once he is dressed he tours the house.

He shuts the lid of the massive toilet and rubs his hands with the ragged towel, and slams the bathroom door. Between it and his room are two bedrooms, an unmade single bed in each. Light through the lampshades steeps his hands in red as he fingers the wall-sockets to reassure himself that they're switched off. As he backs out of each room he turns the light off and shuts the door, holding onto the doorknob until he feels the lock click.

The clatter of his shoes on the uncarpeted staircase tells him how empty the large house is, and reminds him that he doesn't mean it to be empty for much longer. When he has opened the bookshop and customers are selling books to him as well as buying them, he'll store part of his stock in the disused bedrooms. He strides along the L-shaped hall to the kitchen, where fluorescent light smoulders in its tube while he screws the gas taps tight and grovels on the flagstones to examine the electric sockets on the perspiring brownish walls. He needn't check the room next to the kitchen, since it's locked. He looks into the rooms which, once their shared wall is removed, will house the shop. Chairs lean against a dining-table beneath the one live bulb of a chandelier, a lounge suite squats in front of a television tethered to a video recorder. He shuts the doors and lifts his rucksack from the post at the foot of the stairs. Hitching the rucksack over his shoulders, he lets himself out of the house.

The wind has dropped. The poplars are embedded in the tarry sky. Before he reaches the end of his overgrown path and steps into the avenue, his greenish shoes are black with dew. The road leads downhill between buildings which gleam white beyond the trees. Glancing back to reassure himself that he hasn't left a light on by mistake, he sees that all his windows are dark, all the curtains are open except those of the locked room.

He isn't surprised to find himself alone on the road; presumably nobody else rises at this hour. He can't recall ever having met his neighbours, but if they want to avoid him, that suits him. "He's out again," he announces at the top of his voice. "Lock your doors, hide behind the furniture, pull the blankets over your heads or he'll know you're there."

The only response, if it is a response, is the flight of a bird which starts up from among the trees and passes overhead, invisibly black, with a sound like the sweeps of a scythe. When it has gone and he falls silent, he thinks he can hear dew dripping in the trees beside the road. Spider threads caress his face, and he imagines the night as a web in the process of being assembled. He halts on the crown of the tarmac, wondering whether, if he's still enough, he may hear the whisper of the threads. Disturbed by the idea—not so much by the possibility of hearing as by his compulsion to try—he hurries down the avenue, wishing his tread were louder. He's glad when the landing-stage becomes visible at the end of the road.

Perhaps he's too early. Though a ferry is moored there, it's unlit. As he continues downhill, the lights across the bay appear to sink into the black water. Just as he emerges between the last of the poplars, the lights vanish, and he feels as if everything—sky, trees, land, sea—has merged into a single lightless medium. The anchorage creaks as he picks his way to the gangplank and steps onto the deck.

All the stairways to the upper deck are roped off, and the doors of the saloons are locked. He's heading along the narrow strip of deck beside the front saloon when the gangplank is raised with a rattle of chains and the ferry gives a honk which vibrates through the boards underfoot. At once, as if the sound has started the waves up, water slops against the hull as the vessel swings out from the stage.

If it weren't for the occasional creak which reminds him of the sounds a house emits at night, he would hardly know he was on a boat. By the time the engine begins to thump, the ferry is well out from the shore.

From the upper deck he would presumably be able to see the lights of his destination. He grips the sides of the prow and thrusts himself forwards like a figurehead, but can't determine whether the unsteady glow which appears to divide the blackness ahead is real or if it's only the flickering which often manifests itself within his eyelids when he can't sleep. He wedges his thighs in the V of the prow and watches the forest swallowing the buildings on the avenue. He finds the sight oddly satisfying, and so he doesn't face forwards again until the ferry has almost gained the opposite side of the bay. When the steersman, a bust illuminated like a waxwork by the instruments in the wheelhouse, closes down the engine, he slips out of his niche in the prow and turns to look.

The landing-stage is wider than the one below the poplars. Several figures are rising from benches in a shed at the back of the stage. Floodlights bleach the planks and show him the faces of those waiting—flesh white as candles, eyes like glass—as they crowd to meet him at the gangplank. He sidles past the crewman who has let the gangplank down, a burly man whose black beard so resembles the fabric of his balaclava that his eyes and nose look false, and hurries across the shed to the exit ramp.

Only one of the several pay booths at the top of the tunnel is occupied. The woman inside it is poring over an obese dog-eared paperback, its cover hanging open to display a resale stamp. She waits until he pushes a pound coin under the glass of the booth before she raises her flat sleepy face, and he thinks of slot machines in the seaside arcades of his childhood, glass booths containing puppets which tottered alive if one fed them a coin. He's heading for the exit when she swivels on her stool and raps on the glass with the largest wedding ring he has ever seen. "Hey!"

If the fare has gone up, the least she can do is tell him by how much. But she only stares at him and thrusts her hand under the glass, and he thinks she's pointing at him until he notices the coin beneath her fingers. "Too rich to need your change?" she says.

"You've only taken for me."

"That's right, unless you're hiding someone in your bag."

"There's the bicycle."

She stares as if she's refusing to acknowledge a joke, though she can see perfectly well what he means. He gestures at the barrier where he leaned the machine when she called him back, and then he realises with a shock that he has left the bicycle at home. When he apologises and reaches for the coin, her fingers recoil like caterpillars, and she bends the paperback open so fiercely that the bunch of pages she has read loses its grip on the spine and falls inside the booth. He knees the barrier aside and marches out of the tunnel, wondering what else he may have forgotten, feeling as though his very substance has been undermined.

On the far side of a broad deserted road, concrete office buildings catch fragments of the white glare of streetlamps in their multitude of windows. The interiors of the double-decker buses parked in a layby opposite the ferry terminal look moonlit. All six bus-stops have someone waiting at them.

As he crosses the whitened tarmac, the six men watch him silently. All of them are wearing dark suits—black, unless the light is altering the colour of their clothes as much as it's discolouring their faces. They don't respond when he nods to them, and so he does his best to ignore them while he looks for information. The timetables have been wrenched off the bus-stops; even the numbers on the metal flags have been rendered unidentifiable by graffiti which turn sevens into nines, nines into eights, whole numbers into mixed. Computer displays on the fronts of the vehicles announce destinations, but they bewilder him. Are the computers malfunctioning? Flicky Doaky, Eyes End, Cranium, Roly Polytechnic, View Hallow, Pearly Swine—he doesn't believe there are any such places; perhaps the names are jokes the drivers crack after the buses stop running. The men by the bus-stops seem to be waiting for him to react, and he can't help suspecting that they're drivers. He leans against a building to wait for someone to board a bus.

The men turn away from him and exchange glances, and begin to call out to one another. "I'll be gone as soon as I get my head down."

"I'll have mine under the covers before the sun's up."

"Nothing like sleeping when the world's abroad."

"Nothing worse than not being able to switch yourself off."

"You mean the poor bat who couldn't even when he was supposed to have retired."

"And wouldn't let anyone else."

It sounds like a prepared routine, passing systematically along the line from right to left, and he feels as if they're talking at him. He's beginning to experience a rage so black it suffocates his words when another man emerges from a crevice beside him, an alley between the buildings. This one must be a driver, though he is almost a dwarf; he's wearing the uniform. He toddles to the second bus from the left and turns a knob which folds the door open, and it seems clear that he's the person to ask. "Excuse me . . ."

The driver pokes a finger under the brim of his cap. Thick spectacles make his eyes appear to occupy the top half of his wizened face. "Not open yet. You don't see anyone else moving."

True enough, all the dark-suited figures have turned towards the conversation and are frozen in attitudes of listening; some have lifted their hands to their ears. "I only wanted to ask which bus goes to—"

He can't remember. With the loss of the word, his mind seems to shrink and darken. The driver is waiting as though only the word will release him, raising his eyebrows until his eyes fill the lenses of his spectacles. At last a name rises out of the dark. "To Mottershead. Which bus goes to Mottershead?"

"Never heard of it," the driver says triumphantly, and hops onto the bus. "Nothing called that round here."

"Of course there is."

The door flattens into its frame, and he's about to thump on the fingermarked glass when he realises that Mottershead isn't the name of a place: it's his own name. He retreats and presses his spine against the façade of an office in which typewriters are hooded like ranks of cowled heads. He's restraining himself from turning his face to the concrete when the driver, having hoisted himself into the seat behind the wheel, reopens the doors and inclines his torso towards him. "Got another name for me?"

Mottershead thinks he sees a way out of the trap. "Where do you go?"

"Where it says."

Perhaps there really is a district called Eyes End. If Mottershead doesn't board the vehicle he'll be alone with five of the six men who witnessed his discomfiture, the sixth having flashed a rectangle of plastic at the driver and sat in the front downstairs seat. He watches Mottershead with interest and twirls a slow finger in one nostril. "That'll do me," Mottershead tells the driver, and steps onto the platform.

In his pocket is only a twenty-pound note and the change from the ferry. The driver reaches a long arm out of his metal enclosure and plucks the coin from Mottershead's hand. "You'll hear me call when you've run out," he warns, and starts the bus.

Mottershead is on the stairs when the vehicle backs at speed into the road and immediately lurches forwards. He grabs the tubular banister and hauls himself to the top deck, where he lunges at the left-hand front seat and flings himself onto it, jamming his heels against the panel behind the destination indicator.

The view ahead has changed. Buildings which at first he takes for disused offices, their windows broken and their exteriors darkened by age, mirror one another across the road. They're warehouses illuminated by increasingly less frequent streetlamps. Black water glints beyond gaps to his right, while to his left, up slopes no wider than the bus, he glimpses unlit houses crammed together on both sides of alleys which appear to narrow as they climb. He'll make for any second-hand bookshop he sees which is open. Surely he won't be turned off the bus before it brings him to the shops.

When the bus slows, he presses his feet harder against the yielding metal. Two men are standing under an extensively annotated concrete shelter at the corner of an alley, and the foremost of them has extended a white stick like an antenna sensing the approach of the vehicle. The bus screeches to a halt, and Mottershead hears the door flutter open and the stick begin to tap upstairs.

He's assuming that the driver will tone down his driving, but the vehicle jerks forwards like a greyhound out of a trap. He's preparing to help until he hears the man's companion following him upstairs. He watches their reflections on the glass in front of him as the man with the stick fumbles for the seat nearest the stairs and lowers himself onto it. Mottershead is shocked to see the companion mimic these actions, all the more so when he realises why he is acting that way. Both men are blind.

If they don't leave the bus before Mottershead does they'll know that he didn't offer to help. The vehicle slows again, and he's afraid that the driver is about to summon him. No, someone is flagging the bus down, a man craning into the road from beside the stump of a bus-stop.

The door flaps shut, the bus lurches off between the warehouses. The new passenger takes some time to ascend the stairs. At the top he stands gripping the handrail, hunching his shoulders and turning his head tortoise-like. "Who's here?" he demands.

He's blind too. Mottershead is fighting a guilty compulsion to answer him when the man with the stick says "It's us."

"Thought so. Nobody with all their senses is out this early."

He stumbles across the aisle and, placing a hand on each man's scalp to support himself, sits down behind them. It doesn't matter to the three how dark it is, Mottershead reflects, and wonders what job they have been doing. What job has he retired from? Before he can start to remember, the thin voice of the newcomer distracts him. "Has he seen to the electricity?"

"Not him," says the man with the stick. "Too busy thinking of himself."

"Can't spare a thought for his people," his companion adds.

"You'd think he'd attend when they try to let him know his lights are going to fail."

"We'll have some fun when they're out."

"He'll be sorry he needs his eyes."

By now Mottershead's embarrassment has been supplanted by nervousness. Surely they wouldn't say such things if they knew they were being overheard. He peers along the passing alleys in the hope that he may see a better reason than his nerves to quit the bus. "I remember when the lights fused and I got my own back on my dad," the man with the stick laughs, just as Mottershead catches sight of a lit area beyond two consecutive alleys, which looks like the beginning of a wide street lined with shops. If he has to wait for any bookshops there to open, that's decidedly preferable to skulking in his seat. He plants his feet on the ridged floor and, grasping the back of the seat, steers himself into the aisle.

The vehicle provides no means of communicating with the driver. Mottershead could shout or walk noisily, but he doesn't want to startle the three men. He tiptoes to the stairs and is stepping down carefully when the three turn their pale smooth faces to him. All their eyelids are closed, and so flat there might be no eyes behind them. As he falters on the stairs, the trio bursts out laughing.

They've been aware of him all the time. Enraged and bewildered, he clatters downstairs, shouting "Hold on!"

The driver brakes as Mottershead gains the lower deck, and Mottershead has to grab the only handhold within reach—the shoulder of the man in the dark suit. "What's the upheaval?" the driver complains. "Want to give us all a heart attack?"

"Sorry," Mottershead says to the passenger, apologising not only for grabbing him but for discovering his secret. The man's upper arm is unyielding as plastic; he must have an artificial limb. As the bus regains speed Mottershead staggers to the door, seeing the lit area beyond another alley, shouting "Let me off here."

"You're nowhere near where you've paid to go."

"This is where I want," Mottershead says through his teeth.

"I doubt it." Perhaps it's his stature, but the driver has begun to resemble a petulant child thwarted in a game. "You'll get no change," he says.

"Keep the change if it makes you happy. Just open up, or I will."

The driver slams the door open, and a wind howls through the bus. Mottershead is trying to prepare himself to accept the apparent challenge when the driver stamps on the brake, almost flinging him off the platform. "Thank you," Mottershead says heavily, holding onto the bus as he steps down.

The door flutters like a crippled wing, and he hears the driver announce to the passengers "He thinks change makes us happy." The vehicle roars away, trailing oily fumes. When at last the fumes disperse it's still visible, a miniature toy far down the long straight road beneath the low black sky. Down there, perhaps because of the distance, the buildings look windowless. He watches until the bus vanishes as though the perspective has shrunk it to nothing, then he surveys where it has left him.

The nearest alley appears to lead into a lightless tunnel. He's about to retreat towards the openings beyond which he saw light, but then the streetlamp overhead allows him to guess at the contents of a window several hundred yards up the alley—piles of old books.

He steps between the walls and hears his rucksack scraping brick. As the darkness thickens underfoot, the sides of the warehouses tower over him. Where the alley bends beyond them, the window of the first building manages to collect a trace of the light, dimly exhibiting the books. He struggles along the passage, his rucksack flopping against the walls like a disabled pursuer, to the window.

He's tightening the shoulder-straps of the rucksack and skewing his head in an attempt to decipher the spines of the books when he becomes aware that the window belongs to a house. It could be displaying books for sale, but that seems increasingly unlikely as he begins to distinguish the room beyond the books. It's a bedroom, and although the disorder on the bed consists mostly of blankets, he can just discern a head protruding from them, its bald scalp glimmering. Before he has time to step back the eyes flicker open, and the occupant of the bed rises up like a mask on a pole draped with blankets, emitting a cry which seems to voice Mottershead's own panic.

Why has the tenant of the room stacked books in the window if he doesn't want to draw attention? Perhaps they're meant to conceal him, a rampart to keep out the world. It seems not to matter which way Mottershead runs so long as the figure he's disturbed can't see him. By the time he regains some control of himself, he's out of sight of the main road.

Terraced houses crowd on both sides of him, their blackened curtains merging with the black glass of the windows. A hint of light between two houses entices him onward. It's leaking from the mouth of an alley which should lead to the shops he glimpsed from the bus. The high uninterrupted walls of the alley bend left several hundred yards in, towards the source of the light. He dodges into the alley, glancing back for fear that whoever he disturbed may have followed him.

He's heartened by the sight which greets him at the bend. Ahead the alley intersects a lane of unlit terraced houses, on the far side of which it runs straight to a distant pavement illuminated by shops. He's crossing the junction when he notices that the right-hand stretch of the narrow lane is scattered with dozens of dilapidated books and sections of books.

This time there's no doubt that he has found a bookshop. The downstairs windows of two adjacent houses give him a view of a huge room full of shelves stuffed with books. There must be a light in the room, though it's too feeble to locate. Apparently the entrance is in the rear wall. He darts into the passage which divides the shop from the neighbouring houses, and the walls tug at his rucksack as if someone is trying to pull him back.

The passage leads him not to a street but to a back alley alongside the yards of the houses. He has to sidle between the walls to reach the alley he was previously following. There must be a dog in the yard shared by the houses which comprise the bookshop; he hears its claws scrabbling at concrete and scraping the far side of the insecure wall as it leaps repeatedly at him. He can only assume it has lost its voice. A protrusion on the gate of the yard catches a strap of his rucksack, and he almost tears the fabric in his haste to free himself.

At the alley he turns left, determined to find the entrance to the bookshop. As he reaches the junction he grunts with surprise. The glow from the shop has brightened, illuminating the lane, which has been cleared of books. The doorway between the windows is bricked up, but the glow outlines the glass panel of a door to their left. The panel bears an OPEN sign, and the door is ajar.

Since there's no sign of a proprietor or even of a desk where one might sit, Mottershead calls "Hello" as he crosses the threshold. Only an echo of his voice responds, and is immediately suppressed by tons of stale paper, but the presence of so many books is enough of a response. They occupy all four walls to the height of the ceiling, and half a dozen double-sided bookcases extend almost the length of the shop, presenting their ends to him. There's barely room for him to sidle between the volumes which protrude into the dim aisles. Shrugging off his rucksack, he lets it fall beside the door.

He's becoming an expert, he thinks. One glance enables him to locate titles he has seen in every second-hand bookshop he has visited so far: *Closeup, The Riverside Villas Murder, The Birds Fall Down*, sets of the works of Dickens, dozens of issues of the *National Geographic*, editions of Poe. The material which appeals to him will be further from the entrance—books by countless forgotten authors whose work he can enjoy reviving for himself while he sits and waits for customers in his own shop. The notion that although these authors are either dead or as good as dead, he can choose to resurrect whatever they achieved as the fancy guides him, makes him feel as if he has found within himself a power he wasn't aware of possessing.

He's pacing along the line of bookcases in order to decide which aisle looks most promising when the spines of a set of volumes beyond them, on the highest of the shelves on the back wall, catch his eye. The fat spines, patterned like old bark and embossed with golden foliage, appear to be emitting the glow which lights the shop; presumably its source is concealed by the bookcases. Without having read the titles, he knows he wants the trinity of books. Since they're too hefty for even his rucksack to bear, he'll arrange to have them sent once he finds the proprietor.

He doesn't immediately notice that he's hesitating. What did he glimpse as he moved away from the door? He turns to squint at the shelves he initially dismissed, which contain the books whose titles he wouldn't have been able to discern in the gloom if they weren't already so familiar. He sees the book at once, and has the disconcerting impression that its neighbours have rearranged themselves, the better to direct his attention to it. He doesn't understand why the nondescript grubby spine should have any significance for him. Hooking one finger in the stall which the top of the spine has become, he drags the book off the shelf.

The illustration on the rubbed cover depicts a man's face composed of a host of unlikely objects. He hasn't time to examine it in detail, even though the face is familiar, because the words seem to leap at him. The title of the novel is *Cadenza,* and the author's name is Simon Mottershead.

He's able to believe it's only a coincidence until he opens the back cover. Though the photograph may be years or even decades younger than he is, the face which gazes up at him from the flap of the jacket is unquestionably the face he saw in the bathroom mirror.

He slams the cover as if he's crushing a spider. His mind feels dark and crowded; he knows at once that he has forgotten more than the book. He's tempted to replace it on the shelf and run out of the shop, but he mustn't give way to panic. "Is there anyone here but me?" he shouts.

This time not even the echo responds. Someone must have unlocked the door and picked up the books in the lane. Perhaps they're upstairs, but he wonders suddenly if the bookseller may be the person he disturbed by staring into the bedroom. On the whole he thinks he would rather not meet the proprietor face to face. He'll pay for the book in his hand and leave a note asking for the others to be reserved for him until a price has been agreed. He's relieved to see a credit card machine and a dusty sheaf of vouchers on a shelf to the left of the door. He gropes in his pocket for his credit card and a scrap of paper.

There's a solitary folded sheet. He shoves the book into the rucksack and unfolds the page. Two-thirds of it is covered with notes for a lecture. At the top, surrounded by a web of doodling, he has written the word *Library* and a date. "Today," he gasps.

He's supposed to be lecturing to a writers' group. His mind feels as if it's bursting out of his skull. He digs his nails into his scalp, trying to hold onto his memory until he has recaptured all of it, but he can remember nothing else: neither the name nor the whereabouts of the library, not the name of whoever invited him nor of the group itself. Worst of all, he can't recall what time he has undertaken to be there. He's sure he will be late.

He grabs a pencil from beside the credit card machine. Flattening the page against the end of a bookcase, he prints the shortest message he can think of: *Please communicate with me re these.* He adds his details and then squirms along the nearest aisle, tearing off the message as he goes. Floorboards sag, books quiver around him and above him; he's afraid the bookcases will fall and bury him. By craning towards the tomes he's just able to insert the slip of paper into the niche formed by the florid cornice and the top of the leafy oaken binding. He leaves it dangling, a tongue blackened by his name, and retreats towards the door.

He still has to buy his own book. He pins a voucher with finger and thumb against the door, which shakes with every movement of the pencil as though someone crouching out of sight is attempting to fumble it open. A mixture of embarrassment at the small amount and determination to see his name clear makes him press so hard with the pencil that the voucher tears as he signs it, and the plumbago breaks. He lays the voucher in the metal bed and inserts his card in the recess provided, then he drags the handle over them to emboss the voucher. As the handle passes over his card there's a sound like teeth grinding, and he feels the card break.

He wrenches the slide back to its starting point and gapes at the card, which has snapped diagonally in half. He opens his mouth to yell for the proprietor, having forgotten his nervousness, but then he sees that the lead which broke off the pencil was under the card when he used the embosser. Shoving his copy of the voucher into his pocket together with the pointed blades which are the halves of the card, he pokes his arms through the straps of the rucksack and flounces out, his book bumping his spine as if it's trying to climb the bony ladder.

The street is grey with a twilight which appears to seep out of the bricks and the pavement, much as mist seems to rise from the ground. A few windows are lit, but no curtains are open. He runs to the junction of the lane and the alley and listens for traffic. The only noises are the slam of an opened door and a rush of feet which sound as though they're stumbling over parts of themselves. Even if they're wearing slippers too large for them, their approach is enough to send Mottershead fleeing towards the light which was his original destination—fleeing so hastily that his impression of his destination doesn't change until he is almost there.

The area is floodlit, though several of the floodlights have been overturned on the flagstones with which the street is paved. Broken saplings strapped to poles loll in concrete tubs along the centre of the street. All the shops are incomplete, but he can't tell whether they are being built or demolished. The figures which peer over the exposed girders and fragments of walls aren't workmen; they're plastic mannequins, more convincingly flesh-coloured than is usually the case. Vandals must have had some fun with them, because they are all beckoning to Mottershead, or are they gesturing him onward? Their eyes are unpleasantly red. As he blinks at the nearest he sees that someone has painstakingly added crimson veins to the painted eyeballs. A wind from the bay flaps the plastic sheets which have been substituted for roofs, the crippled saplings creak as their elongated shadows grope over the flagstones, and beneath the flapping he thinks he hears the creak of plastic limbs.

To his left the paved area curves out of sight towards the bay. To his right, perhaps half a mile distant, several cars are parked. Mustn't they be on or near a road? Willing the cars to be taxis, he sprints towards them.

The roofs stir as if the skeletons of buildings are trying to awaken. Whenever they do so, the arms of the mannequins wave stiffly at him. The state of the figures grows worse as he progresses: some are hand-less, and brandish rusty prongs protruding from their wrists; most are bald, and those which aren't wear their wigs askew—one wig as grey as matted dust has slipped down to cover a face. All the figures are naked, and sport unlikely combinations of genitalia, presumably thanks to van-dalism. Some of the heads have been turned completely round on the necks, which are mottled as senile flesh. As he passes one such figure it falls forward, rattling the bars of the stranded lift which cages it, and Mottershead claps a hand to his chest as he runs onward.

By now he can see that each of the three cars is occupied, but suppose a car dealer has propped mannequins in each of the drivers' seats? The roofs writhe, and a bald figure sprawls towards him, leaving behind its hand which was supporting it on the back of a solitary dining-chair. Its head is hollow, and empty now that the contents have scuttled away behind a girder. He would cry out if he had breath to do so, but surely there's no need, since the three figures in the cars have sat up and turned towards him. He's no longer alone with the tread, floppy but not quite barefoot, which is following him. He lunges for the foremost vehicle, his eyes so blurred with exertion that he can hardly see the door. He's near to panic before his fingertips snag the handle. He levers it up and, col-lapsing into the back seat, slams the door.

However much of a relief it is just to sit there with his eyes closed, he has to keep moving. "The library," he wheezes.

Either the driver is taciturn by nature or he's losing his voice. "Which?"

At least he seems unlikely to trouble Mottershead with the unnecessary chatter typical of his species, but his response sounds suspiciously like an imitation of Mottershead's wheezing. "The one where a writers' group meets," Mottershead says, interrupting himself twice as he tries to catch his breath.

He's hoping that his words will provoke a further question which may help him clarify his thoughts. To his surprise, the driver starts the car, and Mottershead lets himself sink into the seat, feeling sponge swell to meet his hands through the torn upholstery. When he's no longer aware of having to make himself breathe, he looks where he's going.

The incomplete buildings have been left behind. The car is passing a concrete edifice guarded by railings like fossilised branches and twigs. Despite the stained glass in its windows and the inscriptions carved in scrolls over its broad doorways, it must be a factory rather than a church. Coaches whose windows are impenetrably black are parked inside the gates, and thousands of people, all of them carrying objects which may be toolkits or briefcases and wearing brightly coloured overalls in which they resemble overgrown toddlers, are marching silently into the building. He's trying to decipher the writing on the carved scrolls when he notices that the driver is watching him.

As soon as Mottershead's gaze meets his, the man fixes his attention on the road. Mottershead is almost certain that he is wearing a wig, a curly red wig twice as wide as his neck, above which it perches like a parasite which has drained all colour from the rings of pudgy flesh. The mirror seems to have lent the reflection of his eyes some of its glassiness, for although they're bloodshot, they look dollish—indeed, a flaw in the mirror makes the left eye appear to have been turned inside out.

Mottershead throws himself about on the seat in order to shed the ruck-sack and reach his book.

He intends it both to help him ignore the driver and to revive his ideas for the lecture, but as soon as he reads the opening sentence—"He knows this dark"—he feels threatened by remembering too much. He skims the long paragraphs packed with detail as the unnamed protago-nist listens to the dawn chorus and lets his other senses feast on his surroundings, which sunlight and his awareness of his own mortality are beginning to renew. Mottershead has glanced at only the first few pages when the memory of labouring on the novel begins to form like a charred coal in his mind. He leafs back towards the dedication, but slams the book shut as he realises that the taxi is drawing up at the curb.

He stuffs the book into the rucksack and stares about him. He's out-side the entrance to a shopping mall, a pair of glass doors framed by several neon tubes whose glare is almost blinding. "I want the library," he protests.

"You've got it."

There's no doubt now that the driver is mimicking him, raising the pitch of his voice as Mottershead did. "I can't see it," Mottershead says furiously.

"You will."

Mottershead imagines his own voice being forced to rise as the argument continues, topping the driver's mimicry until it becomes a screech. He flings himself out of the vehicle, almost tripping over the rucksack, and thumps the door shut with his buttocks. "What are you expecting?"

"Two and a big pointed one."

Mottershead produces the twenty-pound note. He wishes he could see the driver's face, but the neon at the entrance to the mall has dazzled him. "I've nothing else to offer you."

"You delight me," says the driver in exactly the same tone. He takes the note and hands Mottershead a smaller one. Mottershead keeps his hand extended, though he isn't looking forward to a repetition of the driver's touch; the man's stubby fingertips seem to lack nails. He's still awaiting change when he hears the driver release the handbrake, and the taxi speeds away.

"Wait," Mottershead neighs, struggling to see past the blur which coats his eyes. He slaps his empty hand over his face and stands crying "Stop thief." The noise of the vehicle fades more swiftly than the blur, until he begins to plead for his sight. Nothing matters more than being able to see. He'll let the driver go if he can only have his vision back.

At last his sight clears. He's beside a dual carriageway, across which the long blank slab of the shopping mall faces acres of waste ground where a few starved shrubs are decorated with litter. Above the carriageway, red lamps grow pale as the light of a glassy sun glares across the waste. There's no sign of the taxi among the traffic which races along both sides of the road, turning grey with the dust in the air. "Good riddance," Mottershead mumbles, and glances at the note in his hand. It's his own twenty-pound note, except that part of it—about an eighth—has been torn off.

He emits a shriek of rage and swivels wildly. His movement prompts the doors of the mall to slide open, and he veers towards them, through an arch of massive concrete blocks reminiscent of the entrance to an ancient tomb. As soon as he has passed between the doors they whisper shut behind him.

The mall is three floors high. Shops and boarded-up rooms surround a wide tiled area on which more than a dozen concrete drums containing flowers and shrubs are arranged in a pattern he can't quite identify. The air is full of a thin sound, either piped music or the twittering of the birds which are flying back and forth under the glassed-in girders of the roof. Escalators rise from the centre of the open space, bearing figures so stiffly posed that they look unreal. He barely notices all this as he dashes into the nearest shop.

It's a video library called Sammy's Hat. Cracked plastic spines are crammed into shelves on the walls which flank the counter, behind which a large man is watching a dwarfish television. If You're Not Happy with Our Service is printed on the front of his T-shirt, which is close to strangling his thick arms and neck beneath his raddled sprawling face. Cassette boxes flaunt their covers behind him: *Don't Look in the Oven*, *The Puncturer*, *Rude and Naked*, *Out of His Head* . . . He acknowledges Mottershead only by ducking closer to the television, which is receiving the credits of a film called *Nasty, Brutish and Short*. "Is it possible for me to phone?" Mottershead says over the buzzing of kazoos.

The shopman's small eyes narrow. "Anything's possible here."

"I mean, may I use your phone?"

The man heaves a sigh which sets boxes rattling on the shelves. "What's it all about?"

"I've been robbed," Mottershead declares, waving the remains of the note. "I just paid my taxi fare with this, and this is what the cabby gave me back."

On the tiny screen a stooge who appears to be wearing a monkish wig is poking two fingers in another's eyes. The shopman throws himself back in his high chair, chortling so grossly that his saliva sizzles on the screen. "Come and see this," he shouts.

A woman tented from neck to feet in gingham squeezes through a doorway behind him. Her ruddy face is even wider than his, her eyes smaller. Mottershead assumes that the shopman has called her to watch the film until the man points at the torn note. "That's what he got when he tried to pay his fare with it," he splutters.

Mottershead feels another screech of rage building up inside him, but it will only waste time; he won't be penniless for long—he'll be paid for the lecture. "Forget it," he says when the hoots and howls of the couple squashed behind the counter begin to relent. "Just tell me where the library is."

The woman lifts her dress, revealing thighs like a pink elephant's, to wipe her eyes. "You're in it, you poor bat."

"Not this kind. The kind with books."

Mottershead intends his tone to be neutral, but the shopman flings himself like a side of beef across the counter and makes a grab for his lapels. "You watch what you're saying to my daughter. Nothing in here to be ashamed of. Stories, that's all they are."

Mottershead backs out of reach, his ankles scraping together. "You don't deserve to have eyes if that's the best you can do with them," he says from the door.

He's hoping to seek help from a security guard, but none is to be seen. At least the couple aren't following him; they've begun to pummel each other, whether because they are choking with laughter or for some more obscure purpose he can't tell. He dodges into the next shop, a tobacconist's full of smoke. "Can you tell me where the library is?"

"At the end."

Perhaps the tobacconist is distracted, having apparently just singed his eyebrows while tuning the flame of a lighter. When Mottershead runs to the far end of the mall he finds only a baker's. "Library?" he wheezes.

"Who says?" The baker looks ready to turn worse than unhelpful. He's digging his fingers into a skull-sized lump of dough which has already been shaped; a swarm of raisins oozes from the sockets into which he has thrust his thumbs. "Thanks anyway," Mottershead blurts, and retreats.

One of the assistants in the adjacent toy shop leaves off playing long enough to direct him. "Up and through," he says, and points a dripping water pistol at him.

Mottershead is afraid that the gun may fire and ruin his lecture notes, and so he makes for the escalators as the assistants recommence chasing one another through the chaos of toys, which reminds him more of a playroom than of a shop. The extravagant threats they're issuing in falsetto voices fade as the deserted stairs lift him towards the roof.

Like the vegetation in the concrete tubs, on closer examination the birds beneath the roof prove to be artificial. Several birds are pursuing their repetitive flights upside down, presumably because of some fault in the mechanism, and their maker appears not to have thought it necessary to provide any of them with eyes. Mottershead finds the spectacle so disagreeably fascinating that he's almost at the top before he notices that someone has stepped forwards to meet him.

She's a woman in her sixties whose hair is dyed precisely the same shade of pale blue as her coat. Her flat chest sports a tray which contains a collecting-tin and a mound of copies of the badge pinned to her lapel. "Is there a library here, do you know?" he pleads.

The woman stares at him. Perhaps she didn't hear him for the mechanical twittering of the birds. The escalator raises him until he's a head taller than she is, and he repeats the question. This time she lifts the tin from its nest of badges, which say Pensioners in Peril in letters red as blood, and rattles it at him. "I'm sorry, I've no money," he complains.

Of course, her stare has grown accusing because he's still holding the remains of the twenty-pound note. "This won't be any use to you. Can't you tell me where the library is?"

Her only response is a look of contempt, and he loses his temper. "Take it if you've got a use for it," he shouts, "if it'll persuade you to answer a simple question."

As he begins to shout, a security guard emerges from a greetings-card shop and jogs towards them. "Is he bothering you?" the guard demands.

"I just want the library," Mottershead wails, seeing himself as the guard must see him, towering over the pensioner and yelling at her. Worse, she has taken the torn note from him, and now she has found her voice. "He tried to pass me this."

"Because you insisted," Mottershead protests, but the guard examines the note before he turns on Mottershead, frowning through the shadow of his peaked cap. "I'd say you owe this lady more than an apology."

"I tried to tell her I've no money." Receiving only stares from both of them, Mottershead blunders on: "I'm a writer. I'm needed at the library. They've asked me to talk."

"So have we," the guard says ponderously. Then the woman stuffs the note into her tin and waves Mottershead away as if he's an insect she can't be bothered to swat, and the guard grasps his shoulder. "Let's make sure you end up where you're wanted."

Before Mottershead quite knows what's happening, he is being marched to the end of the mall above the baker's. Here, invisible from below, is an unmarked door. When the guard leans on a bellpush beside it Mottershead starts to panic, especially when the door is opened by another man in uniform. He can't judge how large the cell beyond the door may be; it's piled with cartons, and the passage between them is scarcely two men wide. The guard who is holding him tells the other "He claims you've invited him to talk."

"Show him through, love. He'll be for the soundproof room."

He flattens himself against the cartons to make way, and the guard pats his plump buttocks with one hand as he shoves Mottershead into the passage. The uniformed man purrs like a big cat and rubs himself against the cartons. "Hold on," Mottershead protests, "where are you taking—" Then the guard reaches past him and opens a door, and

Mottershead's voice booms out beyond it, earning him so many disapproving stares that he would retreat into the cell if it weren't for the guard.

He's reached his destination by a back door. The library is as large as the mall, and disconcertingly similar, except that the walls which overlook the escalators are occupied by books rather than by shops. In front of the multitude of books are more tables for readers than he's able to count, and all the readers are glaring at him. "Where am I meant to go?" he mutters.

"I'll walk you," the guard says, and steers him leftward. "What was the name?"

"Simon Mottershead." He raises his voice in the hope that some of the readers will recognise his name, but they only look hostile. He lets himself be ushered past the tables, trying to think how to convince the readers that he isn't a miscreant. He hasn't succeeded in dredging up a single thought when the guard marshals him left again, through a doorway between shelves of Bibles and other religious tomes, into a room.

The room is white and windowless. Several ranks of seats composed of plastic slabs and metal tubing face away from the door, towards a single chair behind a table bearing a carafe and a glass. About twenty people are scattered among the seats, mostly near the table. Before Mottershead can make for it, the guard leans on his shoulder and sits him in the seat nearest the door. "Simon Mottershead," the guard announces.

Every head glances back and then away. "Not here," someone says.

The guard's hand shifts ominously on Mottershead's shoulder. "I'm Simon Mottershead," Mottershead stammers. "Isn't this the writers' group?"

This time only a few heads respond, and someone murmurs "Who?" Eventually a woman rumbles "Are we expected to turn our seats to you?"

"Not if I'm allowed to move." Mottershead heaves himself to his feet and, shrugging off the guard's grasp, turns to stare him away. The man's expression is so disappointed and wistful that it throws him, and he blunders towards the table, struggling to unstrap his rucksack.

He hears the guard trudge out and close the door, though not before admitting someone else. The latecomer is wearing either slippers or sandals. The sound of footsteps flopping after him makes Mottershead feel pursued, and unwilling to look back. By the time he's past the table, the newcomer is already seated. Mottershead drags the chair out from the table and dumps his rucksack on the floor, seats himself, lifts the inverted glass from the carafe and turns it over. When nobody comes forward to introduce him, he looks up.

He can't identify the latecomer. He doesn't think it would be any of the several elderly women who sit clutching handbags or manuscripts, more than one of which is protected by a knitted cover. It might be one of the young women who are staring hard at him and poising pencils over notepads, or it could be one of the men—not those who resemble army officers, red-faced with suppressing thoughts, but possibly the lanky man who reminds Mottershead of a horse propped on its tailbone, his shoulders almost level with his ears as he grips his knees and crouches low in his seat, or the man whose bald head gleams behind a clump of hatted women. Every eye is on Mottershead, aggravating his awareness that he's meant to speak. He tips the carafe and discovers that it contains not water but a film of dust. "As I say, I'm Simon Mottershead," he says, fumbling for his notes.

His audience looks apathetic, perhaps because they're wondering why he is digging in his pockets with both hands. He must have dropped his notes in the bookshop; his pockets are empty except for the voucher and the pieces of his credit card. "What would you like me to talk about?" he says desperately.

The faces before him turn blank as if their power has been switched off. "Tell us about yourself," says a voice he's unable to locate or to sex.

He feels trapped by the question, bereft of words. "Are you married with children?" the voice says.

"Not any more."

"Did it help your writing?"

At least Mottershead has answers, even if they're almost too quick for him. "Nobody except a writer knows how it feels to be a writer."

"Harrumph har*rumph* humph," a red-faced man on the front row responds.

"I'll tell you how it felt to me," Mottershead says more sharply. "Every day I'd be wakened by a story aching to be told. Writing's a compulsion. By the time you're any good at it you no longer have the choice of giving it up. It won't leave you alone even when you're with people, even when you're desperate to sleep."

By now the faces are so expressionless that he can imagine them fading like masks moulded out of dough. "When it comes to life," he says, anxious to raise his own spirits as much as those of his audience, "it's like seeing everything with new eyes. It's like dreaming while you're awake. It's as if your mind's a spider which is trying to catch reality and spin it into patterns."

"Harrumph harrumph harrumph," the red-faced man enunciates slowly, and leaves it at that. As Mottershead ransacks his mind for memories which don't cause it to flinch, the voice which raised the question of his family speaks. "What's it like to be published?"

"Not as different from not being as you'd think. I used to say I expected the priest at my funeral to ask 'Did he write under his own name?' and 'Should I have heard of him?' and 'How many novels did he write a year?'"

He's hoping to provoke at least a titter, but no face stirs. "Weren't you on television?" says the voice, which is coming from the bald head beyond the hats.

"Exactly," Mottershead laughs. Then the questioner sidles into view, and Mottershead sees that he wasn't suggesting another cliché but trying to remind him. "If you say so," Mottershead says unevenly. "I told a story once about someone who thought he was."

He's closer than ever to panic, and the sight of his questioner doesn't help. He assumes it's a man, even though the appearance of baldness proves to have been achieved by a flesh-coloured hairnet or skullcap. Although nearly all the flesh of his long mottled face has settled into his jowls, this person isn't as thin as he seemed to be when only his scalp was visible; it's as if he somehow rendered himself presentable before letting Mottershead see him. His large dark eyes glisten like bubbles about to pop, and his unwavering gaze makes Mottershead feel in danger of being compelled to speak before he knows what he will say. "Everything's material, anything can start a story growing in your head. Maybe that's our compensation for having to use up so much of ourselves in writing that nobody wants to know us."

The man with the unconvincing scalp looks suspicious and secretly gleeful. When his piebald mouth opens, Mottershead stiffens, though the question sounds innocent enough. "Do you still write?"

"I'm leaving it to people like yourselves."

If that signifies anything beyond allowing Mottershead to feel relatively in control, it ought to encourage the audience, but the questioner smiles as if Mottershead has betrayed himself. The smile causes the upper set of the teeth he's wearing to drop, revealing gums black as a dog's, and he sticks out his tongue to lever the teeth into place. "Wouldn't they give you a chance?"

"Who?"

"The powers that decide what people can read."

Everyone nods in agreement. "I don't think we need to look for conspiracies," Mottershead says, feeling as if his own teeth are exposed.

"Then why did you stop?"

He means stop writing, Mottershead assures himself. The man's gaze is a spotlight penetrating the secret places of his brain. "Because it wasn't worth it. It wasn't worth my expending so much of myself on creating the absolute best I was capable of when nobody cared that I had."

"Don't you think you were lucky to be published at all?"

The man's whitish tongue is ranging about his lips; he's begun to look as mentally unstable as Mottershead suspects he is. Genius may be next to madness, Mottershead thinks, but so is mediocrity and worse where creativity is concerned. "I think that's up to my readers to judge, don't you? What does anyone who's read my books think?"

He lets his attention drift heavenwards, or at least towards the twig-like cracks and peeling leaves of plaster which compose the ceiling. When his pretence of indifference produces no response, he sneaks a glance at his audience. How can the back of every head be facing him? "Anyone who's read anything," he says, attempting a careless laugh. "Someone must have read me or I wouldn't be here."

The pink-scalped man rears up, knotting the belt of his faded and discoloured overcoat which could almost be a dressing-gown. "Remind us," he says.

At least the audience is watching Mottershead, but without warmth. "I expect you'll have heard of *Cadenza*. That was my best book."

"Who says?" his interrogator demands.

"I do." There must have been reviews, and surely Mottershead had friends who gave him their opinions, but where those memories should be is only darkness. "I put everything I could into that book, everything of myself that was worth having. It's about the last days of a man who knows he's dying, and how that gives new life to everything we take for granted."

"How does it end?"

"I'll tell you," Mottershead says, only to discover that the dark has swallowed that information too. "Or perhaps," he corrects himself hastily, "someone who's read it should."

The doughy faces slump. Nobody has read the book. The bald man's stare is probing his thoughts, and he feels as if he's being asked "Why do you write?"—being compelled to answer "Life is shit and that's why I use up so much paper." He's opening his mouth—anything to break the breathless silence—when it occurs to him that he needn't try to recall the end of the book. He grabs the rucksack and, placing it on the table in front of him, unfastens the buckles and opens it towards his audience like a stage magician, displaying the book. "This is me."

It's immediately obvious that he has blundered somehow. "I beg your pardon. This is I," he says, and when their expressions grow more unconvinced: "This am I? I am this?"

The bald man smirks. "I should let it drop."

They needn't quiz Mottershead's grammar; some of them are bound to have perpetrated worse. Losing patience, he lifts the book out of the rucksack, and sees why they are unimpressed. His name is no longer on the cover.

He must have torn the jacket as he shoved the book into the rucksack; it's missing from the front of the book and from the spine, the binding of which is blank. He pulls the rucksack open wide, then forces it inside out, but nothing falls from it except a scattering of soil.

"Har-rumph," the red-faced man pronounces, and several heads nod vigorously. The man with the pink scalp, whose cap fits so snugly that it seems to be flattening flesh as well as any hair which the headgear conceals, stares wide-eyed at Mottershead. By God, he'll show them he wrote the novel. He throws it open, its cover striking the table with a sound like a lid being cast off a box, and finds that the copyright and title pages have been torn out. There's no trace of his name in the book.

He can still display the photograph inside the back cover, which seems impatient to be opened; he's almost sure that he feels the book stir. He picks it up gingerly, but the table beneath it is bare. He squeezes the volume between his hands and lets it fall open.

Perhaps his face is on the flap, but so is an object which has been squashed between the cover and the flyleaf. It's where he remembers the photograph to have been, and the markings on its back are very like a face. Despite its having been flattened, it retains some life. He has barely glimpsed it when it raises itself and, staggering rapidly off the book, drops into his lap.

He screams and leaps to his feet, hurling the book away from him. The object, whose welter of legs makes it appear to have doubled in size, falls to the floor and scuttles through a crack beneath the skirting-board. The audience watch as if they're wondering what further antics Mottershead may perform in a vain attempt to shock them into responding. "I'll show you," he babbles. "Just talk among yourselves while I fetch a book."

Everyone turns to watch him as he heads for the door, forcing himself to walk as though he doesn't feel like running out of the room. Nobody speaks while he struggles with the mechanism of the door, twisting a knob above the handle back and forth until he hears a click and the door swings open. He steps out and pulls it to behind him.

Either the readers at the tables are engrossed in their work or they're consciously ignoring him. He tries to move quietly as he hurries from shelf to shelf. Once he identifies the fiction, surely he'll find one or more of his books. All the shelves on this side of the top floor, however, hold only books about psychology and religion, arranged according to some system he can't crack. He sidles between two tables, ensuring that he doesn't brush against the Bible readers in front of him, and his buttocks bump a woman's head. She's wearing a rain hat which resembles a shower cap, and it must be this which deflates at the contact, but it feels as if her skull has yielded like a dying balloon, a sensation so disconcerting that the apology he means to offer comes out as "My pleasure." Feeling at the mercy of his own words, he blunders to the edge of the balcony and clutches the handrail.

If the fiction is shelved separately from the rest of the stock, he can't see where; every visible shelf holds books larger than any novel, some as thick and knobbly as full-grown branches. As he runs on tiptoe to the down escalator, a sprint which takes him halfway around the perimeter, a few readers glower at him. They would be better employed, he thinks, in complaining about the muffled shouts and thumping, presumably of workmen, which have begun somewhere offstage. A stair crawls out of hiding and catches his heel with a clang that reverberates through the library, and he sails down to the counter.

This is shaped like a symbol of hope, a curve stretching out its arms towards a way of escape. Two librarians with wide flat faces sit shoulder to shoulder at a table behind it, poring over a tome Mottershead takes to be an encyclopaedia of wild animals. He shuffles his feet, clears his throat, knocks on the counter. "Hello?" he pleads.

One librarian removes her steel-framed spectacles and passes them to her colleague, who uses them to peer more closely at an illustration. "Better see what the row is," he suggests.

Mottershead is framing a tart response when he realises that even now they aren't acknowledging him. Both raise their heads towards the shouts and pounding on the top floor. They could be identical twins, and their stubbly scalps, together with the pinstripe suits and shirts and ties they're wearing, seem designed to confuse him. "Can you tell me where to find your fiction?" he says urgently.

"You'll see none of that here," the man says without a glance at him.

"What, nowhere in the library?"

"Only books about it," says the woman, watching someone moving behind and above him.

"No need for fiction here." The man returns her spectacles to her and nods at the book on the desk. It isn't about animals, Mottershead sees now; it's a study of deformed babies, open at a picture of one which appears to have been turned inside out at birth. He's glad to be distracted by a commotion on the top floor, a door releasing a stampede of footsteps and a protesting hubbub—glad, that is, until he looks up.

The uniformed man who admitted him has let the writers out of the room, which is indeed almost soundproof. They glare about the balcony, ignoring the shushing and tutting of the readers, and then several women brandishing handbags and manuscripts catch sight of Mottershead. They rush to the edge and point at him, crying "He locked us in."

"I didn't mean to," Mottershead calls, but the entire library responds with a sound like the dousing of a great fire. "I didn't mean to," he confides to the librarians, who shrug in unison as the writers march away along the balcony. "Where are they going?"

"Where they came from, I expect," the male librarian says with satisfaction.

"But I haven't finished." Mottershead flaps his arms, and is preparing to shout when the stares of all the readers gag him. Perhaps he should let the writers go, especially since he hasn't found a book to show them—but then he realises what he has forgotten. "I haven't been paid."

The female librarian tosses her head to prevent her spectacles from slipping off her rudimentary nose. "No use telling us."

"Don't you know who's in charge?" Mottershead begs.

"You want his holiness."

"The reverend," her colleague explains.

He's pointing at the red-faced man whose entire vocabulary seemed to consist of false coughs, and who is making his way around the balcony towards the down escalator. Mottershead pads to the foot of the escalator, trying to phrase a demand which will be polite but firm. "I believe I'm to be paid now," he rehearses as the red-faced man comes abreast of the escalator. The man marches past without sparing it or Mottershead a glance.

Is there another public exit besides the one beyond the counter? Mottershead groans aloud and sprints to the opposite escalator, dodging irate readers who twist in their seats and try to detain him. He grabs the banister, which squirms as it slithers upwards, and runs up the lumbering stairs.

As soon as he's three stairs short of the balcony he manages to heave himself onto it, using the banisters like parallel bars. The only door he can locate leads to the stockroom through which the guard brought him, but he shouldn't be searching for a door. The red-faced man is returning to the down escalator, having replaced a hymn-book on the shelf.

Mottershead clutches his aching skull. It will take him several minutes to run around the balcony to that escalator, by which time his quarry may well have left the building. "Reverend," he calls desperately. "Reverend! *Reverend!*"

The man seems not to hear him. Either he's experiencing a vision which renders him unaware of his surroundings as he rides towards the ground floor or his title is only the librarians' nickname for him. Mottershead lurches onto the stairs which are climbing doggedly towards him and clatters down, shouting "Hey! Hey! Hey!" Even now the red-faced man doesn't look at him, though all the readers do; many of them start to boo and jeer. While Mottershead is managing to outrun the escalator, his quarry is descending at more than twice his speed. He's only halfway down when the red-faced man steps onto the floor and strides past the counter.

"My fee," Mottershead screams. He lifts his feet and slides down, his heels clanking on the edges of the steps. At the bottom he launches himself between the tables, where at least one reader sticks out a foot for him to jump over. The exit barrier is executing a last few swings, but the red-faced man is already past the doors beyond it. Mottershead is almost at the counter when the man with the pink scalp steps into his path.

"Let me pass," Mottershead cries, but the man widens his glistening eyes and stretches out his arms on either side of him. The librarians are miming indifference, gazing at the roof. "Get away or I'll buffet and belabour you," Mottershead snarls, which earns him admonitory looks from the librarians. He's poising himself to rush his tormentor when the man steps forwards, soles flapping. "Reverend Neverend said to give you this."

Is he protracting a joke which the librarians played on Mottershead? But he's waving an envelope, brown as the wrapper of a book which has something to hide. Mottershead suspects that it contains a text he has no desire to read. "Didn't he even have the grace to serve me with it himself?" Mottershead says for the readers to hear, and snatches the envelope. At once he realises that it's full of coins and notes.

The writers must have held a collection for him. Feeling exposed and clownish, he slips the envelope into his pocket, which he pats to convince himself that he hasn't dropped the envelope, and wills the readers to forget about him. As he tries to sneak past the counter the messenger detains him, seizing his elbow with jittery fingers whose nails are caked with ink. "Can I talk to you?"

"You have done."

"That was for the others. I want to talk about ourselves. We've lots in common, I can tell."

"Some other time," Mottershead says insincerely, trying to pull away without looking at him.

"There won't be."

"So be it, then." Mottershead attempts to stare him into letting go, but can't meet the other's eyes for long; they look as if being compelled to see too much has swollen them almost too large for their sockets. "I want to be left alone," he mutters.

"You know that's not possible."

Mottershead feels black helplessness closing around his mind. He wants to lash out, to thump the man's scalp, which he's sure is plastic disguised not quite successfully as flesh. What would it sound like? The temptation dismays him. "Will you have a word with this person?" he says at the top of his voice.

The librarians frown at him. "What about?" the female says.

"About your dress code, I should think."

The man with the replaced scalp is wearing slippers on his bony feet, and if his buttonless garment belted with old rope isn't a dressing-gown, it might as well be; certainly he's wearing nothing under it except striped trousers like a sleeper's or a convict's. The librarians are still frowning at Mottershead, but he doesn't care, because his outburst has caused his tormentor to flinch and loosen his spidery grip. He pulls himself free and knees the barrier aside, shouting "I think you've got some explaining to do" to freeze the man in case he considers following. He closes both hands around the heavy brass knob of the door and, having opened it just wide enough to sidle through, drags it shut behind him.

He has emerged onto an avenue lined with shops beneath a heavily overcast sky. Display windows shine between tree trunks as far as the eye can see. Though the upper stories are obscured by foliage, it seems to him that the shops have possessed a variety of buildings; through the leaves he glimpses creatures so immobile they must be gargoyles, bricked-up towers like trees pruned to the trunk, domes green as mounds of moss. To his right, in the distance where the trees appear to meet, the sky is clear. He heads for the light, hoping it will help him think.

Before long he sees that he's approaching a bookshop, its windows full of paperbacks as bright and various as packets in a supermarket. Wasn't *Cadenza* put into paperback? The thought of the book makes him shriek through his teeth; he has left the damaged copy and his rucksack in the library. He can't imagine going back, but perhaps there is no need. Dodging the bicycles which are the only traffic, he crosses to the bookshop.

The glass doors are plastered with posters for a book called *Princess the Frog*. The sight of eyes bulging at him from beneath crowned bridal veils confuses him, so that he grapples with the doors for some time before discovering that the right-hand door is locked into position. He shoulders its twin open and thinks he has cracked the glass. No, he has dislodged a poster, which the door crumples and tears. He steps over it and moves quickly into the shop, pretending he was nowhere near.

Fiction is ranged around the walls. Anything by Mottershead ought to be on the shelves at the back of the shop. He's passing the authors beginning with I when someone catches up with him. "May I help you?"

"I'm looking—" Mottershead begins, and then his voice goes to pieces. He has been accosted by a frog in a wedding dress. In a moment he's able to distinguish that the frog is an elderly woman, her leathery skin painted green with the make-up she has used to make her mouth seem wider. She's holding the poster he crumpled. "I can find it myself, thank you," he says in a voice so controlled it feels like suppressing a belch.

"Keep in mind that we're here."

Whether that is meant as a warning or as an offer of assistance, it aggravates the hysteria he's trying to suppress. She has drawn his attention to her colleagues who are scattered about the shop, all of whom, including at least one man, are dressed as bridal frogs. This must be part of a promotion for the book which is advertised on the posters—there's a mound of copies of the book draped with waterweed beside the cash desk. He clutches his mouth as he begins to splutter, and flees deeper into the shop.

The letter M covers the whole of the back wall. He has the impression that the patterns formed by the print on the spines spell out several giant versions of the letter. His name is almost at floor level—Mottershead, in several different typefaces. He digs his fingers into the tops of the pages and tugs at the four books. No wonder nobody has bought them if they're wedged so tightly on the shelf. He manages to tip them towards himself until he's able to grasp the corners of the spines. He heaves at them, and without warning they fly off the shelf and sprawl across the floor.

Before he can pick them up, the frog bride who originally followed him hurries over to him. "It's all right," Mottershead tells her, feeling his mirth coming to the boil again as he stoops to gather the books. "I'll buy these if you'll give me a carrier bag. I wrote them."

Does she think he's lying? Disapproval stretches her mouth wide enough to render her makeup redundant. "Look," he says, no longer wanting to laugh, "I assure you—" Then he sees the covers of the books he's claiming to have written, and his jaw drops.

The author's name is undoubtedly Mottershead; it's spread across the covers in large raised capital letters. The first name, however, is printed small to fit between the thighs of the girls whose naked bottoms are embossed on the covers. The books are called *Eighteen*, *Seventeen*, *Sixteen*, and *Fifteen*, and it's clear from the faces gazing over their shoulders that these are the ages of the girls. He doesn't need to focus on the author's first name to be certain that he could never have entertained such thoughts, let alone admitting them on paper—but how can he convince the princess frog?

"You'd better have them before I do any more damage," he mumbles. If she will only take them, he'll run out of the shop; he no longer cares what she thinks of him. But she shakes her head violently and clenches her greenish fists, further crumpling the poster, and two of her fellow frogs close in behind Mottershead. "Trouble?" the male bride croaks.

"The author of those items claims to have found them on the shelf. One wonders who must have put them there."

"I was mistaken. I didn't write any of these books."

The frog with the poster stares incredulously at Mottershead. "Seems not to know when to stop telling tales," remarks the fattest of the frogs.

"Do I look as if I could be responsible for this stuff?" Mottershead cries. "Why would I be trying to buy books I'd written myself?"

The frogs snigger. "Some people will stop at nothing to promote themselves," says the one with the poster.

Mottershead is overwhelmed by rage which feels distressingly like panic. He tosses the books into the air and is on his way to the exit before they come down. He's fleeing past the shop when the three booksellers appear at the window, hopping up and down and croaking inarticulately as they wave the books at him. All the passing cyclists begin to ring their bells as if to draw attention to him, and he dodges behind a chestnut tree, turning up his collar to hide the parts of his face he can't squash against the trunk.

As soon as the bell-ringing slackens he dodges out from behind the tree and hastens along the avenue, trying to outrun a sound which he has begun to suspect is concealed by the jangle of bells. He has passed only a few buildings, however, when he comes to a bookshop which has taken over a cinema. The compulsion to find himself on the shelves is stronger than ever. Glancing along the deserted pavement, he darts into the shop.

Several life-size cut-out figures, presumably of authors rather than of film stars, loiter inside the entrance. Shelves like exposed girders branch across the walls of the gutted auditorium, and the floor is crowded with tables piled with books: *The Wit of the Answering Machine, 1001 Great Advertising Slogans, Inflate Your Brain* . . . Beside the propped-up figures two young blondes deep in conversation lean against the cash desk. "She has the same hair as me," one says in a voice light as tissue, and her friend responds "I'll have to try it sometime." There's something rather forbidding about the perfection of their young faces, their long eyelashes and blue eyes and pink lips, their unblemished flesh; he can't help thinking of the oldest of the models on the covers of the books he has just disowned. The thought sends words blundering out of his mouth. "Can I have one of you?"

They turn to him with expressions so identically polite that their spuriousness disconcerts him. "I mean, can one of you show me where you keep Simon Mottershead? Not the Mottershead who has fantasies about girls of your age and younger," he adds hastily. "The one who wrote *Cadenza.*"

None of this has made any visible impression on them. He feels as if their perfect surfaces are barriers he can't touch, let alone penetrate. "I'm talking about books, you understand," he says. "I want you to show me some books."

The assistant to his left glances at her colleague. "Better call the manager."

"Is that necessary?" Mottershead says. Apparently it is; before he has finished speaking, the other girl presses a button on the desk. A bell shrills somewhere behind a wall, and a woman several years older than those at the desk but made up to look the same age rises like a figure in a pop-up book from behind a table. "What can I do for you?" she asks Mottershead.

"I'm waiting for the manager."

"I am she."

"Then you can help me," Mottershead says, trying to sound friendly and apologetic and amused by his gaffe. "I'm after Simon Mottershead."

"We have nobody of that name here."

"Books by him, I mean."

"We have none."

"Can you show me where to look? I believe you, obviously," Mottershead lies, "but you've such a large stock . . ."

The woman grunts as though he means that as an insult. "You'd be wasting your time. I know every book in this shop."

Why is she trying to get rid of him? He feels as if the blackness which threatens his mind is darkening the shop, gathering like smoke under the roof. His surroundings, the faces of the women included, appear to be losing depth. "At least," he says desperately, "you must have heard of Simon Mottershead."

"I won't pretend I have."

The blackness is about to swallow everything around him except her cut-out face and those of her assistants. "Well, now you've met him," he almost screams, and flounders towards the exit, which he can barely locate. As he makes a grab for the door, someone who has been waiting in the doorway steps into the shop. It's the man with the false scalp.

He blocks Mottershead's path and holds up one hand, and Mottershead loses control. Seizing the man's shoulders, which feel loose and swollen, he hurls him aside. The man falls headlong, taking two of the propped-up figures with him, and Mottershead is sure he's exaggerating his fall, playing to the audience, who emit cries of outrage and run to help him up. Mottershead knocks over the rest of the propped-up figures to hinder any pursuit and kicks the door shut behind him.

He's hardly out when he sees another bookshop through the trees. Its sign—Everything Worth Reading—is so challenging that he can't resist it. Fewer bicycles are about, and they and their bells seem slowed down. He sprints between them and peers around a tree trunk. When he sees nobody following him he scurries to the third bookshop.

The frontage seems altogether too narrow for the shop to accommodate the stock of which the sign boasts. On the other hand, if the proprietor's standards are higher than those apparent in the other shops, shouldn't this one stock Mottershead's work? He pushes open the black door beside the dim window occupied by a few jacketless leathery books. A bell above the door sounds a low sombre note, and the proprietor raises his head.

His black hair looks spongy and moist as lichen. His whiskers bristle on either side of his long pointed face. He's sitting behind a scratched desk bearing an ancient cash register and a book catalogue, the corners of whose pages have turned up like dead leaves. His wrinkled eyelids rise lethargically as he stares at Mottershead, who strides forwards and sticks out his hand. "Simon Mottershead. *Simon*," he emphasises to ensure there's no mistake.

The man gives the hand a discouraging glance and seems to brace himself as though his instinct is to recoil from his visitor. "Who do you represent?"

"Myself," Mottershead says with a laugh which is meant to be self-deprecating but which comes out sounding wild. "I'm the writer."

"Which writer?"

"Simon Mottershead."

"Congratulations," the bookseller says with a distinct lack of enthusiasm. "To what do I owe such an honor?"

"I was wondering which of my books you might have."

"I can hardly tell you that if they haven't been published."

"They have been," Mottershead wails, struggling to recall titles which will help him fend off the blackness that seems about to consume him; he feels as if he no longer exists. "*Cadenza*. Even if it's out of print, you must have heard of that one."

"No must about it, I fear."

The shop is much longer than was apparent from outside: so long that its depths are almost lightless. The growing darkness might be the absence of his books made visible. "Let me tell you the story," he pleads, "and perhaps it'll come back to you."

The bookseller stands up and gazes past him. "You'll have to excuse me. I've a customer."

A moment later the bell tolls. Should Mottershead take advantage of the diversion and search the shelves for his name? Finding it in the face of the bookseller's denials would be the greatest triumph he can imagine. He edges past the desk and glances at the newcomer, and darkness rushes at him. "He isn't a customer," he says in a throttled voice.

"If he's about to make the same approach to me," the bookseller says, "I must ask you both to leave."

"Of course he isn't," Mottershead manages to articulate rather than lay hands on his pursuer. "How could he?"

The bookseller opens a drawer of the desk and reaches into it. "Please leave or I'll have you excluded."

"You already have," Mottershead says bitterly, and lurches towards the exit, away from the tunnel of blackness which the shop feels like. The bald man is in his way. The top of his scalp is concave now, dented by his recent fall; his eyes have grown luridly bright, perhaps as a result of pressure on his brain. "You're a witness," Mottershead appeals to the bookseller, whose hand is still in the drawer, gripping a weapon or a telephone. "I've told this creature to stay away from me, otherwise I won't be responsible for my actions."

The bookseller shakes his head. "Please fight outside."

Mottershead sees himself and his tormentor as the bookseller is seeing them: two unpublished and probably unpublishable writers, mutually jealous because of their lack of success. The unfairness appals him, and he's about to make a last attempt to persuade the bookseller of his authenticity when the bald man distracts him. "I've got something of yours," he says with a secretive grin.

"Whatever it is, you're welcome to it. Keep it as your fee for leaving me alone," Mottershead tells him, thinking that it must be the damaged copy of *Cadenza*. Since the other doesn't move, Mottershead lunges at him, and is gratified to see him flinch and cover his scalp with both hands. "Stay away or you'll get worse," Mottershead snarls, and marches out of the shop. Then his confidence deserts him, and he flees towards the open space beyond the avenue.

He won't stop for anything, he promises himself. The prospect of failing to find himself in yet another bookshop—of prolonging the black depression which seeps through him like poison—terrifies him, and yet he's unable to refrain from scanning the shopfronts in search of one more bookshop, one more excuse to hope. Didn't he behave like this when *Cadenza* was published? Was that the day when he flustered from bookshop to bookshop, feeling as though just one copy of the book would convince him he existed, until he was ready to do anything that would stop him feeling that way? He's dismayingly grateful that there seem to be no more bookshops on the avenue. Nevertheless a window causes him to falter: the window of a clothes shop.

He's past it—past the full-length mirror among the shirted torsos and bodiless legs dressed in kilts or trousers—before he knows what he has seen. He wavers, stumbles onwards, backtracks reluctantly. He sees himself reappear in the mirror, walking backwards like a figure in a videocassette playing in reverse. Under his suit, which is so faded that its pattern has vanished, he's wearing only a singlet full of ventilation holes through which the grey hairs of his chest sprout: neither a shirt nor socks.

So this is the image of himself which he has been presenting. No wonder everyone was leery of him. His reflection is beginning to tremble before his eyes; his helpless rage is shaking him. He's staring at the mirror as if he is hypnotising himself—he's unable to look away from the sight of himself among the portions of bodies arranged like a work of art composed of dismemberment—when the man with the dented scalp appears behind him.

The reflection shivers like disturbed water. The movement seems to spread beyond the mirror, causing the torsos and severed limbs to stir as if they, or the single dusty head which lurks in one corner of the window, may be dreaming of recomposition. Perhaps one day he'll be able to derive a story from all this, Mottershead thinks desperately, but hasn't he already written something of the kind? His legs are pressing themselves together, his crossed hands are clutching his chest in an attempt to hide the discoloured flesh. The other cranes over his shoulder, and Mottershead feels as if he has grown a second head. "Just a few words," the man whispers moistly in his ear.

"Suck a turd," Mottershead howls and staggers out of reach, bumping into the window as he twists around to face his pursuer. "Will those do? Will that satisfy you?"

The man rolls his eyes and licks his lips. Perhaps he's trying to adjust his teeth, but he looks as though he is asking for more. Mottershead shouts every insult and obscenity and combination of them he can think of, a monologue which seems endless and yet to need no breath. When at last he runs out of words, his victim hasn't even flinched. He raises one hand to his mouth to shove his teeth into place and gives Mottershead a disappointed look. "That didn't sound much like a writer."

"Then I can't be one, can I?" Mottershead says with a kind of hysterical triumph. "Happy now?"

The other reaches for his teeth again as a preamble to responding, but Mottershead won't hear another word. He knocks the hand aside and, digging his fingers into the man's mouth, seizes the upper set of teeth. The tongue pokes bonelessly at his fingers but can't dislodge them until he has taken the teeth, which he shies across the avenue, narrowly missing a lone cyclist. "Fetch," he snarls.

His victim gapes at him as though the weight of his jowls is more than his jaw will sustain. Though he quails at the thought of encountering the tongue again, Mottershead plunges his fingers into the open mouth and grabs the lower set of teeth. Plucking them off the blackened gums, he throws them as high as he can. They lodge in the branches of a chestnut, startling a bird which flaps away along the avenue. "That should keep you busy for a while. Don't even dream of following," he warns, and runs after the bird.

Ahead, beyond a junction which puts an end to the shops, parkland stretches to the horizon. The sky above the park is cloudless, as though cleared by some emanation from the cropped grass. Here and there clumps of trees shade benches, all of which are unoccupied. As Mottershead passes the last shops the bird soars and seems to expand as it flaps blackly towards the zenith. Then it shrinks and vanishes before he expects it to do so, and he squeezes between two of the rusting cars which stand alongside the park.

The gates are held open by bolts driven deep into the path, cracking the concrete. Each of the stone gateposts is carved with a life-size figure which embraces the post and digs its face into the stone as though trying to hide or to see within. Above the scrawny limbs and torsos, the bald heads are pitted and overgrown with moss. Once he is through the gates Mottershead glances back, but the faces aren't emerging from the park-ward sides of the posts, even if the moss on each of them resembles the beginnings of a face. Nor can he see anyone following him.

Beyond the gates the paths fan out. Most of them curve away between the benches, but one leads straight to the horizon, which is furred with trees. As Mottershead strolls along this path he seems to feel the city and everything which has befallen him withdrawing at least as far as the limits of the park. The grass is green as spring and sparkles with rain or dew, drops of which flash like windows to a microscopic world. He won't stop walking until he reaches the trees on the horizon, and per-haps not then unless he has grasped why the park is so familiar.

He's beyond the outermost of the benches when he begins to remem-ber. He was walking with his family, his wife holding his hand and their son's, their daughter holding Mottershead's other hand. Shafts of misty sunlight through the foliage started the trees singing. He felt as if his family were guiding him, keeping him safe while his dreams took pos-session of the woods. He felt that he was being led towards the fulfil-ment of a dream he didn't know he had. Perhaps he was incapable of believing in it or even of conceiving it while he was awake.

In that case, how can he glimpse it now? Too many impressions are crowding it out of his head. Is it a memory, or could it be something he wrote or intended to write? Whichever, he feels certain that he recog-nises the setting—that he has walked with his family through the woods at the far side of the park. They had a house beyond those woods. Isn't it possible that his wife and children still live there? That would mean he has a chance to make it up to them.

He can't think what he needs to put right, but surely he'll remember when he comes face to face with them. Did he use them in a story in some way that distressed them? He begins to jog towards the woods and then, as the trees remain stubbornly distant, to run. He seems to have got nowhere when he stops dead, having heard a toothless voice call his name.

He whirls around, snarling. The sky overhead seems to shrink and blacken, the clumps of trees appear to stiffen, clenching their branches. He can see nobody except a woman dashing through the gateway, dragged by three obese poodles dyed pink and green and purple, each dog wearing a cap and bells. Then the voice calls again, its speech clarified by the lack of teeth. "Here you are."

His tormentor must be hiding among the nearest clump of trees; Mottershead's rucksack is lolling on the bench they shade. He would happily abandon it, but if he doesn't confront his pursuer he's liable to be followed all the way to his family's house. He stalks towards the bench.

The man isn't in the trees around it. Mottershead can only assume that the sight of the rucksack attracted his attention to the wrong clump. He grabs the rucksack and wriggles his arms into the straps, feeling a weight which must be the damaged copy of *Cadenza* settle on his back. "Thank you. Now please go away," he shouts.

The only movement is of the poodles, which are rolling on the grass near the gates so zealously that they've dragged their owner down with them. As Mottershead stares about, he notices that all the houses bordering the park sport television aerials. Was he on television? He seems to remember cameras being poked at him, lights blazing at him, technicians crowding around him. How many people saw him on their screens, and what did they see? Not knowing makes his surroundings feel like a concealed threat. "Stay away from my family, you lunatic," he cries, and runs back to the straight path.

He feels as if the contents of the rucksack are riding him, driving him towards the woods. Whenever he passes another clump of trees around a bench he scrutinises them, though when he does so they appear to draw themselves up, to become identical with the previous clump. He's dizzy from peering around him and behind him by the time he reaches the end of the path.

Two trails lead from it into the woods. One is wide, and ribbed as though outlined by a giant ladder half-buried in the earth. The other winds through a thicket, and he takes it at once, trusting the trees and the undergrowth to betray any attempt to pursue him.

The thicket is more extensive than he anticipates. The trees blot out the sky with branches so closely entangled that it's impossible to tell which foliage belongs to which. The leaves of the shrubs which mass between the trees, narrowing the path, look starved of sunlight; some are pale as the fungi which swell among the roots. Roots encroach on the gloomy path, so that he has to keep glancing down as he sidles through the thicket, peering ahead for the end.

At first he's able to ignore the way the darkness seems to creep closer around him whenever he examines the path, and then he tells himself that it's bound to grow darker as he progresses. But the darkness feels like a sign of pursuit—it feels like a sack which someone is poising over his head. Glaring over his shoulder, he sees that the thicket has closed in behind him, obscuring the view beyond it so thoroughly that the park and the city might never have been there at all.

Though he can neither see nor hear anyone pursuing him, his sense of being followed infests the woods. Foliage gathers overhead like eternal night, fungi goggle at him from beneath the mob of shrubs. He can't keep glancing back, because many of the shrubs between which the path meanders are full of thorns on which he's liable to tear himself. When he fixes his attention on the way ahead, however, he has the impression that he's allowing a pursuer to gain on him—that the dented head is about to crane over his shoulder, protruding its eyes and its discoloured tongue. "Stay out of my mind," he whispers, grabbing at branches and letting them whip savagely past him.

He feels as if he has ventured into a maze of thorns whose points are catching at his mind. He's tempted to retrace his tracks, but when he turns he sees that the branches which he let fly have blocked the path, rendering it indistinguishable in the gloom. At least the way ahead is passable, since initials and whole words are carved on the trees beside the path.

He's less inclined to welcome these signs of life once he succeeds in identifying the words. A tree to his left is inscribed vertically with one word: sockets. A flap of bark has been left hanging from the next tree as though to expose the words dream or scream. Most disconcerting is the message displayed by a trunk on the opposite side of the path—nearly a tree—because when he surveys the woods beyond it, several of the trees seem unconvincing, more like wood carved and assembled to masquerade as trees. He sidles between the thorns as rapidly as he dares in the gathering darkness.

The path bends sharply, and as he approaches the bend he observes that the trees directly ahead of him are carved with words from their roots to their crowns—tree after tree, leading his gaze into the depths of the woods. It seems to him that the thorny gloom must contain words enough to fill at least one book. Should he force his way through the bushes to read them? Perhaps the thorns won't injure him, for he's beginning to identify with them, beginning to think that the thorns themselves must have scratched the words on the trees; he can't imagine anyone struggling through the mass of them to do so. He feels as if the thorns aren't reaching for his mind after all, they're reaching out of it. He tries to grasp that impression, but it's too like an embodiment of the dark for comfort. He drags his gaze away from the engraved trees and edges along the path.

The woods are loath to release him. Thorns snag his rucksack and his shoulders; he feels as if the contents of the rucksack are trying to delay him. How long has he been stumbling through the woods? Will he ever be out of the dark? He's suppressing a fear that the path may have turned back on itself, because wherever he looks in order to pick his way he's confronted with paragraphs gouged out of timber. He's afraid to rest his gaze on them even for a moment, knowing that he'll be compelled to stand and read them while the darkness continues to gather.

Now the thorns ahead are rising above him as though to drive him back. The rucksack tugs at his shoulders, the thorns overhead seem to writhe. He winces from side to side of the path, convinced that he can feel thorns reaching for his eyes. His left eye twinges as if the point of a thorn has touched the surface of the eyeball, and he claps one hand over his eyes and gropes forwards with the other. The skin beneath his fingernails is tingling with apprehension. No thorns have pierced his fingertips, however, when the rucksack slumps against his spine and he flounders into the open.

It's almost as dark outside the forest as it was beneath the trees. Glancing back, he sees that he has emerged through a gap in a hedge which, in the darkness, looks impenetrable. The path, or his deviation from it, has led him into the back garden of a large two-storey house.

Light from a kitchen window and between the curtains of the adjacent ground-floor room lies on the worn grass, trapping him in the intervening darkness. He's preparing to dodge through the narrower ray and sneak around the building to the road when he recognises the house. The curtains may not be familiar, but the gap-toothed look of the arch above the curtained window is, and the tilt of the bricked-up chimney and the droop of the handle of the back door. This was once his house.

The gap in the hedge was his doing. No wonder he was able to place the woods; they were his refuge whenever he found that he couldn't think in the house. He remembers taking care to leave the thorny branches intact, to make it harder for anyone to follow him. He remembers returning from the woods one day to find his children carving their initials on the kitchen doorpost, glancing fearfully towards him as the hedge creaked. His wife ran through the kitchen to rebuke them before he could lose his temper, but listening to her reasoning with them was more than he could bear. "Give me the knife," he said to her, and saw the blade flash in all their eyes. "Maybe one day people will know this was where we lived."

The initials are there on the jamb, all four sets of them. The pile of final letters appears to depict a steady hum, a lullaby which he can almost hear and which makes him feel dreamy and safe, home at last. The situation isn't so simple—he can't assume that he will be received with open arms—but surely once he sees his family he'll recall what happened in the interim. He creeps along the track of darkness, grinning in anticipation of the sight of their faces when they become aware of him. He's halfway across the lawn when a man appears beyond the gap between the curtains of the downstairs room.

Mottershead throws himself flat. The lawn feels like a mattress hardened by age, prickly and full of lumps. Is the man a burglar or some even more dangerous intruder? Mottershead gropes around himself in search of a weapon and finds a rake, its tines upturned a few inches in front of him. If he'd taken one more step before prostrating himself they would have had his eyes. He draws the rake towards him between the strips of light and begins to raise it through the shadow so as to grasp the handle.

The rake is perpendicular in front of him when he wonders if the man, who has passed the gap between the curtains, may be in the house by invitation. He can't assume that, he has to establish that his family is unharmed and not in danger. He has been pressing both hands on the tines of the rake in order to lift the handle; now he lets go with one in order to reach for it. His other hand can't support the weight, and the rake totters. As he tries to grab it with both hands, it falls into the light with a thump and a clang.

He digs his hands and face into the soil and lies absolutely still. The curtains rattle, the light spreads over him, and then the sash of the window bumps up. "Are you all right, old chap?" the man calls. "Stay there and we'll get you."

Mottershead seizes the rake and hauls himself to his feet. The man, who has a long face and a mane of reddish hair, looks concerned until he sees Mottershead clearly; then he frowns. "I lived here," Mottershead gabbles. "I'm just going."

"No hurry, old fellow. Perhaps you still do. Come round the front and we'll see if we can find your room. Shall we put the rake down? It's a bit late for gardening, don't you think? When it's light we can see about finding you your very own plot to look after."

Mottershead lets the rake drop. His embarrassment and discomfiture are giving way to panic, but he has to be certain that he's right to leave. "My wife and children aren't still here, are they?" he says as calmly as he can manage. "The Mottersheads."

"I'm sure they'll be here at visiting time. Let's go round the front now and I'll let you in."

Mottershead makes himself stroll to the corner of the house. As soon as it conceals him he breaks into a run, intending to be past the gates by the time the nurse opens the front door. But he slows to glance through the window in the side of the house.

Beyond the window is the dining-room. All the furniture has been replaced. About a dozen old folk wearing plastic bibs which cover their chests are seated at a trestle table draped with cellophane. Brawny nurses of both sexes stand behind them, spooning greenish slop into their toothless mouths or removing slices of bread which two of the diners have placed on their own heads. One nurse seems about to knock with her knuckles on a balding woman's skull but desists, simpering, when she catches sight of Mottershead. He puts on speed again, too tardily. As he rounds the house, the male nurse opens the front door.

He raises his long face towards Mottershead like a hound on the scent. "Sorry to have bothered you," Mottershead calls to him, backing towards the gates. "I should be somewhere else by now. I'll be on my way."

The man's face seems to elongate as his mouth opens. "We've someone who's a bit confused here. I don't think we want him wandering off."

He's addressing two of his colleagues who have just stepped into the drive. Their eyes gleam with the light of the streetlamp outside the gates; the rest of their faces are covered with surgical masks. They move to either side of the drive and advance on Mottershead like mirror images, each stretching out a hand to take him by the arms.

He waits until they're almost upon him, his neck twitching as he watches them over his shoulder. At the last moment he dodges around them, leaping and nearly falling over what's left of his wife's rockery, and dashes across the car park which most of the front garden has become. He swings himself around an upright of a sign naming the Wild Rest Home and manages to drag the right-hand gate open as the concrete catches at its bolt. Struggling through the gap, he clashes the gate shut and looks back.

The nurses have already caught up with him. Though he didn't hear them following, all three are close enough to touch. The eyes of the masked nurses are far too large; their masks are so flat it seems impossible for them to be concealing any features. Their companion's face points like a hound's towards Mottershead, and he poises himself, eager for the chase, as they each seize one of the gates. "Stay," Mottershead cries, and flees into the dark beyond the streetlamp.

Has he strayed back into the woods? Surely the suburban street ought to lead to a main road, but he's having to dodge around trees which sprout thickly from the pavement and even, it seems, from the roadway. There must be houses; he sees the flickering of televisions, though their screens appear to be among the trees themselves rather than in rooms. If he has turned the wrong way at the gates, it's too late to rectify his error. The single lamp has already been blotted out by trees dripping with mist, but he knows his pursuers are behind him. He runs towards the sound of an engine revving somewhere ahead.

It's a bus, and he doesn't care where it's going so long as it helps him escape. When he glances round he sees that the nurses are gaining on him, the long-faced man's nose quivering above the bared teeth, the others flanking him, their lack of faces glimmering. The sound of the engine is moving gradually to Mottershead's left, and he sprints in that direction, trying to avoid the patches of unsteady light where he glimpses figures watching televisions, unless the shapes are monumental statues which have collapsed in front of marble slabs. Then the long-faced nurse draws level with him, leaping over the source of one patch of flickering, which seems to freeze him for a moment so that Mottershead can see him clearly: face like a hound's skull, pallid flapping belly, limbs white and thin as bones. He drops to all fours and bounds ahead, ranging back and forth while he waits to see which way Mottershead will dodge.

Mottershead runs straight at him, praying that will make him falter. Instead the man leaps to meet him, his eyes bulging as whitely as his teeth. Mottershead lurches aside and puts on a final desperate burst of speed, which takes him away from the sound of the bus. There are no lights where he's running, only trees which loom in front of him whichever way he stumbles. "I won't go back," he tells himself, unable to say it aloud for the clamping of his jaw, feeling as though even his voice has deserted him. He swerves around another tree and another, and suddenly he's in a narrow passage where weeds and branches overhang the high walls. He dashes along it, tripping over bricks which have fallen from the walls, and at last it lets him into the open.

He's on a street which winds between dark dumpy houses. All the houses are derelict, as are the cars parked beneath smashed lamps along both sides of the road. Nevertheless the street isn't entirely lifeless; he hears the creaks of rusty springs, and several bunches of heads rise to watch him through the glassless windscreens, their tiny eyes glittering like raindrops. He peers along the brick passage, which for the moment is empty, and tries frantically to judge which way to run. The groaning of the engine becomes audible once more, and the bus grinds into view between the houses to his right.

The vehicle is dark except for its guttering headlamps. He stares at the passage again and sees three figures racing towards him, stretching out their arms until it seems they could finger the ground without stooping. He forces his way between two cars. They crumble when he brushes against them, and he feels them shake as he disturbs their occupants. He staggers into the road, waving his hands wildly at the bus.

Is it really bound for somewhere called Frosty Biceps? He hasn't time to reread the destination, he's too busy trying to catch the attention of the driver, who is bent so low over the steering-wheel that his forehead appears to overhang his eyes. The driver sees him and lifts his expressionless face, whose features are squashed into a concavity between the jutting forehead and prominent chin. The vehicle slows, and Mottershead digs in his pocket for the envelope of money. The bus halts a few feet away from him and the door wavers open.

He hasn't reached the platform when the vehicle starts to coast forwards. Glancing behind him, he sees hands drumming their fingers on the walls at the end of the passage, three hands on each wall, as if his pursuers are only waiting for the bus to forsake him before they run him down. "Help me," he pleads.

The driver doesn't brake or look away from the road, but his forehead and chin relax sufficiently to let him open his mouth. "Get if you're getting," he mutters.

Mottershead clutches at the metal pole beyond the door and hauls himself onto the platform. At once the bus sways around the next curve, barely missing two derelict cars and almost throwing Mottershead off. He hangs onto the pole until the door drags shut like a curtain rusty with disuse, then he takes one hand from the pole to reach for the envelope. "Ferry?" he says hopefully.

"You'll end up where you have to go."

The driver seems to begrudge him even that response. Mottershead wraps his legs around the pole, feeling like a monkey, and tries to hold the envelope steady while he inserts a finger beneath the flap. "How much is it?"

The driver jerks his head, vaguely indicating the depths of the bus. "You'll have to deal with him."

Presumably he's referring to a conductor, but the vehicle is too dark for Mottershead to locate him. No doubt he'll come to Mottershead, who clambers upstairs as the bus sways onwards. As soon as he's on the top deck he clings to the banister above the stairs and peers through the grimy windows.

The passage down which he was chased is already out of sight, and the road is deserted. Otherwise the view behind him and ahead of him is less reassuring. The spaces between the houses are piled high with refuse: crumpled cars, bent supermarket trolleys, handless grandfather clocks hollow as coffins, huge verdigrised bells, television sets with doll-sized figures stuffed inside them, their faces and hands flattened against the cracked screens. He can't tell whether the hulks beyond the houses closest to the road are buildings or abandoned buses. He staggers to the front seat and falls into it, sitting forwards to let the contents of the rucksack settle themselves, and then he sinks back.

There's movement above him. A round mirror is set in the ceiling over the cabin, allowing the driver to survey the top deck through a spyhole. Having spied Mottershead, the driver returns his attention to the windings of the road, and Mottershead looks back. As far as he can distinguish in the thick gloom, he's alone on the upper deck. He gazes ahead, willing the landing-stage not to be far.

He rather wishes he hadn't noticed the mirror. Its bulbousness stretches the driver's forehead and chin so that his dwarfed eyes and nose and mouth appear to be set in a crescent of flesh surmounted by a tuft of whitish hair. The feeble headlights flicker over the derelict sub-urb, and Mottershead has the impression that the houses themselves are stuffed to their roofs with refuse; certainly the figures in the gaping windows are being thrust towards the sills by the tangled masses within. As the bus swings around a curve, scraping several cars, he thinks he sees a figure lose its hold on the second-floor sill where it's perched and fall headfirst onto the concrete. He can't be seeing all this, he tells him-self; it's just that he hasn't had a chance to recover from the day, from the effect which the man with the unreal pate had on his mind. Another figure plummets from a window, the impact flinging its head and all its limbs in different directions, and he realises that the figures are dum-mies. He shouldn't even be watching, he hasn't sorted out his fare. He tears open the envelope and brings it to his eyes.

It contains half-a-dozen coins and several folded notes. As he pulls out the notes and smooths them on his palm, the coins rattle together. Surely he has misheard the sound. He leafs through the notes, peering so hard at them that his vision shivers, then he glares at the coins. All of the latter are plastic, and apart from a note in some unrecognisably foreign currency, the notes are from a board game too.

He clenches his fists in helpless rage, crushing the notes, splintering the coins. So the writers' group never held a collection for him. The man who handed him the envelope must be responsible for its contents, and Mottershead is certain now that the man has been doing his best to drive him mad. When did he begin? He followed Mottershead into the room in the library, but from where? Perhaps from the bookshop where Mottershead found the copy of *Cadenza*—perhaps from the bedroom which Mottershead thought was a bookshop. The further back he tries to remember, the further and deeper the madness seems to reach; it's like a black pit into which he's falling with increasing speed. Then a glimpse of movement jerks him back into full awareness of his situation, and he glares at the mirror.

At first he thinks it may have been only the driver who moved. The man's face looks more misshapen than ever, the brow drawn further forwards than the chin by the globular mirror. Beyond him, however, Mottershead can just discern the reflection of the lower deck, which is no longer empty. Some way down the aisle there's a hint of a face in the air, a glimmering of eyes and teeth.

The eyes and the grin must be dismayingly large to be visible at such a distance in the dark. They look deserted by flesh. He can see nothing of the head they occupy except for a pale scrawny blur, but he sees movement below them, in front of them. It has begun to reach two hands towards the stairs.

It's as though the mirror is a transparent egg inside which an embryo is forming. That image seems to clarify his vision, and he thinks the eyes are about to hatch or otherwise transform. Though neither the head nor the blur which is presumably its body has advanced, the thin white hands are much closer to the stairs. He can't tell whether the spindly arms or the hands themselves are lengthening, but he feels as if his see-ing the shape is allowing it to reach out—as if his inability to look away or to stop seeing is attracting it to him. His fists close convulsively on useless paper and plastic. He shies everything he's holding at the mirror and scrabbles in his pockets. As the last of the notes flutters to the floor he finds the sharp portions of his broken credit card.

He takes them out and holds them between fingers and thumbs. There's one blade for each of his eyes. In the mirror the huge unblinking eyes above the knowing grin watch him. He lifts the points towards his face, trying to take aim despite the tremors which are spreading from his fingers to the rest of him. He'll have to apply the blades one at a time, he thinks. He tears his gaze away from the mirror, from the sight of the driver crouching over the wheel as if determined to ignore the presence in the aisle, the hands which appear to be drawing the rest of it towards the stairs. Mottershead grabs the back of his own head so that it can't flinch out of range, and poises the first blade in front of his left eye.

The bus has arrived at the brow of a hill, where the houses come to an end. Beyond the last ruins, whose walls are almost buried in refuse, the road snakes down a bare slope into blackness. At the foot of the hill is a looming mass relieved only by a few lit windows. His thinking is so constricted that at first he doesn't understand why the two lines of win-dows, one above the other, are identical. The lower rank is a reflection in black water; the windows are those of a boat.

Dare he risk heading for the stairs if that means the shape in the aisle may touch him? He'll never reach the ferry otherwise. The point wavers in front of his eye, his hand grasps the back of his skull. The bus accel-erates downhill, and the sudden movement jerks his head towards the blade. With a choked scream he opens both hands just in time for it to scrape his cheekbone.

The plastic skates across the floor and clatters down the stairs. He still has a weapon, if such a defence will be any use. He mustn't imagine the worst or he'll be lost. The bus is more than halfway down the slope. He shoves himself off the seat and turns towards the stairs, bracing himself to confront what may be waiting at the bottom. But it isn't there, it's in the aisle behind him.

The rudimentary face grins with delight. The thin white fingers are visibly lengthening, and he has stumbled almost within their grasp. They're moving not so much like fingers as like the legs of spiders dangling in the gloom. If he hadn't stood up when he did they would have closed over his eyes. That thought and the sight of them paralyses him, but another swerve of the vehicle throws him forwards. A convulsion of panic sends him sideways, where he manages to duck away from them, onto the stairs. He's two steps down when they swoop over the banisters and touch him.

They touch his eyes. They feel like tongues composed of material softer than flesh. He hurls himself backwards, colliding with the metal wall, hacking at them with the blade. In the moment before they recoil from his attack he seems to feel a fingertip penetrating the surface of each eyeball. Blinking wildly, he slashes at the fingers as they retreat. Their substance tatters like wet paper, and he wonders if any of it is left in his eyes. As the remnants of the hands shrink back over the banister he staggers downstairs, moaning in his throat. "Stop," he screams.

If his plea has any effect on the driver, it causes him only to mime indifference. As he leans over the wheel, his features seem to retreat into the hollow between his forehead and chin. Mottershead lunges at the door and wrenches at the handle. Either as a result of his violence or because the driver has released the mechanism, the door folds inwards, but the vehicle maintains its speed. It swerves towards the landing-stage, which consists of no more than a few planks embedded in glistening mud. The bus is travelling so fast that it almost skids onto the planks. The driver brakes, and Mottershead seizes his chance. As the bus slows momentarily, he launches himself onto the stage.

His impetus carries him across the planks at a helpless run. They shift alarmingly, sliding sideways. Some of them aren't even set in the earth, they're floating in water which looks thick as mud. Before any of this has registered he's stumbling headlong onto the ferry as it bumps against the stage. By grabbing at the banister of the staircase which leads to the upper deck, he manages to halt himself. He clings to the rusty metal and stares back.

The bus is veering up the hill. Nothing appears to have followed him or to be about to follow. Though he can't hear or feel the working of the engine, the boat is drifting away from the stage, several dislodged planks of which are trailing in its wake. He feels hollow with relief, and so the boat is some way out before he notices that it has ceased to show any lights.

Could the crew have abandoned it while he was on the hill? Even being cast adrift seems preferable to his encounter on the bus. All the same, he would like to see where he's going. He scrambles upstairs to the top deck.

Several benches stand by the rail on either side of the deck. Ventilators rise above them, fat pipes whose wide mouths are turned towards the rail. Two pairs of double doors lead to a lounge below the wheelhouse. The sky and the water might be a single medium, a stagnant darkness which coats the surfaces of the vessel and fills the lounge and wheelhouse. He sits on a bench and watches the ruined suburb on the hill withdraw like a stage set and sink as though the blackness is consuming it, and then he sits and waits.

He isn't sure what he's waiting for: perhaps for daylight, or the appearance of another shore, or—best of all—of another boat with a crew to take him on board. He hopes he won't have to wait long, because it's beginning to prey on his nerves; he feels as if he isn't alone on the boat after all. The doors to the lounge keep stirring furtively as if someone is peeping between them. That could be due to the motion of the vessel, though its rocking is imperceptible, but what has he begun to glimpse in the mouths of the ventilators, ducking out of sight whenever he glares at them? Whatever is keeping him company, everything seems to conceal it; even the benches, which remind him increasingly of boxes with concealed lids. Perhaps the lids are about to shift. Certainly he senses movement close to him.

He grabs the rail and pulls himself to his feet. As he stares about the deck in the midst of the shoreless water he feels something dodge behind him. He presses his spine against the rail. The deck is deserted, but something is behind him. He's about to twist around until he catches sight of it, even though his instincts tell him that he won't succeed, that he'll go on spinning until he can't stop. Instead he makes himself stay as he is, and grips the rail to hold himself still. Before long he senses movement at his back.

He knows where it is. He might have known sooner, he thinks, if it hadn't been infecting his perceptions. He shoves himself away from the rail and strides to the middle of the deck, an expression which feels like a grin breaking out on his face. Planting his legs wide to steady himself, he shrugs off the rucksack and dumps it on the end of a bench. As he unbuckles it, the contents stir uneasily. He pulls it wide open and stoops to peer within.

There's no book inside. The only contents are a naked doll about two feet high. Though it's composed of whitish mottled plastic, it looks starved and withered. He inverts the rucksack, and the doll clatters in two pieces to the deck, the unscrewed top of the skull rolling away between the benches, the limbs twitching as the rest of the doll sprawls.

What has emerged from the head scuttles into the depths of the ruck-sack and tries to burrow into a corner. Mottershead slams the rucksack onto the deck and stamps on it until the struggling inside it weakens and eventually ceases, then he kicks it and the doll overboard.

He hangs onto the rail and gazes at the water. Something is reluctant to let go of him. It feels like teeth buried in his brain, gnawing rat-like at its substance. As sluggish ripples spread through the water the teeth seem to burrow deeper and to lose their sharpness. The ripples fade as the doll and the rucksack sink, and he feels as if a toothless mouth has lodged in his skull, its enfeebled tongue poking at the fleshy petals of his brain. The ripples vanish, and so does the kiss in his brain, as if the mouth has starved of brain matter. Now that his mind is clear he turns to see where the boat is approaching.

It's an island covered with trees and illuminated faintly by a crescent moon. Is it the place which feels as much like a dream as a memory? He has dreamed of being guided through the forest, following shafts of sunlight which appear to be both marking out his path and lingering on secrets of the forest: trees inscribed with messages of lichen; a glade encircled by mounds composed of moss and tiny blossoms as if the pro-cesses of growth are performing an arcane ritual; an avenue of pines whose trunks, which are straight as telephone poles, are surrounded by golden flakes of themselves as though sunlight has solidified in the piny chill and settled to the earth. Surely all this is more than a dream, despite his impression that the forest never ends—and then he sees that the ferry has brought him home.

The prow is pivoting towards the stage where he embarked before dawn. He can just see the avenue of poplars which leads to his house. Couldn't the forest which seems to cover most of the island be the source of his vision? There's no telling in the dark. At least the vessel isn't drifting aimlessly; someone is in the wheelhouse after all, steering the boat to the shore.

As the ferry nudges the stage Mottershead descends the stairs. Since there's nobody to moor the craft, he waits until the hull scrapes the tyres at the edge of the stage, then he runs at the gap where the gangplank should be, and jumps. The ferry swings away at once and sails into the blackness, but he has time to glimpse the helmsman. Is it the bearded sailor from the earlier ferry? He's wearing a balaclava, though he seems to have pulled it down over the whole of his face. If its dim silhouette represents the outline of the skull, then surely Mottershead ought to have noticed how odd the shape was. It's the fault of the darkness, he thinks, or else his perceptions aren't as undistorted as he has allowed himself to hope. He'll feel better once he's home. He turns away from the water and strides towards the house.

The poplars creak and sway as though they're about to collapse beneath the burden of the low thick sky. All the houses among the trees are unlit, and he can't locate any of them by the glow of the moon, within whose curve he seems to glimpse a hint of features. He feels as though he can sense the growth of the forest around him; he keeps his gaze fixed on the tarmac for fear of straying once again into the woods. When he sees the lights of his house ahead he sprints towards them.

It doesn't matter that he can't recall leaving the lights on. He runs up the overgrown path, fishing for his keys, which rattle out of his pocket like the chain of a miniature anchor. He's almost at the front door when he hears a voice beyond the curtains of the lounge: his own voice.

Worse yet, it sounds terrified. He feels as if he isn't really outside the house—as if only his terror is. He's tempted to flee into the woods rather than learn what the voice may have to tell him, but if he takes to his heels now he knows he will never be able to stop. He aims the key at the lock and grips his wrist with his other hand to steady it. At last the key finds the slot, and he eases the door open.

The bulb above the L-shaped hall is lit. The hall and the uncarpeted staircase look faded with disuse. Beyond the door to the lounge his voice is babbling incomprehensibly as if it's unable to stop. He retrieves his key and creeps into the hall, inching the door shut behind him.

He isn't stealthy enough. The voice is suddenly cut off, and he hears the whir of a speeding videotape. He slams the front door and, racing across the hall, flings open the door to the lounge.

Three people are sitting in the slumped armchairs: a woman who may be about his age, a younger woman, a man her age or slightly older. All have greying hair, which seems premature in at least two of them, and faces so wide that their foreheads appear lower than they should. As Mottershead strides into the room the man jumps up and snatches a tape out of the video recorder while his sister clears away a board game strewn with plastic coins and toy notes. "Darling," the woman says to Mottershead, "we were just coming to fetch you."

"We've been wondering where you'd got to," says her daughter.

"Have you been working all this time, dad?" the man says gently, as if Mottershead isn't already beset by enough questions of his own. Have they come to visit him, or are they living with him despite what he told the writers' group? Were they somewhere in the house when he left it, or did they let themselves in later? "I've been using my mind all right," he tells his son, to get rid of at least that question.

"Then I should put your feet up now," his wife advises.

"Take it easy," says his daughter. "You've earned the rest."

"Try and get some sleep," his son says. "We're here."

Why isn't Mottershead reassured? Part of him yearns to embrace them, and perhaps he'll be able to once he has watched the video cassette—once he no longer feels that they're keeping a secret from him.

He knows they'll try to dissuade him from watching if they realise he means to do so. "Aren't we eating?" he suggests.

"If you're ready to put some flesh on yourself," says his wife.

"I'll help you," his daughter tells her, and they both go out. His son has slipped the video cassette into its case and is trying to pretend he isn't holding it. "I'll put that away," Mottershead informs him, staring hard at him until he hands over the cassette and trudges out of the room. "Close the door," Mottershead calls after him. "I'd like to be alone for a while."

The cassette has been recorded from a television broadcast. Hand-written on the label is the title, *Out of His Head*. Does that refer to the creative process? Might he just have heard himself reading one of his stories aloud? Again he seems to remember cameras and lights surrounding him, but now he has the disconcerting notion that it isn't the memory which is vague—it's rather that he was unsure at the time whether the crew and their equipment were actually present. He shoves the cassette into the expressionless black mouth of the player and turns the sound of the television low as the image shivers into focus.

The cassette hasn't been rewound completely; the programme is under way. One of his books is hovering in space. *Postpone the Stone*—of course that was a title of his; why couldn't he have called it to mind when he needed to? A trick of the camera flips the book over like a playing card and transforms it into another of his novels, *Make No Bones*, and then into *Cadenza*. He's about to run the tape back to remind himself of his work when he hears what the commentary is saying about him.

"—speculate with an intensity best described as neurotic," an unctuous male voice is saying. "In one of his stories a man who's obsessed with the impossibility of knowing if he has died in his sleep convinces himself that he has, and is dreaming. Another concerns a man who believes he is being followed by a schizophrenic whose hallucinations are affecting his own perceptions, but the hallucinations prove to be the reality he has tried to avoid seeing. The reader is left suspecting that the schizophrenic is really a projection of the man himself."

Did Mottershead write that? He's reaching out to halt the tape, so as to have time to think, when he sees himself appear on the screen. The sight freezes him, his hands outstretched.

He's walking back and forth across a glade—whether in the forest on the island or behind his old home isn't clear—and muttering to himself as rapidly as he is walking. Now and then he lurches at trees to examine the bark or squats to scrutinise the grass, and then he's off again, muttering and scurrying. His grin is so fixed, and his eyes are so wide, that he looks afraid to do anything but grin. Every few seconds he digs his fingers into his unkempt scalp as if he feels it slipping.

While he has been straining unsuccessfully to distinguish his own words Mottershead has ceased to hear the commentary, but now he becomes conscious of it. "—in the last of his rare interviews," the voice is saying. "The price of such intense commitment to his work may have been an inability to stop. At first this took the form of a compulsion to tell his stories to anyone who could be persuaded to listen. Later, immediately prior to his breakdown, he appears to have been unable to grasp reality except as raw material to be shaped. The breakdown may have been precipitated by the creative urge continuing to make demands on him after he had lost the power to write."

He can almost remember telling stories to people in the street, to anyone who wasn't swift enough to elude him. He has the impression that the last such encounter may have been very recent indeed. Before he can seize the impression, his family enters the glade. They look younger, though their hair is already greying. They're trying to coax him home from the woods, but he keeps dodging them, both his gait and his voice speeding up. His babbling sounds more like the voice he overheard on his way in. He is still failing to understand its words when he hears his family murmuring outside the room.

He drags the cassette out of the player. He hasn't remembered every-thing; he's at the edge of a deeper blackness. He doesn't want to face his family until he has managed to remember. He hugs the cassette to his chest with both hands as if someone is about to take it from him. When the plastic carapace begins to crack, he's afraid that its contents may escape. He shoves the cassette into its case and stuffs the case into his pocket as he tiptoes to the door to hear what his family is murmuring about him. Before he reaches it, the voices cease.

He clasps the doorknob and presses his ear against a panel, but can hear nothing. He throws the door open, and the women turn to gaze at him from the kitchen at the far end of the hall, while his son comes to the doorway of the dining-room. "Anything we can do, dad?" he says. "Want someone to sit with you?"

"I'm fine the way I am," Mottershead retorts, wondering how they can all have withdrawn so quickly from discussing him outside the lounge. He advances on his son, expecting to find that he has only been pretending to busy himself. But the table is laid; all four places on the dim tablecloth are set, except for one from which the steak knife is miss-ing. He knows instinctively that it's his place. "You aren't finished," he stammers, and makes for the stairs.

The women continue to watch him. Under the fluorescent tube their hair looks grey with dust, their foreheads appear squashed by shadows. It seems to Mottershead that they may be about to transform, to reveal their true nature, of which these details are merely hints. His mind hasn't quite cleared itself, he thinks. He mustn't let this happen, not to them. "I'll be upstairs," he shouts. "No need to come looking."

"That's right, you put your feet up," his daughter says.

"You've earned it," his son adds.

"Get some rest," says his wife.

Even this unnerves him; it revives an impression of his life with them, of how it became a monotonous descent by excruciatingly minute stages into a banality with which he felt they were doing their best to smother him. Or was that something he tried to write? He dashes upstairs to his room.

He lies on the mattress and gazes at the branching cracks and peeling plaster overhead. The sight makes him uneasy, but so does the rest of the room: the shapeless bulging contents of the chest of drawers, the eternally open wardrobe, the blurred shapes in the wallpaper, where he can see figures flattened like insects if he lets himself. He closes his eyes, but shapes gather behind the lids at once. Should he switch off the light? He feels as if his sole means of finding peace may be to retreat into the dark. He hasn't opened his eyes when his family enters the room.

They must have come through the door from the corridor. Even if he sees them standing on the side of the room furthest from the door, they can't have emerged from the wardrobe. "Having a snooze?" his son says. "That's the ticket. We were just wondering if you'd seen a knife."

"Why should I know where it is?"

"We aren't saying you do," his daughter assures him. "You have your snooze while we see if it's anywhere."

He shouldn't have admitted that he knows what they're searching for; he feels that the admission has made them wary of him. As they peer into the wardrobe and poke through the drawers full of unwashed clothes and fumble at the heavy curtains, he's sure that they are surreptitiously watching him. He inches his hands out on both sides of him and gropes under the mattress, but the knife isn't there. Suddenly afraid to find it, he shoves himself off the bed.

The three of them swing towards him as though they are affecting not to move. "We won't be long," his wife murmurs. "Just pretend we aren't here."

"Bathroom," Mottershead cries, thinking that he'll be alone in there if anywhere. He sprints along the corridor, past the rooms whose shaded light-bulbs steep the single beds in crimson, and into the bathroom, clawing at the bolt until it finds the socket. He crosses his wrists and clutches his shoulders as he stares around him.

The room is less of a refuge than he hoped, but at first he doesn't understand why. Is it the sound like a faint choked gurgling, not quite able to form words, which is making him reluctant to sit on the lid of the toilet or lie in the rusty bath? Though it can only be the plumbing, it seems like a memory, or at least reminiscent of one. His gaze roams the bathroom and is caught by a gleam beside the sink: his open razor. If he's made to feel trapped in the room, he doesn't know what he might do. He scrabbles at the bolt, to get the door open before his family starts murmuring outside. The door bangs against the wall, and the heads crane out of the other rooms. His children appear flayed by the crimson light behind them, his wife's hair looks matted with dust; they seem to have hardly any foreheads. The sight appals him, and he flees past them, flinching out of reach. There's still somewhere he thinks he may be safe—the locked room.

The key was in the lock earlier, but suppose it has been removed while he was wandering? As he runs downstairs and along the corridor, he feels as though his nerves are all he is. He glances into the dining-room in case the knife has reappeared, but now the other knives are missing too. Even seeing the key in the locked door doesn't help; indeed, he wants to rush out of the house and never come back. But his hand is reaching with uncontrollable smoothness for the key. He turns it and pushes the door open, and switches on the light in the room.

A thought arrests him on the threshold of the bare room, which is so brightly lit by a shadeless bulb that it seems to contain nothing but illumination. Does he mean to lock the door in order to keep his family out, or himself in? Have they hidden the other knives from him? His vision begins to adjust, and he sees the walls white as blank pages, glaring like the walls of an interrogation room. Someone is lying on the floorboards under the bulb.

He can't immediately distinguish who it is, but he thinks that whoever has been persecuting him and his perceptions has managed to hide in the room. Since they are lying where the light is brightest, why can't he see them clearly? It occurs to him that he may not want to see. At once, before he has time to cover his eyes, he does. His family is in the room.

They're lying face up on the boards, their hands folded on their chests. His children's heads are nearest the door, his wife's feet are between them. At each of their throats a book lies open, pinned there by one of the knives driven deep. Their faces look as if someone has tried unsuccessfully to pull and knead and pummel them into a semblance of calm.

For a moment he believes they're watching him, though their eyes are dull with dust. But he's unable to waken any life in their eyes, even when he grabs the flex and moves the light-bulb back and forth, making their eyes gleam and go out, gleam and go out. Falling to his knees achieves nothing; all he can see is the book at his wife's throat. He finds himself reading and rereading one sentence: *As a child he hoped life would never end; when he grew up he was afraid it might not.*

He's rather proud of having phrased that. Did he once write about doing away with his family, or wasn't he able to write it? In either case, having already imagined the act and his ensuing grief may be the reason why he feels empty now, and growing emptier. He feels as if he's about to come to an end. Anything is preferable to the lifelessness of the room, even the kind of day he has been through.

He rises unsteadily and wavers to the door, where he switches off the light. That seems to help a little, and so does locking the door from the outside. "I'm better now," he mumbles, and then he shouts it through the house.

There's no response. He can't blame them for hiding from him while the fourth knife is at large, but if they'll only stay with him they'll be able to ensure that he doesn't find it first. He runs through the ground floor, hoping to meet them in each room, switching off the light in each to remind him where he has already looked for them. He darkens the stairs and runs up, he turns off the lights in the bathroom, in his son's bedroom and his daughter's. Now only his and his wife's room remains, and mustn't he have had a reason to leave it until last? "Surprise," he cries, starting to laugh and weep as he throws the door open. But nobody is in the room.

He stares at the desertion, one hand on the light-switch. Even the meagre furniture seems hardly present. If he finds the knife he'll use it on himself. Why does the thought seem to contain a revelation? He clutches at his eyes with his free hand as if to adjust his vision, then he gazes ahead, barely seeing the room, not needing to see. He'll never find the knife, he thinks, because he has already turned it on himself.

Perhaps only he is dead. Perhaps everything else was a story which he has been telling to keep himself company in the dark or to convince himself that he still has some grasp of the world. He has to believe that of at least the contents of the locked room. No wonder his search for his family has shown him empty rooms; dreams can't be forced to appear. At least his instincts haven't failed him, since he has been darkening the house. He needs the dark so that his story can take shape.

He turns off the last light and, pacing blindly to the bed, sinks onto the mattress. The room already seems less substantial. He lies back and crosses his hands on his chest, he closes his eyes and waits for them to fill with blank darkness. If he lies absolutely still, perhaps his family will come to him. Hasn't he tried this before, more than once, many times? Perhaps this time there will be light to lead them into the endless sunlit forest. It does no good to wish that he could return to a time when he might have been cured of his visions—when he was only mad.

For Penny and Alan
and Timmy and Robin

—SOME OF MY DARK TO FIND
YOUR WAY THROUGH

ABOUT THE EDITOR

Stephen Jones lives in London, England. A Hugo Award nominee, he is the winner of four World Fantasy Awards, three International Horror Guild Awards, five Bram Stoker Awards, twenty-one British Fantasy Awards and a Lifetime Achievement Award from the Horror Writers Association. One of Britain's most acclaimed horror and dark fantasy writers and editors, he has more than 145 books to his credit, including *The Art of Horror Movies: An Illustrated History*, the film books of Neil Gaiman's *Coraline* and *Stardust*, *The Illustrated Monster Movie Guide* and *The Hellraiser Chronicles*; the non-fiction studies *Horror: 100 Best Books* and *Horror: Another 100 Best Books* (both with Kim Newman); the single-author collections *Necronomicon* and *Eldritch Tales* by H. P. Lovecraft, *The Complete Chronicles of Conan* and *Conan's Brethren* by Robert E. Howard, and *Curious Warnings: The Great Ghost Stories of M. R. James*; plus such anthologies as *Horrorology: The Lexicon of Fear*, *Fearie Tales: Stories of the Grimm and Gruesome*, *A Book of Horrors*, *The Mammoth Book of Halloween Stories*, *The Lovecraft Squad* and *Zombie Apocalypse!* series, and twenty-nine volumes of *Best New Horror*. You can visit his web site at www.stephenjoneseditor.com or follow him on Facebook at "Stephen Jones-Editor."